PENGUIN BOOKS

THE MYSTERY OF EDWIN DROOD

Charles Dickens was born at Portsmouth on 7 February 1812, the second of eight children. Dickens's childhood experiences were similar to those depicted in *David Copperfield*. His father, who was a government clerk, was imprisoned for debt and Dickens was sent to work at the age of twelve. The memories of this period were to haunt him until his death. He taught himself shorthand and became a reporter of parliamentary debates for the *Morning Chronicle*. He began to publish sketches in various periodicals, which were subsequently republished as *Sketches of Boz*. *The Pickwick Papers* were published in 1836–7 and after a slow start became a publishing phenomenon and Dickens's characters the centre of a popular cult. Part of the secret of his success was the method of cheap serial publication, which Dickens used for all his novels. He began *Oliver Twist* in 1837, followed by *Nicholas Nickleby* (1838–9) and *The Old Curiosity Shop* (1840–41). After finishing *Barnaby Rudge* (1841) Dickens set off for America; he went full of enthusiasm for the young republic but, in spite of a triumphant reception, he returned disillusioned. His experiences are recorded in *American Notes* (1842). *Martin Chuzzlewit* (1843–4) did not repeat its predecessors' success but this was quickly redressed by the huge popularity of the *Christmas Books*, of which the first, *A Christmas Carol*, appeared in 1843. *Dombey and Son* (1844–6) and *David Copperfield* (1849–50) were more serious in theme and more carefully planned than his early novels. In his later work Dickens's social criticism became more radical and his comedy more savage. *Bleak House* was published in 1853 and was followed by *Hard Times* (1854), *Little Dorrit* (1855–7), *A Tale of Two Cities* (1859), *Great Expectations* (1860–61) and *Our Mutual Friend* (1864–5). His last novel, *The Mystery of Edwin Drood*, was never completed and Dickens died on 9 June 1870.

Angus Wilson, the distinguished novelist, was Emeritus Professor of English Literature at the University of East Anglia. He wrote the introduction for *Oliver Twist* in the Penguin Classics. His *The World of Charles Dickens* is also published in Penguin. He died in 1991.

Arthur Cox is a civil servant in the United States of America, and has written a number of articles for literary magazines on the works of Dickens. He has contributed to the *Dickensian*.

CHARLES DICKENS

THE MYSTERY OF
EDWIN DROOD

Edited by Arthur J. Cox
with an introduction by
Angus Wilson

PENGUIN BOOKS

PENGUIN BOOKS

Published by the Penguin Group
Penguin Books Ltd, 27 Wrights Lane, London W8 5TZ, England
Penguin Books USA Inc., 375 Hudson Street, New York, New York 10014, USA
Penguin Books Australia Ltd, Ringwood, Victoria, Australia
Penguin Books Canada Ltd, 10 Alcorn Avenue, Toronto, Ontario, Canada M4V 3B2
Penguin Books (NZ) Ltd, 182–190 Wairau Road, Auckland 10, New Zealand

Penguin Books Ltd, Registered Offices: Harmondsworth, Middlesex, England

First published 1870
Published in the Penguin English Library 1974
Reprinted in Penguin Classics 1985
Penguin Film and TV Tie-in edition published 1993
10

Printed in England by Clays Ltd, St Ives plc
Set in Monotype Fournier

CONTENTS

CHARLES DICKENS

A NOTE BY ANGUS CALDER

CHARLES DICKENS was born at Portsmouth on 7 February 1812. He was the second of the eight children of John Dickens, a clerk in the Naval Pay Office, whose mother had been in service to Lord Crewe. Although John Dickens was hard-working, he was rarely able to live within his income, and this brought a series of crises upon his family, which lived under the shadow of menacing social insecurity.

John Dickens's work took him from place to place, so that Charles spent his early childhood in Portsmouth, London, and Chatham. He was happiest at Chatham, where he attended a school run by a young Baptist minister, who recognized his abilities and paid him special attention. In 1823 the family moved to London, faced with financial disaster, and, to help out, a relative of Mrs Dickens offered Charles work in a blacking business which he managed. Two days before his twelfth birthday the boy began work at a factory at Hungerford Stairs, labelling bottles for six shillings a week.

Shortly before this, John Dickens had been arrested for debt, and soon the whole family, except for Charles, who was found lodgings, joined him in the Marshalsea Debtors' Prison. The double blow – his menial job and the family shame – gave Charles a shock which transformed him. In later years he told only his wife and his closest friend, John Forster, of these experiences, which haunted him till his death.

After three months in prison, John Dickens was released by process of having himself declared an Insolvent Debtor, but it was not until weeks later that he withdrew Charles from work and sent him to school, where he did well. At fifteen, Charles began work in the office of a firm of Gray's Inn attorneys. Sensing a vocation elsewhere, he taught himself shorthand, and eighteen months later began to work as a freelance reporter in the court of Doctors' Commons.

In 1829 or 1830 he fell passionately in love with Maria Beadnell, the daughter of a banker. Their affair staggered fruitlessly on until the summer of 1833. Meanwhile, he began to report parliamentary debates, and won himself a high reputation for speed and accuracy. His first *Sketches by Boz* appeared in magazines soon after he was twenty-one. In 1834 he joined the reporting staff of the *Morning Chronicle*. A well-received volume of his *Sketches* appeared on his twenty-fourth birthday.

His growing reputation secured him a commission from the publishers, Chapman and Hall, to provide the text to appear in monthly instalments beside sporting plates by a popular artist, Seymour. He 'thought of Mr Pickwick'. Two days after the first number appeared he married Catherine Hogarth, the daughter of a fellow-journalist, on the prospect. Although early sales were disappointing, *Pickwick Papers* (1836–7) soon became a publishing phenomenon, and Dickens's characters the centre of a popular cult. Part of the secret was the method of cheap serial publication, which Dickens used for all his subsequent novels (some, however, being serialized in weekly magazines edited by himself), and which was copied by other writers.

While *Pickwick* was still running, Dickens began *Oliver Twist* (1837). *Nicholas Nickleby* (1838–9) provided him with a third success, and sales of *The Old Curiosity Shop* (1840–41) reached 100,000. After finishing *Barnaby Rudge* (1841), Dickens set off with his wife for the United States. He went full of enthusiasm for the young republic, but returned heartily disillusioned, in spite of a triumphant reception. His experiences are recorded in *American Notes* (1842).

His first setback came when *Martin Chuzzlewit* (1843–4) did not repeat the extraordinary success of its predecessors, though he promptly inaugurated his triumphant series of *Christmas Books* with *A Christmas Carol* (1843). He now travelled abroad, first to Italy (1844–5) and then to Switzerland and Paris (1846). During a brief interlude in England he projected, not another novel, but a paper, the *Daily News*. This first appeared in January 1846, but Dickens resigned after only seventeen days as editor.

His next novel, *Dombey and Son* (1846–8), was more wholly serious and more carefully planned than his early work. In *David Copperfield* (1849–50), he explored his own childhood and youth, thinly disguised. In the 1850s he increased his already intense interest in public affairs. He founded *Household Words*, a weekly magazine which combined entertainment with social purpose; it was succeeded in 1859 by *All the Year Round*, which sold as many as 300,000 copies. *Bleak House* (1852–3) and *Hard Times* (1854) have strong social themes, and *Little Dorrit* (1855–7) continues Dickens's bitter public denunciation of the whole framework of government and administration which had mismanaged the Crimean War.

In 1858 he separated from his wife. Although Kate, a shadowy, slow person, had given him ten children, she had never suited his exuberant temperament very well. He befriended a young actress, Ellen Ternan, who may have become his mistress. He was now living mainly in Kent, at Gad's Hill, near his boyhood home of Chatham. *A Tale of Two Cities* (1859), *Great Expectations* (1860–61), and *Our Mutual Friend* (1864–5) completed his life's main work of fourteen major novels. By the mid 1860s his health was failing, partly under the strain of his successful but exhausting public readings from his own work, which had begun in 1858. An immensely profitable but physically shattering series of readings in America (1867–8) speeded his decline, and he collapsed during a 'farewell' series in England. His last novel, *Edwin Drood* (1870), was never completed; he suffered a stroke after a full day's work at Gad's Hill on 8 June 1870 and died the following day. Lamentation was demonstrative and universal, and he was buried in the Poets' Corner of Westminster Abbey.

Dickens's extreme energy was not exhausted by his unique success as a novelist. His weekly journalism made heavy demands on his time after 1850, and he constantly turned to the stage, first in many amateur theatricals, given privately or for charity, where he produced and took leading roles with great brilliance, and, later, in his public readings. His concern with social reform in his novels and journalism was matched by an active personal interest in several charitable projects.

Furthermore, as Lionel Trilling puts it, 'the mere record of his conviviality is exhausting'. His typical relaxation was a long walk at great speed, and he was dedicated to any and every sort of game or jollification. In the early days of his success, observers were sometimes displeased by his flamboyant dress and a hint of vulgarity in his manners, but he had powerful, magnetizing eyes and over- whelming charm. Beneath his high spirits, friends could detect a permanent emotional insecurity and restlessness, which flavours the tragi-comic world of his novels.

Two biographies stand out among many: John Forster's *Life* (1872–4, many times reprinted); and Edgar Johnson's *Charles Dickens, His Tragedy and Triumph* (London: Gollancz, 1953), which embodies material neglected or suppressed by Forster. Readers interested in Dickens's methods as a novelist will be enlightened by John Butt's and Kathleen Tillotson's *Dickens at Work* (London: Methuen, 1957). There are innumerable specialized studies of his work, life and views. A magazine exclusively devoted to the subject, *The Dickensian*, is published three times a year by the Dickens Fellowship.

INTRODUCTION

THE first monthly number of *The Mystery of Edwin Drood* was published in April 1870. The novel was designed to be complete in twelve parts – a short novel by Victorian standards, a very short novel by Dickens's standards. It was, in fact, to prove even shorter, for on 8 June Charles Dickens suffered an apoplectic stroke. He died the next day. Six numbers only of *The Mystery of Edwin Drood* were completed.

This fact is central to the mass of discussion that the novel has aroused in later generations. A half-finished book by a man of genius is not something which it is easy for critics to assess. It is doubtful whether we truly can judge the literary value of *The Mystery of Edwin Drood*, we can only point to individual merits or imperfections, and try to put them into perspective beside those of the complete novels which had gone before.

Until quite recently most critics have evaded even this comparatively satisfying approach to what is inevitably a tantalizing, unsatisfying thing – an unfinished product of an artist of genius. They have attempted to compensate by laying exceptional stress on the circumstances under which the book was written.

Some few, knowing that Dickens's health was in serious decline in the last years of his life, have dismissed the book altogether. His friend, Wilkie Collins, later declared it to be 'Dickens' last laboured effort, the melancholy work of a worn-out brain.' Bernard Shaw spoke of it as 'a gesture by a man who was already three quarters dead.' This is not the view of most modern critics. More relevant, perhaps, it was not the view of critics in *The Times*, *The Athenaeum*, or *The Graphic* at the date of the publication of the first number. Then *The Mystery of Edwin Drood* was not seen as the book of a dying man, but as a remarkable sign of the persistence of Dickens's vitality, evidence that he could entertain a whole new generation as he had entertained their fathers. There *were* hostile notices of the new novel. Most of Dickens's novels had received some. But the general reception of *The Mystery of Edwin Drood* when it first appeared was far more friendly, far more sure of his continued artistic vitality than it had been on the publication of *Our Mutual*

Friend in 1865, four and a half years before, or, indeed, than it had been of *Little Dorrit* between 1855 and 1857, or, certainly, of *Martin Chuzzlewit* in 1843–4. The dismissive view of Collins and Shaw may be itself dismissed as an easy and insufficient hindsight.

The more usual approach to *Edwin Drood* is, I think, almost as insufficient, but not so easy to dismiss. For decades, from around the turn of the century until the outbreak of the last war, the concern of Dickens's admirers was entirely with the mystery aspect of the story – who killed Edwin Drood? Sometimes, was Edwin Drood really dead at all? And, in addition, who was the mysterious Datchery, the stranger who visits Cloisterham after Drood's disappearance? Certainly these questions come into our minds when we read the book, and, as they are not answered, they are bound to nag us. The title of the book, too, seems to lay emphasis on this purely 'whodunnit' aspect of the novel. But Dickens's titles do not as a rule run deep into the heart of the significance of his novels; and about this one, as Appendix A in this edition shows, he was very undecided. There had been mysteries in all his novels since *Oliver Twist* (1837–9). If he had died before finishing *Barnaby Rudge*, certainly before he had reached Book Two of that novel, we might be asking, who killed Barnaby's father, or was his father really dead at all? These seem minor questions now beside that novel's extraordinary insight into the nature of violent revolution. And so with the murder of Mr Tulkinghorn in *Bleak House*, or the mystery of Rigaud's hold over Mrs Clenham in *Little Dorrit*; it would be an absurdity to see those two great social novels in such narrow terms. These mysteries are the essence of Dickens's plots. These plots are indeed essential to the novels, but they are only the mechanism by which the great imaginative magic lantern works; the total significance of what Dickens shows us in his novels is a hundred times greater than his plots. In fact he was a very clumsy contriver of plots, and often, as in *Little Dorrit*, the 'mysteries' are only unravelled in the last chapters in a mass of complicated and suddenly revealed events that have taken place before the action of the novel began. There is a hint of something of the sort in the complicated family relationships in *The Mystery of Edwin Drood*.

Nevertheless, it has to be admitted that the book, as we have it, *is* organized around Edwin's disappearance; and the book was to be a short one – perhaps, as a result, what might have been his next most skilfully organized novel after *Great Expectations*, another comparatively short novel. The mystery, the plot, that is, in so condensed a book, inevitably becomes more identical with the whole of the work of art than in the more sprawling novels, where digression, sub-plot and sheer comic performance may take off from the central story without at all reducing the profundity of the book's total insight. To this extent, the conventional detective-story concern of most commentators on *Edwin Drood* in the first half of our century has some justification, but only if by asking about Edwin's murder or Jasper's guilt we are exploring the deeper nature of the novel. There is really no evidence that Charles Dickens in his last novel had departed completely from the kind of novels that he had previously produced, nothing to suggest that he was intent upon creating a novel whose major interest lay solely in suspense and mystery, like his friend Wilkie Collins's *The Moonstone*, which had appeared as a serial in *All the Year Round* in 1868, less still upon writing the sort of complex technical mystery story which so many of the ingenious unravellers of Drood's puzzle have invented. Such technical perfections do not indeed belong to the Victorian period, they are the products of our century's mastery of the detective-story form. It is not surprising that at the height of the Dickensian passion for solving Drood's mystery, Sir Arthur Conan Doyle, and even Sherlock Holmes himself, to say nothing of the spirits with whom Sir Arthur was in touch in 'the world beyond the grave', should all have shown interest in how and if Edwin Drood met his end. From 1905, in its first issue, until at least 1930, contributors to the *Dickensian*, the journal of the Dickens Fellowship, were preoccupied with Jasper's guilt or innocence, and the real identity of Datchery. A bibliography by Matz of such Droodiana in 1911 gives eighty-two such items, including whole books; and his daughter's continuation in 1928 and 1929 lists 135. And since that date there has been much further controversy. Perhaps Sir Felix Aylmer's book, *The Drood Case* of 1964, defending Jasper's innocence in a complicated, closely argued, but to me inherently improbable solution based upon the old Islamic family feud code, may be seen as the last magnificent rocket in this long firework display of detective ingenuity that has dazzled and distracted the readers of Dickens's novel. Most of this today seems hardly more than an enjoyable but irrelevant parlour

game. All too few of these mystery solvers are concerned with the
fact that the mystery was invented by Dickens and not by themselves; none are content to discuss the unfinished book as a part of
his whole canon.

Here once again it is interesting to turn to contemporary reviews
of the unfinished novel. What struck contemporaries as new was its
un-Dickensian cathedral setting and clerical cast. Comparisons
were made with Trollope rather than with Wilkie Collins's world
of oriental mysteries and hypnotic powers. I do not myself think
that the changed social setting of *Edwin Drood* is the absolute core
of the book's significance, but it is certainly quite as unexpected in
his work as the elements of the exotic. The latter are surely to be
seen only as a new aspect of the gothic and the supernatural that
had persisted – especially in his short magazine tales – from the
days of the interpolated stories in *The Pickwick Papers* back in
1836.

Such evidence of Dickens's intentions in *Edwin Drood* as we
have from his relations and friends is all agreed upon the simple
solution to the mystery that Jasper murdered his nephew Edwin
Drood. Such a solution is naturally not satisfying to those who
look to the book for the kind of cleverly designed false clues and
motives that mark twentieth-century detective fiction. In most
cases these critics have found it possible to dismiss contemporary
evidence in favour of certain very tantalizing puzzles in the half-
finished text, and, above all, in the implications of the designs for
the cover of the monthly parts. These puzzles are both genuine and
fascinating. Yet I cannot feel that they should outweigh the account
of the book given by those who knew Dickens, particularly as this
account, though unsatisfactory to readers who are looking for
a brilliant 'whodunnit', accords most satisfactorily with that
concentration upon the fight between the forces of Good and Evil
as exemplified in contemporary society, with particular emphasis
upon the analysis and personification of Evil, which had been
Dickens's preoccupation in all his novels.

Perhaps the most satisfactory approach, then, to *The Mystery
of Edwin Drood* is to examine the evidence for its inception and
construction in relation to the rest of Dickens's life and work, and
to relate this all the while to the facts of the novel itself.

Dickens's previous novel, *Our Mutual Friend*, had ended serial

publication in November 1865. There is, therefore, a four and a
half year gap between the two novels, the longest in Dickens's
writing life. This fact itself has been used by those who dismiss
Edwin Drood as the work of a dying man to bolster their opinion.
Yet the gap between *Our Mutual Friend* and its predecessor *Great
Expectations* is about three and a half years, almost as long. It
would be easy to suggest that, despite all the social and meta-
physical profundity, above all the extraordinary 'modernity' of
Our Mutual Friend, its spun-out length and its periodic slackness
of texture after the remarkable tautness of *Great Expectations* was
the work of an ailing man, only, of course, Charles Dickens did
not die before he completed it. Beside *Our Mutual Friend, The
Mystery of Edwin Drood* is a model of compression and, above all,
a continuously and rapidly active book. I suspect that this compression and its consequent vitality were the product of Dickens's
recognition of the need to conserve his energies in view of his
physical weakening – but this only rebukes those who write off
Edwin Drood, supporting rather Doctor Johnson's view that
'when a man knows he is to be hanged in a fortnight, it concentrates his mind wonderfully.' Evidence for the first stirring afresh
of Dickens's literary imagination comes from George Dolby, the
manager of the reading tours. He is a good and reliable witness,
for his admiration and support of the seriously ailing novelist
through the long, exacting journeys in America and all over Great
Britain had made them very close to one another. 'He began to
cast about for a subject for a new book,' Dolby tells us, soon after
his lecture tours had been brought to an end by his doctor's orders
at Preston in April 1869. The value of this evidence is that it
shows Dickens, as had usually been the case, in search of a novel,
not waiting passively for inspiration to come to him, searching no
doubt anxiously to fill up the great vacuum left in his emotional
satisfaction by the end of the readings that had so obsessed him.
It, therefore, ties *Edwin Drood* to his usual imaginative course but
with added stimulus. It also gives credence to the next evidence
that follows.

   This is the central testimony of his lifelong friend and biographer
John Forster. Forster says that in July Dickens wrote to him:
'What should you think of the idea of a story beginning in this
way? – Two people, boy and girl, or very young, going apart

from one another, pledged to be married after many years – at the end of the book. The interest to arise out of the tracing of their separate ways, and the impossibility of what will be done with that impending fate.' He tells us that this idea was discarded, but my experience as a novelist tells me that first ideas (unless they are *wholly* discarded, which is clearly not the case here) have a powerful influence on books. I think that Forster's account should urge us to give full weight to Rosebud in this novel. It is obvious, of course, that her relation to Edwin is no longer central in the finished work, that the scheme suggested to Forster here leaves out the all important figure of Jasper. Nevertheless, I think that it gives considerable importance to Dickens's concern in this novel for the inner truths of the loves and attachments of the young people. This is something which in his early career he had only been able to bring alive autobiographically in *David Copperfield*; but which he later conceived with increasing truth and with consequent increasing depth in the portrayal of his heroes and heroines, who had once been only lay figures. In this respect, *The Mystery of Edwin Drood* with Edwin and Rosa and Neville and Helena is the natural successor to *Our Mutual Friend* with Eugene Wrayburn and Bella Wilfer, or to *Great Expectations* with Pip and Estella.

Solvers of the Drood mystery for whom Forster's later evidence is inconvenient have pointed out that this first idea he attributes to Dickens is, in fact, to be found in Dickens's Memoranda Book, which he kept between 1855 and 1865 and cannot be dated later than 1862. They usually add, quite truthfully, that Forster is not so good a witness for Dickens's last years as he had been from 1840 to 1860, since domestic events in the lives of both had somewhat dissolved their close intimacy, and Dickens resented Forster's dislike of his public readings. But it is, after all, suggested that Forster, wishing to appear party to all his friend's ideas, copied this suggested plot out of the old Memoranda Book and then attributed it to a letter from Dickens. This is not merely a charge of faulty memory, but one of bad faith which would surely throw doubts upon the whole of Forster's famous biography, for a man who will insert fabrication where he has no fact can hardly be trusted to be true to the facts of all that he does know. Yet Forster's work is and remains, with many imperfections and biased stresses, our principal recognized account of Dickens's life. I doubt if these solvers of the Drood mystery who impugn Forster's integrity realize the implications of their charge. In any case, that Dickens, in search, as Dolby has said, of a new idea, should have turned to his Memoranda Book seems highly probable. I have never kept a memoranda book. But if I had one, I should consult it. That Dickens did so is made more likely by the fact that a metaphor from the same Memoranda Book appeared in *The Mystery of Edwin Drood* in the Billickin's dialogue.

Refutation of Forster's account of this earliest idea of Dickens for his new novel is really only important to those with whose solutions it does not agree, because of the much more complete and positive account with which he follows it. In the biography he writes:

I first heard of the later design in a letter dated Friday the 6th of August 1869, in which ... he spoke of the change that had occurred to him for the new tale by himself: 'I laid aside the fancy I told you of, and have a very curious and new idea for my new story. Not a communicable idea (or the interest of the story would be gone) but a very strong one, though difficult to work.' The story, I learnt, immediately afterward, was to be that of a murder of a nephew by his uncle; the originality of which was to consist in the review of the murderer's career by himself at the close, when its temptations were to be dwelt upon as if, not he the culprit, but some other man, were the tempted. The last chapters were to be written in the condemned cell, to which his wickedness, all elaborately elicited from him as if told of another, had brought him. Discovery by the murderer of the utter needlessness of the murder for its object, was to follow hard upon commission of the deed; but all discovery of the murder was to be baffled till towards the close, when by the means of a gold ring which had resisted the corrosive effects of the lime into which he had thrown the body, not only the person murdered was to be identified but the locality of the crime and the man who committed it. So much was told me before any of the book was written; and it will be recollected that the ring, taken by Drood to be given to his betrothed only if their engagement went on, was brought away with him from their last interview. Rosa was to marry Tartar, and Crisparkle the sister of Landless, who was himself, I think, to have perished in assisting Tartar finally to unmask and seize the murderer.

Those who reject this account note the seeming contradiction between Dickens's supposed statement that his idea was in-communicable and the 'immediately afterward' communication. I am not convinced that such contradiction in behaviour by Dickens or any other author, during the period of gestation of a book, is so inherently improbable. There may even be a touch of amusement in Forster's tone. But even if the timing is not quite as Forster suggests, I find it hard to reject his account of what Dickens told him, even if Dickens may well have altered his scheme somewhat in the course of writing (and would no doubt have altered it further had he lived). The apparent contradiction may well be resolved if we consider the 'not communicable idea' to relate to the psychological state (connected with drug-taking or mesmeric powers, or both) of Jasper which created the split in his personality. If the interest of the novel was psychological rather than mysterious, it is this aspect that Dickens would have kept to himself. As to the charge usually made that Forster's account is based only upon what he imagined the novel to be from his reading of what was already written, this seems to me nonsensical. One can hardly suppose that any account of the novel which did *not* accord with what had been published would be acceptable to anyone. Yet all too many solvers of the Edwin Drood mystery have been led into elaborate fantasies far away from the half-novel we possess. In consequence they have been forced to reject Forster's account on the absurd ground that it is too near to what he might have concluded from reading the text.

Forster's account of what the novel was to be seems to me, in fact, entirely in consonance with Dickens's life-long obsession and with the social and ethical application of this obsession, which had greatly changed in the last two decades of his life.

That Jasper was intended to have murdered Edwin is supported by Charles Dickens junior, Dickens's eldest son, in his account of a conversation with his father during a walk at Gad's Hill. Kate Perugini, Dickens's younger daughter and former wife of the first illustrator of the novel, Charles Collins, backed up Forster's view in an article in the *Pall Mall Magazine* for June 1906, in which she wrote:

I do not mean to imply that the mystery itself had no strong hold on my father's imagination; but greatly as he was interested in the intricacies of that tangled skein, the information that he gave to Mr Forster, from whom he had withheld nothing for thirty three years, certainly points to the fact that he was quite as deeply fascinated and absorbed in the study of the criminal Jasper, as in the dark and sinister crime that has given the book its title.

The year previously, 1905, an attack in *The Times Literary Supplement*, asserting that no reported statements by Dickens about the outcome of *Edwin Drood* could be relied upon, had drawn a fierce letter to *The Times* from the novel's illustrator, Luke Fildes. He reported a conversation with Dickens, in which he had asked the importance of Jasper's double necktie (in fact, a black scarf in the novel). Dickens replied, 'Can you keep a secret? I must have the double necktie. It is necessary for Jasper strangles Edwin Drood with it.' It is also very relevant to Forster's account that Dickens had already proposed to take the illustrator to see the inside of Maidstone jail. Those who favour a more complicated murder or supposed murder than these testimonies support have dismissed them as Dickens's deliberate misleading or teasing of his friend, his family, and his illustrator. I agree with the present editor, Mr Arthur Cox, in his comment upon Dickens's notes for the novel that they, like much else, are cryptic, but I do not believe that what he concealed was anything so commonplace as a whodunnit solution. A remark of his about his previous novel, *Our Mutual Friend*, is relevant here. Speaking of the simple revelation at the end of that book about John Harmon's identity, he said, 'I foresaw the likelihood that a class of readers and commentators would suppose that I was at great pains to conceal exactly what I was at great pains to suggest.' Dickens changed and developed greatly in his social ideas, in his treatment of language, in the organization of his novels, but in literary devices he was fairly constant. I suspect that it was not his family and his friends he fooled when he said that Jasper killed Edwin, but rather, as with *Our Mutual Friend*, a class of readers and commentators that couldn't believe things were as simple as they seemed.

There is little substance in conjectures as to where or how the murdered Edwin may reappear – Lieutenant Tartar was at one time a favoured suggestion; nor do I see much point in speculating about which character (if any) is disguised as Datchery, although the idea that he is Helena Landless seems more peculiarly un-

Dickensian than any of the other favourites like Bazzard, Grew-gious, or even, surely rather improbably, Tartar. Nevertheless, some of the more complete and bizarre solutions to the mystery do rest upon aspects of the book that deserve attention. The two most relevant theories are those of Duffield and of Aylmer. The idea that Jasper is connected with the Thuggee followers of Kali, a conjecture associated with the American Droodian expert Duffield, can be supported by Jasper's black scarf, by the passage where Grewgious refuses refreshment at Jasper's house, by Dickens's acquaintance with Captain Meadows Taylor whose *Confessions of a Thug* he had surely read, above all by the presence of another person (Neville) at a feast which precedes Edwin's presumed murder (all marks of Thuggee practice). There is both external and internal evidence here. Far more important, the de-velopment of the Thuggee theory lays stress upon a very new and marked aspect of the novel – its connection with the Orient. Equally Aylmer's more improbable but highly complex treatment of the book as an exculpation of Jasper and the story of an Egyptian family blood-feud is valuable not so much for its details as for its attachment to an undoubtedly important aspect of the novel often overlooked – the relation of its plot to complex past histories in the Jasper, the Drood, the Bud and the Landless families, an extremely familiar but always important element in Dickens's novels. In short all this puzzle-solving, however bizarre its answers, is valuable when it highlights either something unexpected or something so familiar as to escape notice. It is virtually valueless, as with all the many guesses at who Datchery was, when it throws no light upon the half-book by Charles Dickens which it seeks to elucidate.

One other aspect of *The Mystery of Edwin Drood* has led to much speculation, even though it is unlikely that it can ever be solved. Dickens's cover designs for the monthly parts always embodied hints or allegories concerning the novels they contained. *Edwin Drood* is no exception. The design published as frontispiece to this edition is the final one carried out by Luke Fildes, then a young, largely unknown artist, new to co-operation with Dickens. Its allegory of the rosy path leading up to Rosebud's marriage seems clear enough, though not perhaps its ascent from the pipe of Princess Puffer, who appears on the side of Evil in the novel.

The thorny ascent leads up in all probability to Jasper, though the smoking Chinaman can only be identified as the apparently unimportant opium-seller rival to the Princess. Who Rosebud's bridegroom may be we can't tell, though he has been compared on surely dubious evidence to Edwin in the plates of the book. Certainly he seems to be the same person who someone (Jasper?) confronts in alarm by lamplight. The meaning of this bottom picture is inevitably the source of endless speculation – is it Edwin returned, or Neville dressed as Edwin, or Helena dressed as Edwin, and so on. Such difficulties of interpretation exist even for some of Dickens's complete novels, where his cover designs appear later to be contradicted by what he wrote, so perhaps we should not be too teased by the puzzle. Yet it is complicated for this novel by one curious fact: the original designer was his son-in-law, Charles Collins, brother to Wilkie. Charles Collins was already ill with a chest complaint, probably cancer of the lung, when he undertook the commission. He drew the cover design and a few plates under Dickens's instructions, and then was forced to give up because of physical pain. But the cover design he made, although shaped like Fildes's, has material differences. Two policemen are in pursuit on the stairs on the thorny side instead of two civilians; the Chinaman appears to be a young woman (not necessarily Chinese); the bridegroom and the man in the lantern light are, as in the final design, the same person, but in Collins's drawing the young man has no moustache. Speculation about all this has been considerable. I doubt myself if we can answer any of it. But we can certainly say that Dickens's ideas about the novel had changed substantially between October when Collins was first commissioned and November or December when Fildes was appointed. By this time the first two numbers of the novel were completed.

The editor's notes and appendixes to this edition draw attention to various difficulties that Dickens met in the creation of this novel – underwriting the first two numbers (a hitherto unknown experience in the long years of serial writing), suppressing the early introduction of Princess Puffer to Cloisterham, and so on. Rudolph Lehmann in his autobiography, *An Artist's Reminiscence*, of 1926, says that 'Henry Wills [Dickens's co-editor of *All the Year Round*] told me that Dickens, while in the midst of serial publication of "Edwin Drood," altered the plot and found himself hope-

lessly entangled as in a maze of which he could not find the issue.'
This is a second-hand witness speaking many years after the event.
But if Wills *did* say this, we should pay attention, for he is one of
the most reliable and straightforward of all the Dickens circle. My
own belief is that Dickens did find himself more than usually in a
maze with the development of the plot, and that he did so, para-
doxically, because of the particular virtues of *Edwin Drood*. This
is one of the móst compact and rapidly moving of all his novels.
That may be, as I have suggested, his conscious insurance against a
long novel that his health could not support – a tragic insurance, if
Lehmann's report of Wills is true, for he makes Wills add that the
anxieties attendant upon the difficulties of the book led up to
Dickens's collapse. This is pure surmise, of course, but one thing
can be said – the complicated plots suggested by the Droodians
seem likely to spill over the six parts still to come, and yet the
convincing, essentially Dickensian story put forward by Forster
as Dickens's own account seems likely barely to fill them.

So much for the work as a whole as it might or might not have
been. What of the half-book we have? Its opening is one of the
most dramatic of Dickens's many arresting first pages. Yet – and
here we see the extraordinary value of textual work like that of the
present editor – in true reproduction of the manuscript version as
given in this Penguin text, with first a vision of the whole cathedral
town, then moving down to the cathedral tower, we have a familiar
Dickensian literary device, highly cinematic, as in *Bleak House*
where the camera moves down through the fog to London, and
at last on down to the Chancery and into its court in session. The
merging of the oriental dream with the cathedral town brings two
unfamiliar worlds together and both are unique in a novel by
Dickens.

We know that he had been fascinated since childhood with *The
Arabian Nights*, but we also know that the Orient, always a matter
of disgust for him, as embodied in the ancient, static, opium-laden
civilization of 'John Chinaman', had become doubly hateful since
the treachery of the Indian Mutiny in 1857. We can therefore expect
the horror-attraction of Jasper's oriental vision. And, on the whole,
the horror of the actual Asia of England's experience in the Mutiny
is likely by this time consciously to outweigh his childhood
fascination with *The Arabian Nights*.

I believe that in this embodiment of evil in Jasper's opium dreams, we penetrate very deeply into developments within Dickens's imaginative consciousness. There is little doubt, surely, that the oriental dream *is* evil – it is both erotic and violent, and, more important, it is the outcome of that necessary preliminary dream journey of Jasper's, mysteriously described in the last chapter, which surely relates closely to murder. Now, in identifying this oriental world – and the dream is Turkish rather than Indian or Chinese – Dickens is identifying the world of *The Arabian Nights* with the erotic and the violent, those parts of it of which we may suppose he was unconscious when as a child he so loved it that it remained (with Shakespeare) his main source of quotation well on into his maturity. It is worth noting that the other literary reference of *Edwin Drood* is *Macbeth* – the darkest, most murderous of all Shakespeare's plays, though it is quoted very characteristically in a facetious context more than once in Dickens's novel. Now, if we take Jasper to be the symbol of evil, we must then conclude that his evil dreams are identified with one of the earliest sources of Dickens's literary imagination.

That, in this source, Dickens has picked out the erotic and the violent, perhaps, backs up Edmund Wilson's suspicion that Jasper embodies the submerged part of Dickens himself. It is certainly likely that a fear of his own violent side (we need not stress the erotic) may lie under Dickens's obsession with murder as the supreme evil. Mr Dyson, who gives us a fine account of Jasper as the embodiment of evil, is deeply shocked at Wilson's attempt to see any part of so great a creative genius as Dickens in his evil fictive creation. I believe that Wilson's thesis does have some validity and need not shock us so greatly, if, first, we consider that a great number of responsible Englishmen of the last century spent much of their energies in suppressing the erotic-violent side of their natures, and, more particularly, if we accept Forster's account of Dickens's intentions with Jasper, namely that he was a divided man whose evil side was cut off from his everyday self. This does not mean that Dickens would have condemned him the less, for he was by this time an implacable foe to any excuse for crime.

In any case, for me, the important thing about this identification of the Arabian Night dream with evil does not lie in Dickens's fear, conscious or otherwise, of his own animal nature, but in its sug-

gestion – a suggestion amplified in the whole treatment of opium
escape and dreams – that Dickens had, perhaps partly consciously,
become very mistrustful of fiction, of the art he practised, of the
fancy and the imagination as weapons on behalf of the Good in
life. If this is so, it corroborates or extends my detection of the
same distrust of storytelling and art in *Great Expectations* when
Pip's invented fantasies about Miss Havisham's house (so akin to
Dickens's own fanciful powers) are reprehended by Jo as 'Lies'.
Whether this reflects regrets by Dickens about his own life as an
artist, a fiction-maker, is the concern of the speculative biographer;
what we are concerned with here is its relation to the view of life
embodied in his fiction, his fictional identification of the forces of
good and evil as they worked in the world around him. I think it
suggests a continuing, perhaps even a final disillusionment with
childlikeness, with wonder and fancy as adequate positive forces.
His idea of Sleary's circus folk as the antidote to the deadening
factual world of Gradgrind – the armies of Good and Evil as he saw
them back in 1854 in *Hard Times*, the logical culmination of all his
early work – is now quite changed. Fancy and wonder have been
taken over by the black, the gothic and the evil forces of Jasper.
Good has shrunk to the small world of private responsible in-
dividuals ready to pit their courage against the forces of dark
fancy – Rosebud's courage, Tartar's naval manliness and powers
of practical invention, Helena's tough pride, and, most unlikely
of all Dickensian 'good' people, a lawyer, Mr Grewgious, and a
clergyman, the muscular, classically trained Canon Crisparkle –
for in his earlier books all lawyers had been villains or, at least,
ambiguous characters associated with crime like Jaggers, and until
his previous novel, *Our Mutual Friend*, so had all clergymen.

This small army of the good, strong in its resolution, even, like
Rosebud in flight from Jasper, ready to give way in order to
oppose, is primarily middle-class and primarily private. It does not
preclude Dickens's continued concern with the poor and the out-
cast, whom he had championed all his life, although in this novel
their form is ambiguous – Puffer, Tope, above all, Deputy. But it
does directly continue that small world of private doing of good,
of professional-class heroes and heroines, that we see in the close
of *Bleak House* or *Little Dorrit*.

Does this private good mean the world of Cloisterham close,

so small compared with Dickens's previous vast social canvases?
Not entirely, I think, for Cloisterham is not wholly good – the
progressive, radical Dickens is not so changed that an old mouldering cathedral can be a positive value for him; and the Orient, too,
as represented by England's Imperial Mission has also its good side.
Let me take the last point first. Professor Edgar Johnson has seen in
The Mystery of Edwin Drood a radical anti-imperial attitude by
Dickens. He speaks of 'India, China, the victims of the opium
trade, subject peoples everywhere, falling prey to a greedy
Imperialism.' 'Young Drood', he says, 'mouths the catchwords
of that imperialism in their most infuriating form. He is "going to
wake Egypt up a little", he says patronisingly.' Dickens's suggestion in all this is surely quite the opposite. He believed firmly
in the superiority of the white races over the brown and the black.
His dislike for missionary activities, and what he thought to be
some sentimentalization of the negroes of Africa among the
members of the anti-slavery lobby, had originally been due to his
feeling that concern for the black race abroad had made good men
and women neglectful of the evils and poverty at home in England.
That is the meaning of Mrs Jellyby in *Bleak House*. But gradually,
and markedly after the Indian Mutiny in 1857, he had gone further
and had come to believe that the white man must dominate and
order the world of the blacks and the browns. This surely is the
meaning of his support for Governor Eyre's harsh measures in
Jamaica in 1865. His views expressed in letters about the basic
racial inferiority of the blacks after his 1867–8 visit to the United
States were definite. *The Mystery of Edwin Drood* continues to
state these views, hence the absurd rumours against Neville in
Cloisterham – 'Before coming to England he had caused to be
whipped to death sundry "Natives" – nomadic persons, encamping
now in Asia, now in Africa, now in the West Indies, and now at the
North Pole – vaguely supposed in Cloisterham to be always black,
always of great virtue, always calling themselves Me, and everybody else Massa or Missie (according to sex)', and so on – the
typical heavy irony about those who misguidedly respected black
people. Edwin's fault is not, I am sure, to have an Imperial mission,
but rather, in his youthful callowness, to make light of it. Perhaps
Dickens had in mind the failure his son Walter had made in India,
to which Dickens had sent him with such high hopes. In any case,

if there is a public dimension to the little band of those who do good, it lies beyond seas, fighting the treacherous, colourful Oriental source of Jasper's dreams.

Certainly it does not lie at home. There are only three public figures in the book and all are stupid, bullying and cowardly. First we have Mr Honeythunder. We should note that he is a *general* philanthropist, for, although in *Bleak House* (1852), Dickens had confined his satire to Exeter House missionaries and Tractarian busybodies, in the last decade of his life he extended his attacks to include all penal reformers, anti-Imperialists, supporters of women's rights and a host of other wrong-meaning enthusiasts. Second comes the Mayor, Mr Sapsea, the representative of reaction, the oldest of Dickens's enemies – the Tories. The 'Sapsea Fragment', printed as an appendix to this volume, is very important in this respect, for it underlines Mayor Sapsea's Tory prejudices, his devotion to the old order, his snobbery. Without that, we might fear that the old radical Dickens had gone altogether, but this is not so. For the same reason the authority of the Cathedral is represented so odiously in the Dean.

The Mystery of Edwin Drood, as well as telling us much about Dickens's developing attitude to the young and to the Empire, also speaks of that very evasive thing, his religious beliefs. Dickens's faith was always strong but he preferred not to examine sacred subjects too closely. He was always a simple New Testament Christian. In earlier times a Unitarian, he had been increasingly reconciled to the Church of England he was baptized in, by the emergence of a broad church school without the Calvinism of Exeter Hall or the Romanism of the Tractarians; especially was he attracted by the muscular Christianity of Tom Hughes and Charles Kingsley. Canon Crisparkle is surely a tribute to this. But, of the Church as an institution, he still preserved, as he did towards all institutions, an instinctive radical suspicion; it is this that the Dean represents. Even more he remained, what he had been when he wrote *A Child's History of England* (published in 1852) to prevent his eldest boy growing up into a High Church Tory, an unshakeable hater of the past, especially of the Middle Ages. We are reminded again and again in the novel of the unnaturalness of the cloistered life for men and women. The Cathedral is not a force for good, except in the last chapter, when it is seen through the believer

Canon Crisparkle's good eyes. Because Jasper hates it as a prison does not mean that we should revere it. Indeed Cloisterham itself is a place from which the good characters must escape. And here we have a final paradox, typical of the unresolved tensions which underlie the greatness of Charles Dickens's art. We know that in his last years Dickens sought refuge at Gad's Hill from a London he had come to loathe, but we also know that, as in the winter preceding his death, he was drawn to the bustle of London. So it is in the novel: the good characters, save for the Crisparkles, are more and more collected in London, have fled from the petty meanness of Cloisterham; yet London is the scene of the evil opium dreams of Jasper, though Cloisterham is the scene of his black deed. In London, too, is to be found the only purely comic character, the Billickin; but it is to be noted that her verbal comedy is the most stale thing in the novel, a repetition of Mrs Gamp and David Copperfield's London landlady, creations of the 1840s.

We are left, at last, with Jasper at the centre. Much has been written about the nature of his evil. Certainly mesmerism would seem to be part of his evil powers – mesmerism which Dickens had used beneficently to heal Mrs De La Rue, the consul's wife in Genoa, in 1844. Jasper's dissatisfaction, however, his willingness neither to endure the cathedral monotony manfully nor to make another life for himself, but to seek refuge in drugged dreams, are what set him apart among the damned in Dickens's world, where the good forces are always energetic and outward-looking, but never more so than at the end of his life. Some critics of the novel at the time of its publication dismissed Jasper as a melodramatic gesture. I could not do that, but neither could I take the character as we have it in this half-book for the tremendous achievement of depicting evil that it is sometimes said to be nowadays. This is one more reason for me to accept Forster's version of the book's entirety, for surely the last scenes as he suggests them, with Jasper's confession in the condemned cell, would have been tremendous and entirely Jasper's own. The character might well have been more terrible than any of Dickens's previous men of violence.

In fact, all unwillingly, one is always brought back to the simple distress that the book was not finished. We could have known more had Queen Victoria only been more inquisitive. In March 1870, two months and a half before his death, he had been received by

the Queen in an hour and a half private interview. He wrote afterwards to his friend, Sir Arthur Helps, the Clerk of the Privy
Council, 'If Her Majesty should ever be sufficiently interested in
my tale to desire to know a little more of it in advance of her
subjects, you know how proud I shall be to anticipate publication.'
Alas, she was not.

ANGUS WILSON

A NOTE ON THE TEXT

CHARLES DICKENS began work on what was to prove his last book in August 1869. It was to be published in monthly parts, or numbers, of roughly sixteen thousand words (or thirty-two pages) each, as had most of his previous books; but this time it was intended that there should be only twelve numbers, rather than the usual twenty. As it happened, even this much was not to be. Three numbers had been published and there was not quite enough letter-press and manuscript on hand for three more when the author was felled by the stroke that ended his life. The result is one of the curiosities of literature.

The text of the present edition has been compared with the manuscript and partial proofs in the Forster Collection at the Victoria and Albert Museum, and with the text of the first edition, published in 1870. It differs in three ways from the 1870 text and from the texts of most other editions.

First: Dickens found that he had over-written the manuscript for the fifth number and so struck out of the proofs of that number a sufficient quantity of text so that his four chapters would fit into the thirty-two pages. But he died before the number went into print, and his literary executor John Forster re-inserted the deletions. This necessarily made too much written matter and he carried this excess matter forward into the next number in the guise of a chapter – Chapter 21, 'A Recognition' – and changed the title of Chapter 20 from 'Divers Flights' to 'A Flight'. The present edition restores the author's chapter titles and divisions, but follows Forster's example in retaining the deleted material, as it was removed only in the interest of saving space.

Second: The last two chapters were in Dickens's handwriting only when he died. He never saw the proofs for these pages – the last that ever flowed from his pen – and his printers passed a great many misreadings of the manuscript into the published text. The last two chapters of the present book are founded on a new reading of the manuscript. (Several small errors in the first printing, made while the author was still alive but uncaught by him, are corrected here.)

Third: The author's original spelling and punctuation have been restored, except in those cases in which it seemed impractical to do so. Where Dickens's spelling of a word varied from instance to instance, I have chosen the more conventional spelling.

I have marked with a star the break between each monthly part of the novel.

Included in this edition (Appendix A) is a reproduction, in type, of Dickens's notes and number plans for *The Mystery of Edwin Drood*. Also included (Appendix B) is the so-called 'Sapsea Fragment', a portion of manuscript relevant to *Drood*, that was discovered after the author's death and which Forster published in his *Life of Charles Dickens*, with a misleading description of its general nature and some misconstruction of the text. A new reading is supplied.

Grateful acknowledgement is made to the Keeper of the Library, Victoria and Albert Museum, for permission to examine the manuscript, and the proofs of the fifth number, of *The Mystery of Edwin Drood*.

A. J. C.

SELECTED FURTHER READING

THE literature on *The Mystery of Edwin Drood* is extremely extensive, though much of it is of doubtful value. Besides various continuations, sequels, adaptations, there are eleven book-length – and several hundred shorter – serious discussions of the novel. For works published to 1928, see '*The Mystery of Edwin Drood:* a Bibliography', compiled by B. W. Matz, *Dickensian*, VII (1911), pp. 130–33; and 'A Bibliography of *Edwin Drood*: Part II', compiled by Winifred Matz, *Dickensian*, XXIV (1928), p. 236; XXV (1928/9), pp. 42–4 and 185–7. There is no comprehensive bibliography of works on the subject published since 1928. A few titles are listed below.

John Forster, *Life of Charles Dickens*. 1872–4. See Book XI, Chapter 2.

H[enry] J[ackson], *About Edwin Drood*. 1911. And see his letter in *The Times Literary Supplement*, 7 August 1919, p. 425.

W. Robertson Nicoll, *The Problem of Edwin Drood*. 1912. Reprints the B. W. Matz bibliography.

J. Cuming Walters, *The Complete Mystery of Edwin Drood*. 1912.

Montagu Saunders, *The Mystery in the Drood Family*. 1914.

Aubrey Boyd, 'A New Angle on the Drood Mystery', in *Humanistic Series: Social Studies*, IX (October 1921), pp. 35–85; reprinted as a pamphlet, 1922. Discusses the part played in the story by 'animal magnetism'.

Howard Duffield, 'John Jasper: Strangler', in *The Bookman*, February 1930. Argues that Jasper is an adherent of the Hindu sect of Thuggee and has murdered Drood according to the dictates of its ritual.

Edmund Wilson, 'Dickens: The Two Scrooges', in *The Wound and the Bow*. 1941. Possibly the most influential essay written on Dickens. Concludes with a theory on *Drood* combining the ideas of Boyd and Duffield, above.

Edgar Johnson, *Charles Dickens. His Tragedy and Triumph*. 1952. See Part Ten, Chapter 4.

Philip Collins, *Dickens and Crime*. 1962.

Felix Aylmer, *The Drood Case*. 1964. The most recent book on the subject.
A. E. Dyson, *The Inimitable Dickens*. 1970. Last chapter.

Facsimile of the title-page of the first edition (1870)

THE MYSTERY

OF

EDWIN DROOD

BY

CHARLES DICKENS.

LONDON:

CHAPMAN & HALL, 193, PICCADILLY.

CONTENTS

The Dawn

AN ancient English Cathedral town? How can the ancient English Cathedral town be here! The well-known massive grey square tower of its old Cathedral? How can that be here! There is no spike of rusty iron in the air, between the eye and it, from any point of the real prospect. What IS the spike that intervenes, and who has set it up? Maybe, it is set up by the Sultan's orders for the impaling of a horde of Turkish robbers, one by one. It is so, for cymbals clash, and the Sultan goes by to his palace in long procession. Ten thousand scimitars flash in the sunlight, and thrice ten thousand dancing-girls strew flowers. Then, follow white elephants caparisoned in countless gorgeous colors, and infinite in number and attendants. Still, the Cathedral tower rises in the background, where it cannot be, and still no writhing figure is on the grim spike. Stay! Is the spike so low a thing as the rusty spike on the top of a post of an old bedstead that has tumbled all awry? Some vague period of drowsy laughter must be devoted to the consideration of this possibility.

Shaking from head to foot, the man whose scattered consciousness has thus fantastically pieced itself together, at length rises, supports his trembling frame upon his arms, and looks around. He is in the meanest and closest of small rooms. Through the ragged window-curtain, the light of early day steals in from a miserable court. He lies, dressed, across a large unseemly bed, upon a bedstead that has indeed given way under the weight upon it. Lying, also dressed and also across the bed, not longwise, are a Chinaman, a Lascar, and a haggard woman. The two first are in a sleep or stupor; the last is blowing at a kind of pipe, to kindle it. And as she blows, and shading it with her lean hand, concentrates its red spark of light, it serves in the dim morning as a lamp to show him what he sees of her.

'Another?' says this woman,[1] in a querulous, rattling whisper. 'Have another?'

He looks about him, with his hand to his forehead.

'Ye've smoked as many as five since ye come in at midnight,' the woman goes on, as she chronically complains. 'Poor me, poor me, my head is so bad. Them two come in after ye. Ah, poor me, the business is slack, is slack! Few Chinamen about the Docks, and fewer Lascars, and no ships coming in, these say! Here's another ready for ye, deary. Ye'll remember like a good soul, won't ye, that the market price is dreffle high just now? More nor three shillings and sixpence for a thimbleful! And ye'll remember that nobody but me (and Jack Chinaman t'other side the court; but he can't do it as well as me) has the true secret of mixing it? Ye'll pay up according, deary, won't ye?'

She blows at the pipe as she speaks, and, occasionally bubbling at it, inhales much of its contents.

'O me, O me, my lungs is weak, my lungs is bad! It's nearly ready for ye, deary. Ah, poor me, poor me, my poor hand shakes like to drop off! I see ye coming-to, and I ses to my poor self, "I'll have another ready for him, and he'll bear in mind the market price of opium, and pay according." O my poor head! I makes my pipes of old penny ink-bottles, ye see, deary – this is one – and I fits in a mouthpiece, this way, and I takes my mixter out of this thimble with this little horn spoon; and so I fills, deary. Ah, my poor nerves! I got Heavens-hard drunk for sixteen year afore I took to this; but this don't hurt me, not to speak of. And it takes away the hunger as well as wittles, deary.'

She hands him the nearly-emptied pipe, and sinks back, turning over on her face.

He rises unsteadily from the bed, lays the pipe upon the hearth-stone, draws back the ragged curtain, and looks with repugnance at his three companions. He notices that the woman has opium-smoked herself into a strange likeness of the Chinaman. His form of cheek, eye, and temple, and his color, are repeated in her. Said Chinaman convulsively wrestles with one of his many Gods, or Devils, perhaps, and snarls horribly. The Lascar laughs and dribbles at the mouth. The hostess is still.

'What visions can *she* have?' the waking man muses, as he turns her face towards him, and stands looking down at it. 'Visions of many butchers' shops, and public-houses, and much credit? Of an increase of hideous customers, and this horrible bedstead set up-right again, and this horrible court swept clean? What can she rise to, under any quantity of opium, higher than that! – Eh?'

He bends down his ear, to listen to her mutterings.

'Unintelligible!'

As he watches the spasmodic shoots and darts that break out of her face and limbs, like fitful lightning out of a dark sky, some contagion in them seizes upon him: insomuch that he has to withdraw himself to a lean arm-chair by the hearth – placed there, perhaps, for such emergencies – and to sit in it, holding tight, until he has got the better of this unclean spirit of imitation.

Then he comes back, pounces on the Chinaman, and, seizing him with both hands by the throat, turns him violently on the bed. The Chinaman clutches the aggressive hands, resists, gasps, and protests.

'What do you say?'

A watchful pause.

'Unintelligible!'

Slowly loosening his grasp as he listens to the incoherent jargon with an attentive frown, he turns to the Lascar and fairly drags him forth upon the floor. As he falls, the Lascar starts into a half-risen attitude, glares with his eyes, lashes about him fiercely with his arms, and draws a phantom knife. It then becomes apparent that the woman has taken possession of his knife, for safety's sake; for, she too starting up, and restraining and expostulating with him, the knife is visible in her dress, not in his, when they drowsily drop back, side by side.

There has been chattering and clattering enough between them, but to no purpose. When any distinct word has been flung into the air, it has had no sense or sequence. Wherefore 'unintelligible!' is again the comment of the watcher, made with some reassured nodding of his head, and a gloomy smile. He then lays certain silver money on the table, finds his hat, gropes his way down the broken stairs, gives a good morning to some rat-ridden door-keeper, in bed in a black hutch beneath the stairs, and passes out.

That same afternoon, the massive grey square tower of an old Cathedral rises before the sight of a jaded traveller. The bells are going for daily vesper service, and he must needs attend it, one would say, from his haste to reach the open Cathedral door. The choir are getting on their sullied white robes, in a hurry, when he arrives among them, gets on his own robe, and falls into the procession filing in to service. Then, the Sacristan locks the iron-barred gates that divide the sanctuary from the chancel, and all of the procession having scuttled into their places, hide their faces; and then the intoned words, 'WHEN THE WICKED MAN —'² rise among groins of arches and beams of roof, awakening muttered thunder.

CHAPTER 2

A Dean, and a Chapter Also

WHOSOEVER has observed that sedate and clerical bird, the rook, may perhaps have noticed that when he wings his way homeward towards nightfall, in a sedate and clerical company, two rooks will suddenly detach themselves from the rest, will retrace their flight for some distance, and will there poise and linger; conveying to mere men the fancy that it is of some occult importance to the body politic, that this artful couple should pretend to have re-nounced connexion with it.

Similarly, service being over in the old Cathedral with the square tower, and the choir scuffling out again, and divers venerable persons of rook-like aspect dispersing, two of these latter retrace their steps, and walk together in the echoing Close.

Not only is the day waning, but the year. The low sun is fiery and yet cold behind the monastery ruin, and the Virginia creeper on the Cathedral wall has showered half its deep-red leaves down on the pavement. There has been rain this afternoon, and a wintry shudder goes among the little pools on the cracked uneven flag-stones, and through the giant elm trees as they shed a gust of tears. Their fallen leaves lie strewn thickly about. Some of these leaves, in a timid rush, seek sanctuary within the low arched Cathedral door; but two men coming out, resist them, and cast them forth again with their feet; this done, one of the two locks the door with a goodly key, and the other flits away with a folio music book.

'Mr Jasper was that, Tope?'

'Yes, Mr Dean.'

'He has stayed late.'

'Yes, Mr Dean. I have stayed for him, your Reverence. He has been took a little poorly.'

'Say "taken," Tope – to the Dean,' the younger rook interposes in a low tone with this touch of correction, as who should say: 'You may offer bad grammar to the laity, or the humbler clergy, not to the Dean.'

Mr Tope, Chief Verger and Showman, and accustomed to be high with excursion parties, declines with a silent loftiness to perceive that any suggestion has been tendered to him.

'And when and how has Mr Jasper been taken – for, as Mr Crisparkle has remarked, it is better to say taken – taken –' repeats the Dean; 'when and how has Mr Jasper been Taken –'

'Taken, sir,' Tope deferentially murmurs.

'– Poorly, Tope?'

'Why, sir, Mr Jasper was that breathed –'

'I wouldn't say "That breathed," Tope,' Mr Crisparkle interposes, with the same touch as before. 'Not English – to the Dean.'

'Breathed to that extent,' the Dean (not unflattered by this indirect homage) condescendingly remarks, 'would be preferable.'

'Mr Jasper's breathing was so remarkably short' – thus discreetly does Mr Tope work his way round the sunken rock – 'when he came in, that it distressed him mightily to get his notes out: which was perhaps the cause of his having a kind of fit on him after a little. His memory grew DAZED.' Mr Tope, with his eyes on the Reverend Mr Crisparkle, shoots this word out, as defying him to improve upon it: 'and a dimness and giddiness crept over him as strange as ever I saw: though he didn't seem to mind it particularly, himself. However, a little time and a little water brought him out of his DAZE.' Mr Tope repeats the word and its emphasis, with the air of saying: 'As I *have* made a success, I'll make it again.'

'And Mr Jasper has gone home quite himself, has he?' asks the Dean.

'Your Reverence, he has gone home quite himself. And I'm glad to see he's having his fire kindled up, for it's chilly after the wet, and the Cathedral had both a damp feel and a damp touch this afternoon, and he was very shivery.'

They all three look towards an old stone gatehouse[1] crossing the Close, with an arched thoroughfare passing beneath it. Through its latticed window, a fire shines out upon the fast-darkening scene, involving in shadow the pendent masses of ivy and creeper covering the building's front. As the deep Cathedral-bell strikes the hour, a ripple of wind goes through these at their distance, like a ripple of the solemn sound that hums through tomb and tower, broken niche and defaced statue, in the pile close at hand.

'Is Mr Jasper's nephew with him?' the Dean asks.

'No, sir,' replies the Verger, 'but expected. There's his own solitary shadow betwixt his two windows – the one looking this way, and the one looking down into the High Street – drawing his own curtains now.'

'Well, well,' says the Dean, with a sprightly air of breaking up the little conference, 'I hope Mr Jasper's heart may not be too much set upon his nephew. Our affections, however laudable, in this transitory world, should never master us; we should guide them, guide them. I find I am not disagreeably reminded of my dinner, by hearing my dinner-bell. Perhaps, Mr Crisparkle, you will, before going home, look in on Jasper?'

'Certainly, Mr Dean. And tell him that you had the kindness to desire to know how he was?'

'Aye; do so, do so. Certainly. Wished to know how he was. By all means. Wished to know how he was.'

With a pleasant air of patronage, the Dean as nearly cocks his quaint hat as a Dean in good spirits may, and directs his comely gaiters towards the ruddy dining-room of the snug old red-brick house where he is at present 'in residence' with Mrs Dean and Miss Dean.

Mr Crisparkle, Minor Canon, fair and rosy, and perpetually pitching himself head-foremost into all the deep running water in the surrounding country; Mr Crisparkle, Minor Canon, early riser, musical, classical, cheerful, kind, good-natured, social, contented, and boy-like; Mr Crisparkle, Minor Canon and good man, lately 'Coach' upon the chief Pagan high roads, but since promoted by a patron (grateful for a well-taught son) to his present Christian beat; betakes himself to the gatehouse, on his way home to his early tea.

'Sorry to hear from Tope that you have not been well, Jasper.'

'Oh, it was nothing, nothing!'

'You look a little worn.'

'Do I? Oh, I don't think so. What is better, I don't feel so. Tope has made too much of it, I suspect. It's his trade to make the most of everything appertaining to the Cathedral, you know.'

'I may tell the Dean – I call expressly from the Dean – that you are all right again?'

The reply, with a slight smile, is: 'Certainly; with my respects and thanks to the Dean.'

'I'm glad to hear that you expect young Drood.'

'I expect the dear fellow every moment.'

'Ah! He will do you more good than a doctor, Jasper.'

'More good than a dozen doctors. For I love him dearly, and I don't love doctors, or doctors' stuff.'

Mr Jasper is a dark man of some six-and-twenty, with thick, lustrous, well-arranged black hair and whisker. He looks older than he is, as dark men often do. His voice is deep and good, his face and figure are good, his manner is a little sombre. His room is a little sombre, and may have had its influence in forming his manner. It is mostly in shadow. Even when the sun shines brilliantly, it seldom touches the grand piano in the recess, or the folio music-books on the stand, or the bookshelves on the wall, or the unfinished picture of a blooming schoolgirl hanging over the chimneypiece; her flowing brown hair tied with a blue riband, and her beauty remarkable for a quite childish, almost babyish, touch of saucy discontent, comically conscious of itself. (There is not the least artistic merit in this picture, which is a mere daub; but it is clear that the painter has made it humorously – one might almost say, revengefully – like the original.)

'We shall miss you, Jasper, at the "Alternate Musical Wednesdays" to-night; but no doubt you are best at home. Good-night. God bless you! "Tell me, shep-herds,[2] te-e-ell me; tell me-e-e, have you seen (have you seen, have you seen, have you seen) my-y-y Flo-o-ora-a pass this way!"' Melodiously good Minor Canon the Reverend Septimus Crisparkle thus delivers himself, in musical rhythm, as he withdraws his amiable face from the doorway and conveys it down stairs.

Sounds of recognition and greeting pass between the Reverend Septimus and somebody else, at the stair-foot. Mr Jasper listens, starts from his chair, and catches a young fellow in his arms, exclaiming:

'My dear Edwin!'

'My dear Jack! So glad to see you!'

'Get off your greatcoat, bright boy, and sit down here in your own corner. Your feet are not wet? Pull your boots off. Do pull your boots off.'

'My dear Jack, I am as dry as a bone. Don't moddley-coddley, there's a good fellow. I like anything better than being moddley-coddleyed.'

With the check upon him of being unsympathetically restrained in a genial outburst of enthusiasm, Mr Jasper stands still, and looks on intently at the young fellow, divesting himself of his outer coat, hat, gloves, and so forth. Once for all, a look of intentness and intensity – a look of hungry, exacting, watchful, and yet devoted affection – is always, now and ever afterwards, on the Jasper face whenever the Jasper face is addressed in this direction. And whenever it is so addressed, it is never, on this occasion or on any other, dividedly addressed; it is always concentrated.

'Now I am right, and now I'll take my corner, Jack. Any dinner, Jack?'

Mr Jasper opens a door at the upper end of the room, and discloses a small inner room pleasantly lighted and prepared, wherein a comely dame is in the act of setting dishes on table.

'What a jolly old Jack it is!' cries the young fellow, with a clap of his hands. 'Look here, Jack; tell me; whose birthday is it?'

'Not yours, I know,' Mr Jasper answers, pausing to consider.

'Not mine, you know? No; not mine, *I* know! Pussy's!'

Fixed as the look the young fellow meets is, there is yet in it some strange power of suddenly including the sketch over the chimneypiece.

'Pussy's, Jack! We must drink Many happy returns to her. Come, uncle; take your dutiful and sharp-set nephew in to dinner.'

As the boy (for he is little more) lays a hand on Jasper's shoulder, Jasper cordially and gaily lays a hand on *his* shoulder, and so Marseillaise-wise they go in to dinner.

'And, Lord! Here's Mrs Tope!' cries the boy. 'Lovelier than ever!'

'Never you mind me, Master Edwin,' retorts the Verger's wife; 'I can take care of myself.'

'You can't. You're much too handsome. Give me a kiss, because it's Pussy's birthday.'

'I'd Pussy you, young man, if I was Pussy, as you call her,' Mrs Tope blushingly retorts, after being saluted. 'Your uncle's too much wrapt up in you, that's where it is. He makes so much of you, that it's my opinion you think you've only to call your Pussys by the dozen, to make 'em come.'

'You forget, Mrs Tope,' Mr Jasper interposes, taking his place at table with a genial smile, 'and so do you, Ned, that Uncle and Nephew are words prohibited here by common consent and express agreement. For what we are going to receive His holy name be praised!'

'Done like the Dean! Witness, Edwin Drood! Please to carve, Jack, for I can't.'

This sally ushers in the dinner. Little to the present purpose, or to any purpose, is said, while it is in course of being disposed of. At length the cloth is drawn, and a dish of walnuts and a decanter of rich-colored sherry are placed upon the table.

'I say! Tell me, Jack,' the young fellow then flows on: 'do you really and truly feel as if the mention of our relationship divided us at all? *I* don't.'

'Uncles as a rule, Ned, are so much older than their nephews,' is the reply, 'that I have that feeling instinctively.'

'As a rule? Ah, may-be! But what is a difference in age of half a dozen years or so? And some uncles, in large families, are even younger than their nephews. By George, I wish it was the case with us!'

'Why?'

'Because if it was, I'd take the lead with you, Jack, and be as wise as Begone dull care[3] that turned a young man grey, and begone dull care that turned an old man to clay. – Halloa, Jack! Don't drink.'

'Why not?'

'Asks why not, on Pussy's birthday, and no Happy Returns proposed! Pussy, Jack, and many of 'em! Happy returns, I mean.'

Laying an affectionate and laughing touch on the boy's extended hand, as if it were at once his giddy head and his light heart, Mr Jasper drinks the toast in silence.

'Hip, hip, hip, and nine times nine, and one to finish with, and all that, understood. Hooray, hooray, hooray! And now, Jack, let's have a little talk about Pussy. Two pairs of nut-crackers? Pass me one, and take the other.' Crack. 'How's Pussy getting on, Jack?'

'With her music? Fairly.'

'What a dreadfully conscientious fellow you are, Jack. But *I* know, Lord bless you! Inattentive, isn't she?'

'She can learn anything, if she will.'

'*If* she will! Egad, that's it. But if she won't?'

Crack. On Mr Jasper's part.

'How's she looking, Jack?'

Mr Jasper's concentrated face again includes the portrait as he returns: 'Very like your sketch indeed.'

'I *am* a little proud of it,' says the young fellow, glancing up at the sketch with complacency, and then shutting one eye, and taking a corrected prospect of it over a level bridge of nut-cracker in the air: 'Not badly hit off from memory. But I ought to have caught that expression pretty well, for I have seen it often enough.'

Crack. On Edwin Drood's part.

Crack. On Mr Jasper's part.

'In point of fact,' the former resumes, after some silent dipping among his fragments of walnut with an air of pique, 'I see it whenever I go to see Pussy. If I don't find it on her face, I leave it there. – You know I do, Miss Scornful Pert. Booh!' With a twirl of the nut-crackers at the portrait.

Crack. Crack. Crack. Slowly, on Mr Jasper's part.

Crack. Sharply, on the part of Edwin Drood.

Silence on both sides.

'Have you lost your tongue, Jack?'

'Have you found yours, Ned?'

'No, but really; – isn't it, you know, after all?'

Mr Jasper lifts his dark eyebrows enquiringly.

'Isn't it unsatisfactory to be cut off from choice in such a matter? There, Jack! I tell you! If I could choose, I would choose Pussy from all the pretty girls in the world.'

'But you have not got to choose.'

'That's what I complain of. My dead and gone father and Pussy's dead and gone father must needs marry us together by anticipation. Why the – Devil, I was going to say, if it had been respectful to their memory – couldn't they leave us alone?'

'Tut, tut, dear boy,' Mr Jasper remonstrates, in a tone of gentle deprecation.

'Tut, tut? Yes, Jack, it's all very well for *you*. *You* can take it easily. *Your* life is not laid down to scale, and lined and dotted out for you, like a surveyor's plan. *You* have no uncomfortable suspicion that you are forced upon anybody, nor has anybody an uncomfortable suspicion that she is forced upon you, or that you are forced upon her. *You* can choose for yourself. Life, for *you*, is a plum with the natural bloom on; it hasn't been over-carefully wiped off for *you* –'

'Don't stop, dear fellow. Go on.'

'Can I anyhow have hurt your feelings, Jack?'

'How can you have hurt my feelings?'

'Good Heaven, Jack, you look frightfully ill! There's a strange film come over your eyes.'

Mr Jasper, with a forced smile, stretches out his right hand, as if at once to disarm apprehension and gain time to get better. After a while he says faintly:

'I have been taking opium for a pain[4] – an agony – that some-times overcomes me. The effects of the medicine steal over me like a blight or a cloud, and pass. You see them in the act of passing; they will be gone directly. Look away from me. They will go all the sooner.'

With a scared face, the younger man complies, by casting his eyes downward at the ashes on the hearth. Not relaxing his own gaze at the fire, but rather strengthening it with a fierce, firm grip upon his elbow-chair, the elder sits for a few moments rigid, and then, with thick drops standing on his forehead, and a sharp catch of his breath, becomes as he was before. On his so subsiding in his chair, his nephew gently and assiduously tends him while he quite recovers. When Jasper is restored, he lays a tender hand upon his nephew's shoulder, and, in a tone of voice less troubled than the purport of his words – indeed with something of raillery or banter in it – thus addresses him:

'There is said to be a hidden skeleton in every house; but you thought there was none in mine, dear Ned.'

'Upon my life, Jack, I did think so. However, when I come to consider that even in Pussy's house – if she had one – and in mine – if I had one –'

'You were going to say (but that I interrupted you in spite of myself) what a quiet life mine is. No whirl and uproar around me, no distracting commerce or calculation, no risk, no change of place, myself devoted to the art I pursue, my business my pleasure.'

'I really was going to say something of the kind, Jack; but you see, you, speaking of yourself, almost necessarily leave out much that I should have put in. For instance: I should have put in the foreground your being so much respected as Lay Precentor, or Lay Clerk, or whatever you call it, of this Cathedral; your enjoying the reputation of having done such wonders with the choir; your choosing your society, and holding such an independent position in this queer old place; your gift of teaching (why, even Pussy, who don't like being taught, says there never was such a Master as you are!); and your connexion.'

'Yes; I saw what you were tending to. I hate it.'

'Hate it, Jack?' (Much bewildered.)

'I hate it. The cramped monotony of my existence grinds me away by the grain. How does our service sound to you?'

'Beautiful! Quite celestial!'

'It often sounds to me quite devilish. I am so weary of it. The echoes of my own voice among the arches seem to mock me with my daily drudging round. No wretched monk who droned his life away in that gloomy place, before me, can have been more tired of it than I am. He could take for relief (and did take) to carving demons out of the stalls and seats and desks. What shall I do? Must I take to carving them out of my heart?'

'I thought you had so exactly found your niche in life, Jack,' Edwin Drood returns, astonished, bending forward in his chair to lay a sympathetic hand on Jasper's knee, and looking at him with an anxious face.

'I know you thought so. They all think so.'

'Well; I suppose they do,' says Edwin, meditating aloud. 'Pussy thinks so.'

'When did she tell you that?'

'The last time I was here. You remember when. Three months ago.'

'How did she phrase it?'

'Oh! She only said that she had become your pupil, and that you were made for your vocation.'

The younger man glances at the portrait. The elder sees it in him.

'Anyhow, my dear Ned,' Jasper resumes, as he shakes his head with a grave cheerfulness: 'I must subdue myself to my vocation: which is much the same thing outwardly. It's too late to find another now. This is a confidence between us.'

'It shall be sacredly preserved, Jack.'

'I have reposed it in you, because –'

'I feel it, I assure you. Because we are fast friends, and because you love and trust me, as I love and trust you. Both hands, Jack.'

As each stands looking into the other's eyes, and as the uncle holds the nephew's hands, the uncle thus proceeds:

'You know now, don't you, that even a poor monotonous chorister and grinder of music – in his niche – may be troubled with some stray sort of ambition, aspiration, restlessness, dissatisfaction, what shall we call it?'

'Yes, dear Jack.'

'And you will remember?'

'My dear Jack, I only ask you, am I likely to forget what you have said with so much feeling?'

'Take it as a warning, then.'

In the act of having his hands released, and of moving a step back, Edwin pauses for an instant to consider the application of these last words. The instant over, he says, sensibly touched:

'I am afraid I am but a shallow, surface kind of fellow, Jack, and that my headpiece is none of the best. But I needn't say I am young; and perhaps I shall not grow worse as I grow older. At all events, I hope I have something impressible within me, which feels – deeply feels – the disinterestedness of your painfully laying your inner self bare, as a warning to me.'

Mr Jasper's steadiness of face and figure becomes so marvellous that his breathing seems to have stopped.

'I couldn't fail to notice, Jack, that it cost you a great effort, and that you were very much moved, and very unlike your usual self. Of course I knew that you were extremely fond of me, but I really was not prepared for your, as I may say, sacrificing yourself to me, in that way.'

Mr Jasper, becoming a breathing man again without the smallest stage of transition between the two extreme states, lifts his shoulders, laughs, and waves his right arm.

'No; don't put the sentiment away, Jack; please don't; for I am very much in earnest. I have no doubt that that unhealthy state of mind which you have so powerfully described is attended with some real suffering, and is hard to bear. But let me reassure you, Jack, as to the chances of its overcoming Me. I don't think I am in the way of it. In some few months less than another year, you know, I shall carry Pussy off from school as Mrs Edwin Drood. I shall then go engineering into the East, and Pussy with me. And although we have our little tiffs now, arising out of a certain unavoidable flatness that attends our love-making, owing to its end being all settled beforehand, still I have no doubt of our getting on capitally then, when it's done and can't be helped. In short, Jack, to go back to the old song I was freely quoting at dinner (and who knows old songs better than you!), my wife shall dance and I will sing, so merrily pass the day. Of Pussy's being beautiful there cannot be a doubt; – and when you are good besides, Little Miss Impudence,' once more apostrophizing the portrait, 'I'll burn your comic likeness and paint your music-master another.'

Mr Jasper, with his hand to his chin, and with an expression of musing benevolence on his face, has attentively watched every animated look and gesture attending the delivery of these words. He remains in that attitude after they are spoken, as if in a kind of fascination attendant on his strong interest in the youthful spirit that he loves so well. Then, he says with a quiet smile:

'You won't be warned, then?'

'No, Jack.'

'You can't be warned, then?'

'No, Jack, not by you. Besides that I don't really consider myself in danger, I don't like your putting yourself in that position.'

'Shall we go and walk in the churchyard?'

'By all means. You won't mind my slipping out of it for half a moment to the Nuns' House, and leaving a parcel there? Only gloves for Pussy; as many pairs of gloves as she is years old to-day. Rather poetical, Jack?'

Mr Jasper, still in the same attitude, murmurs: '"Nothing half so sweet in life,"⁵ Ned!'

'Here's the parcel in my greatcoat pocket. They must be presented to-night, or the poetry is gone. It's against regulations for me to call at night, but not to leave a packet. I am ready, Jack!'

Mr Jasper dissolves his attitude, and they go out together.

CHAPTER 3

The Nuns' House

FOR sufficient reasons which this narrative will itself unfold as it advances, a fictitious name must be bestowed upon the old Cathedral town. Let it stand in these pages as Cloisterham.[1] It was once possibly known to the Druids by another name, and certainly to the Romans by another, and to the Saxons by another, and to the Normans by another; and a name more or less in the course of many centuries can be of little moment to its dusty chronicles.

An ancient city, Cloisterham, and no meet dwelling-place for any one with hankerings after the noisy world. A monotonous, silent city, deriving an earthy flavor throughout, from its Cathedral crypt, and so abounding in vestiges of monastic graves, that the Cloisterham children grow small salad in the dust of abbots and abbesses, and make dirt-pies of nuns and friars; while every ploughman in its outlying fields renders to once puissant Lord Treasurers, Archbishops, Bishops, and such-like, the attention which the Ogre in the story-book desired to render to his unbidden visitor, and grinds their bones to make his bread.

A drowsy city, Cloisterham, whose inhabitants seem to suppose, with an inconsistency more strange than rare, that all its changes lie behind it, and that there are no more to come. A queer moral to derive from antiquity, yet older than any traceable antiquity. So silent are the streets of Cloisterham (though prone to echo on the smallest provocation), that of a summer-day the sunblinds of its shops scarce dare to flap in the south wind; while the sun-browned tramps, who pass along and stare, quicken their limp a little, that they may the sooner get beyond the confines of its oppressive respectability. This is a feat not difficult of achievement, seeing that the streets of Cloisterham city are little more than one narrow street by which you get into it and get out of it: the rest being mostly disappointing yards with pumps in them and no thoroughfare – exception made of the Cathedral-close, and a paved Quaker settlement, in color and general conformation very like a Quakeress's bonnet, up in a shady corner.

In a word, a city of another and a bygone time is Cloisterham, with its hoarse Cathedral-bell, its hoarse rooks hovering about the

Cathedral tower, its hoarser and less distinct rooks in the stalls far beneath. Fragments of old wall, saint's chapel, chapter-house, convent and monastery, have got incongruously or obstructively built into many of its houses and gardens, much as kindred jumbled notions have become incorporated into many of its citizens' minds. All things in it are of the past. Even its single pawnbroker takes in no pledges, nor has he for a long time, but offers vainly an un-redeemed stock for sale, of which the costlier articles are dim and pale old watches apparently in a slow perspiration, tarnished sugar-tongs with ineffectual legs, and odd volumes of dismal books. The most abundant and the most agreeable evidences of progressing life in Cloisterham are the evidences of vegetable life in its many gardens; even its drooping and despondent little theatre has its poor strip of garden, receiving the foul fiend, when he ducks from its stage into the infernal regions, among scarlet beans or oyster-shells, according to the season of the year.

In the midst of Cloisterham stands the Nuns' House;[2] a venerable brick edifice, whose present appellation is doubtless derived from the legend of its conventual uses. On the trim gate enclosing its old courtyard is a resplendent brass plate flashing forth the legend: 'Seminary for Young Ladies. Miss Twinkleton.' The house-front is so old and worn, and the brass plate is so shining and staring, that the general result has reminded imaginative strangers of a battered old beau with a large modern eye-glass stuck in his blind eye.

Whether the nuns of yore, being of a submissive rather than a stiff-necked generation, habitually bent their contemplative heads to avoid collision with the beams in the low ceilings of the many chambers of their House; whether they sat in its long low windows, telling their beads for their mortification instead of making neck-laces of them for their adornment; whether they were ever walled up alive in odd angles and jutting gables of the building for having some ineradicable leaven of busy mother Nature in them which has kept the fermenting world alive ever since; these may be matters of interest to its haunting ghosts (if any), but constitute no item in Miss Twinkleton's half-yearly accounts. They are neither of Miss Twinkleton's inclusive regulars, nor of her extras. The lady who undertakes the poetical department of the establishment at so much (or so little) a quarter has no pieces in her list of recitals bearing on such unprofitable questions.

As, in some cases of drunkenness, and in others of animal magnetism, there are two states of consciousness which never clash, but each of which pursues its separate course as though it were continuous instead of broken (thus, if I hide my watch when I am drunk, I must be drunk again before I can remember where), so Miss Twinkleton has two distinct and separate phases of being. Every night, the moment the young ladies have retired to rest, does Miss Twinkleton smarten up her curls a little, brighten up her eyes a little, and become a sprightly Miss Twinkleton whom the young ladies have never seen. Every night, at the same hour, does Miss Twinkleton resume the topics of the previous night, comprehending the tenderer scandal of Cloisterham, of which she has no knowledge whatever by day, and references to a certain season at Tunbridge Wells (airily called by Miss Twinkleton in this state of her existence 'The Wells'), notably the season wherein a certain finished gentleman (compassionately called by Miss Twinkleton, in this state of her existence, 'Foolish Mr Porters') revealed a homage of the heart, whereof Miss Twinkleton, in her scholastic state of existence, is as ignorant as a granite pillar. Miss Twinkleton's companion in both states of existence, and equally adaptable to either, is one Mrs Tisher: a deferential widow with a weak back, a chronic sigh, and a suppressed voice, who looks after the young ladies' wardrobes, and leads them to infer that she has seen better days. Perhaps this is the reason why it is an article of faith with the servants, handed down from race to race, that the departed Tisher was a hairdresser.

The pet pupil of the Nuns' House is Miss Rosa Bud, of course called Rosebud; wonderfully pretty, wonderfully childish, wonderfully whimsical. An awkward interest (awkward because romantic) attaches to Miss Bud in the minds of the young ladies, on account of its being known to them that a husband has been chosen for her by will and bequest, and that her guardian is bound down to bestow her on that husband when he comes of age. Miss Twinkleton, in her seminarial state of existence, has combated the romantic aspect of this destiny by affecting to shake her head over it behind Miss Bud's dimpled shoulders, and to brood on the unhappy lot of that doomed little victim. But with no better effect – possibly some unfelt touch of foolish Mr Porters has undermined the endeavour – than to evoke from the young ladies an unanimous bedchamber cry of 'Oh! what a pretending old thing Miss Twinkle-ton is, my dear!'

The Nuns' House is never in such a state of flutter as when this allotted husband calls to see little Rosebud. (It is unanimously understood by the young ladies that he is lawfully entitled to this privilege, and that if Miss Twinkleton disputed it she would be instantly taken up and transported.) When his ring at the gate bell is expected, or takes place, every young lady who can, under any pretence, look out of window, looks out of window: while every young lady who is 'practising,' practises out of time; and the French class becomes so demoralized that the Mark goes round as briskly as the bottle at a convivial party in the last century.

On the afternoon of the day next after the dinner of two at the Gate House, the bell is rung with the usual fluttering results.

'Mr Edwin Drood to see Miss Rosa.'

This is the announcement of the parlor-maid in chief. Miss Twinkleton, with an exemplary air of melancholy on her, turns to the sacrifice, and says: 'You may go down, my dear.' Miss Bud goes down, followed by all eyes.

Mr Edwin Drood is waiting in Miss Twinkleton's own parlor: a dainty room, with nothing more directly scholastic in it than a terrestrial and a celestial globe. These expressive machines imply (to parents and guardians) that even when Miss Twinkleton retires into the bosom of privacy, duty may at any moment compel her to become a sort of Wandering Jewess, scouring the earth and soaring through the skies in search of knowledge for her pupils.

The last new maid, who has never seen the young gentleman Miss Rosa is engaged to, and who is making his acquaintance between the hinges of the open door, left open for the purpose, stumbles guiltily down the kitchen stairs, as a charming little apparition, with its face concealed by a little silk apron thrown over its head, glides into the parlor.

'Oh! It *is* so ridiculous!' says the apparition, stopping and shrinking. 'Don't, Eddy!'

'Don't what, Rosa?'

'Don't come any nearer, please. It *is* so absurd.'

'What is absurd, Rosa?'

'The whole thing is. It *is* so absurd to be an engaged orphan; and it *is* so absurd to have the girls and the servants scuttling about after one, like mice in the wainscot; and it *is* so absurd to be called upon!'

The apparition appears to have a thumb in the corner of its mouth while making this complaint.

'You give me an affectionate reception, Pussy, I must say.'

'Well, I will in a minute, Eddy, but I can't just yet. How are you?' (very shortly.)

'I am unable to reply that I am much the better for seeing you, Pussy, inasmuch as I see nothing of you.'

This second remonstrance brings a dark bright pouting eye out from a corner of the apron; but it swiftly becomes invisible again, as the apparition exclaims: 'Oh! Good Gracious, you have had half your hair cut off!'

'I should have done better to have had my head cut off, I think,' says Edwin, rumpling the hair in question, with a fierce glance at the looking-glass, and giving an impatient stamp. 'Shall I go?'

'No; you needn't go just yet, Eddy. The girls would all be asking questions why you went.'

'Once for all, Rosa, will you uncover that ridiculous little head of yours and give me a welcome?'

The apron is pulled off the childish head, as its wearer replies: 'You're very welcome, Eddy. There! I'm sure that's nice. Shake hands. No, I can't kiss you, because I've got an acidulated drop in my mouth.'

'Are you at all glad to see me, Pussy?'

'Oh, yes, I'm dreadfully glad. − Go and sit down. − Miss Twinkleton.'

It is the custom of that excellent lady, when these visits occur, to appear every three minutes, either in her own person or in that of Mrs Tisher, and lay an offering on the shrine of Propriety by affecting to look for some desiderated article. On the present occasion, Miss Twinkleton, gracefully gliding in and out, says, in passing: 'How do you do, Mr Drood? Very glad indeed to have the pleasure. Pray excuse me. Tweezers. Thank you!'

'I got the gloves last evening, Eddy, and I like them very much. They are beauties.'

'Well, that's something,' the affianced replies, half grumbling. 'The smallest encouragement thankfully received. And how did you pass your birthday, Pussy?'[3]

'Delightfully! Everybody gave me a present. And we had a feast. And we had a ball at night.'

'A feast and a ball, eh? These occasions seem to go off tolerably well without me, Pussy.'

'De-lightfully!' cries Rosa, in a quite spontaneous manner, and without the least pretence of reserve.

'Hah! And what was the feast?'

'Tarts, oranges, jellies, and shrimps.'

'Any partners at the ball?'

'We danced with one another, of course, sir. But some of the girls made game to be their brothers. It *was* so droll!'

'Did anybody make game to be –'

'To be you? Oh dear yes!' cries Rosa, laughing with great enjoyment. 'That was the first thing done.'

'I hope she did it pretty well,' says Edwin, rather doubtfully.

'Oh! It was excellent! – I wouldn't dance with you, you know.'

Edwin scarcely seems to see the force of this; begs to know if he may take the liberty to ask why?

'Because I was so tired of you,' returns Rosa. But she quickly adds, and pleadingly too, seeing displeasure in his face: 'Dear Eddy, you were just as tired of me, you know.'

'Did I say so, Rosa?'

'Say so! Do you ever say so? No, you only showed if. Oh, she did it so well!' cries Rosa, in a sudden ecstasy with her counterfeit betrothed.

'It strikes me that she must be a devilish impudent girl,' says Edwin Drood. 'And so, Pussy, you have passed your last birthday in this old house.'

'Ah, yes!' Rosa clasps her hands, looks down with a sigh, and shakes her head.

'You seem to be sorry, Rosa.'

'I am sorry for the poor old place. Somehow, I feel as if it would miss me, when I am gone so far away, so young.'

'Perhaps we had better stop short, Rosa?'

She looks up at him with a swift bright look; next moment shakes her head, sighs, and looks down again.

'That is to say, is it, Pussy, that we are both resigned?'

She nods her head again, and after a short silence, quaintly bursts out with: 'You know we must be married, and married from here, Eddy, or the poor girls will be so dreadfully disappointed!'

For the moment there is more of compassion, both for her and for himself, in her affianced husband's face, than there is of love. He checks the look, and asks: 'Shall I take you out for a walk, Rosa dear?'

Rosa dear does not seem at all clear on this point, until her face, which has been comically reflective, brightens. 'Oh, yes, Eddy; let us go for a walk! And I tell you what we'll do. You shall pretend that you are engaged to somebody else, and I'll pretend that I am not engaged to anybody, and then we shan't quarrel.'

'Do you think that will prevent our falling out, Rosa?'

'I know it will. Hush! Pretend to look out of window. – Mrs Tisher!'

Through a fortuitous concourse of accidents, the matronly Tisher heaves in sight, says, in rustling through the room like the legendary ghost of a Dowager in silken skirts: 'I hope I see Mr Drood well; though I needn't ask, if I may judge from his complexion? I trust I disturb no one; but there *was* a paper-knife – Oh, thank you, I am sure!' and disappears with her prize.

'One other thing you must do, Eddy, to oblige me,' says Rosebud. 'The moment we get into the street, you must put me outside, and keep close to the house yourself – squeeze and graze yourself against it.'

'By all means, Rosa, if you wish it. Might I ask why?'

'Oh! because I don't want the girls to see you.'

'It's a fine day; but would you like me to carry an umbrella up?'

'Don't be foolish, sir. You haven't got polished leather boots on,' pouting, with one shoulder raised.

'Perhaps that might escape the notice of the girls, even if they did see me,' remarks Edwin, looking down at his boots with a sudden distaste for them.

'Nothing escapes their notice, sir. And then I know what would happen. Some of them would begin reflecting on me by saying (for *they* are free) that they never will on any account engage themselves to lovers without polished leather boots. Hark! Miss Twinkleton. I'll ask for leave.'

That discreet lady being indeed heard without, enquiring of nobody in a blandly conversational tone as she advances: 'Eh?

Indeed! Are you quite sure you saw my mother-of-pearl button-holder on the work-table in my room?' is at once solicited for walking leave, and graciously accords it. And soon the young couple go out of the Nuns' House, taking all precautions against the discovery of the so vitally defective boots of Mr Edwin Drood: precautions, let us hope, effective for the peace of Mrs Edwin Drood that is to be.

'Which way shall we take, Rosa?'

Rosa replies: 'I want to go to the Lumps-of-Delight shop.'

'To the –?'

'A Turkish sweetmeat, sir. My gracious me, don't you understand anything? Call yourself an Engineer, and not know *that*?'

'Why, how should I know it, Rosa?'

'Because I am very fond of them. But oh! I forgot what we are to pretend. No, you needn't know anything about them; never mind.'

So he is gloomily borne off to the Lumps-of-Delight shop, where Rosa makes her purchase, and, after offering some to him (which he rather indignantly declines), begins to partake of it with great zest: previously taking off and rolling up a pair of little pink gloves, like rose-leaves, and occasionally putting her little pink fingers to her rosy lips, to cleanse them from the Dust of Delight that comes off the Lumps.

'Now, be a good-tempered Eddy, and pretend. And so you are engaged?'

'And so I am engaged.'

'Is she nice?'

'Charming.'

'Tall?'

'Immensely tall!' (Rosa being short.)

'Must be gawky, I should think,' is Rosa's quiet commentary.

'I beg your pardon; not at all,' contradiction rising in him. 'What is termed a fine woman; a splendid woman.'

'Big nose, no doubt,' is the quiet commentary again.

'Not a little one, certainly,' is the quick reply. (Rosa's being a little one.)

'Long pale nose, with a red knob in the middle, *I* know the sort of nose,' says Rosa, with a satisfied nod, and tranquilly enjoying the Lumps.

'You *don't* know the sort of nose, Rosa,' with some warmth; 'because it's nothing of the kind.'

'Not a pale nose, Eddy?'

'No.' Determined not to assent.

'A red nose? Oh! I don't like red noses. However, to be sure, she can always powder it.'

'She would scorn to powder it,' says Edwin, becoming heated.

'Would she? What a stupid thing she must be! Is she stupid in everything?'

'No. In nothing.'

After a pause, in which the whimsically wicked face has not been unobservant of him, Rosa says:

'And this most sensible of creatures likes the idea of being carried off to Egypt; does she, Eddy?'

'Yes. She takes a sensible interest in triumphs of engineering skill: especially when they are to change the whole condition of an undeveloped country.'

'Lor!' says Rosa, shrugging her shoulders, with a little laugh of wonder.

'Do you object,' Edwin enquires, with a majestic turn of his eyes downward upon the fairy figure: 'do you object, Rosa, to her feeling that interest?'

'Object? My dear Eddy! But really. Doesn't she hate boilers and things?'

'I can answer for her not being so idiotic as to hate Boilers,' he returns with angry emphasis; 'though I cannot answer for her views about Things; really not understanding what Things are meant.'

'But don't she hate Arabs, and Turks, and Fellahs, and people?'

'Certainly not.' Very firmly.

'At least, she *must* hate the Pyramids? Come, Eddy?'

'Why should she be such a little – tall, I mean – Goose, as to hate the Pyramids, Rosa?'

'Ah! you should hear Miss Twinkleton,' often nodding her head, and much enjoying the Lumps, 'bore about them, and then you wouldn't ask. Tiresome old burying-grounds! Isises, and Ibises, and Cheopses, and Pharaohses; who cares about them? And then there was Belzoni or somebody,[4] dragged out by the legs, half choked with bats and dust. All the girls say serve him right, and hope it hurt him, and wish he had been quite choked.'

The two youthful figures, side by side, but not now arm-in-arm, wander discontentedly about the old Close; and each sometimes stops and slowly imprints a deeper footstep in the fallen leaves.

'Well!' says Edwin, after a lengthy silence. 'According to custom. We can't get on, Rosa.'

Rosa tosses her head, and says she don't want to get on.

'That's a pretty sentiment, Rosa, considering.'

'Considering what?'

'If I say what, you'll go wrong again.'

'*You*'ll go wrong, you mean, Eddy. Don't be ungenerous.'

'Ungenerous! I like that!'

'Then I *don't* like that, and so I tell you plainly,' Rosa pouts.

'Now, Rosa, I put it to you. Who disparaged my profession, my destination –'

'You are not going to be buried in the Pyramids, I hope?' she interrupts, arching her delicate eyebrows. 'You never said you were. If you are, why haven't you mentioned it to me? I can't find out your plans by instinct.'

'Now, Rosa; you know very well what I mean, my dear.'

'Well then, why did you begin with your detestable red-nosed Giantesses? And she would, she would, she would, she would, she WOULD powder it!' cries Rosa, in a little burst of comical contradictory spleen.

'Somehow or other, I never can come right in these discussions,' says Edwin, sighing and becoming resigned.

'How is it possible, sir, that you ever can come right when you're always wrong? And as to Belzoni, I suppose he's dead; – I'm sure I hope he is – and how can his legs or his chokes concern you?'

'It is nearly time for your return, Rosa. We have not had a very happy walk, have we?'

'A happy walk? A detestably unhappy walk, sir. If I go upstairs the moment I get in and cry till I can't take my dancing-lesson, you are responsible, mind!'

'Let us be friends, Rosa.'

'Ah!' cries Rosa, shaking her head and bursting into real tears. 'I wish we *could* be friends! It's because we can't be friends, that we try one another so. I am a young little thing, Eddy, to have an old heartache; but I really, really have, sometimes. Don't be angry.

I know you have one yourself, too often. We should both of us have done better, if What is to be had been left What might have been. I am quite a serious little thing now, and not teasing you. Let each of us forbear, this one time, on our own account, and on the other's!'

Disarmed by this glimpse of a woman's nature in the spoilt child, though for an instant disposed to resent it as seeming to involve the enforced infliction of himself upon her, Edwin Drood stands watching her as she childishly cries and sobs, with both hands to the handkerchief at her eyes, and then – she becoming more composed, and indeed beginning in her young inconstancy to laugh at herself for having been so moved – leads her to a seat hard by, under the elm trees.

'One clear word of understanding, Pussy dear. I am not clever out of my own line – now I come to think of it, I don't know that I am particularly clever in it – but I want to do right. There is not – there may be – I really don't see my way to what I want to say, but I must say it before we part – there is not any other young –'

'Oh no, Eddy! It's generous of you to ask me; but no, no, no!'

They have come very near to the Cathedral windows, and at this moment the organ and the choir sound out sublimely. As they sit listening to the solemn swell, the confidence of last night rises in young Edwin Drood's mind, and he thinks how unlike this music is to that discordance.

'I fancy I can distinguish Jack's voice,' is his remark in a low tone in connexion with the train of thought.

'Take me back at once, please,' urges his Affianced, quickly laying her light hand upon his wrist. 'They will all be coming out directly; let us get away. Oh, what a resounding chord! But don't let us stop to listen to it; let us get away!'

Her hurry is over, as soon as they have passed out of the Close. They go, arm-in-arm now, gravely and deliberately enough, along the old High Street, to the Nuns' House. At the gate, the street being within sight empty, Edwin bends down his face to Rosebud's.

She remonstrates, laughing, and is a childish schoolgirl again.

'Eddy, no! I'm too stickey to be kissed. But give me your hand, and I'll blow a kiss into that.'

He does so. She breathes a light breath into it and asks, retaining it and looking into it:

'Now say, what do you see?'

'See, Rosa?'

'Why, I thought you Egyptian boys could look into a hand and see all sorts of phantoms? Can't you see a happy Future?'

For certain, neither of them sees a happy Present, as the gate opens and closes, and one goes in and the other goes away.

CHAPTER 4

Mr Sapsea

ACCEPTING the jackass as the type of self-sufficient stupidity and conceit – a custom, perhaps, like some few other customs, more conventional than fair – then the purest Jackass in Cloisterham is Mr Thomas Sapsea, Auctioneer.

Mr Sapsea 'dresses at' the Dean; has been bowed to for the Dean, in mistake; has even been spoken to in the street as My Lord, under the impression that he was the Bishop come down unexpectedly, without his chaplain. Mr Sapsea is very proud of this, and of his voice, and of his style. He has even (in selling landed property) tried the experiment of slightly intoning in his pulpit, to make himself more like what he takes to be the genuine ecclesiastical article. So, in ending a Sale by Public Auction, Mr Sapsea finishes off with an air of bestowing a benediction on the assembled brokers, which leaves the real Dean – a modest and worthy gentleman – far behind.

Mr Sapsea has many admirers; indeed, the proposition is carried by a large local majority, even including non-believers in his wisdom, that he is a credit to Cloisterham. He possesses the great qualities of being portentous and dull, and of having a roll in his speech, and another roll in his gait; not to mention a certain gravely flowing action with his hands, as if he were presently going to Confirm the individual with whom he holds discourse. Much nearer sixty years of age than fifty, with a flowing outline of stomach, and horizontal creases in his waistcoat; reputed to be rich; voting at elections in the strictly respectable interest; morally satisfied that nothing but he himself has grown since he was a baby; how can dunder-headed Mr Sapsea be otherwise than a credit to Cloisterham, and society?

Mr Sapsea's premises are in the High Street, over against the Nuns' House. They are of about the period of the Nuns' House, irregularly modernized here and there, as steadily deteriorating generations found, more and more, that they preferred air and light to Fever and the Plague. Over the doorway is a wooden effigy,[1] about half life-size, representing Mr Sapsea's father, in a curly wig and toga, in the act of selling. The chastity of the idea, and the natural appearance of the little finger, hammer, and pulpit, have been much admired.

Mr Sapsea sits in his dull ground-floor sitting-room, giving first on his paved back yard, and then on his railed-off garden. Mr Sapsea has a bottle of port wine on a table before the fire – the fire is an early luxury, but pleasant on the cool, chilly autumn evening – and is characteristically attended by his portrait, his eight-day clock, and his weather-glass. Characteristically, because he would uphold himself against mankind, his weather-glass against weather, and his clock against time.

By Mr Sapsea's side on the table are a writing-desk and writing materials. Glancing at a scrap of manuscript, Mr Sapsea reads it to himself with a lofty air, and then, slowly pacing the room with his thumbs in the arm-holes of his waistcoat, repeats it from memory: so internally, though with much dignity, that the word 'Ethelinda' is alone audible.

There are three clean wineglasses in a tray on the table. His serving-maid entering, and announcing 'Mr Jasper is come, sir,' Mr Sapsea waves 'Admit him' and draws two wineglasses from the rank, as being claimed.

'Glad to see you, sir. I congratulate myself on having the honor of receiving you here for the first time.' Mr Sapsea does the honors of his house in this wise.

'You are very good. The honor is mine and the self-congratulation is mine.'

'You are pleased to say so, sir. But I do assure you that it is a satisfaction to me to receive you in my humble home. And that is what I would not say to everybody.' Ineffable loftiness on Mr Sapsea's part accompanies these words, as leaving the sentence to be understood: 'You will not easily believe that your society can be a satisfaction to a man like myself; nevertheless, it is.'

'I have for some time desired to know you, Mr Sapsea.'

'And I, sir, have long known you by reputation as a man of taste. Let me fill your glass. I will give you, sir,' says Mr Sapsea, filling his own:

> 'When the French come over,
> May we meet them at Dover!'

This was a patriotic toast in Mr Sapsea's infancy, and he is therefore fully convinced of its being appropriate to any subsequent era.

'You can scarcely be ignorant, Mr Sapsea,' observes Jasper, watching the auctioneer with a smile as the latter stretches out his legs before the fire, 'that you know the world.'

'Well, sir,' is the chuckling reply, 'I think I know something of it; something of it.'

'Your reputation for that knowledge has always interested and surprised me, and made me wish to know you. For, Cloisterham is a little place. Cooped up in it myself, I know nothing beyond it, and feel it to be a very little place.'

'If I have not gone to foreign countries, young man,' Mr Sapsea begins, and then stops: – 'You will excuse my calling you young man, Mr Jasper? You are much my junior.'

'By all means.'

'If I have not gone to foreign countries, young man, foreign countries have come to me. They have come to me in the way of business, and I have improved upon my opportunities. Put it that I take an inventory, or make a catalogue. I see a French clock. I never saw him before, in my life, but I instantly lay my finger on him and say "Paris!" I see some cups and saucers of Chinese make, equally strangers to me personally: I put my finger on them, then and there, and I say "Pekin, Nankin, and Canton." It is the same with Japan, with Egypt, and with bamboo and sandal-wood from the East Indies; I put my finger on them all. I have put my finger on the North Pole before now, and said, "Spear of Esquimaux make, for half a pint of pale sherry!"'

'Really? A very remarkable way, Mr Sapsea, of acquiring a knowledge of men and things.'

'I mention it, sir,' Mr Sapsea rejoins, with unspeakable complacency, 'because, as I say, it don't do to boast of what you are; but show how you came to be it, and then you prove it.'

'Most interesting. We were to speak of the late Mrs Sapsea.'

'We were, sir.' Mr Sapsea fills both glasses, and takes the decanter into safe keeping again. 'Before I consult your opinion as a man of taste on this little trifle' – holding it up – 'which is *but* a trifle, and still has required some thought, sir, some little fever of the brow, I ought perhaps to describe the character of the late Mrs Sapsea, now dead three quarters of a year.'

Mr Jasper, in the act of yawning behind his wineglass, puts down that screen and calls up a look of interest. It is a little impaired in its expressiveness by his having a shut-up gape still to dispose of, with watering eyes.

'Half a dozen years ago, or so,' Mr Sapsea proceeds, 'when I had enlarged my mind up to – I will not say to what it now is, for that might seem to aim at too much, but up to the pitch of wanting another mind to be absorbed in it – I cast my eye about me for a nuptial partner. Because, as I say, it is not good for man to be alone.'

Mr Jasper appears to commit this original idea to memory.

'Miss Brobity at that time kept, I will not call it the rival establishment to the establishment at the Nuns' House opposite, but I will call it the other parallel establishment down town. The world did have it that she showed a passion for attending my sales, when they took place on half-holidays, or in vacation time. The world did put it about, that she admired my style. The world did notice that as time flowed by, my style became traceable in the dictation-exercises of Miss Brobity's pupils. Young man, a whisper even sprang up in obscure malignity, that one ignorant and besotted Churl (a parent) so committed himself as to object to it by name. But I do not believe this. For is it likely that any human creature in his right senses would so lay himself open to be pointed at, by what I call the finger of scorn?'

Mr Jasper shakes his head. Not in the least likely. Mr Sapsea, in a grandiloquent state of absence of mind, seems to refill his visitor's glass, which is full already; and does really refill his own, which is empty.

'Miss Brobity's Being, young man, was deeply imbued with

homage to Mind. She revered Mind, when launched, or, as I say, precipitated, on an extensive knowledge of the world. When I made my proposal, she did me the honor to be so overshadowed with a species of Awe, as to be able to articulate only the two words, "O Thou!" – meaning myself. Her limpid blue eyes were fixed upon me, her semi-transparent hands were clasped together, pallor overspread her aquiline features, and, though encouraged to proceed, she never did proceed a word further. I disposed of the parallel establishment, by private contract, and we became as nearly one as could be expected under the circumstances. But she never could, and she never did, find a phrase satisfactory to her perhaps-too-favorable estimate of my intellect. To the very last (feeble action of liver), she addressed me in the same unfinished terms.'

Mr Jasper has closed his eyes as the auctioneer has deepened his voice. He now abruptly opens them, and says, in unison with the deepened voice 'Ah!' – rather as if stopping himself on the extreme verge of adding – 'men!'

'I have been since,' says Mr Sapsea, with his legs stretched out, and solemnly enjoying himself with the wine and the fire, 'what you behold me; I have been since a solitary mourner; I have been since, as I say, wasting my evening conversation on the desert air. I will not say that I have reproached myself; but there have been times when I have asked myself the question: What if her husband had been nearer on a level with her? If she had not had to look up quite so high, what might the stimulating action have been upon the liver?'

Mr Jasper says, with an appearance of having fallen into dread-fully low spirits, that he 'supposes it was to be.'

'We can only suppose so, sir,' Mr Sapsea coincides. 'As I say, Man proposes, Heaven disposes. It may or may not be putting the same thought in another form; but that is the way I put it.'

Mr Jasper murmurs assent.

'And now, Mr Jasper,' resumes the auctioneer, producing his scrap of manuscript, 'Mrs Sapsea's monument having had full time to settle and dry, let me take your opinion, as a man of taste, on the inscription I have (as I before remarked, not without some little fever of the brow) drawn out for it. Take it in your own hand. The setting out of the lines requires to be followed with the eye, as well as the contents with the mind.'

Mr Jasper complying, sees and reads as follows:

ETHELINDA,
Reverential Wife of
MR THOMAS SAPSEA,
AUCTIONEER, VALUER, ESTATE AGENT, &c.,
OF THIS CITY.
Whose Knowledge of the World,
Though somewhat extensive,
Never brought him acquainted with
A SPIRIT
More capable of
LOOKING UP TO HIM.
STRANGER PAUSE
And ask thyself the Question,
CANST THOU DO LIKEWISE?
If Not,
WITH A BLUSH RETIRE.

Mr Sapsea having risen and stationed himself with his back to the fire, for the purpose of observing the effect of these lines on the countenance of a man of taste, consequently has his face towards the door, when his serving-maid, again appearing, announces, 'Durdles is come, sir!' He promptly draws forth and fills the third wineglass, as being now claimed, and replies, 'Show Durdles in.'

'Admirable!' quoth Mr Jasper, handing back the paper.

'You approve, sir?'

'Impossible not to approve. Striking, characteristic, and complete.'

The auctioneer inclines his head, as one accepting his due and giving a receipt; and invites the entering Durdles to take off that glass of wine (handing the same), for it will warm him.

Durdles is a stonemason; chiefly in the gravestone, tomb, and monument way, and wholly of their color from head to foot. No man is better known in Cloisterham. He is the chartered libertine of the place. Fame trumpets him a wonderful workman – which, for aught that anybody knows, he may be (as he never works); and a wonderful sot – which everybody knows he is. With the Cathedral crypt he is better acquainted than any living authority; it may even be than any dead one. It is said that the intimacy of this acquaintance began in his habitually resorting to that secret place, to lock out the Cloisterham boy-populace, and sleep off the fumes of liquor: he having ready access to the Cathedral, as contractor for rough repairs. Be this as it may, he does know much about it, and, in the demolition of impedimental fragments of wall, buttress, and pavement, has seen strange sights. He often speaks of himself in the third person; perhaps being a little misty as to his own identity when he narrates; perhaps impartially adopting the Cloisterham nomenclature in reference to a character of acknowledged distinc-tion. Thus he will say, touching his strange sights: 'Durdles come upon the old chap,' in reference to a buried magnate of ancient time and high degree, 'by striking right into the coffin with his pick. The old chap gave Durdles a look with his open eyes, as much as to say "Is your name Durdles? Why, my man, I've been waiting for you a Devil of a time!" And then he turned to pow-der.' With a two-foot rule always in his pocket, and a mason's hammer all but always in his hand, Durdles goes continually sounding and tapping[2] all about and about the Cathedral; and whenever he says to Tope: 'Tope, here's another old 'un in here!' Tope announces it to the Dean as an established discovery.

In a suit of coarse flannel with horn buttons, a yellow neckerchief with draggled ends, an old hat more russet-colored than black, and laced boots of the hue of his stony calling, Durdles leads a hazy, gipsy sort of life, carrying his dinner about with him in a small bundle, and sitting on all manner of tombstones to dine. This dinner of Durdles's has become quite a Cloisterham institution: not only because of his never appearing in public without it, but because of its having been, on certain renowned occasions, taken into custody along with Durdles (as drunk and incapable), and exhibited before the Bench of Justices at the Town Hall. These occasions, however, have been few and far apart: Durdles being as seldom drunk as sober. For the rest, he is an old bachelor, and he lives in a little antiquated hole of a house that was never finished: supposed to be built, so far, of stones stolen from the city wall. To this abode there is an approach, ankle-deep in stone chips, resembling a petrified grove of tombstones, urns, draperies, and broken columns, in all stages of sculpture. Herein, two journey-men incessantly chip, while other two journeymen, who face each other, incessantly saw stone; dipping as regularly in and out of their sheltering sentry-boxes, as if they were mechanical figures emblematical of Time and Death.

To Durdles, when he has consumed his glass of port, Mr Sapsea entrusts that precious effort of his Muse. Durdles unfeelingly takes out his two-foot rule, and measures the lines calmly, alloying them with stone-grit.

'This is for the monument, is it, Mr Sapsea?'

'The Inscription. Yes.' Mr Sapsea waits for its effect on a common mind.

'It'll come in to a eighth of a inch,' says Durdles. 'Your servant, Mr Jasper. Hope I see you well.'

'How are you, Durdles?'

'I've got a touch of the Tombatism on me, Mr Jasper, but that I must expect.'

'You mean the Rheumatism,' says Sapsea, in a sharp tone. (He is nettled by having his composition so mechanically received.)

'No, I don't. I mean, Mr Sapsea, the Tombatism. It's another sort from Rheumatism. Mr Jasper knows what Durdles means. You get among them Tombs afore it's well light on a winter morning, and keep on, as the Catechism says, a walking in the same all the days of your life, and *you*'ll know what Durdles means.'

'It is a bitter cold place,' Mr Jasper assents, with an antipathetic shiver.

'And if it's bitter cold for you, up in the chancel, with a lot of live breath smoking out about you, what the bitterness is to Durdles, down in the crypt among the earthy damps there, and the dead breath of the old 'uns,' returns that individual, 'Durdles leaves you to judge. – Is this to be put in hand at once, Mr Sapsea?'

Mr Sapsea, with an Author's anxiety to rush into publication, replies that it cannot be out of hand too soon.

'You had better let me have the key, then,' says Durdles.

'Why, man, it is not to be put inside the monument!'

'Durdles knows where it's to be put, Mr Sapsea; no man better. Ask 'ere a man in Cloisterham whether Durdles knows his work.'

Mr Sapsea rises, takes a key from a drawer, unlocks an iron safe let into the wall, and takes from it another key.

'When Durdles puts a touch or a finish upon his work, no matter where, inside or outside, Durdles likes to look at his work

all round, and see that his work is a doing him credit,' Durdles
explains, doggedly.

The key proffered him by the bereaved widower being a large
one, he slips his two-foot rule into a side pocket of his flannel
trousers made for it, and deliberately opens his flannel coat, and
opens the mouth of a large breast-pocket within it before taking
the key to place in that repository.

'Why, Durdles!' exclaims Jasper, looking on amused. 'You are
undermined with pockets!'

'And I carries weight in 'em too, Mr Jasper. Feel those;' producing two other large keys.

'Hand me Mr Sapsea's likewise. Surely this is the heaviest of the
three.'

'You'll find 'em much of a muchness, I expect,' says Durdles.
'They all belong to monuments. They all open Durdles's work.
Durdles keeps the keys of his work mostly. Not that they're much
used.'

'By the bye,' it comes into Jasper's mind to say, as he idly
examines the keys; 'I have been going to ask you, many a day,
and have always forgotten. You know they sometimes call you
Stony Durdles, don't you?'

'Cloisterham knows me as Durdles, Mr Jasper.'

'I am aware of that, of course. But the boys sometimes –'

'Oh! If you mind them young Imps of boys –' Durdles gruffly
interrupts.

'I don't mind them, any more than you do. But there was a
discussion the other day among the Choir, whether Stony stood
for Tony;' clinking one key against another.

('Take care of the wards, Mr Jasper.')

'Or whether Stony stood for Stephen;' clinking with a change of
keys.

('You can't make a pitch-pipe of 'em, Mr Jasper.')

'Or whether the name comes from your trade. How stands the
fact?'

Mr Jasper weighs the three keys in his hand, lifts his head from
his idly stooping attitude over the fire, and delivers the keys to
Durdles with an ingenuous and friendly face.

But the stony one is a gruff one likewise, and that hazy state of
his is always an uncertain state, highly conscious of its dignity, and

prone to take offence. He drops his two keys back into his pocket one by one, and buttons them up; he takes his dinner-bundle from the chair-back on which he hung it when he came in; he distributes the weight he carries, by tying the third key up in it, as though he were an Ostrich, and liked to dine off cold iron; and he gets out of the room, deigning no word of answer.[3]

Mr Sapsea then proposes a hit at backgammon, which, seasoned with his own improving conversation, and terminating in a supper of cold roast beef and salad, beguiles the golden evening until pretty late. Mr Sapsea's wisdom being, in its delivery to mortals, rather of the diffuse than the epigrammatic order, is by no means expended even then; but his visitor intimates that he will come back for more of the precious commodity on future occasions, and Mr Sapsea lets him off for the present, to ponder on the instalment he carries away.

CHAPTER 5

Mr Durdles and Friend[1]

JOHN Jasper, on his way home through the Close, is brought to a standstill by the spectacle of Stony Durdles, dinner-bundle and all, leaning his back against the iron railing of the burial-ground enclosing it from the old cloister-arches; and a hideous small boy in rags flinging stones at him as a well-defined mark in the moon-light. Sometimes the stones hit him, and sometimes they miss him, but Durdles seems indifferent to either fortune. The hideous small boy, on the contrary, whenever he hits Durdles, blows a whistle of triumph through a jagged gap, convenient for the purpose, in the front of his mouth, where half his teeth are wanting; and whenever he misses him, yelps out 'Mulled agin!' and tries to atone for the failure by taking a more correct and vicious aim.

'What are you doing to the man?' demands Jasper, stepping out into the moonlight from the shade.

'Making a cock-shy of him,' replies the hideous small boy.

'Give me those stones in your hand.'

'Yes, I'll give 'em you down your throat, if you come a-ketching hold of me,' says the small boy, shaking himself loose, and backing. 'I'll smash your eye, if you don't look out!'

'Baby-Devil that you are, what has the man done to you?'

'He won't go home.'

'What is that to you?'

'He gives me a 'apenny to pelt him home if I ketches him out too late,' says the boy. And then chants, like a little savage, half stumbling and half dancing among the rags and laces of his dilapidated boots:

> 'Widdy widdy wen!
> I – ket – ches – Im – out – ar – ter – ten,
> Widdy widdy wy!
> Then – E – don't – go – then – I – shy –
> Widdy Widdy Wake-cock warning!'

– with a comprehensive sweep on the last word, and one more delivery at Durdles.

This would seem to be a poetical note of preparation, agreed upon, as a caution to Durdles to stand clear if he can, or to betake himself homeward.

John Jasper invites the boy with a beck of his head to follow him (feeling it hopeless to drag him, or coax him) and crosses to the iron railing where the Stony (and stoned) One is profoundly meditating.

'Do you know this thing, this child?' asks Jasper, at a loss for a word that will define this thing.

'Deputy,' said Durdles, with a nod.

'Is that its – his – name?'

'Deputy,' assents Durdles.

'I'm man-servant up at the Travellers' Twopenny in Gas Works Garding,' this thing explains. 'All us man-servants at Travellers' Lodgings is named Deputy. When we're chock full and the Travellers is all a-bed I come out for my 'elth.' Then withdrawing into the road, and taking aim, he resumes:

> 'Widdy widdy wen!
> I – ket – ches – Im – out – ar – ter——'

'Hold your hand,' cries Jasper, 'and don't throw while I stand so near him, or I'll kill you! Come, Durdles; let me walk home with you to-night. Shall I carry your bundle?'

'Not on any account,' replies Durdles, adjusting it. 'Durdles was making his reflections here when you come up, sir, surrounded by his works, like a poplar Author. – Your own brother-in-law;' introducing a sarcophagus within the railing, white and cold in the moonlight. 'Mrs Sapsea;' introducing the monument of that devoted wife.[2] 'Late Incumbent;' introducing the Reverend Gentleman's broken column. 'Departed Assessed Taxes;' introducing a vase and towel, standing on what might represent the cake of soap. 'Former pastrycook and muffin-maker, much respected;' introducing gravestone. 'All safe and sound here, sir, and all Durdles's work! Of the common folk that is merely bundled up in turf and brambles, the less said, the better. A poor lot, soon forgot.'

'This creature, Deputy, is behind us,' says Jasper, looking back. 'Is he to follow us?'

The relations between Durdles and Deputy are of a capricious kind; for, on Durdles's turning himself about with the slow gravity of beery soddenness, Deputy makes a pretty wide circuit into the road and stands on the defensive.

'You never cried Widdy Warning before you begun to-night,' says Durdles, unexpectedly reminded of, or imagining, an injury.

'Yer lie, I did,' says Deputy, in his only form of polite contradiction.

'Own brother, sir,' observes Durdles, turning himself about again, and as unexpectedly forgetting his offence as he had recalled or conceived it; 'own brother to Peter the Wild Boy! But I gave him an object in life.'

'At which he takes aim?' Mr Jasper suggests.

'That's it, sir,' returns Durdles, quite satisfied; 'at which he takes aim. I took him in hand and gave him an object. What was he before? A destroyer. What work did he do? Nothing but destruction. What did he earn by it? Short terms in Cloisterham Jail. Not a person, not a piece of property, not a winder, not a horse, nor a dog, nor a cat, nor a bird, nor a fowl, nor a pig, but what he stoned, for want of an enlightened object. I put that enlightened object before him, and now he can turn his honest halfpenny by the three penn'orth a week.'

'I wonder he has no competitors.'

'He has plenty, Mr Jasper, but he stones 'em all away. Now, I don't know what this scheme of mine comes to,' pursues Durdles, considering about it with the same sodden gravity; 'I don't know what you may precisely call it. It ain't a sort of a – scheme of a – National Education?'

'I should say not,' replies Jasper.

'*I* should say not,' assents Durdles; 'then we won't try to give it a name.'

'He still keeps behind us,' repeats Jasper, looking over his shoulder; 'is he to follow us?'

'We can't help going round by the Travellers' Twopenny, if we go the short way, which is the back way,' Durdles answers, 'and we'll drop him there.'

So they go on; Deputy, as a rear rank of one, taking open order, and invading the silence of the hour and place by stoning every wall, post, pillar, and other inanimate object, by the deserted way.

'Is there anything new down in the crypt, Durdles?' asks John Jasper.

'Anything old, I think you mean,' growls Durdles. 'It ain't a spot for novelty.'

'Any new discovery on your part, I meant.'

'There's a old 'un under the seventh pillar on the left as you go down the broken steps of the little underground chapel as formerly was; I make him out (so fur as I've made him out yet) to be one of them old 'uns with a crook. To judge from the size of the passages in the walls, and of the steps and doors, by which they come and went, them crooks must have been a good deal in the way of the old 'uns! Two on 'em meeting promiscuous must have hitched one another by the mitre, pretty often, I should say.'

Without any endeavour to correct the literality of this opinion, Jasper surveys his companion – covered from head to foot with old mortar, lime, and stone grit – as though he, Jasper, were getting imbued with a romantic interest in his weird life.

'Yours is a curious existence.'

Without furnishing the least clue to the question, whether he receives this as a compliment or as quite the reverse, Durdles gruffly answers: 'Yours is another.'

'Well! Inasmuch as my lot is cast in the same old earthy, chilly, never-changing place, Yes. But there is much more mystery and interest in your connexion with the Cathedral than in mine. Indeed,

I am beginning to have some idea of asking you to take me on as a sort of student, or free 'prentice, under you, and to let me go about with you sometimes, and see some of these odd nooks in which you pass your days.'

The Stony One replies, in a general way, All right. Everybody knows where to find Durdles, when he's wanted. Which, if not strictly true, is approximately so, if taken to express that Durdles may always be found in a state of vagabondage somewhere.

'What I dwell upon most,' says Jasper, pursuing his subject of romantic interest, 'is the remarkable accuracy with which you would seem to find out where people are buried. – What is the matter? That bundle is in your way; let me hold it.'

Durdles has stopped and backed a little (Deputy, attentive to all his movements, immediately skirmishing into the road), and was looking about for some ledge or corner to place his bundle on, when thus relieved of it.

'Just you give me my hammer out of that,' says Durdles, 'and I'll show you.'

Clink, clink. And his hammer is handed him.

'Now, lookee here. You pitch your note, don't you, Mr Jasper?'

'Yes.'

'So I sound for mine. I take my hammer, and I tap.' (Here he strikes the pavement, and the attentive Deputy skirmishes at a rather wider range, as supposing that his head may be in requisition.) 'I tap, tap, tap. Solid! I go on tapping. Solid still! Tap again. Holloa! Hollow! Tap again, persevering. Solid in hollow! Tap, tap, tap, to try it better. Solid in hollow; and inside solid, hollow again! There you are! Old 'un crumbled away in stone coffin, in vault!'

'Astonishing!'

'I have even done this,' says Durdles, drawing out his two-foot rule (Deputy meanwhile skirmishing nearer, as suspecting that Treasure may be about to be discovered, which may somehow lead to his own enrichment, and the delicious treat of the discoverers being hanged by the neck, on his evidence, until they are dead). 'Say that hammer of mine's a wall – my work. Two; four; and two is six,' measuring on the pavement. 'Six foot inside that wall is Mrs Sapsea.'

'Not really Mrs Sapsea?'

'Say Mrs Sapsea. Her wall's thicker, but say Mrs Sapsea. Durdles taps that wall represented by that hammer, and says, after good sounding: "Something betwixt us!" Sure enough, some rubbish has been left in that same six foot space by Durdles's men!'

Jasper opines that such accuracy 'is a gift.'

'I wouldn't have it as a gift,' returns Durdles, by no means receiving the observation in good part. 'I worked it out for myself. Durdles comes by *his* knowledge through grubbing deep for it, and having it up by the roots when it don't want to come. – Halloa you Deputy!'

'Widdy!' is Deputy's shrill response, standing off again.

'Catch that ha'penny. And don't let me see any more of you to-night, after we come to the Travellers' Twopenny.'

'Warning!' returns Deputy, having caught the halfpenny, and appearing by this mystic word to express his assent to the arrangement.

They have but to cross what was once the vineyard, belonging to what was once the Monastery, to come into the narrow back lane wherein stands the crazy wooden house of two low stories currently known as the Travellers' Twopenny: – a house all warped and distorted, like the morals of the travellers, with scant remains of a lattice-work porch over the door, and also of a rustic fence before its stamped-out garden; by reason of the travellers being so bound to the premises by a tender sentiment (or so fond of having a fire by the roadside in the course of the day), that they can never be persuaded or threatened into departure, without violently possessing themselves of some wooden forget-me-not, and bearing it off.

The semblance of an inn is attempted to be given to this wretched place by fragments of conventional red curtaining in the windows, which rags are made muddily transparent in the night-season by feeble lights of rush or cotton dip burning dully in the close air of the inside. As Durdles and Jasper come near,[3] they are addressed by an inscribed paper lantern over the door, setting forth the purport of the house. They are also addressed by some half-dozen other hideous small boys – whether twopenny lodgers or followers or hangers-on of such, who knows! – who, as if attracted by some carrion-scent of Deputy in the air, start into the moonlight, as vultures might gather in the desert, and instantly fall to stoning him and one another.

'Stop, you young brutes,' cries Jasper, angrily, 'and let us go by!'

This remonstrance being received with yells and flying stones, according to a custom of late years comfortably established among the police regulations of our English communities, where Christians are stoned on all sides, as if the days of Saint Stephen were revived, Durdles remarks of the young savages, with some point, that 'they haven't got an object,' and leads the way down the lane.

At the corner of the lane, Jasper, hotly enraged, checks his companion and looks back. All is silent. Next moment, a stone coming rattling at his hat, and a distant yell of 'Wake-cock! Warning!' followed by a crow, as from some infernally-hatched Chanticleer, apprising him under whose victorious fire he stands, he turns the corner into safety, and takes Durdles home: Durdles stumbling among the litter of his stony yard as if he were going to turn head foremost into one of the unfinished tombs.

John Jasper returns by another way to his Gate House, and entering softly with his key, finds his fire still burning. He takes from a locked press a peculiar-looking pipe, which he fills – but not with tobacco – and, having adjusted the contents of the bowl, very carefully, with a little instrument, ascends an inner staircase of only a few steps, leading to two rooms. One of these is his own sleeping chamber: the other is his nephew's. There is a light in each.

His nephew lies asleep, calm and untroubled. John Jasper stands looking down upon him, his unlighted pipe in his hand, for some time, with a fixed and deep attention. Then, hushing his footsteps, he passes to his own room, lights his pipe, and delivers himself to the Spectres it invokes at midnight.

*

CHAPTER 6

Philanthropy in Minor Canon Corner

THE Reverend Septimus Crisparkle (Septimus, because six little brother Crisparkles before him went out, one by one, as they were born, like six weak little rushlights, as they were lighted), having broken the thin morning ice near Cloisterham Weir with his amiable head, much to the invigoration of his frame, was now assisting his circulation by boxing at a looking-glass with great science and prowess. A fresh and healthy portrait the looking-glass presented of the Reverend Septimus, feinting and dodging with the utmost artfulness, and hitting out from the shoulder with the utmost straightness, while his radiant features teemed with innocence, and soft-hearted benevolence beamed from his boxing-gloves.

It was scarcely breakfast time yet, for Mrs Crisparkle – mother, not wife, of the Reverend Septimus – was only just down, and waiting for the urn. Indeed, the Reverend Septimus left off at this very moment to take the pretty old lady's entering face between his boxing-gloves and kiss it. Having done so with tenderness, the Reverend Septimus turned to again, countering with his left, and putting in his right, in a tremendous manner.

'I say, every morning of my life, that you'll do it at last, Sept,' remarked the old lady, looking on; 'and so you will.'

'Do what, Ma dear?'

'Break the pier-glass, or burst a blood-vessel.'

'Neither, please God, Ma dear. Here's wind, Ma. Look at this!'

In a concluding round of great severity, the Reverend Septimus administered and escaped all sorts of punishment, and wound up by getting the old lady's cap into Chancery[1] – such is the technical term used in scientific circles by the learned in the Noble Art – with a lightness of touch that hardly stirred the lightest lavender or cherry riband on it. Magnanimously releasing the defeated, just in time to get his gloves into a drawer and feign to be looking out of window in a contemplative state of mind when a servant entered, the Reverend Septimus then gave place to the urn and other preparations for breakfast. These completed, and the two alone again, it was pleasant to see (or would have been, if there had been any one to see it, which there never was), the old lady standing to say the Lord's Prayer aloud, and her son, Minor Canon nevertheless, standing with bent head to hear it, he being within five years of forty: much as he had stood to hear the same words from the same lips when he was within five months of four.

What is prettier than an old lady – except a young lady – when her eyes are bright, when her figure is trim and compact, when her face is cheerful and calm, when her dress is as the dress of a china shepherdess: so dainty in its colors, so individually assorted to herself, so neatly moulded on her? Nothing is prettier, thought the good Minor Canon frequently, when taking his seat at table opposite his long-widowed mother. Her thought at such times may be condensed into the two words that oftenest did duty together in all her conversations: 'My Sept!'

They were a good pair to sit breakfasting together in Minor Canon Corner,[2] Cloisterham. For, Minor Canon Corner was a quiet place in the shadow of the Cathedral, which the cawing of the rooks, the echoing footsteps of rare passers, the sound of the Cathedral bell, or the roll of the Cathedral organ, seemed to render more quiet than absolute silence. Swaggering fighting men had had their centuries of ramping and raving about Minor Canon Corner, and beaten serfs had had their centuries of drudging and dying there, and powerful monks had had their centuries of being sometimes useful and sometimes harmful there, and behold they were all gone out of Minor Canon Corner, and so much the better. Perhaps one of the highest uses of their ever having been there, was, that there might be left behind, that blessed air of tranquillity which pervaded Minor Canon Corner, and that serenely romantic state of the mind – productive for the most part of pity and for-bearance – which is engendered by a sorrowful story that is all told, or a pathetic play that is played out.

Red-brick walls harmoniously toned down in color by time, strong-rooted ivy, latticed windows, panelled rooms, big oaken beams in little places, and stone-walled gardens where annual fruit yet ripened upon monkish trees were the principal surroundings of pretty old Mrs Crisparkle and the Reverend Septimus as they sat at breakfast.

'And what, Ma dear,' enquired the Minor Canon, giving proof of a wholesome and vigorous appetite, 'does the letter say?'

80 THE MYSTERY OF EDWIN DROOD

The pretty old lady, after reading it, had just laid it down upon the breakfast-cloth. She handed it over to her son.

Now, the old lady was exceedingly proud of her bright eyes being so clear that she could read writing without spectacles. Her son was also so proud of the circumstance, and so dutifully bent on her deriving the utmost possible gratification from it, that he had invented the pretence that he himself could *not* read writing without spectacles. Therefore he now assumed a pair, of grave and prodigious proportions, which not only seriously inconvenienced his nose and his breakfast, but seriously impeded his perusal of the letter. For, he had the eyes of a microscope and a telescope combined, when they were unassisted.

'It's from Mr Honeythunder, of course,' said the old lady, folding her arms.

'Of course,' assented her son. He then lamely read on:

> '"Haven of Philanthropy,
> '"Chief Offices, London, Wednesday.

'"DEAR MADAM,

'"I write in the –;" In the what's this? What does he write in?'

'In the chair,' said the old lady.

The Reverend Septimus took off his spectacles, that he might see her face, as he exclaimed:

'Why, what should he write in?'

'Bless me, bless me, Sept,' returned the old lady, 'you don't see the context! Give it back to me, my dear.'

Glad to get his spectacles off (for they always made his eyes water), her son obeyed: murmuring that his sight for reading manuscript got worse and worse daily.

'"I write,"' his mother went on, reading very perspicuously and precisely, '"from the chair, to which I shall probably be confined for some hours."'

Septimus looked at the row of chairs against the wall, with a half-protesting and half-appealing countenance.

'"We have,"' the old lady read on with a little extra emphasis, '"a meeting of our Convened Chief Composite Committee of Central and District Philanthropists, at our Head Haven as above; and it is their unanimous pleasure that I take the chair."'

Septimus breathed more freely, and muttered: 'Oh! If he comes to *that*, let him.'

'"Not to lose a day's post, I take the opportunity of a long report being read, denouncing a public miscreant –"'

'It is a most extraordinary thing,' interposed the gentle Minor Canon, laying down his knife and fork to rub his ear in a vexed manner, 'that these Philanthropists are always denouncing somebody. And it is another most extraordinary thing that they are always so violently flush of miscreants!'

'"Denouncing a public miscreant!"' – the old lady resumed, '"to get our little affair of business off my mind. I have spoken with my two wards, Neville and Helena Landless, on the subject of their defective education, and they give in to the plan proposed; as I should have taken good care they did, whether they liked it or not."'

'And it is another most extraordinary thing,' remarked the Minor Canon in the same tone as before, 'that these Philanthropists are so given to seizing their fellow-creatures by the scruff of the neck, and (as one may say) bumping them into the paths of peace. – I beg your pardon, Ma dear, for interrupting.'

'"Therefore, dear Madam, you will please prepare your son, the Rev. Mr Septimus, to expect Neville as an inmate to be read with, on Monday next. On the same day Helena will accompany him to Cloisterham, to take up her quarters at the Nuns' House, the establishment recommended by yourself and son jointly. Please likewise to prepare for her reception and tuition there. The terms in both cases are understood to be exactly as stated to me in writing by yourself, when I opened a correspondence with you on this subject, after the honor of being introduced to you at your sister's house in town here. With compliments to the Rev. Mr Septimus, I am, Dear Madam, Your affectionate brother (In Philanthropy), LUKE HONEYTHUNDER."'

'Well, Ma,' said Septimus, after a little more rubbing of his ear, 'we must try it. There can be no doubt that we have room for an inmate, and that I have time to bestow upon him, and inclination too. I must confess to feeling rather glad that he is not Mr Honeythunder himself. Though that seems wretchedly prejudiced – does it not? – for I never saw him. Is he a large man, Ma?'

'I should call him a large man, my dear,' the old lady replied after some hesitation, 'but that his voice is so much larger.'

'Than himself?'

'Than anybody.'

'Hah!' said Septimus. And finished his breakfast as if the flavor of the Superior Family Souchong, and also of the ham and toast and eggs, were a little on the wane.

Mrs Crisparkle's sister, another piece of Dresden china, and matching her so neatly that they would have made a delightful pair of ornaments for the two ends of any capacious old-fashioned chimneypiece, and by right should never have been seen apart, was the childless wife of a clergyman holding Corporation preferment in London City. Mr Honeythunder in his public character of Professor of Philanthropy had come to know Mrs Crisparkle during the last re-matching of the china ornaments (in other words during her last annual visit to her sister), after a public occasion of a philanthropic nature, when certain devoted orphans of tender years had been glutted with plum buns, and plump bumptiousness. These were all the antecedents known in Minor Canon Corner of the coming pupils.

'I am sure you will agree with me, Ma,' said Mr Crisparkle, after thinking the matter over, 'that the first thing to be done, is, to put these young people as much at their ease as possible. There is nothing disinterested in the notion, because we cannot be at our ease with them unless they are at their ease with us. Now, Jasper's nephew is down here at present; and like takes to like, and youth takes to youth. He is a cordial young fellow, and we will have him to meet the brother and sister at dinner. That's three. We can't think of asking him, without asking Jasper. That's four. Add Miss Twinkleton and the fairy bride that is to be, and that's six. Add our two selves, and that's eight. Would eight at a friendly dinner at all put you out, Ma?'

'Nine would, Sept,' returned the old lady, visibly nervous.

'My dear Ma, I particularize eight.'

'The exact size of the table and the room, my dear.'

So it was settled that way; and when Mr Crisparkle called with his mother upon Miss Twinkleton, to arrange for the reception of Miss Helena Landless at the Nuns' House, the two other invitations having reference to that establishment were proffered and accepted. Miss Twinkleton did, indeed, glance at the globes, as regretting that they were not formed to be taken out into society; but became reconciled to leaving them behind. Instructions were then despatched to the Philanthropist for the departure and arrival, in good time for dinner, of Mr Neville and Miss Helena; and stock for soup became fragrant in the air of Minor Canon Corner.

In those days[3] there was no railway to Cloisterham, and Mr Sapsea said there never would be. Mr Sapsea said more; he said there never should be. And yet, marvellous to consider, it has come to pass, in these days, that Express Trains don't think Cloisterham worth stopping at, but yell and whirl through it on their larger errands, casting the dust off their wheels as a testimony against its insignificance. Some remote fragment of Main Line to somewhere else, there was, which was going to ruin the Money Market if it failed, and Church and State if it succeeded, and (of course), the Constitution, whether or no; but even that had already so unsettled Cloisterham traffic, that the traffic, deserting the high road, came sneaking in from an unprecedented part of the country by a back stable-way, for many years labelled at the corner: 'Beware of the Dog.'

To this ignominious avenue of approach, Mr Crisparkle repaired, awaiting the arrival of a short squat omnibus, with a disproportionate heap of luggage on the roof – like a little Elephant with infinitely too much Castle – which was then the daily service between Cloisterham and external mankind. As this vehicle lumbered up, Mr Crisparkle could hardly see anything else of it for a large outside passenger seated on the box, with his elbows squared, and his hands on his knees, compressing the driver into a most uncomfortably small compass, and glowering about him with a strongly marked face.

'Is this Cloisterham?' demanded the passenger, in a tremendous voice.

'It is,' replied the driver, rubbing himself as if he ached, after throwing the reins to the ostler. 'And I never was so glad to see it.'

'Tell your master to make his box seat wider, then,' returned the passenger. 'Your master is morally bound – and ought to be legally, under ruinous penalties – to provide for the comfort of his fellow-man.'

The driver instituted, with the palms of his hands, a superficial perquisition into the state of his skeleton; which seemed to make him anxious.

'Have I sat upon you?' asked the passenger.

'You have,' said the driver, as if he didn't like it at all.

'Take that card, my friend.'

'I think I won't deprive you on it,' returned the driver, casting his eyes over it with no great favor, without taking it. 'What's the good of it to me?'

'Be a Member of that Society,' said the passenger.

'What shall I get by it?' asked the driver.

'Brotherhood,' returned the passenger, in a ferocious voice.

'Thankee,' said the driver, very deliberately, as he got down; 'my mother was contented with myself, and so am I. I don't want no brothers.'

'But you must have them,' replied the passenger, also descending, 'whether you like it or not. I am your brother.'

'I say!' expostulated the driver, becoming more chafed in temper; 'not too fur! The worm *will*, when –'

But here Mr Crisparkle interposed, remonstrating aside, in a friendly voice: 'Joe, Joe, Joe!⁴ don't forget yourself, Joe, my good fellow!' and then, when Joe peaceably touched his hat, accosting the passenger with: 'Mr Honeythunder?'

'That is my name, sir.'

'My name is Crisparkle.'

'Reverend Mr Septimus? Glad to see you, sir. Neville and Helena are inside. Having a little succumbed of late, under the pressure of my public labors, I thought I would take a mouthful of fresh air, and come down with them, and return at night. So you are the Reverend Mr Septimus, are you?' surveying him on the whole with disappointment, and twisting a double eye-glass by its ribbon, as if he were roasting it; but not otherwise using it. 'Hah! I expected to see you older, sir.'

'I hope you will,' was the good-humored reply.

'Eh?' demanded Mr Honeythunder.

'Only a poor little joke. Not worth repeating.'

'Joke? Aye; I never see a joke,' Mr Honeythunder frowningly retorted. 'A joke is wasted upon me, sir. Where are they? Helena and Neville, come here! Mr Crisparkle has come down to meet you.'

An unusually handsome lithe young fellow, and an unusually handsome lithe girl; much alike; both very dark, and very rich in color; she of almost the gipsy type; something untamed about them both; a certain air upon them of hunter and huntress; yet withal a certain air of being the objects of the chase, rather than the followers. Slender, supple, quick of eye and limb; half shy, half defiant; fierce of look; an indefinable kind of pause coming and going on their whole expression, both of face and form, which might be equally likened to the pause before a crouch, or a bound. The rough mental notes made in the first five minutes by Mr Crisparkle would have read thus, *verbatim*.

He invited Mr Honeythunder to dinner, with a troubled mind (for the discomfiture of the dear old china shepherdess lay heavy on it), and gave his arm to Helena Landless. Both she and her brother, as they walked all together through the ancient streets, took great delight in what he pointed out of the Cathedral and the Monastery-ruin, and wondered – so his notes ran on – much as if they were beautiful barbaric captives brought from some wild tropical dominion. Mr Honeythunder walked in the middle of the road, shouldering the natives out of his way, and loudly developing a scheme he had, for making a raid on all the unemployed persons in the United Kingdom, laying them every one by the heels in jail, and forcing them, on pain of prompt extermination, to become philanthropists.

Then they came to Minor Canon Corner.[5] Mrs Crisparkle had need of her own share of philanthropy when she beheld this very large and very loud excrescence on the little party. Always something in the nature of a Boil upon the face of society, Mr Honeythunder expanded into an inflammatory Wen in Minor Canon Corner. Though it was not literally true, as was facetiously charged against him by public unbelievers, that he called aloud to his fellow-creatures: 'Curse your souls and bodies, come here and be blessed!' still his philanthropy was of that gunpowderous sort that the difference between it and animosity was hard to determine. You were to abolish military force, but you were first to bring all commanding officers who had done their duty, to trial by court martial for that offence, and shoot them. You were to abolish war, but were to make converts by making war upon them, and charging them with loving war as the apple of their eye. You were to have no capital punishment, but were first to sweep off the face of the earth all legislators, jurists, and judges, who were of the contrary opinion. You were to have universal concord, and were to get it by eliminating all the people who wouldn't, or conscientiously couldn't, be concordant. You were to love your brother as yourself, but after an indefinite interval of maligning him (very much as if you hated him), and calling him all manner of names. Above all things, you were to do nothing in private, or on your own account. You were to go to the offices of the Haven of Philanthropy, and put your name down as a Member and a Professing Philanthropist. Then, you were to pay up your subscription, get your card of membership and your riband and medal, and were evermore to live upon a platform, and evermore to say what Mr Honeythunder said, and what the Treasurer said, and what the sub-Treasurer said, and what the Committee said, and what the sub-Committee said, and what the Secretary said, and what the Vice Secretary said. And this was usually said in the unanimously carried resolution under hand and seal, to the effect: 'That this assembled Body of Professing Philanthropists views, with indignant scorn and contempt, not unmixed with utter detestation and loathing abhorrence,' – in short, the baseness of all those who do not belong to it, and pledges itself to make as many obnoxious statements as possible about them, without being at all particular as to facts.

The dinner was a most doleful breakdown. The philanthropist deranged the symmetry of the table, sat himself in the way of the waiting, blocked up the thoroughfare, and drove Mr Tope (who assisted the parlor-maid) to the verge of distraction by passing plates and dishes on, over his own head. Nobody could talk to anybody, because he held forth to everybody at once, as if the company had no individual existence, but were a Meeting. He impounded the Reverend Mr Septimus, as an official personage to be addressed, or kind of human peg to hang his oratorical hat on, and fell into the exasperating habit, common among such orators, of impersonating him as a wicked and weak opponent. Thus, he would ask: 'And will you, sir, now stultify yourself by telling me' – and so forth, when the innocent man had not opened his lips, nor meant to open them. Or he would say: 'Now see, sir, to what a position you are reduced. I will leave you no escape. After exhausting all the resources of fraud and falsehood, during years upon years; after exhibiting a combination of dastardly meanness with ensanguined daring, such as the world has not often witnessed; you have now the hypocrisy to bend the knee before the most degraded of mankind, and to sue and whine and howl for mercy!' Whereat the unfortunate Minor Canon would look, in part indignant and in part perplexed: while his worthy mother sat bridling, with tears in her eyes, and the remainder of the party lapsed into a sort of gelatinous state, in which there was no flavor or solidity, and very little resistance.

But the gush of philanthropy that burst forth when the departure of Mr Honeythunder began to impend, must have been highly gratifying to the feelings of that distinguished man.[6] His coffee was produced, by the special activity of Mr Tope, a full hour before he wanted it. Mr Crisparkle sat with his watch in his hand, for about the same period, lest he should overstay his time. The four young people were unanimous in believing that the Cathedral clock struck three-quarters, when it actually struck but one. Miss Twinkleton estimated the distance to the omnibus at five-and-twenty minutes' walk, when it was really five. The affectionate kindness of the whole circle hustled him into his great-coat, and shoved him out into the moonlight, as if he were a fugitive traitor with whom they sympathized, and a troop of horse were at the back door. Mr Crisparkle and his new charge, who took him to the omnibus, were so fervent in their apprehensions of his catching cold, that they shut him up in it instantly and left him, with still half an hour to spare.

CHAPTER 7

More Confidences than One

'I KNOW very little of that gentleman, sir,' said Neville to the Minor Canon as they turned back.

'You know very little of your guardian?' the Minor Canon repeated.

'Almost nothing.'

'How came he –'

'To *be* my guardian? I'll tell you, sir. I suppose you know that we come (my sister and I) from Ceylon?'

'Indeed, no.'

'I wonder at that. We lived with a stepfather there. Our mother died there, when we were little children. We have had a wretched existence. She made him our guardian, and he was a miserly wretch who grudged us food to eat, and clothes to wear. At his death, he passed us over to this man; for no better reason that I know of, than his being a friend or connexion of his, whose name was always in print and catching his attention.'

'That was lately, I suppose?'

'Quite lately, sir. This stepfather of ours was a cruel brute as well as a grinding one. It was well he died when he did, or I might have killed him.'

Mr Crisparkle stopped short in the moonlight and looked at his hopeful pupil in consternation.

'I surprise you, sir?' he said, with a quick change to a submissive manner.

'You shock me; unspeakably shock me.'

The pupil hung his head for a little while, as they walked on, and then said: 'You never saw him beat your sister. I have seen him beat mine, more than once or twice, and I never forgot it.'

'Nothing,' said Mr Crisparkle, 'not even a beloved and beautiful sister's tears under dastardly ill-usage;' he became less severe, in spite of himself, as his indignation rose; 'could justify those horrible expressions that you used.'

'I am sorry I used them, and especially to you, sir. I beg to recall them. But permit me to set you right on one point. You spoke of my sister's tears. My sister would have let him tear her to pieces, before she would have let him believe that he could make her shed a tear.'

Mr Crisparkle reviewed those mental notes of his, and was neither at all surprised to hear it, nor at all disposed to question it.

'Perhaps you will think it strange, sir,' – this was said in a hesitating voice – 'that I should so soon ask you to allow me to confide in you, and to have the kindness to hear a word or two from me in my defence?'

'Defence?' Mr Crisparkle repeated. 'You are not on your defence, Mr Neville.'

'I think I am, sir. At least I know I should be, if you were better acquainted with my character.'

'Well, Mr Neville,' was the rejoinder. 'What if you leave me to find it out?'

'Since it is your pleasure, sir,' answered the young man, with a quick change in his manner to sullen disappointment: 'since it is your pleasure to check me in my impulse, I must submit.'

There was that in the tone of this short speech which made the conscientious man to whom it was addressed uneasy. It hinted to him that he might, without meaning it, turn aside a trustfulness beneficial to a mis-shapen young mind and perhaps to his own power of directing and improving it. They were within sight of the lights in his windows, and he stopped.

'Let us turn back and take a turn or two up and down, Mr Neville, or you may not have time to finish what you wish to say to me. You are hasty in thinking that I mean to check you. Quite the contrary. I invite your confidence.'

'You have invited it, sir, without knowing it, ever since I came here. I say "ever since," as if I had been here a week! The truth is, we came here (my sister and I) to quarrel with you, and affront you, and break away again.'

'Really?' said Mr Crisparkle, at a dead loss for anything else to say.

'You see, we could not know what you were beforehand, sir; could we?'

'Clearly not,' said Mr Crisparkle.

'And having liked no one else with whom we have ever been brought into contact, we had made up our minds not to like you.'

'Really?' said Mr Crisparkle again.

'But we do like you, sir, and we see an unmistakable difference between your house and your reception of us, and anything else we have ever known. This – and my happening to be alone with you – and everything around us seeming so quiet and peaceful after Mr Honeythunder's departure – and Cloisterham being so old and grave and beautiful, with the moon shining on it – these things inclined me to open my heart.'

'I quite understand, Mr Neville. And it is salutary to listen to such influences.'

'In describing my own imperfections, sir, I must ask you not to suppose that I am describing my sister's. She has come out of the

disadvantages of our miserable life, as much better than I am, as
that Cathedral tower is higher than those chimneys.'

Mr Crisparkle in his own breast was not so sure of this.

'I have had, sir, from my earliest remembrance, to suppress a
deadly and bitter hatred. This has made me secret and revengeful.
I have been always tyrannically held down by the strong hand. This
has driven me, in my weakness, to the resource of being false and
mean. I have been stinted of education, liberty, money, dress, the
very necessaries of life, the commonest pleasures of childhood, the
commonest possessions of youth. This has caused me to be utterly
wanting in I don't know what emotions, or remembrances, or good
instincts – I have not even a name for the thing, you see! – that you
have had to work upon in other young men to whom you have
been accustomed.'

'This is evidently true. But this is not encouraging,' thought Mr
Crisparkle as they turned again.

'And to finish with, sir: I have been brought up among abject
and servile dependents, of an inferior race,[1] and I may easily have
contracted some affinity with them. Sometimes, I don't know but
that it may be a drop of what is tigerish in their blood.'

'As in the case of that remark just now,' thought Mr Crisparkle.

'In a last word of reference to my sister, sir (we are twin children), you ought to know, to her honor, that nothing in our
misery ever subdued her, though it often cowed me. When we
ran away from it (we ran away four times in six years, to be soon
brought back and cruelly punished), the flight was always of her
planning and leading. Each time she dressed as a boy, and showed
the daring of a man. I take it we were seven years old when we first
decamped; but I remember, when I lost the pocket-knife with
which she was to have cut her hair short, how desperately she
tried to tear it out, or bite it off. I have nothing further to say, sir,
except that I hope you will bear with me and make allowance for
me.'

'Of that, Mr Neville, you may be sure,' returned the Minor
Canon. 'I don't preach more than I can help, and I will not repay
your confidence with a sermon. But I entreat you to bear in mind,
very seriously and steadily, that if I am to do you any good, it can
only be with your own assistance; and that you can only render
that, efficiently, by seeking aid from Heaven.'

'I will try to do my part, sir.'

'And, Mr Neville, I will try to do mine. Here is my hand on it. May God bless our endeavours!'

They were now standing at his house-door, and a cheerful sound of voices and laughter was heard within.

'We will take one more turn before going in,' said Mr Crisparkle, 'for I want to ask you a question. When you said you were in a changed mind concerning me, you spoke, not only for yourself, but for your sister too?'

'Undoubtedly I did, sir.'

'Excuse me, Mr Neville, but I think you have had no opportunity of communicating with your sister, since I met you. Mr Honeythunder was very eloquent; but perhaps I may venture to say, without ill-nature, that he rather monopolized the occasion. May you not have answered for your sister without sufficient warrant?'

Neville shook his head with a proud smile.

'You don't know, sir, yet, what a complete understanding can exist between my sister and me, though no spoken word – perhaps hardly as much as a look – may have passed between us. She not only feels as I have described, but she very well knows that I am taking this opportunity of speaking to you, both for her and for myself.'

Mr Crisparkle looked in his face, with some incredulity; but his face expressed such absolute and firm conviction of the truth of what he said, that Mr Crisparkle looked at the pavement, and mused, until they came to his door again.

'I will ask for one more turn, sir, this time,' said the young man, with a rather heightened color rising in his face. 'But for Mr Honeythunder's – I think you called it eloquence, sir?' (somewhat slyly).

'I – yes, I called it eloquence,' said Mr Crisparkle.

'But for Mr Honeythunder's eloquence, I might have had no need to ask you what I am going to ask you. This Mr Edwin Drood, sir: I think that's the name?'

'Quite correct,' said Mr Crisparkle. 'D-r-double o-d.'

'Does he – or did he – read with you, sir?'

'Never, Mr Neville. He comes here visiting his relation, Mr Jasper.'

'Is Miss Bud his relation too, sir?'

('Now, why should he ask that, with sudden superciliousness!' thought Mr Crisparkle.) Then he explained, aloud, what he knew of the little story of their betrothal.

'Oh! *That's* it, is it?' said the young man. 'I understand his air of proprietorship now!'

This was said so evidently to himself, or to anybody rather than Mr Crisparkle, that the latter instinctively felt as if to notice it would be almost tantamount to noticing a passage in a letter which he had read by chance over the writer's shoulder. A moment afterwards they re-entered the house.

Mr Jasper was seated at the piano as they came into his drawing-room, and was accompanying Miss Rosebud while she sang. It was a consequence of his playing the accompaniment without notes, and of her being a heedless little creature very apt to go wrong, that he followed her lips most attentively, with his eyes as well as hands; carefully and softly hinting the key-note from time to time. Standing with an arm drawn round her, but with a face far more intent on Mr Jasper than on her singing, stood Helena, between whom and her brother an instantaneous recognition passed, in which Mr Crisparkle saw, or thought he saw, the understanding that had been spoken of, flash out. Mr Neville then took his admiring station, leaning against the piano, opposite the singer; Mr Crisparkle sat down by the china shepherdess; Edwin Drood gallantly furled and unfurled Miss Twinkleton's fan; and that lady passively claimed that sort of exhibitor's proprietorship in the accomplishment on view, which Mr Tope, the Verger, daily claimed in the Cathedral service.

The song went on. It was a sorrowful strain of parting, and the fresh young voice was very plaintive and tender. As Jasper watched the pretty lips, and ever and again hinted the one note, as though it were a low whisper from himself, the voice became less steady, until all at once the singer broke into a burst of tears, and shrieked out, with her hands over her eyes: 'I can't bear this! I am frightened! Take me away!'

With one swift turn of her lithe figure, Helena laid the little beauty on a sofa, as if she had never caught her up. Then, on one knee beside her, and with one hand upon her rosy mouth, while with the other she appealed to all the rest, Helena said to them:

'It's nothing; it's all over; don't speak to her for one minute, and she is well!'

Jasper's hands had, in the same instant, lifted themselves from the keys, and were now poised above them, as though he waited to resume. In that attitude he yet sat quiet: not even looking round, when all the rest had changed their places and were re-assuring one another.

'Pussy's not used to an audience; that's the fact,' said Edwin Drood. 'She got nervous, and couldn't hold out. Besides, Jack, you are such a conscientious master, and require so much, that I believe you make her afraid of you. No wonder.'

'No wonder,' repeated Helena.

'There, Jack, you hear! You would be afraid of him, under similar circumstances, wouldn't you, Miss Landless?'

'Not under any circumstances,' returned Helena.

Jasper brought down his hands, looked over his shoulder, and begged to thank Miss Landless for her vindication of his character. Then he fell to dumbly playing, without striking the notes, while his little pupil was taken to an open window for air, and was otherwise petted and restored. When she was brought back, his place was empty. 'Jack's gone, Pussy,' Edwin told her. 'I am more than half afraid he didn't like to be charged with being the Monster who had frightened you.' But she answered never a word, and shivered, as if they had made her a little too cold.

Miss Twinkleton now opining that indeed these were late hours, Mrs Crisparkle, for finding ourselves outside the walls of the Nuns' House, and that we who undertook the formation of the future wives and mothers of England (the last words in a lower voice, as requiring to be communicated in confidence) were really bound (voice coming up again) to set a better example than one of rakish habits, wrappers were put in requisition, and the two young cavaliers volunteered to see the ladies home. It was soon done, and the gate of the Nuns' House closed upon them.

The boarders had retired, and only Mrs Tisher in solitary vigil awaited the new pupil. Her bedroom being within Rosa's, very little introduction or explanation was necessary, before she was placed in charge of her new friend, and left for the night.

'This is a blessed relief, my dear,' said Helena. 'I have been dreading all day, that I should be brought to bay at this time.'

'There are not many of us,' returned Rosa, 'and we are good-natured girls; at least the others are; I can answer for them.'

'I can answer for you,' laughed Helena, searching the lovely little face with her dark fiery eyes, and tenderly caressing the small figure. 'You will be a friend to me, won't you?'

'I hope so. But the idea of my being a friend to you seems too absurd, though.'

'Why?'

'Oh! I am such a mite of a thing, and you are so womanly and handsome. You seem to have resolution and power enough to crush me. I shrink into nothing by the side of your presence even.'

'I am a neglected creature, my dear, unacquainted with all accomplishments, sensitively conscious that I have everything to learn, and deeply ashamed to own my ignorance.'

'And yet you acknowledge everything to me!' said Rosa.

'My pretty one, can I help it? There is a fascination in you.'

'Oh! Is there though?' pouted Rosa, half in jest and half in earnest. 'What a pity Master Eddy doesn't feel it more!'

Of course her relations towards that young gentleman had been already imparted, in Minor Canon Corner.

'Why, surely he must love you with all his heart!' cried Helena, with an earnestness that threatened to blaze into ferocity if he didn't.

'Eh? Oh, well, I suppose he does,' said Rosa, pouting again; 'I am sure I have no right to say he doesn't. Perhaps it's my fault. Perhaps I am not as nice to him as I ought to be. I don't think I am. But it *is* so ridiculous!'

Helena's eyes demanded what was.

'*We* are,' said Rosa, answering as if she had spoken. 'We are such a ridiculous couple. And we are always quarrelling.'

'Why?'

'Because we both know we are ridiculous, my dear!' Rosa gave that answer as if it were the most conclusive answer in the world.

Helena's masterful look was intent upon her face for a few moments, and then she impulsively put out both her hands and said:

'You will be my friend and help me?'

'Indeed, my dear, I will,' replied Rosa, in a tone of affectionate childishness that went straight and true to her heart; 'I will be as good a friend as such a mite of a thing can be to such a noble creature as you. And be a friend to me, please; for I don't understand myself: and I want a friend who can understand me, very much indeed.'

Helena Landless kissed her, and retaining both her hands, said: 'Who is Mr Jasper?'

Rosa turned aside her head in answering: 'Eddy's uncle, and my music-master.'

'You do not love him?'

'Ugh!' She put her hands up to her face, and shook with fear or horror.

'You know that he loves you?'

'Oh, don't, don't, don't!' cried Rosa, dropping on her knees, and clinging to her new resource. 'Don't tell me of it! He terrifies me. He haunts my thoughts, like a dreadful ghost. I feel that I am never safe from him. I feel as if he could pass in through the wall when he is spoken of.' She actually did look round, as if she dreaded to see him standing in the shadow behind her.

'Try to tell me more about it, darling.'

'Yes, I will, I will. Because you are so strong. But hold me the while, and stay with me afterwards.'

'My child! You speak as if he had threatened you in some dark way.'

'He has never spoken to me about – that. Never.'

'What has he done?'

'He has made a slave of me with his looks. He has forced me to understand him, without his saying a word; and he has forced me to keep silence, without his uttering a threat. When I play, he never moves his eyes from my hands. When I sing, he never moves his eyes from my lips. When he corrects me, and strikes a note, or a chord, or plays a passage, he himself is in the sounds, whispering that he pursues me as a lover, and commanding me to keep his secret. I avoid his eyes, but he forces me to see them without looking at them. Even when a glaze comes over them (which is sometimes the case), and he seems to wander away into a frightful sort of dream in which he threatens most, he obliges me to know it, and to know that he is sitting close at my side, more terrible to me then than ever.'

'What is this imagined threatening, pretty one? What is threatened?'

'I don't know. I have never even dared to think or wonder what it is.'

'And was this all, to-night?'

'This was all; except that to-night when he watched my lips so closely as I was singing, besides feeling terrified I felt ashamed and passionately hurt. It was as if he kissed me, and I couldn't bear it, but cried out. You must never breathe this to any one. Eddy is devoted to him. But you said to-night that you would not be afraid of him, under any circumstances, and that gives me – who am so much afraid of him – courage to tell only you. Hold me! Stay with me! I am too frightened to be left by myself.'

The lustrous gipsy-face drooped over the clinging arms and bosom, and the wild black hair fell down protectingly over the childish form. There was a slumbering gleam of fire in the intense dark eyes, though they were then softened with compassion and admiration. Let whomsoever it most concerned look well to it!

CHAPTER 8

Daggers Drawn

THE two young men, having seen the damsels, their charges, enter the courtyard of the Nuns' House, and finding themselves coldly stared at by the brazen door-plate, as if the battered old beau with the glass in his eye were insolent, look at one another, look along the perspective of the moonlit street, and slowly walk away together.

'Do you stay here long, Mr Drood?' says Neville.

'Not this time,' is the careless answer. 'I leave for London again, to-morrow. But I shall be here, off and on, until next Midsummer; then I shall take my leave of Cloisterham, and England too; for many a long day, I expect.'

'Are you going abroad?'

'Going to wake up Egypt a little,' is the condescending answer.

'Are you reading?'

'Reading!' repeats Edwin Drood, with a touch of contempt. 'No. Doing, working, engineering. My small patrimony was left a part of the capital of the Firm I am with, by my father, a former partner; and I am a charge upon the Firm until I come of age; and then I step into my modest share in the concern. Jack – you met him at dinner – is, until then, my guardian and trustee.'

'I heard from Mr Crisparkle of your other good fortune.'

'What do you mean by my other good fortune?'

Neville has made his remark in a watchfully advancing, and yet furtive and shy manner, very expressive of that peculiar air already noticed, of being at once hunter and hunted. Edwin has made his retort with an abruptness not at all polite. They stop and interchange a rather heated look.

'I hope,' says Neville, 'there is no offence, Mr Drood, in my innocently referring to your betrothal?'

'By George!' cries Edwin, leading on again at a somewhat quicker pace. 'Everybody in this chattering old Cloisterham refers to it. I wonder no Public House has been set up, with my portrait for the sign of The Betrothed's Head. Or Pussy's portrait. One or the other.'

'I am not accountable for Mr Crisparkle's mentioning the matter to me, quite openly,' Neville begins.

'No; that's true; you are not,' Edwin Drood assents.

'But,' resumes Neville, 'I am accountable for mentioning it to you. And I did so, on the supposition that you could not fail to be highly proud of it.'

Now, there are these two curious touches of human nature working the secret springs of this dialogue. Neville Landless is already enough impressed by Little Rosebud, to feel indignant that Edwin Drood (far below her) should hold his prize so lightly. Edwin Drood is already enough impressed by Helena, to feel indignant that Helena's brother (far below her) should dispose of him so coolly, and put him out of the way so entirely.

However, the last remark had better be answered. So, says Edwin:

'I don't know, Mr Neville' (adopting that mode of address from Mr Crisparkle), 'that what people are proudest of, they usually talk most about; I don't know either, that what they are proudest of, they most like other people to talk about. But I live a busy life, and I speak under correction by you readers, who ought to know everything, and I dare say do.'

By this time they have both become savage; Mr Neville out in the open; Edwin Drood under the transparent cover of a popular tune, and a stop now and then to pretend to admire picturesque effects in the moonlight before him.

'It does not seem to me very civil in you,' remarks Neville, at length, 'to reflect upon a stranger who comes here, not having had your advantages, to try to make up for lost time. But, to be sure, *I* was not brought up in "busy life," and my ideas of civility were formed among Heathens.'

'Perhaps, the best civility, whatever kind of people we are brought up among,' retorts Edwin Drood, 'is to mind our own business. If you will set me that example, I promise to follow it.'

'Do you know that you take a great deal too much upon yourself,' is the angry rejoinder; 'and that in the part of the world I come from, you would be called to account for it?'

'By whom, for instance?' asks Edwin Drood, coming to a halt, and surveying the other with a look of disdain.

But, here a startling right hand is laid on Edwin's shoulder, and Jasper stands between them. For it would seem that he, too, has strolled round by the Nuns' House, and has come up behind them on the shadowy side of the road.

'Ned, Ned, Ned!' he says. 'We must have no more of this. I don't like this. I have overheard high words between you two. Remember, my dear boy, you are almost in the position of host to-night. You belong, as it were, to the place, and in a manner represent it towards a stranger. Mr Neville is a stranger, and you should respect the obligations of hospitality. And, Mr Neville:' laying his left hand on the inner shoulder of that young gentleman, and thus walking on between them, hand to shoulder on either side: 'you will pardon me; but I appeal to you to govern your temper too. Now, what is amiss? But why ask! Let there be nothing amiss, and the question is superfluous. We are all three on a good understanding, are we not?'

After a silent struggle between the two young men who shall speak last, Edwin Drood strikes in with: 'So far as I am concerned, Jack, there is no anger in me.'

'Nor in me,' says Neville Landless, though not so freely; or perhaps so carelessly. 'But if Mr Drood knew all that lies behind me, far away from here, he might know better how it is that sharp-edged words have sharp edges to wound me.'

'Perhaps,' says Jasper, in a smoothing manner, 'we had better not qualify our good understanding. We had better not say anything having the appearance of a remonstrance or condition; it might not seem generous. Frankly and freely, you see there is no anger in Ned. Frankly and freely, there is no anger in you, Mr Neville?'

'None at all, Mr Jasper.' Still, not quite so frankly or so freely; or, be it said once again, not quite so carelessly perhaps.

'All over then! Now, my bachelor Gate House is a few yards from here, and the heater is on the fire, and the wine and glasses are on the table, and it is not a stone's throw from Minor Canon Corner. Ned, you are up and away to-morrow. We will carry Mr Neville in with us, to take a stirrup-cup.'

'With all my heart, Jack.'

'And with all mine, Mr Jasper.' Neville feels it impossible to say less, but would rather not go. He has an impression upon him that he has lost hold of his temper; feels that Edwin Drood's coolness, so far from being infectious, makes him red hot.

Mr Jasper, still walking in the centre, hand to shoulder on either side, beautifully turns the Refrain of a drinking-song, and they all go to his rooms. There, the first object visible, when he adds the light of a lamp to that of the fire, is the portrait over the chimney-piece. It is not an object calculated to improve the understanding between the two young men, as rather awkwardly reviving the subject of their difference. Accordingly, they both glance at it consciously, but say nothing. Jasper, however (who would appear from his conduct to have gained but an imperfect clue to the cause of their late high words), directly calls attention to it.

'You recognize that picture, Mr Neville?' shading the lamp to throw the light upon it.

'I recognize it, but it is far from flattering the original.'

'Oh, you are hard upon it! It was done by Ned, who made me a present of it.'

'I am sorry for that, Mr Drood,' Neville apologizes, with a real intention to apologize; 'if I had known I was in the artist's presence –'

'Oh, a joke, sir, a mere joke,' Edwin cuts in, with a provoking yawn. 'A little humoring of Pussy's points! I'm going to paint her gravely, one of these days, if she's good.'

The air of leisurely patronage and indifference with which this is said, as the speaker throws himself back in a chair and clasps his hands at the back of his head, as a rest for it, is very exasperating to the excitable and excited Neville. Jasper looks observantly from the one to the other, slightly smiles, and turns his back to mix a jug of mulled wine at the fire. It seems to require much mixing and compounding.

'I suppose, Mr Neville,' says Edwin, quick to resent the indignant protest against himself in the face of young Landless, which is fully as visible as the portrait, or the fire, or the lamp: 'I suppose that if you painted the picture of your lady love –'

'I can't paint,' is the hasty interruption.

'That's your misfortune, and not your fault. You would if you could. But if you could, I suppose you would make her (no matter what she was in reality) Juno, Minerva, Diana, and Venus, all in one. Eh?'

'I have no lady love, and I can't say.'

'If I were to try my hand,' says Edwin, with a boyish boastfulness getting up in him, 'on a portrait of Miss Landless – in earnest, mind you; in earnest – you should see what I could do!'

'My sister's consent to sit for it being first got, I suppose? As it never will be got, I am afraid I shall never see what you can do. I must bear the loss.'

Jasper turns round from the fire, fills a large goblet glass for Neville, fills a large goblet glass for Edwin, and hands each his own; then fills for himself, saying:

'Come, Mr Neville, we are to drink to my Nephew, Ned. As it is his foot that is in the stirrup – metaphorically – our stirrup-cup is to be devoted to him. Ned, my dearest fellow, my love!'

Jasper sets the example of nearly emptying his glass, and Neville follows it. Edwin Drood says, 'Thank you both very much,' and follows the double example.

'Look at him!' cries Jasper, stretching out his hand admiringly and tenderly, though rallyingly too. 'See where he lounges so easily, Mr Neville! The world is all before him where to choose. A life of stirring work and interest, a life of change and excitement, a life of domestic ease and love! Look at him!'

Edwin Drood's face has become quickly and remarkably flushed by the wine; so has the face of Neville Landless. Edwin still sits thrown back in his chair, making that rest of clasped hands for his head.

'See how little he heeds it all!' Jasper proceeds in a bantering vein. 'It hardly is worth his while to pluck the golden fruit that hangs ripe on the tree for him. And yet consider the contrast, Mr Neville. You and I have no prospect of stirring work and interest, or of change and excitement, or of domestic ease and love. You and I have no prospect (unless you are more fortunate than I am, which may easily be), but the tedious, unchanging round of this dull place.'

'Upon my soul, Jack,' says Edwin, complacently, 'I feel quite apologetic for having my way smoothed as you describe. But you know what I know, Jack, and it may not be so very easy as it seems, after all. May it, Pussy?' To the portrait, with a snap of his thumb and finger. 'We have got to hit it off yet; haven't we, Pussy? You know what I mean, Jack.'

His speech has become thick and indistinct. Jasper, quiet and self-possessed, looks to Neville, as expecting his answer or comment. When Neville speaks, *his* speech is also thick and indistinct.

'It might have been better for Mr Drood to have known some hardships,' he says, defiantly.

'Pray,' retorts Edwin, turning merely his eyes in that direction, 'pray why might it have been better for Mr Drood to have known some hardships?'

'Aye,' Jasper assents with an air of interest; 'let us know why?'

'Because they might have made him more sensible,' says Neville, 'of good fortune that is not by any means necessarily the result of his own merits.'

Mr Jasper quickly looks to his nephew for his rejoinder.

'Have *you* known hardships, may I ask?' says Edwin Drood, sitting upright.

Mr Jasper quickly looks to the other for his retort.

'I have.'

'And what have they made *you* sensible of?'

Mr Jasper's play of eyes between the two holds good throughout the dialogue, to the end.

'I have told you once before to-night.'

'You have done nothing of the sort.'

'I tell you I have. That you take a great deal too much upon yourself.'

'You added something else to that, if I remember?'

'Yes, I did say something else.'

'Say it again.'

'I said that in the part of the world I come from, you would be called to account for it.'

'Only there?' cries Edwin Drood, with a contemptuous laugh. 'A long way off, I believe? Yes; I see! That part of the world is at a safe distance.'

'Say here, then,' rejoins the other, rising in a fury. 'Say anywhere! Your vanity is intolerable, your conceit is beyond endurance, you talk as if you were some rare and precious prize, instead of a common boaster. You are a common fellow, and a common boaster.'

'Pooh, pooh,' says Edwin Drood, equally furious, but more collected; 'how should you know? You may know a black common fellow, or a black common boaster, when you see him (and no doubt you have a large acquaintance that way); but you are no judge of white men.'

This insulting allusion to his dark skin infuriates Neville to that violent degree, that he flings the dregs of his wine at Edwin Drood, and is in the act of flinging the goblet after it, when his arm is caught in the nick of time by Jasper.

'Ned, my dear fellow!' he cries in a loud voice; 'I entreat you, I command you, to be still!' There has been a rush of all the three, and a clattering of glasses and overturning of chairs. 'Mr Neville, for shame! Give this glass to me. Open your hand, sir. I WILL have it!'

But Neville throws him off, and pauses for an instant, in a raging passion, with the goblet yet in his uplifted hand. Then, he dashes it down under the grate, with such force that the broken splinters fly out again in a shower; and he leaves the house.

When he first emerges into the night air, nothing around him is still or steady; nothing around him shows like what it is; he only knows that he stands with a bare head in the midst of a blood-red whirl, waiting to be struggled with, and to struggle to the death.

But, nothing happening, and the moon looking down upon him as if he were dead after a fit of wrath, he holds his steam-hammer beating head and heart, and staggers away. Then, he becomes half conscious of having heard himself bolted and barred out, like a dangerous animal; and thinks what shall he do?

Some wildly passionate ideas of the river dissolve under the spell of the moonlight on the Cathedral and the graves, and the re-membrance of his sister, and the thought of what he owes to the good man who has but that very day won his confidence and given him his pledge. He repairs to Minor Canon Corner, and knocks softly at the door.

It is Mr Crisparkle's custom to sit up last of the early household, very softly touching his piano and practising his favorite parts in concerted vocal music. The south wind that goes where it lists, by way of Minor Canon Corner on a still night, is not more subdued than Mr Crisparkle at such times, regardful of the slumbers of the china shepherdess.

His knock is immediately answered by Mr Crisparkle himself. When he opens the door, candle in hand, his cheerful face falls, and disappointed amazement is in it.

'Mr Neville! In this disorder! Where have you been?'

'I have been to Mr Jasper's, sir. With his nephew.'

'Come in.'

The Minor Canon props him by the elbow with a strong hand (in a strictly scientific manner, worthy of his morning trainings), and turns him into his own little book-room, and shuts the door.

'I have begun ill, sir. I have begun dreadfully ill.'

'Too true. You are not sober, Mr Neville.'

'I am afraid I am not, sir, though I can satisfy you at another time that I have had very little indeed to drink, and that it overcame me in the strangest and most sudden manner.'

'Mr Neville, Mr Neville,' says the Minor Canon, shaking his head with a sorrowful smile; 'I have heard that said before.'

'I think – my mind is much confused, but I think – it is equally true of Mr Jasper's nephew, sir.'

'Very likely,' is the dry rejoinder.

'We quarrelled, sir. He insulted me most grossly. He had heated that tigerish blood I told you of to-day, before then.'

'Mr Neville,' rejoins the Minor Canon, mildly, but firmly: 'I request you not to speak to me with that clenched right hand. Unclench it, if you please.'

'He goaded me, sir,' pursues the young man, instantly obeying, 'beyond my power of endurance. I cannot say whether or no he meant it at first, but he did it. He certainly meant it at last. In short, sir,' with an irrepressible outburst, 'in the passion into which he lashed me, I would have cut him down if I could, and I tried to do it.'

'You have clenched that hand again,' is Mr Crisparkle's quiet commentary.

'I beg your pardon, sir.'

'You know your room, for I showed it to you before dinner; but I will accompany you to it once more. Your arm, if you please. Softly, for the house is all a-bed.'

Scooping his hand into the same scientific elbow-rest as before, and backing it up with the inert strength of his arm, as skilfully as a Police Expert, and with an apparent repose quite unattainable by Novices, Mr Crisparkle conducts his pupil to the pleasant and orderly old room prepared for him. Arrived there, the young man throws himself into a chair, and, flinging his arms upon his reading-table, rests his head upon them with an air of wretched self-reproach.

The gentle Minor Canon has had it in his thoughts to leave the room, without a word. But, looking round at the door, and seeing this dejected figure, he turns back to it, touches it with a mild hand, and says 'Good night!' A sob is his only acknowledgment. He might have had many a worse; perhaps, could have had few better.

Another soft knock at the outer door attracts his attention as he goes down stairs. He opens it to Mr Jasper, holding in his hand the pupil's hat.

'We have had an awful scene with him,' says Jasper, in a low voice.

'Has it been so bad as that?'

'Murderous!'

Mr Crisparkle remonstrates: 'No, no, no. Do not use such strong words.'

'He might have laid my dear boy dead at my feet. It is no fault of his, that he did not. But that I was, through the mercy of God, swift and strong with him, he would have cut him down on my hearth.'

The phrase smites home. 'Ah!' thinks Mr Crisparkle. 'His own words!'

'Seeing what I have seen to-night, and hearing what I have heard,' adds Jasper, with great earnestness, 'I shall never know peace of mind when there is danger of those two coming together with no one else to interfere. It was horrible. There is something of the tiger in his dark blood.'

'Ah!' thinks Mr Crisparkle. 'So he said!'

'You, my dear sir,' pursues Jasper, taking his hand, 'even you, have accepted a dangerous charge.'[1]

'You need have no fear for me, Jasper,' returns Mr Crisparkle, with a quiet smile. 'I have none for myself.'

'I have none for myself,' returns Jasper, with an emphasis on the last pronoun, 'because I am not, nor am I in the way of being, the object of his hostility. But you may be, and my dear boy has been. Good night!'

Mr Crisparkle goes in, with the hat that has so easily, so almost imperceptibly, acquired the right to be hung up in his hall; hangs it up; and goes thoughtfully to bed.

CHAPTER 9

Birds in the Bush[1]

ROSA, having no relation that she knew of in the world, had, from the seventh year of her age, known no home but the Nuns' House, and no mother but Miss Twinkleton. Her remembrance of her own mother was of a pretty little creature like herself (not much older than herself, it seemed to her), who had been brought home in her father's arms, drowned. The fatal accident had happened at a party of pleasure. Every fold and color in the pretty summer dress, and even the long wet hair, with scattered petals of ruined flowers still clinging to it, as the dead young figure, in its sad, sad beauty lay upon the bed, were fixed indelibly in Rosa's recollection. So were the wild despair and the subsequent bowed-down grief of her poor young father, who died brokenhearted on the first anniversary of that hard day.

The betrothal of Rosa grew out of the soothing of his year of mental distress by his fast friend and old college companion, Drood: who likewise had been left a widower in his youth. But he, too, went the silent road into which all earthly pilgrimages merge, some sooner, and some later; and thus the young couple had come to be as they were.

The atmosphere of pity surrounding the little orphan girl when she first came to Cloisterham, had never cleared away. It had taken brighter hues as she grew older, happier, prettier; now it had been golden, now roseate, and now azure; but it had always adorned her with some soft light of its own. The general desire to console and caress her, had caused her to be treated in the beginning as a child much younger than her years; the same desire had caused her to be still petted when she was a child no longer. Who should be her favorite, who should anticipate this or that small present, or do her this or that small service; who should take her home for the holidays; who should write to her the oftenest when they were separated, and whom she would most rejoice to see again when they were reunited; even these gentle rivalries were not without their slight dashes of bitterness in the Nuns' House. Well for the poor Nuns in their day, if they hid no harder strife under their veils and rosaries!

Thus Rosa had grown to be an amiable, giddy, wilful, winning little creature; spoilt, in the sense of counting upon kindness from all around her; but not in the sense of repaying it with indifference. Possessing an exhaustless well of affection in her nature, its sparkling waters had freshened and brightened the Nuns' House for years, and yet its depths had never yet been moved: what might betide when that came to pass; what developing changes might fall upon the heedless head, and light heart then; remained to be seen.

By what means the news that there had been a quarrel between the two young men over-night, involving even some kind of onslaught by Mr Neville upon Edwin Drood, got into Miss Twinkleton's establishment before breakfast, it is impossible to say.

Whether it was brought in by the birds of the air, or came blowing in with the very air itself, when the casement windows were set open; whether the baker brought it kneaded into the bread, or the milkman delivered it as part of the adulteration of his milk; or the housemaids, beating the dust out of their mats against the gateposts, received it in exchange deposited on the mats by the town atmosphere; certain it is that the news permeated every gable of the old building before Miss Twinkleton was down, and that Miss Twinkleton herself received it through Mrs Tisher, while yet in the act of dressing; or (as she might have expressed the phrase to a parent or guardian of a mythological turn) of sacrificing to the Graces.

Miss Landless's brother had thrown a bottle at Mr Edwin Drood.

Miss Landless's brother had thrown a knife at Mr Edwin Drood.

A knife became suggestive of a fork, and Miss Landless's brother had thrown a fork at Mr Edwin Drood.

As in the governing precedent of Peter Piper, alleged to have picked the peck of pickled pepper, it was held physically desirable to have evidence of the existence of the peck of pickled pepper which Peter Piper was alleged to have picked: so, in this case, it was held psychologically important to know Why Miss Landless's brother threw a bottle, knife, or fork – or bottle, knife, *and* fork – for the cook had been given to understand it was all three – at Mr Edwin Drood?

Well, then. Miss Landless's brother had said he admired Miss Bud. Mr Edwin Drood had said to Miss Landless's brother that he had no business to admire Miss Bud. Miss Landless's brother had then 'up'd' (this was the cook's exact information) with the bottle, knife, fork, and decanter (the decanter now coolly flying at everybody's head, without the least introduction), and thrown them all at Mr Edwin Drood.

Poor little Rosa put a forefinger into each of her ears when these rumors began to circulate, and retired into a corner, beseeching not to be told any more; but Miss Landless, begging permission of Miss Twinkleton to go and speak with her brother, and pretty plainly showing that she would take it if it were not given, struck out the more definite course of going to Mr Crisparkle's for accurate intelligence.

When she came back (being first closeted with Miss Twinkleton, in order that anything objectionable in her tidings might be retained by that discreet filter), she imparted to Rosa only, what had taken place; dwelling with a flushed cheek on the provocation her brother had received, but almost limiting it to that last gross affront as crowning 'some other words between them,' and, out of consideration for her new friend, passing lightly over the fact that the other words had originated in her lover's taking things in general so very easily. To Rosa direct, she brought a petition from her brother that she would forgive him; and, having delivered it with sisterly earnestness, made an end of the subject.

It was reserved for Miss Twinkleton to tone down the public mind of the Nuns' House. That lady, therefore, entering in a stately manner what plebeians might have called the school-room, but what, in the patrician language of the head of the Nuns' House, was euphuistically, not to say round-aboutedly, denominated 'the apartment allotted to study,' and saying with a forensic air, 'Ladies!' all rose. Mrs Tisher at the same time grouped herself behind her chief, as representing Queen Elizabeth's first historical female friend at Tilbury Fort.[2] Miss Twinkleton then proceeded to remark that Rumor, Ladies, had been represented by the bard of Avon – needless were it to mention the immortal SHAKESPEARE, also called the Swan of his native river, not improbably with some reference to the ancient superstition that that bird of graceful plumage (Miss Jennings will please stand upright) sang sweetly on the approach of death, for which we have no ornithological authority, – Rumor, Ladies, had been represented by that bard – hem! –

'who drew
The celebrated Jew,'

as painted full of tongues. Rumor in Cloisterham (Miss Ferdinand will honor me with her attention) was no exception to the great limner's portrait of Rumor elsewhere. A slight *fracas* between two young gentlemen occurring last night within a hundred miles of these peaceful walls (Miss Ferdinand, being apparently incorrigible, will have the kindness to write out this evening, in the original language, the first four fables of our vivacious neighbour, Monsieur La Fontaine[3]) had been very grossly exaggerated by Rumor's voice. In the first alarm and anxiety arising from our sympathy with

a sweet young friend, not wholly to be dissociated from one of the
gladiators in the bloodless arena in question (the impropriety of
Miss Reynolds's appearing to stab herself in the band with a pin,
is far too obvious, and too glaringly unlady-like, to be pointed out),
we descended from our maiden elevation to discuss this uncongenial and this unfit theme. Responsible enquiries having assured
us that it was but one of those 'airy nothings' pointed at by the
Poet (whose name and date of birth Miss Giggles will supply
within half an hour), we would now discard the subject, and con-
centrate our minds upon the grateful labors of the day.

But the subject so survived all day, nevertheless, that Miss
Ferdinand got into new trouble by surreptitiously clapping on a
paper moustache at dinner-time, and going through the motions of
aiming a water-bottle at Miss Giggles, who drew a table-spoon in
defence.

Now, Rosa thought of this unlucky quarrel a great deal, and
thought of it with an uncomfortable feeling that she was involved
in it, as cause, or consequence, or what not, through being in a
false position altogether as to her marriage engagement. Never free
from such uneasiness when she was with her affianced husband, it
was not likely that she would be free from it when they were apart.
To-day, too, she was cast in upon herself, and deprived of the
relief of talking freely with her new friend, because the quarrel
had been with Helena's brother, and Helena undisguisedly avoided
the subject as a delicate and difficult one to herself. At this critical
time, of all times, Rosa's guardian was announced as having come
to see her.

Mr Grewgious had been well selected for his trust, as a man of
incorruptible integrity, but certainly for no other appropriate
quality discernible on the surface. He was an arid, sandy man, who,
if he had been put into a grinding-mill, looked as if he would have
ground immediately into high-dried snuff. He had a scanty flat
crop of hair, in color and consistency like some very mangy yellow
fur tippet; it was so unlike hair, that it must have been a wig, but
for the stupendous improbability of anybody's voluntarily sporting
such a head. The little play of feature that his face presented, was
cut deep into it, in a few hard curves that made it more like work;
and he had certain notches in his forehead, which looked as though
Nature had been about to touch them into sensibility or refinement,

when she had impatiently thrown away the chisel, and said: 'I really cannot be worried to finish off this man; let him go as he is.'

With too great length of throat at his upper end, and too much ankle-bone and heel at his lower; with an awkward and hesitating manner; with a shambling walk, and with what is called a near sight – which perhaps prevented his observing how much white cotton stocking he displayed to the public eye, in contrast with his black suit – Mr Grewgious still had some strange capacity in him of making on the whole an agreeable impression.

Mr Grewgious was discovered by his ward, much discomfited by being in Miss Twinkleton's company in Miss Twinkleton's own sacred room. Dim forebodings of being examined in something, and not coming well out of it, seemed to oppress the poor gentleman when found in these circumstances.

'My dear, how do you do? I am glad to see you. My dear, how much improved you are. Permit me to hand you a chair, my dear.'

Miss Twinkleton rose at her little writing-table, saying, with general sweetness, as to the polite Universe: 'Will you permit me to retire?'

'By no means, madam, on my account. I beg that you will not move.'

'I must entreat permission to *move*,' returned Miss Twinkleton, repeating the word with a charming grace; 'but I will not withdraw, since you are so obliging. If I wheel my desk to this corner window, shall I be in the way?'

'Madam! In the way!'

'You are very kind. Rosa, my dear, you will be under no restraint, I am sure.'

Here Mr Grewgious, left by the fire with Rosa, said again: 'My dear, how do you do? I am glad to see you, my dear.' And having waited for her to sit down, sat down himself.

'My visits,' said Mr Grewgious, 'are, like those of the angels – not that I compare myself to an angel.'

'No, sir,' said Rosa.

'Not by any means,' assented Mr Grewgious. 'I merely refer to my visits, which are few and far between. The angels are, we know very well, upstairs.'

Miss Twinkleton looked round with a kind of stiff stare.

'I refer, my dear,' said Mr Grewgious, laying his hand on Rosa's, as the possibility thrilled through his frame of his otherwise seeming to take the awful liberty of calling Miss Twinkleton my dear; 'I refer to the other young ladies.'

Miss Twinkleton resumed her writing.

Mr Grewgious, with a sense of not having managed his opening point quite as neatly as he might have desired, smoothed his head from back to front as if he had just dived, and were pressing the water out – this smoothing action, however superfluous, was habitual with him – and took a pocket-book from his coat-pocket, and a stump of black-lead pencil from his waistcoat pocket.

'I made,' he said, turning the leaves: 'I made a guiding memorandum or so – as I usually do, for I have no conversational powers whatever – to which I will, with your permission, my dear, refer. "Well and happy." Truly. You are well and happy, my dear? You look so.'

'Yes, indeed, sir,' answered Rosa.

'For which,' said Mr Grewgious, with a bend of his head towards the corner window, 'our warmest acknowledgments are due, and I am sure are rendered, to the maternal kindness and the constant care and consideration of the lady whom I have now the honor to see before me.'

This point, again, made but a lame departure from Mr Grewgious, and never got to its destination; for, Miss Twinkleton, feeling that the courtesies required her to be by this time quite outside the conversation, was biting the end of her pen, and looking upward, as waiting for the descent of an idea from any member of the Celestial Nine who might have one to spare.

Mr Grewgious smoothed his smooth head again, and then made another reference to his pocket-book; lining out 'well and happy' as disposed of.

'"Pounds, shillings, and pence" is my next note. A dry subject for a young lady, but an important subject too. Life is pounds, shillings, and pence. Death is –' A sudden recollection of the death of her two parents seemed to stop him, and he said in a softer tone, and evidently inserting the negative as an after-thought: 'Death is *not* pounds, shillings, and pence.'

His voice was as hard and dry as himself, and Fancy might have ground it straight, like himself, into high-dried snuff. And yet, through the very limited means of expression that he possessed, he seemed to express kindness. If Nature had but finished him off, kindness might have been recognizable in his face at this moment. But if the notches in his forehead wouldn't fuse together, and if his face would work and couldn't play, what could he do, poor man!

'"Pounds, shillings, and pence." You find your allowance always sufficient for your wants, my dear?'

Rosa wanted for nothing, and therefore it was ample.

'And you are not in debt?'

Rosa laughed at the idea of being in debt. It seemed, to her inexperience, a comical vagary of the imagination. Mr Grewgious stretched his near sight to be sure that this was her view of the case. 'Ah!' he said, as comment, with a furtive glance towards Miss Twinkleton, and lining out 'pounds, shillings, and pence': 'I spoke of having got among the angels! So I did!'

Rosa felt what his next memorandum would prove to be, and was blushing and folding a crease in her dress with one embarrassed hand, long before he found it.

'"Marriage." Hem!' Mr Grewgious carried his smoothing hand down over his eyes and nose, and even chin, before drawing his chair a little nearer, and speaking a little more confidentially: 'I now touch, my dear, upon the point that is the direct cause of my troubling you with the present visit. Otherwise, being a particularly Angular man, I should not have intruded here. I am the last man to intrude into a sphere for which I am so entirely unfitted. I feel, on these premises, as if I was a bear – with the cramp – in a youthful Cotillon.'⁴

His ungainliness gave him enough of the air of his simile to set Rosa off laughing heartily.

'It strikes you in the same light,' said Mr Grewgious, with perfect calmness. 'Just so. To return to my memorandum. Mr Edwin has been to and fro here, as was arranged. You have mentioned that, in your quarterly letters to me. And you like him, and he likes you.'

'I *like* him very much, sir,' rejoined Rosa.

'So I said, my dear,' returned her guardian, for whose ear the timid emphasis was much too fine. 'Good. And you correspond.'

'We write to one another,' said Rosa, pouting, as she recalled their epistolary differences.

'Such is the meaning that I attach to the word "correspond"

in this application, my dear,' said Mr Grewgious. 'Good. All goes well, time works on, and at this next Christmas-time it will become necessary, as a matter of form, to give the exemplary lady in the corner window, to whom we are so much indebted, business notice of your departure in the ensuing half-year. Your relations with her are far more than business relations, no doubt; but a residue of business remains in them, and business is business ever. I am a particularly Angular man,' proceeded Mr Grewgious, as if it suddenly occurred to him to mention it, 'and I am not used to give anything away. If, for these two reasons, some competent Proxy would give *you* away, I should take it very kindly.'

Rosa intimated, with her eyes on the ground, that she thought a substitute might be found, if required.

'Surely, surely,' said Mr Grewgious. 'For instance, the gentleman who teaches Dancing here – he would know how to do it with graceful propriety. He would advance and retire in a manner satisfactory to the feelings of the officiating clergyman, and of yourself, and the bridegroom, and all parties concerned. I am – I am a particularly Angular man,' said Mr Grewgious, as if he had made up his mind to screw it out at last: 'and should only blunder.'

Rosa sat still and silent. Perhaps her mind had not quite got so far as the ceremony yet, but was lagging on the way there.

'Memorandum. "Will." Now, my dear,' said Mr Grewgious, referring to his notes, disposing of 'marriage' with his pencil, and taking a paper from his pocket: 'although I have before possessed you with the contents of your father's will, I think it right at this time to leave a certified copy of it in your hands. And although Mr Edwin is also aware of its contents, I think it right at this time likewise to place a certified copy of it in Mr Jasper's hands –'

'Not in his own!' asked Rosa, looking up quickly. 'Cannot the copy go to Eddy himself?'

'Why, yes, my dear, if you particularly wish it; but I spoke of Mr Jasper as being his trustee.'

'I do particularly wish it, if you please,' said Rosa, hurriedly and earnestly; 'I don't like Mr Jasper to come between us, in any way.'

'It is natural, I suppose,' said Mr Grewgious, 'that your young husband should be all in all. Yes. You observe that I say, I suppose.

The fact is, I am a particularly Unnatural man, and I don't know from my own knowledge.'

Rosa looked at him with some wonder.

'I mean,' he explained, 'that young ways were never my ways. I was the only offspring of parents far advanced in life, and I half believe I was born advanced in life myself. No personality is intended towards the name you will so soon change, when I re-mark that while the general growth of people seem to have come into existence, buds, I seem to have come into existence a chip. I was a chip – and a very dry one – when I first became aware of myself. Respecting the other certified copy, your wish shall be complied with. Respecting your inheritance, I think you know all. It is an annuity of two hundred and fifty pounds. The savings upon that annuity, and some other items to your credit, all duly carried to account, with vouchers, will place you in possession of a lump-sum of money, rather exceeding Seventeen Hundred Pounds. I am empowered to advance the cost of your preparations for your marriage out of that fund. All is told.'

'Will you please tell me,' said Rosa, taking the paper with a prettily knitted brow, but not opening it: 'whether I am right in what I am going to say? I can understand what you tell me, so very much better than what I read in law-writings. My poor papa and Eddy's father made their agreement together, as very dear and firm and fast friends, in order that we, too, might be very dear and firm and fast friends after them?'

'Just so.'

'For the lasting good of both of us, and the lasting happiness of both of us?'

'Just so.'

'That we might be to one another even much more than they had been to one another?'

'Just so.'

'It was not bound upon Eddy, and it was not bound upon me, by any forfeit, in case –'

'Don't be agitated, my dear. In the case that it brings tears into your affectionate eyes even to picture to yourself – in the case of your not marrying one another – no, no forfeiture on either side. You would then have been my ward until you were of age. No worse would have befallen you. Bad enough perhaps!'

'And Eddy?'

'He would have come into his partnership derived from his father, and into its arrears to his credit (if any), on attaining his majority, just as now.'

Rosa, with her perplexed face and knitted brow, bit the corner of her attested copy, as she sat with her head on one side, looking abstractedly on the floor, and smoothing it with her foot.

'In short,' said Mr Grewgious, 'this betrothal is a wish, a sentiment, a friendly project, tenderly expressed on both sides. That it was strongly felt, and that there was a lively hope that it would prosper, there can be no doubt. When you were both children, you began to be accustomed to it, and it *has* prospered. But circumstances alter cases; and I made this visit to-day, partly, indeed principally, to discharge myself of the duty of telling you, my dear, that two young people can only be betrothed in marriage (except as a matter of convenience, and therefore mockery and misery) of their own free will, their own attachment, and their own assurance (it may or it may not prove a mistaken one, but we must take our chance of that), that they are suited to each other and will make each other happy. Is it to be supposed, for example, that if either of your fathers were living now, and had any mistrust on that subject, his mind would not be changed by the change of circumstances involved in the change of your years? Untenable, unreasonable, inconclusive, and preposterous!'

Mr Grewgious said all this, as if he were reading it aloud; or, still more, as if he were repeating a lesson. So expressionless of any approach to spontaneity were his face and manner.

'I have now, my dear,' he added, blurring out 'Will' with his pencil, 'discharged myself of what is doubtless a formal duty in this case, but still a duty in such a case. Memorandum, "Wishes:" My dear, is there any wish of yours that I can further?'

Rosa shook her head, with an almost plaintive air of hesitation in want of help.

'Is there any instruction that I can take from you with reference to your affairs?'

'I – I should like to settle them with Eddy first, if you please,' said Rosa, plaiting the crease in her dress.

'Surely. Surely,' returned Mr Grewgious. 'You two should be of one mind in all things. Is the young gentleman expected shortly?'

'He has gone away only this morning. He will be back at Christmas.'

'Nothing could happen better. You will, on his return at Christmas, arrange all matters of detail with him; you will then communicate with me; and I will discharge myself (as a mere business acquittance) of my business responsibilities towards the accomplished lady in the corner window. They will accrue at that season.' Blurring pencil once again. 'Memorandum. "Leave." Yes. I will now, my dear, take my leave.'

'Could I,' said Rosa, rising, as he jerked out of his chair in his ungainly way: 'could I ask you, most kindly to come to me at Christmas, if I had anything particular to say to you?'

'Why, certainly, certainly,' he rejoined; apparently – if such a word can be used of one who had no apparent lights or shadows about him – complimented by the question. 'As a particularly Angular man, I do not fit smoothly into the social circle, and consequently I have no other engagement at Christmas-time than to partake, on the twenty-fifth, of a boiled turkey and celery sauce with a – with a particularly Angular clerk I have the good fortune to possess, whose father, being a Norfolk farmer, sends him up (the turkey up), as a present to me, from the neighbourhood of Norwich. I should be quite proud of your wishing to see me, my dear. As a professional Receiver of rents, so very few people *do* wish to see me, that the novelty would be bracing.'

For his ready acquiescence, the grateful Rosa put her hands upon his shoulders, stood on tiptoe, and instantly kissed him.

'Lord bless me!' cried Mr Grewgious. 'Thank you, my dear! The honor is almost equal to the pleasure. Miss Twinkleton, Madam, I have had a most satisfactory conversation with my ward, and I will now release you from the incumbrance of my presence.'

'Nay, sir,' rejoined Miss Twinkleton, rising with a gracious condescension: 'say not incumbrance. Not so, by any means. I cannot permit you to say so.'

'Thank you, Madam. I have read in the newspapers,' said Mr Grewgious, stammering a little, 'that when a distinguished visitor (not that I am one: far from it) goes to a school (not that this is one: far from it), he asks for a holiday, or some sort of grace. It being now the afternoon in the – College – of which you are the eminent head, the young ladies might gain nothing, except in name, by having the rest of the day allowed them. But if there is any young lady at all under a cloud, might I solicit –?'

'Ah, Mr Grewgious, Mr Grewgious!' cried Miss Twinkleton, with a chastely-rallying forefinger. 'Oh, you gentlemen, you gentlemen! Fie for shame, that you are so hard upon us poor maligned disciplinarians of our sex, for your sakes! But as Miss Ferdinand is at present weighed down by an incubus' – Miss Twinkleton might have said a pen-and-ink-ubus[5] of writing out Monsieur La Fontaine – 'go to her, Rosa my dear, and tell her the penalty is remitted, in deference to the intercession of your guardian, Mr Grewgious.'

Miss Twinkleton here achieved a curtsey, suggestive of marvels happening to her respective legs, and which she came out of nobly, three yards behind her starting-point.

As he held it incumbent upon him to call on Mr Jasper before leaving Cloisterham, Mr Grewgious went to the Gate House, and climbed its postern stair. But Mr Jasper's door being closed, and presenting on a slip of paper the word 'Cathedral,' the fact of its being service-time was borne into the mind of Mr Grewgious. So he descended the stair again, and, crossing the Close, paused at the great western folding-door of the Cathedral, which stood open on the fine and bright, though short-lived, afternoon, for the airing of the place.

'Dear me,' said Mr Grewgious, peeping in, 'it's like looking down the throat of Old Time.'

Old Time heaved a mouldy sigh from tomb and arch and vault; and gloomy shadows began to deepen in corners; and damps began to rise from green patches of stone; and jewels, cast upon the pavement of the nave from stained glass by the declining sun, began to perish. Within the grill-gate of the chancel, up the steps surmounted loomingly by the fast darkening organ, white robes could be dimly seen, and one feeble voice, rising and falling in a cracked monotonous mutter, could at intervals be faintly heard. In the free outer air, the river, the green pastures, and the brown arable lands, the teeming hills and dales, were reddened by the sunset: while the distant little windows in windmills and farm homesteads, shone, patches of bright beaten gold. In the Cathedral, all became grey, murky, and sepulchral, and the cracked monoton-ous mutter went on like a dying voice, until the organ and the choir burst forth, and drowned it in a sea of music. Then the sea fell, and the dying voice made another feeble effort, and then the sea rose high, and beat its life out, and lashed the roof, and surged among the arches, and pierced the heights of the great tower; and then the sea was dry, and all was still.

Mr Grewgious had by that time walked to the chancel-steps, where he met the living waters coming out.

'Nothing is the matter?' Thus Jasper accosted him, rather quickly. 'You have not been sent for?'

'Not at all, not at all. I came down of my own accord. I have been to my pretty ward's, and am now homeward bound again.'

'You found her thriving?'

'Blooming indeed. Most blooming. I merely came to tell her, seriously, what a betrothal by deceased parents is.'

'And what is it – according to your judgment?'

Mr Grewgious noticed the whiteness of the lips that asked the question, and put it down to the chilling account of the Cathedral.

'I merely came to tell her that it could not be considered binding, against any such reason for its dissolution as a want of affection, or want of disposition to carry it into effect, on the side of either party.'

'May I ask, had you any especial reason for telling her that?'

Mr Grewgious answered somewhat sharply: 'The especial reason of doing my duty, sir. Simply that.' Then he added: 'Come, Mr Jasper; I know your affection for your nephew, and that you are quick to feel on his behalf. I assure you that this implies not the least doubt of, or disrespect to, your nephew.'

'You could not,' returned Jasper, with a friendly pressure of his arm, as they walked on side by side, 'speak more handsomely.'

Mr Grewgious pulled off his hat to smooth his head, and, having smoothed it, nodded it contentedly, and put his hat on again.

'I will wager,' said Jasper, smiling – his lips were still so white that he was conscious of it, and bit and moistened them while speaking: 'I will wager that she hinted no wish to be released from Ned.'

'And you will win your wager, if you do,' retorted Mr Grewgious. 'We should allow some margin for little maidenly delicacies in a young motherless creature, under such circumstances, I suppose; it is not in my line; what do you think?'

'There can be no doubt of it.'

'I am glad you say so. Because,' proceeded Mr Grewgious, who had all this time very knowingly felt his way round to action on his remembrance of what she had said of Jasper himself: 'because she seems to have some little delicate instinct that all preliminary arrangements had best be made between Mr Edwin Drood and herself, don't you see? She don't want us, don't you know?'

Jasper touched himself on the breast, and said, somewhat indistinctly: 'You mean me.'

Mr Grewgious touched himself on the breast, and said: 'I mean us. Therefore, let them have their little discussions and councils together, when Mr Edwin Drood comes back here at Christmas, and then you and I will step in, and put the final touches to the business.'

'So, you settled with her that you would come back at Christmas?' observed Jasper.[6] 'I see! Mr Grewgious, as you quite fairly said just now, there is such an exceptional attachment between my nephew and me, that I am more sensitive for the dear, fortunate, happy, happy fellow than for myself. But it is only right that the young lady should be considered, as you have pointed out, and that I should accept my cue from you. I accept it. I understand that at Christmas they will complete their preparations for May, and that their marriage will be put in final train by themselves, and that nothing will remain for us but to put ourselves in train also, and have everything ready for our formal release from our trusts, on Edwin's birthday.'

'That is my understanding,' assented Mr Grewgious, as they shook hands to part. 'God bless them both!'

'God save them both!' cried Jasper.

'I said, bless them,' remarked the former, looking back over his shoulder.

'I said, save them,' returned the latter. 'Is there any difference?'

*

CHAPTER 10

Smoothing the Way

IT has been often enough remarked that women have a curious power of divining the characters of men, which would seem to be innate and instinctive; seeing that it is arrived at through no patient process of reasoning, that it can give no satisfactory or sufficient account of itself, and that it pronounces in the most confident manner even against accumulated observation on the part of the other sex. But it has not been quite so often remarked that this power (fallible, like every other human attribute) is for the most part absolutely incapable of self-revision; and that when it has delivered an adverse opinion which by all human lights is subsequently proved to have failed, it is undistinguishable from prejudice, in respect of its determination not to be corrected. Nay, the very possibility of contradiction or disproof, however remote, communicates to this feminine judgment from the first, in nine cases out of ten, the weakness attendant on the testimony of an interested witness: so personally and strongly does the fair diviner connect herself with her divination.

'Now, don't you think, Ma dear,' said the Minor Canon to his mother one day as she sat at her knitting in his little book-room, 'that you are rather hard on Mr Neville?'

'No, I do *not*, Sept,' returned the old lady.

'Let us discuss it, Ma.'

'I have no objection to discuss it, Sept. I trust, my dear, I am always open to discussion.' There was a vibration in the old lady's cap, as though she internally added: 'and I should like to see the discussion that would change *my* mind!'

'Very good, Ma,' said her conciliatory son. 'There is nothing like being open to discussion.'

'I hope not, my dear,' returned the old lady, evidently shut to it.

'Well! Mr Neville, on that unfortunate occasion, commits himself under provocation.'

'And under mulled wine,' added the old lady.

'I must admit the wine. Though I believe the two young men were much alike in that regard.'

'I don't!' said the old lady.

'Why not, Ma?'

'Because I *don't*,' said the old lady. 'Still, I am quite open to discussion.'

'But, my dear Ma, I cannot see how we are to discuss, if you take that line.'

'Blame Mr Neville for it, Sept, and not me,' said the old lady, with stately severity.

'My dear Ma! Why Mr Neville?'

'Because,' said Mrs Crisparkle, retiring on first principles, 'he came home intoxicated, and did great discredit to this house, and showed great disrespect to this family.'

'That is not to be denied, Ma. He was then, and he is now, very sorry for it.'

'But for Mr Jasper's well-bred consideration in coming up to me, next day, after service, in the Nave itself, with his gown still on, and expressing his hope that I had not been greatly alarmed or had my rest violently broken, I believe I might never had heard of that disgraceful transaction,' said the old lady.

'To be candid, Ma, I think I should have kept it from you if I could: though I had not decidedly made up my mind. I was following Jasper out, to confer with him on the subject, and to consider the expediency of his and my jointly hushing the thing up on all accounts, when I found him speaking to you. Then it was too late.'

'Too late, indeed, Sept. He was still as pale as gentlemanly ashes at what had taken place in his rooms over-night.'

'If I *had* kept it from you, Ma, you may be sure it would have been for your peace and quiet, and for the good of the young men, and in my best discharge of my duty according to my lights.'

The old lady immediately walked across the room and kissed him; saying, 'Of course, my dear Sept, I am sure of that.'

'However, it became the town-talk,' said Mr Crisparkle, rubbing his ear, as his mother resumed her seat, and her knitting, 'and passed out of my power.'

'And I said then, Sept,' returned the old lady, 'that I thought ill of Mr Neville. And I say now, that I think ill of Mr Neville. And I said then, and I say now, that I hope Mr Neville may come to good, but I don't believe he will.' Here the cap vibrated again, considerably.

'I am sorry to hear you say so, Ma –'

'I am sorry to say so, my dear,' interposed the old lady, knitting on firmly, 'but I can't help it.'

'– For,' pursued the Minor Canon, 'it is undeniable that Mr Neville is exceedingly industrious and attentive, and that he improves apace, and that he has – I hope I may say – an attachment to me.'

'There is no merit in the last article, my dear,' said the old lady, quickly; 'and if he says there is, I think the worse of him for the boast.'

'But, my dear Ma, he never said there was.'

'Perhaps not,' returned the old lady; 'still, I don't see that it greatly signifies.'

There was no impatience in the pleasant look with which Mr Crisparkle contemplated the pretty old piece of china as it knitted; but there was, certainly, a humorous sense of its not being a piece of china to argue with very closely.

'Besides, Sept. Ask yourself what he would be without his sister. You know what an influence she has over him; you know what a capacity she has; you know that whatever he reads with you, he reads with her. Give her her fair share of your praise, and how much do you leave for him?'

At these words Mr Crisparkle fell into a little reverie, in which he thought of several things. He thought of the times he had seen the brother and sister together in deep converse over one of his own old college books; now, in the rimy mornings, when he made those sharpening pilgrimages to Cloisterham Weir; now, in the sombre evenings, when he faced the wind at sunset, having climbed his favorite outlook, a beetling fragment of monastery ruin;[1] and the two studious figures passed below him along the margin of the river, in which the town fires and lights already shone, making the landscape bleaker. He thought how the consciousness had stolen upon him that in teaching one, he was teaching two; and how he had almost insensibly adapted his explanations to both minds – that with which his own was daily in contact, and that which he only approached through it. He thought of the gossip that had reached him from the Nuns' House, to the effect that Helena, whom he had mistrusted as so proud and fierce, submitted herself to the fairy-bride (as he called her), and learnt from her what she knew. He thought of the picturesque alliance between those two, externally so very different. He thought – perhaps most of all – could it be that these things were yet but so many weeks old, and had become an integral part of his life?

As, whenever the Reverend Septimus fell a-musing, his good mother took it to be an infallible sign that he 'wanted support,' the blooming old lady made all haste to the dining-room closet, to produce from it the support embodied in a glass of Constantia and a home-made biscuit. It was a most wonderful closet, worthy of Cloisterham and of Minor Canon Corner. Above it, a portrait of Handel in a flowing wig beamed down at the spectator, with a knowing air of being up to the contents of the closet, and a musical air of intending to combine all its harmonies in one delicious fugue. No common closet with a vulgar door on hinges, openable all at once, and leaving nothing to be disclosed by degrees, this rare closet had a lock in mid-air, where two perpendicular slides met: the one falling down, and the other pushing up. The upper slide, on being pulled down (leaving the lower a double mystery), revealed deep shelves of pickle-jars, jam-pots, tin canisters, spice boxes, and agreeably outlandish vessels of blue and white, the luscious lodgings of preserved tamarinds and ginger. Every benevolent inhabitant of this retreat had his name inscribed upon his stomach. The pickles, in a uniform of rich brown double-breasted buttoned coat, and yellow or sombre drab continuations, announced their portly forms, in printed capitals, as Walnut, Gherkin, Onion, Cabbage, Cauliflower, Mixed, and other members of that noble family. The jams, as being of a less masculine temperament, and as wearing curl-papers, announced themselves in feminine calligraphy, like a soft whisper, to be Raspberry, Gooseberry, Apricot, Plum, Damson, Apple, and Peach. The scene closing on these charmers, and the lower slide ascending, oranges were revealed, attended by a mighty japanned sugar-box, to temper their acerbity if unripe. Home-made biscuits waited at the Court of these Powers, accompanied by a goodly fragment of plum-cake, and various slender ladies' fingers, to be dipped into sweet wine and kissed. Lowest of all, a compact leaden vault enshrined the sweet wine and a stock of cordials: whence issued whispers of Seville Orange, Lemon, Almond, and

Caraway-seed. There was a crowning air upon this closet of closets, of having been for ages hummed through by the Cathedral bell and organ, until those venerable bees had made sublimated honey of everything in store; and it was always observed that every dipper among the shelves (deep, as has been noticed, and swallowing up head, shoulders, and elbows) came forth again mellow-faced, and seeming to have undergone a saccharine transfiguration.

The Reverend Septimus yielded himself up quite as willing a victim to a nauseous medicinal herb-closet, also presided over by the china shepherdess, as to this glorious cupboard. To what amazing infusions of gentian, peppermint, gilliflower, sage, parsley, thyme, rue, rosemary, and dandelion, did his courageous stomach submit itself! In what wonderful wrappers, enclosing layers of dried leaves, would he swathe his rosy and contented face, if his mother suspected him of a toothache! What botanical blotches would he cheerfully stick upon his cheek, or forehead, if the dear old lady convicted him of an imperceptible pimple there! Into this herbaceous penitentiary, situated on an upper staircase-landing: a low and narrow whitewashed cell, where bunches of dried leaves hung from rusty hooks in the ceiling, and were spread out upon shelves, in company with portentous bottles: would the Reverend Septimus submissively be led, like the highly-popular lamb[2] who has so long and unresistingly been led to the slaughter, and there would he, *un*like that lamb, bore nobody but himself. Not even doing that much, so that the old lady were busy and pleased, he would quietly swallow what was given him, merely taking a corrective dip of hands and face into the great bowl of dried rose-leaves, and into the other great bowl of dried lavender, and then would go out, as confident in the sweetening powers of Cloisterham Weir and a wholesome mind, as Lady Macbeth was hopeless of those of all the seas that roll.

In the present instance the good Minor Canon took his glass of Constantia with an excellent grace, and, so supported to his mother's satisfaction, applied himself to the remaining duties of the day. In their orderly and punctual progress they brought round Vesper Service and twilight. The Cathedral being very cold, he set off for a brisk trot after service; the trot to end in a charge at his favorite fragment of ruin, which was to be carried by storm, without a pause for breath.

He carried it in a masterly manner, and, not breathed even then, stood looking down upon the river. The river at Cloisterham is sufficiently near the sea to throw up oftentimes a quantity of sea-weed. An unusual quantity had come in with the last tide, and this, and the confusion of the water, and the restless dipping and flapping of the noisy gulls, and an angry light out seaward beyond the brown-sailed barges that were turning black, foreshadowed a stormy night. In his mind he was contrasting the wild and noisy sea with the quiet harbor of Minor Canon Corner, when Helena and Neville Landless passed below him. He had had the two together in his thoughts all day, and at once climbed down to speak to them together. The footing was rough in an uncertain light for any tread save that of a good climber; but the Minor Canon was as good a climber as most men, and stood beside them before many good climbers would have been half-way down.

'A wild evening, Miss Landless! Do you not find your usual walk with your brother too exposed and cold for the time of year? Or at all events, when the sun is down, and the weather is driving in from the sea?'

Helena thought not. It was their favorite walk. It was very retired.

'It is very retired,' assented Mr Crisparkle, laying hold of his opportunity straightway, and walking on with them. 'It is a place of all others where one can speak without interruption, as I wish to do. Mr Neville, I believe you tell your sister everything that passes between us?'

'Everything, sir.'

'Consequently,' said Mr Crisparkle, 'your sister is aware that I have repeatedly urged you to make some kind of apology for that unfortunate occurrence which befell, on the night of your arrival here.'

In saying it he looked to her, and not to him; therefore it was she, and not he, who replied:

'Yes.'

'I call it unfortunate, Miss Helena,' resumed Mr Crisparkle, 'forasmuch as it certainly has engendered a prejudice against Neville. There is a notion about, that he is a dangerously passionate fellow, of an uncontrollable and furious temper: he is really avoided as such.'

'I have no doubt he is, poor fellow,' said Helena, with a look of proud compassion at her brother, expressing a deep sense of his being ungenerously treated. 'I should be quite sure of it, from your saying so; but what you tell me is confirmed by suppressed hints and references that I meet with every day.'

'Now,' Mr Crisparkle again resumed, in a tone of mild though firm persuasion, 'is not this to be regretted, and ought it not to be amended? These are early days of Neville's in Cloisterham, and I have no fear of his outliving such a prejudice, and proving himself to have been misunderstood. But how much wiser to take action at once, than to trust to uncertain time! Besides; apart from its being politic, it is right. For there can be no question that Neville was wrong.'

'He was provoked,' Helena submitted.

'He was the assailant,' Mr Crisparkle submitted.

They walked on in silence, until Helena raised her eyes to the Minor Canon's face, and said, almost reproachfully: 'Oh, Mr Crisparkle, would you have Neville throw himself at young Drood's feet, or at Mr Jasper's, who maligns him every day! In your heart you cannot mean it. From your heart you could not do it, if his case were yours.'

'I have represented to Mr Crisparkle, Helena,' said Neville, with a glance of deference towards his tutor, 'that if I could do it from my heart, I would. But I cannot, and I revolt from the pretence. You forget, however, that to put the case to Mr Crisparkle as his own, is to suppose Mr Crisparkle to have done what I did.'

'I ask his pardon,' said Helena.

'You see,' remarked Mr Crisparkle, again laying hold of his opportunity, though with a moderate and delicate touch, 'you both instinctively acknowledge that Neville did wrong! Then why stop short, and not otherwise acknowledge it?'

'Is there no difference,' asked Helena, with a little faltering in her manner, 'between submission to a generous spirit, and submission to a base or trivial one?'

Before the worthy Minor Canon was quite ready with his argument in reference to this nice distinction, Neville struck in:

'Help me to clear myself with Mr Crisparkle, Helena. Help me to convince him that I cannot be the first to make concessions without mockery and falsehood. My nature must be changed before

I can do so, and it is not changed. I am sensible of inexpressible affront, and deliberate aggravation of inexpressible affront, and I am angry. The plain truth is, I am still as angry when I recall that night as I was that night.'

'Neville,' hinted the Minor Canon, with a steady countenance, 'you have repeated that former action of your hands, which I so much dislike.'

'I am sorry for it, sir, but it was involuntary. I confessed that I was still as angry.'

'And I confess,' said Mr Crisparkle, 'that I hoped for better things.'

'I am sorry to disappoint you, sir, but it would be far worse to deceive you, and I should deceive you grossly if I pretended that you had softened me in this respect. The time may come when your powerful influence will do even that with the difficult pupil whose antecedents you know; but it has not come yet. Is this so, and in spite of my struggles against myself, Helena?'

She, whose dark eyes were watching the effect of what he said on Mr Crisparkle's face, replied – to Mr Crisparkle; not to him: 'It is so.' After a short pause, she answered the slightest look of enquiry conceivable, in her brother's eyes, with as slight an affirmative bend of her own head; and he went on:

'I have never yet had the courage to say to you, sir, what in full openness I ought to have said when you first talked with me on this subject. It is not easy to say, and I have been withheld by a fear of its seeming ridiculous, which is very strong upon me down to this last moment, and might, but for my sister, prevent my being quite open with you even now. – I admire Miss Bud, sir, so very much, that I cannot bear her being treated with conceit or in-difference; and even if I did not feel that I had an injury against young Drood on my own account, I should feel that I had an injury against him on hers.'

Mr Crisparkle, in utter amazement, looked at Helena for cor-roboration, and met in her expressive face full corroboration, and a plea for advice.

'The young lady of whom you speak is, as you know, Mr Neville, shortly to be married,' said Mr Crisparkle, gravely; 'there-fore your admiration, if it be of that special nature which you seem to indicate, is outrageously misplaced. Moreover, it is monstrous that you should take upon yourself to be the young lady's champion against her chosen husband. Besides, you have seen them only once. The young lady has become your sister's friend; and I wonder that your sister, even on her behalf, has not checked you in this irrational and culpable fancy.'

'She has tried, sir, but uselessly. Husband or no husband, that fellow is incapable of the feeling with which I am inspired towards the beautiful young creature whom he treats like a doll. I say he is as incapable of it, as he is unworthy of her. I say she is sacrificed in being bestowed upon him. I say that I love her, and despise and hate him!' This with a face so flushed, and a gesture so violent, that his sister crossed to his side, and caught his arm, remonstrating, 'Neville, Neville!'

Thus recalled to himself, he quickly became sensible of having lost the guard he had set upon his passionate tendency, and covered his face with his hand, as one repentant, and wretched.

Mr Crisparkle, watching him attentively, and at the same time meditating how to proceed, walked on for some paces in silence. Then he spoke:

'Mr Neville, Mr Neville, I am sorely grieved to see in you more traces of a character as sullen, angry, and wild, as the night now closing in. They are of too serious an aspect to leave me the resource of treating the infatuation you have disclosed, as undeserving serious consideration. I give it very serious consideration, and I speak to you accordingly. This feud between you and young Drood must not go on. I cannot permit it to go on, any longer, knowing what I now know from you, and you living under my roof. Whatever prejudiced and unauthorized constructions your blind and envious wrath may put upon his character, it is a frank, good-natured character. I know I can trust to it for that. Now, pray observe what I am about to say. On reflection, and on your sister's representation, I am willing to admit that, in making peace with young Drood, you have a right to be met half way. I will engage that you shall be, and even that young Drood shall make the first advance. This condition fulfilled, you will pledge me the honor of a Christian gentleman that the quarrel is for ever at an end on your side. What may be in your heart when you give him your hand, can only be known to the Searcher of all hearts; but it will never go well with you, if there be any treachery there. So far, as to that;

next as to what I must again speak of as your infatuation. I understand it to have been confided to me, and to be known to no other person save your sister and yourself. Do I understand aright?'

Helena answered in a low voice: 'It is only known to us three who are here together.'

'It is not at all known to the young lady, your friend?'

'On my soul, no!'

'I require you, then, to give me your similar and solemn pledge, Mr Neville, that it shall remain the secret it is, and that you will take no other action whatsoever upon it than endeavouring (and that most earnestly) to erase it from your mind. I will not tell you that it will soon pass; I will not tell you that it is the fancy of the moment; I will not tell you that such caprices have their rise and fall among the young and ardent every hour; I will leave you undisturbed in the belief that it has few parallels or none, that it will abide with you a long time, and that it will be very difficult to conquer. So much the more weight shall I attach to the pledge I require from you, when it is unreservedly given.'

The young man twice or thrice essayed to speak, but failed.

'Let me leave you with your sister, whom it is time you took home,' said Mr Crisparkle. 'You will find me alone in my room by-and-bye.'

'Pray do not leave us yet,' Helena implored him. 'Another minute.'

'I should not,' said Neville, pressing his hand upon his face, 'have needed so much as another minute, if you had been less patient with me, Mr Crisparkle, less considerate of me, and less unpretendingly good and true. Oh, if in my childhood I had known such a guide!'

'Follow your guide now, Neville,' murmured Helena, 'and follow him to Heaven!'

There was that in her tone which broke the good Minor Canon's voice, or it would have repudiated her exaltation of him. As it was, he laid a finger on his lips, and looked towards her brother.

'To say that I give both pledges, Mr Crisparkle, out of my innermost heart, and to say that there is no treachery in it, is to say nothing!' Thus Neville, greatly moved, 'I beg your forgiveness for my miserable lapse into a burst of passion.'

'Not mine, Neville, not mine. You know with whom forgiveness lies, as the highest attribute conceivable. Miss Helena, you and your brother were twin children. You came into this world with the same dispositions, and you passed your younger days together surrounded by the same adverse circumstances. What you have overcome in yourself, can you not overcome in him? You see the rock that lies in his course. Who but you can keep him clear of it?'

'Who but you, sir?' replied Helena. 'What is my influence, or my weak wisdom, compared with yours!'

'You have the wisdom of Love,' returned the Minor Canon, 'and it was the highest wisdom ever known upon this earth, remember. As to mine – but the less said of that commonplace commodity the better. Good night!'

She took the hand he offered her, and gratefully and almost reverently raised it to her lips.

'Tut!' said the Minor Canon, softly, 'I am much overpaid!' And turned away.

Retracing his steps towards the Cathedral Close, he tried, as he went along in the dark, to think out the best means of bringing to pass what he had promised to effect, and what must somehow be done. 'I shall probably be asked to marry them,' he reflected, 'and I would they were married and gone! But this presses first.' He debated principally, whether he should write to young Drood, or whether he should speak to Jasper. The consciousness of being popular with the whole Cathedral establishment inclined him to the latter course, and the well-timed sight of the lighted Gate House decided him to take it. 'I will strike while the iron is hot,' he said, 'and see him now.'

Jasper was lying asleep on a couch before the fire, when, having ascended the postern-stair, and received no answer to his knock at the door, Mr Crisparkle gently turned the handle and looked in. Long afterwards he had cause to remember how Jasper sprang from the couch in a delirious state between sleeping and waking, crying out: 'What is the matter? Who did it?'

'It is only I, Jasper. I am sorry to have disturbed you.'

The glare of his eyes settled down into a look of recognition, and he moved a chair or two, to make a way to the fireside.

'I was dreaming at a great rate, and am glad to be disturbed from an indigestive after-dinner sleep. Not to mention that you are always welcome.'

'Thank you. I am not confident,' returned Mr Crisparkle as he sat himself down in the easy chair placed for him, 'that my subject will at first sight be quite as welcome as myself; but I am a minister of peace, and I pursue my subject in the interests of peace. In a word, Jasper, I want to establish peace between these two young fellows.'

A very perplexed expression took hold of Mr Jasper's face; a very perplexing expression too, for Mr Crisparkle could make nothing of it.

'How?' was Jasper's enquiry, in a low and slow voice, after a silence.

'For the "How" I come to you. I want to ask you to do me the great favor and service of interposing with your nephew (I have already interposed with Mr Neville), and getting him to write you a short note, in his lively way, saying that he is willing to shake hands. I know what a good-natured fellow he is, and what influence you have with him. And without in the least defending Mr Neville, we must all admit that he was bitterly stung.'

Jasper turned that perplexed face towards the fire. Mr Crisparkle continuing to observe it, found it even more perplexing than before, inasmuch as it seemed to denote (which could hardly be) some close internal calculation.

'I know that you are not prepossessed in Mr Neville's favor,' the Minor Canon was going on, when Jasper stopped him:

'You have cause to say so. I am not, indeed.'

'Undoubtedly, and I admit his lamentable violence of temper, though I hope he and I will get the better of it between us. But I have exacted a very solemn promise from him as to his future demeanour towards your nephew, if you do kindly interpose; and I am sure he will keep it.'

'You are always responsible and trustworthy, Mr Crisparkle. Do you really feel sure that you can answer for him so confidently?'

'I do.'

The perplexed and perplexing look vanished.

'Then you relieve my mind of a great dread, and a heavy weight,' said Jasper; 'I will do it.'

Mr Crisparkle, delighted by the swiftness and completeness of his success, acknowledged it in the handsomest terms.

'I will do it,' repeated Jasper, 'for the comfort of having your

guarantee against my vague and unformed fears. You will laugh –
but do you keep a Diary?'

'A line for a day; not more.'

'A line for a day would be quite as much as my uneventful life
would need, Heaven knows,' said Jasper, taking a book from a
desk; 'but that my Diary is, in fact, a Diary of Ned's life too. You
will laugh at this entry; you will guess when it was made:

'Past midnight. – After what I have just now seen, I have a morbid
dread upon me of some horrible consequences resulting to my dear
boy, that I cannot reason with or in any way contend against. All my
efforts are vain. The demoniacal passion of this Neville Landless, his
strength in his fury, and his savage rage for the destruction of its object,
appal me. So profound is the impression, that twice since have I gone
into my dear boy's room, to assure myself of his sleeping safely, and
not lying dead in his blood.

'Here is another entry next morning:

'Ned up and away. Light-hearted and unsuspicious as ever. He
laughed when I cautioned him, and said he was as good a man as
Neville Landless any day. I told him that might be, but he was not as
bad a man. He continued to make light of it, but I travelled with him
as far as I could, and left him most unwillingly. I am unable to shake
off these dark intangible presentiments of evil – if feelings founded
upon staring facts are to be so called.

'Again and again,' said Jasper, in conclusion, twirling the leaves
of the book before putting it by, 'I have relapsed into these moods,
as other entries show. But I have now your assurance at my back,
and shall put it in my book, and make it an antidote to my black
humors.'

'Such an antidote, I hope,' returned Mr Crisparkle, 'as will in-
duce you before long to consign the black humors to the flames. I
ought to be the last to find any fault with you this evening, when
you have met my wishes so freely; but I must say, Jasper, that
your devotion to your nephew has made you exaggerative here.'

'You are my witness,' said Jasper, shrugging his shoulders,
'what my state of mind honestly was, that night, before I sat down
to write, and in what words I expressed it. You remember objecting
to a word I used, as being too strong? It was a stronger word than
any in my Diary.'

'Well, well. Try the antidote,' rejoined Mr Crisparkle, 'and may it give you a brighter and better view of the case! We will discuss it no more now. I have to thank you for myself, and I thank you sincerely.'

'You shall find,' said Jasper, as they shook hands, 'that I will not do the thing you wish me to do, by halves. I will take care that Ned, giving way at all, shall give way thoroughly.'

On the third day after this conversation, he called on Mr Crisparkle with the following letter:

MY DEAR JACK,

I am touched by your account of your interview with Mr Crisparkle, whom I much respect and esteem. At once I openly say that I forgot myself on that occasion quite as much as Mr Landless did, and that I wish that byegone to be a byegone, and all to be right again.

Look here, dear old boy. Ask Mr Landless to dinner on Christmas Eve (the better the day the better the deed), and let there be only we three, and let us shake hands all round there and then, and say no more about it.

My Dear Jack,
Ever your most affectionate,
EDWIN DROOD

P.S. – Love to Miss Pussy at the next music lesson.

'You expect Mr Neville, then?' said Mr Crisparkle.
'I count upon his coming,' said Mr Jasper.

CHAPTER II

A Picture and a Ring

BEHIND the most ancient part of Holborn, London, where certain gabled houses some centuries of age still stand looking on the public way, as if disconsolately looking for the Old Bourne that has long run dry, is a little nook composed of two irregular quad-rangles, called Staple Inn. It is one of those nooks, the turning into which out of the clashing street, imparts to the relieved pedestrian the sensation of having put cotton in his ears, and velvet soles on his boots. It is one of those nooks where a few smoky sparrows twitter in smoky trees, as though they called to one another, 'Let us play at country,' and where a few feet of garden mould and a few yards of gravel enable them to do that refreshing violence to their tiny understandings. Moreover, it is one of those nooks which are legal nooks; and it contains a little Hall, with a little lantern in its roof: to what obstructive purposes devoted, and at whose expense, this history knoweth not.

In the days when Cloisterham took offence at the existence of a railroad afar off, as menacing that sensitive Constitution, the property of us Britons, the odd fortune of which sacred institution it is to be in exactly equal degrees croaked about, trembled for, and boasted of, whatever happens to anything, anywhere in the world: in those days no neighbouring architecture of lofty proportions had arisen to overshadow Staple Inn. The westering sun bestowed bright glances on it, and the south-west wind blew into it un-impeded.

Neither wind nor sun, however, favored Staple Inn, one December afternoon towards six o'clock, when it was filled with fog, and candles shed murky and blurred rays through the windows of all its then-occupied sets of chambers; notably, from a set of chambers in a corner house in the little inner quadrangle, presenting in black and white over its ugly portal the mysterious inscription:

$$P$$
$$J \qquad T$$
1747.

In which set of chambers, never having troubled his head about the inscription, unless to bethink himself at odd times on glancing up at it, that haply it might mean Perhaps John Thomas,[1] or Perhaps Joe Tyler, sat Mr Grewgious writing by his fire.

Who could have told, by looking at Mr Grewgious, whether he had ever known ambition or disappointment? He had been bred to the Bar, and had laid himself out for chamber practice; to draw deeds; 'convey the wise it call,' as Pistol says. But Conveyancing and he had made such a very indifferent marriage of it that they had separated by consent - if there can be said to be separation where there has never been coming together.

No. Coy Conveyancing would not come to Mr Grewgious. She was wooed, not won, and they went their several ways. But an

Arbitration being blown towards him by some unaccountable wind, and he gaining great credit in it as one indefatigable in seeking out right and doing right, a pretty fat Receivership was next blown into his pocket by a wind more traceable to its source. So, by chance, he had found his niche. Receiver and Agent now, to two rich estates, and deputing their legal business, in an amount worth having, to a firm of solicitors on the floor below, he had snuffed out his ambition (supposing him to have ever lighted it) and had settled down with his snuffers for the rest of his life under the dry vine and fig-tree of P. J. T., who planted in seventeen-forty-seven.

Many accounts and account-books, many files of correspondence, and several strong boxes, garnished Mr Grewgious's room. They can scarcely be represented as having lumbered it, so conscientious and precise was their orderly arrangement. The apprehension of dying suddenly, and leaving one fact or one figure with any incompleteness or obscurity attaching to it, would have stretched Mr Grewgious stone dead any day. The largest fidelity to a trust was the life-blood of the man. There are sorts of life-blood that course more quickly, more gaily, more attractively; but there is no better sort in circulation.

There was no luxury in his room. Even its comforts were limited to its being dry and warm, and having a snug though faded fireside. What may be called its private life was confined to the hearth, and an easy chair, and an old-fashioned occasional round table that was brought out upon the rug after business hours, from a corner where it elsewise remained turned up like a shining mahogany shield. Behind it, when standing thus on the defensive, was a closet, usually containing something good to drink. An outer room was the clerk's room; Mr Grewgious's sleeping-room was across the common stair; and he held some not empty cellarage at the bottom of the common stair. Three hundred days in the year, at least, he crossed over to the hotel in Furnival's Inn[2] for his dinner, and after dinner crossed back again, to make the most of these simplicities until it should become broad business day once more, with P. J. T., date seventeen-forty-seven.

As Mr Grewgious sat and wrote by his fire that afternoon, so did the clerk of Mr Grewgious sit and write by *his* fire. A pale, puffy-faced, dark-haired person of thirty, with big dark eyes that wholly wanted lustre, and a dissatisfied doughy complexion, that seemed to ask to be sent to the baker's, this attendant was a mysterious being, possessed of some strange power over Mr Grewgious. As though he had been called into existence, like a fabulous Familiar, by a magic spell which had failed when required to dismiss him, he stuck tight to Mr Grewgious's stool, although Mr Grewgious's comfort and convenience would manifestly have been advanced by dispossessing him. A gloomy person with tangled locks, and a general air of having been reared under the shadow of that baleful tree of Java[3] which has given shelter to more lies than the whole botanical kingdom, Mr Grewgious, nevertheless, treated him with unaccountable consideration.

'Now, Bazzard,' said Mr Grewgious, on the entrance of his clerk: looking up from his papers as he arranged them for the night: 'what is in the wind besides fog?'

'Mr Drood,' said Bazzard.

'What of him?'

'Has called,' said Bazzard.

'You might have shown him in.'

'I am doing it,' said Bazzard.

The visitor came in accordingly.

'Dear me!' said Mr Grewgious, looking round his pair of office candles. 'I thought you had called and merely left your name, and gone. How do you do, Mr Edwin? Dear me, you're choking!'

'It's this fog,' returned Edwin; 'and it makes my eyes smart, like Cayenne pepper.'

'Is it really so bad as that? Pray undo your wrappers. It's fortunate I have so good a fire; but Mr Bazzard has taken care of me.'

'No I haven't,' said Mr Bazzard at the door.

'Ah! Then it follows that I must have taken care of myself without observing it,' said Mr Grewgious. 'Pray be seated in my chair. No. I beg! Coming out of such an atmosphere, in *my* chair.'

Edwin took the easy chair in the corner; and the fog he had brought in with him, and the fog he took off with his great-coat and neck-shawl, was speedily licked up by the eager fire.

'I look,' said Edwin, smiling, 'as if I had come to stop.'

'— By-the-bye,' cried Mr Grewgious; 'excuse my interrupting you; do stop. The fog may clear in an hour or two. We can have dinner in from just across Holborn. You had better take your Cayenne pepper here than outside; pray stop and dine.'

'You are very kind,' said Edwin, glancing about him, as though attracted by the notion of a new and relishing sort of gipsy-party.

'Not at all,' said Mr Grewgious; 'you are very kind to join issue with a bachelor in chambers, and take pot-luck. And I'll ask,' said Mr Grewgious, dropping his voice, and speaking with a twinkling eye, as if inspired with a bright thought: 'I'll ask Bazzard. He mightn't like it else. Bazzard!'

Bazzard reappeared.

'Dine presently with Mr Drood and me.'

'If I am ordered to dine, of course I will, sir,' was the gloomy answer.

'Save the man!' cried Mr Grewgious. 'You're not ordered; you're invited.'

'Thank you, sir,' said Bazzard; 'in that case I don't care if I do.'

'That's arranged. And perhaps you wouldn't mind,' said Mr Grewgious, 'stepping over to the hotel in Furnival's, and asking them to send in materials for laying the cloth. For dinner we'll have a tureen of the hottest and strongest soup available, and we'll have the best made-dish that can be recommended, and we'll have a joint (such as a haunch of mutton), and we'll have a goose, or a turkey, or any little stuffed thing of that sort that may happen to be in the bill of fare – in short, we'll have whatever there is on hand.'

These liberal directions Mr Grewgious issued with his usual air of reading an inventory, or repeating a lesson, or doing anything else by rote. Bazzard, after drawing out the round table, withdrew to execute them.

'I was a little delicate, you see,' said Mr Grewgious, in a lower tone, after his clerk's departure, 'about employing him in the foraging or commissariat department. Because he mightn't like it.'

'He seems to have his own way, sir,' remarked Edwin.

'His own way?' returned Mr Grewgious. 'Oh, dear no! Poor fellow, you quite mistake him. If he had his own way, he wouldn't be here.'

'I wonder where he would be!' Edwin thought. But he only thought it, because Mr Grewgious came and stood himself with his back to the other corner of the fire, and his shoulder-blades against the chimney-piece, and collected his skirts for easy conversation.

'I take it, without having the gift of prophecy, that you have done me the favor of looking in to mention that you are going down yonder – where I can tell you, you are expected – and to offer to execute any little commission from me to my charming ward, and perhaps to sharpen me up a bit in any proceedings? Eh, Mr Edwin?'

'I called, sir, before going down, as an act of attention.'

'Of attention!' said Mr Grewgious. 'Ah! of course, not of impatience?'

'Impatience, sir?'

Mr Grewgious had meant to be arch – not that he in the remotest degree expressed that meaning – and had brought himself into scarcely supportable proximity with the fire, as if to burn the fullest effect of his archness into himself, as other subtle impressions are burnt into hard metals. But his archness suddenly flying before the composed face and manner of his visitor, and only the fire remaining, he started and rubbed himself.

'I have lately been down yonder,' said Mr Grewgious, re-arranging his skirts; 'and that was what I referred to, when I said I could tell you you are expected.'

'Indeed, sir! Yes; I knew that Pussy was looking out for me.'

'Do you keep a cat down there?' asked Mr Grewgious.

Edwin colored a little, as he explained: 'I call Rosa Pussy.'

'Oh, really,' said Mr Grewgious, smoothing down his head; 'that's very affable.'

Edwin glanced at his face, uncertain whether or no he seriously objected to the appellation. But Edwin might as well have glanced at the face of a clock.

'A pet name, sir,' he explained again.

'Umps,' said Mr Grewgious, with a nod. But with such an extra-ordinary compromise between an unqualified assent and a qualified dissent, that his visitor was much disconcerted.

'Did PRosa –' Edwin began, by way of recovering himself.

'PRosa?' repeated Mr Grewgious.

'I was going to say Pussy, and changed my mind; – did she tell you anything about the Landlesses?'

'No,' said Mr Grewgious. 'What is the Landlesses? An estate? A villa? A farm?'

'A brother and sister. The sister is at the Nuns' House, and has become a great friend of P—'

'PRosa's,' Mr Grewgious struck in, with a fixed face.

'She is a strikingly handsome girl, sir, and I thought she might have been described to you, or presented to you, perhaps?'

'Neither,' said Mr Grewgious. 'But here is Bazzard.'

Bazzard returned, accompanied by two waiters – an immoveable waiter, and a flying waiter; and the three brought in with them as much fog as gave a new roar to the fire. The flying waiter, who had brought everything on his shoulders, laid the cloth with amazing rapidity and dexterity; while the immoveable waiter, who had brought nothing, found fault with him. The flying waiter then highly polished all the glasses he had brought, and the immoveable waiter looked through them. The flying waiter then flew across Holborn for the soup, and flew back again, and then took another flight for the made-dish, and flew back again, and then took another flight for the joint and poultry, and flew back again, and between whiles took supplementary flights for a great variety of articles, as it was discovered from time to time that the immoveable waiter had forgotten them all. But let the flying waiter cleave the air as he might, he was always reproached on his return by the immoveable waiter for bringing fog with him, and being out of breath. At the conclusion of the repast, by which time the flying waiter was severely blown, the immoveable waiter gathered up the tablecloth under his arm with a grand air, and having sternly (not to say with indignation) looked on at the flying waiter while he set clean glasses round, directed a valedictory glance towards Mr Grewgious, conveying: 'Let it be clearly understood between us that the reward is mine, and that Nil is the claim of this slave,' and pushed the flying waiter before him out of the room.

It was like a highly finished miniature painting representing My Lords of the Circumlocutional Department,[4] Commandership-in-Chief of any sort, Government. It was quite an edifying little picture to be hung on the line in the National Gallery.

As the fog had been the proximate cause of this sumptuous repast, so the fog served for its general sauce. To hear the outdoor clerks sneezing, wheezing, and beating their feet on the gravel was a zest far surpassing Doctor Kitchener's. To bid, with a shiver, the unfortunate flying waiter shut the door before he had opened it, was a condiment of a profounder flavor than Harvey. And here let it be noticed, parenthetically, that the leg of this young man, in its application to the door, evinced the finest sense of touch: always preceding himself and tray (with something of an angling air about it), by some seconds: and always lingering after he and the tray had disappeared, like Macbeth's leg when accompanying him off the stage with reluctance to the assassination of Duncan.

The host had gone below to the cellar, and had brought up bottles of ruby, straw-colored, and golden drinks, which had ripened long ago in lands where no fogs are, and had since lain slumbering in the shade. Sparkling and tingling after so long a nap, they pushed at their corks to help the corkscrew (like prisoners helping rioters to force their gates), and danced out gaily. If P. J. T. in seventeen-forty-seven, or in any other year of his period, drank such wines – then, for a certainty P. J. T. was Pretty Jolly Too.

Externally, Mr Grewgious showed no signs of being mellowed by these glowing vintages. Instead of his drinking them, they might have been poured over him in his high-dried snuff form, and run to waste, for any lights and shades they caused to flicker over his face. Neither was his manner influenced. But, in his wooden way, he had observant eyes for Edwin; and when, at the end of dinner, he motioned Edwin back to his own easy chair in the fire-side corner, and Edwin luxuriously sank into it after very brief remonstrance, Mr Grewgious, as he turned his seat round towards the fire too, and smoothed his head and face, might have been seen looking at his visitor between his smoothing fingers.

'Bazzard!' said Mr Grewgious, suddenly turning to him.

'I follow you, sir,' returned Bazzard; who had done his work of consuming meat and drink in a workmanlike manner, though mostly in speechlessness.

'I drink to you, Bazzard; Mr Edwin, success to Mr Bazzard!'

'Success to Mr Bazzard!' echoed Edwin, with a totally unfounded appearance of enthusiasm, and with the unspoken addition: – 'What in, I wonder!'

'And May!' pursued Mr Grewgious – 'I am not at liberty to be definite – May! – my conversational powers are so very limited that I know I shall not come well out of this – May! – it ought to be put imaginatively, but I have no imagination – May! – the thorn of anxiety is as near the mark as I am likely to get – May it come out at last!'

Mr Bazzard, with a frowning smile at the fire, put a hand into his tangled locks, as if the thorn of anxiety were there; then into his waistcoat, as if it were there; then into his pockets, as if it were there. In all these movements he was closely followed by the eyes of Edwin, as if that young gentleman expected to see the thorn in action. It was not produced, however, and Mr Bazzard merely said: 'I follow you, sir, and I thank you.'

'I am going,' said Mr Grewgious, jingling his glass on the table with one hand, and bending aside under cover of the other, to whisper to Edwin, 'to drink to my ward. But I put Bazzard first. He mightn't like it else.'

This was said with a mysterious wink; or what would have been a wink, if, in Mr Grewgious's hands, it could have been quick enough. So Edwin winked responsively, without the least idea what he meant by doing so.

'And now,' said Mr Grewgious, 'I devote a bumper to the fair and fascinating Miss Rosa. Bazzard, the fair and fascinating Miss Rosa!'

'I follow you, sir,' said Bazzard, 'and I pledge you!'

'And so do I!' said Edwin.

'Lord bless me!' cried Mr Grewgious, breaking the blank silence which of course ensued: though why these pauses *should* come upon us when we have performed any small social rite, not directly inducive of self-examination or mental despondency, who can tell! 'I am a particularly Angular man, and yet I fancy (if I may use the word, not having a morsel of fancy), that I could draw a picture of a true lover's state of mind, to-night.'

'Let us follow you, sir,' said Bazzard, 'and have the picture.'

'Mr Edwin will correct it where it's wrong,' resumed Mr Grewgious, 'and will throw in a few touches from the life. I dare say it is wrong in many particulars, and wants many touches from the life, for I was born a Chip, and have neither soft sympathies nor soft experiences. Well! I hazard the guess that the true lover's mind is completely permeated by the beloved object of his affections. I hazard the guess that her dear name is precious to him, cannot be heard or repeated without emotion, and is preserved sacred. If he has any distinguishing appellation of fondness for her, it is reserved for her, and is not for common ears. A name that it would be a privilege to call her by, being alone with her own bright self, it would be a liberty, a coldness, an insensibility, almost a breach of good faith, to flaunt elsewhere.'

It was wonderful to see Mr Grewgious sitting bolt upright, with his hands on his knees, continuously chopping this discourse out of himself: much as a charity boy with a very good memory might get his catechism said: and evincing no correspondent emotion whatever, unless in a certain occasional little tingling perceptible at the end of his nose.

'My picture,' Mr Grewgious proceeded, 'goes on to represent (under correction from you, Mr Edwin) the true lover as ever impatient to be in the presence or vicinity of the beloved object of his affections; as caring very little for his ease in any other society; and as constantly seeking that. If I was to say seeking that, as a bird seeks its nest, I should make an ass of myself, because that would trench upon what I understand to be poetry; and I am so far from trenching upon poetry at any time, that I never, to my knowledge, got within ten thousand miles of it. And I am besides totally unacquainted with the habits of birds, except the birds of Staple Inn, who seek their nests on ledges, and in gutter-pipes and chimneypots, not constructed for them by the beneficent hand of Nature. I beg, therefore, to be understood as foregoing the bird's-nest. But my picture does represent the true lover as having no existence separable from that of the beloved object of his affections, and as living at once a double life and a halved life. And if I do not clearly express what I mean by that, it is either for the reason that having no conversational powers, I cannot express what I mean, or that having no meaning, I do not mean what I fail to express. Which, to the best of my belief, is not the case.'

Edwin had turned red and turned white, as certain points of this picture came into the light. He now sat looking at the fire, and bit his lip.

'The speculations of an Angular man,' resumed Mr Grewgious, still sitting and speaking exactly as before, 'are probably erroneous on so globular a topic. But I figure to myself (subject, as before, to Mr Edwin's correction), that there can be no coolness, no lassitude, no doubt, no indifference, no half fire and half smoke state of mind, in a real lover. Pray am I at all near the mark in my picture?'

As abrupt in his conclusion as in his commencement and progress, he jerked this enquiry at Edwin, and stopped when one might have supposed him in the middle of his oration.

'I should say, sir,' stammered Edwin, 'as you refer the question to me –'

'Yes,' said Mr Grewgious, 'I refer it to you, as an authority.'

'I should say, then, sir,' Edwin went on, embarrassed, 'that the picture you have drawn is generally correct; but I submit that perhaps you may be rather hard upon the unlucky lover.'

'Likely so,' assented Mr Grewgious, 'likely so. I am a hard man in the grain.'

'He may not show,' said Edwin, 'all he feels; or he may not –'

There he stopped so long, to find the rest of his sentence, that Mr Grewgious rendered his difficulty a thousand times the greater, by unexpectedly striking in with:

'No, to be sure; he *may* not!'

After that, they all sat silent; the silence of Mr Bazzard being occasioned by slumber.

'His responsibility is very great, though,' said Mr Grewgious at length, with his eyes on the fire.

Edwin nodded assent, with *his* eyes on the fire.

'And let him be sure that he trifles with no one,' said Mr Grewgious; 'neither with himself, nor with any other.'

Edwin bit his lip again, and still sat looking at the fire.

'He must not make a plaything of a treasure. Woe betide him if he does! Let him take that well to heart,' said Mr Grewgious.

Though he said these things in short sentences, much as the supposititious charity boy just now referred to might have repeated a verse or two from the Book of Proverbs, there was something dreamy (for so literal a man) in the way in which he now shook his right forefinger at the live coals in the grate, and again fell silent.

But not for long. As he sat upright and stiff in his chair, he suddenly rapped his knees, like the carved image of some queer Joss or other coming out of its reverie, and said: 'We must finish this bottle, Mr Edwin. Let me help you. I'll help Bazzard too, though he *is* asleep. He mightn't like it else.'

He helped them both, and helped himself, and drained his glass, and stood it bottom upward on the table, as though he had just caught a bluebottle in it.

'And now, Mr Edwin,' he proceeded, wiping his mouth and hands upon his handkerchief: 'to a little piece of business. You received from me, the other day, a certified copy of Miss Rosa's father's will. You knew its contents before, but you received it from me as a matter of business. I should have sent it to Mr Jasper, but for Miss Rosa's wishing it to come straight to you, in preference. You received it?'

'Quite safely, sir.'

'You should have acknowledged its receipt,' said Mr Grewgious, 'business being business all the world over. However, you did not.'

'I meant to have acknowledged it when I first came in this evening, sir.'

'Not a business-like acknowledgment,' returned Mr Grewgious; 'however, let that pass. Now, in that document you have observed a few words of kindly allusion to its being left to me to discharge a little trust, confided to me in conversation, at such time as I in my discretion may think best.'

'Yes, sir.'

'Mr Edwin, it came into my mind just now, when I was looking at the fire, that I could, in my discretion, acquit myself of that trust at no better time than the present. Favor me with your attention, half a minute.'

He took a bunch of keys from his pocket, singled out by the candle-light the key he wanted, and then, with a candle in his hand, went to a bureau or escritoire, unlocked it, touched the spring of a little secret drawer, and took from it an ordinary ring-case made for a single ring. With this in his hand, he returned to his chair. As he held it up for the young man to see, his hand trembled.

'Mr Edwin, this rose of diamonds and rubies delicately set in gold, was a ring belonging to Miss Rosa's mother. It was removed from her dead hand, in my presence, with such distracted grief as I hope it may never be my lot to contemplate again. Hard man as I am, I am not hard enough for that. See how bright these stones shine!' opening the case. 'And yet the eyes that were so much brighter, and that so often looked upon them with a light and a proud heart, have been ashes among ashes, and dust among dust, some years! If I had any imagination (which it is needless to say I have not), I might imagine that the lasting beauty of these stones was almost cruel.'

He closed the case again as he spoke.

'This ring was given to the young lady who was drowned so early in her beautiful and happy career, by her husband, when they first plighted their faith to one another. It was he who removed it from her unconscious hand, and it was he who, when his death drew very near, placed it in mine. The trust in which I received it, was, that, you and Miss Rosa growing to manhood and womanhood, and your betrothal prospering and coming to maturity, I should give it to you to place upon her finger. Failing those desired results, it was to remain in my possession.'

Some trouble was in the young man's face, and some indecision was in the action of his hand, as Mr Grewgious, looking steadfastly at him, gave him the ring.

'Your placing it on her finger,' said Mr Grewgious, 'will be the solemn seal upon your strict fidelity to the living and the dead. You are going to her, to make the last irrevocable preparations for your marriage. Take it with you.'

The young man took the little case, and placed it in his breast.

'If anything should be amiss, if anything should be even slightly wrong, between you; if you should have any secret consciousness that you are committing yourself to this step for no higher reason than because you have long been accustomed to look forward to it; then,' said Mr Grewgious, 'I charge you once more, by the living and by the dead, to bring that ring back to me!'

Here Bazzard awoke himself by his own snoring; and, as is usual in such cases, sat apoplectically staring at vacancy, as defying vacancy to accuse him of having been asleep.

'Bazzard!' said Mr Grewgious, harder than ever.

'I follow you, sir,' said Bazzard, 'and I have been following you.'

'In discharge of a trust, I have handed Mr Edwin Drood a ring of diamonds and rubies. You see?'

Edwin reproduced the little case, and opened it; and Bazzard looked into it.

'I follow you both, sir,' returned Bazzard, 'and I witness the transaction.'

Evidently anxious to get away and be alone, Edwin Drood now resumed his outer clothing, muttering something about time and appointments. The fog was reported no clearer (by the flying waiter, who alighted from a speculative flight in the coffee interest), but he went out into it; and Bazzard, after his manner, 'followed' him.

Mr Grewgious, left alone, walked softly and slowly to and fro, for an hour and more. He was restless to-night, and seemed dispirited.

'I hope I have done right,' he said. 'The appeal to him seemed necessary. It was hard to lose the ring, and yet it must have gone from me very soon.'

He closed the empty little drawer with a sigh, and shut and locked the escritoire, and came back to the solitary fireside.

'Her ring,' he went on. 'Will it come back to me? My mind hangs about her ring very uneasily to-night. But that is explainable. I have had it so long, and I have prized it so much! I wonder –'

He was in a wondering mood as well as a restless; for, though he checked himself at that point, and took another walk, he resumed his wondering when he sat down again.

'I wonder (for the ten thousandth time, and what a weak fool I, for what can it signify now!) whether he confided the charge of their orphan child to me, because he knew – Good God, how like her mother she has become!

'I wonder whether he ever so much as suspected that some one doted on her, at a hopeless, speechless distance, when he struck in and won her. I wonder whether it ever crept into his mind who that unfortunate some one was!

'I wonder whether I shall sleep to-night! At all events, I will shut out the world with the bedclothes, and try.'

Mr Grewgious crossed the staircase to his raw and foggy bedroom, and was soon ready for bed. Dimly catching sight of his face in the misty looking-glass, he held his candle to it for a moment.

'A likely some one, *you*, to come into anybody's thoughts in such an aspect!' he exclaimed. 'There, there! there! Get to bed, poor man, and cease to jabber!'

With that, he extinguished his light, pulled up the bedclothes around him, and with another sigh shut out the world. And yet there are such unexplored romantic nooks in the unlikeliest men, that even old tinderous and touch-woody P. J. T. Possibly Jabbered Thus, at some odd times, in or about seventeen-forty-seven.

CHAPTER 12

A Night with Durdles

WHEN Mr Sapsea has nothing better to do, towards evening, and finds the contemplation of his own profundity becoming a little monotonous in spite of the vastness of the subject, he often takes an airing in the Cathedral Close and thereabout. He likes to pass the churchyard with a swelling air of proprietorship, and to encourage in his breast a sort of benignant-landlord feeling, in that he has been bountiful towards that meritorious tenant, Mrs Sapsea, and has publicly given her a prize. He likes to see a stray face or two looking in through the railings, and perhaps reading his inscription. Should he meet a stranger coming from the churchyard with a quick step, he is morally convinced that the stranger is 'with a blush retiring,' as monumentally directed.

Mr Sapsea's importance has received enhancement, for he has become Mayor of Cloisterham. Without mayors, and many of them, it cannot be disputed that the whole framework of society – Mr Sapsea is confident that he invented that forcible figure – would fall to pieces. Mayors have been knighted for 'going up' with addresses: explosive machines intrepidly discharging shot and shell into the English Grammar. Mr Sapsea may 'go up' with an address. Rise, Sir Thomas Sapsea! Of such is the salt of the earth.

Mr Sapsea has improved the acquaintance of Mr Jasper, since their first meeting to partake of port, epitaph, backgammon, beef, and salad. Mr Sapsea has been received at the Gate House with kindred hospitality; and on that occasion Mr Jasper seated himself at the piano, and sang to him, tickling his ears – figuratively, long enough to present a considerable area for tickling. What Mr Sapsea likes in that young man is, that he is always ready to profit by the wisdom of his elders, and that he is sound, sir, at the core. In proof of which, he sang to Mr Sapsea that evening no kickshaw ditties, favorites with national enemies, but gave him the genuine George the Third home-brewed; exhorting him (as 'my brave boys') to reduce to a smashed condition all other islands but this island, and all continents, peninsulas, isthmuses, promontories, and other geographical forms of land soever, besides sweeping the seas in all directions. In short, he rendered it pretty clear that Providence made a distinct mistake in originating so small a nation of hearts of oak, and so many other verminous peoples.

Mr Sapsea, walking slowly this moist evening near the church-yard with his hands behind him, on the look out for a blushing and retiring stranger, turns a corner, and comes instead into the goodly presence of the Dean, conversing with the Verger and Mr Jasper. Mr Sapsea makes his obeisance, and is instantly stricken far more ecclesiastical than any Archbishop of York, or Canterbury.

'You are evidently going to write a book about us, Mr Jasper,' quoth the Dean; 'to write a book about us. Well! We are very ancient, and we ought to make a good book. We are not so richly endowed in possessions as in age; but perhaps you will put *that* in your book, among other things, and call attention to our wrongs.'

Mr Tope, as in duty bound, is greatly entertained by this.

'I really have no intention at all, sir,' replies Jasper, 'of turning author, or archæologist. It is but a whim of mine. And even for my whim, Mr Sapsea here is more accountable than I am.'

'How so, Mr Mayor?' says the Dean, with a nod of good-natured recognition of his Fetch. 'How is that, Mr Mayor?'

'I am not aware,' Mr Sapsea remarks, looking about him for information, 'to what the Very Reverend the Dean does me the honor of referring.' And then falls to studying his original in minute points of detail.

'Durdles,' Mr Tope hints.

'Aye!' the Dean echoes; 'Durdles, Durdles!'

'The truth is, sir,' explains Jasper, 'that my curiosity in the man was first really stimulated by Mr Sapsea. Mr Sapsea's know-ledge of mankind, and power of drawing out whatever is recluse or odd around him, first led to my bestowing a second thought upon the man: though of course I had met him constantly about. You would not be surprised by this, Mr Dean, if you had seen Mr Sapsea deal with him in his own parlor, as I did.'

'Oh!' cries Sapsea, picking up the ball thrown to him with ineffable complacency and pomposity; 'yes, yes. The Very Rever-end the Dean refers to that? Yes. I happened to bring Durdles and Mr Jasper together. I regard Durdles as a Character.'

'A character, Mr Sapsea, that with a few skilful touches you turn inside out,' says Jasper.

'Nay, not quite that,' returns the lumbering auctioneer. 'I may have a little influence over him, perhaps; and a little insight into his character, perhaps. The Very Reverend the Dean will please to bear in mind that I have seen the world.' Here Mr Sapsea gets a little behind the Dean, to inspect his coat-buttons.

'Well!' says the Dean, looking about him to see what has become of his copyist: 'I hope, Mr Mayor, you will use your study and knowledge of Durdles to the good purpose of exhorting him not to break our worthy and respected Choir Master's neck; we cannot afford it; his head and voice are much too valuable to us.'

Mr Tope is again highly entertained, and, having fallen into respectful convulsions of laughter, subsides into a deferential murmur, importing that surely any gentleman would deem it a pleasure and an honor to have his neck broken, in return for such a compliment from such a source.

'I will take it upon myself, sir,' observes Sapsea, loftily, 'to answer for Mr Jasper's neck. I will tell Durdles to be careful of it. He will mind what *I* say. How is it at present endangered?' he enquires, looking about him with magnificent patronage.

'Only by my making a moonlight expedition with Durdles among the tombs, vaults, towers, and ruins,' returns Jasper. 'You remember suggesting, when you brought us together, that, as a lover of the picturesque, it might be worth my while?'

'*I* remember!' replies the auctioneer. And the solemn idiot really believes that he does remember.

'Profiting by your hint,' pursues Jasper, 'I have had some day-rambles with the extraordinary old fellow, and we are to make a moonlight hole-and-corner exploration to-night.'

'And here he is,' says the Dean.

Durdles, with his dinner-bundle in his hand, is indeed beheld slouching towards them. Slouching nearer, and perceiving the Dean, he pulls off his hat, and is slouching away with it under his arm, when Mr Sapsea stops him.

'Mind you take care of my friend,' is the injunction Mr Sapsea lays upon him.

'What friend o' yourn is dead?' asks Durdles. 'No orders has come in for any friend o' yourn.'

'I mean my live friend, there.'

'Oh! Him?' says Durdles. 'He can take care of himself, can Mister Jarsper.'

'But do you take care of him too,' says Sapsea.

Whom Durdles (there being command in his tone) surlily surveys from head to foot.

'With submission to his Reverence the Dean, if you'll mind what concerns you, Mr Sapsea, Durdles he'll mind what concerns him.'

'You're out of temper,' says Mr Sapsea, winking to the company to observe how smoothly he will manage him. 'My friend concerns me, and Mr Jasper is my friend. And you are my friend.'

'Don't you get into a bad habit of boasting,' retorts Durdles, with a grave cautionary nod. 'It'll grow upon you.'[1]

'You are out of temper,' says Sapsea again; reddening, but again winking to the company.

'I own to it,' returns Durdles; 'I don't like liberties.'

Mr Sapsea winks a third wink to the company, as who should say: 'I think you will agree with me that I have settled *his* business;' and stalks out of the controversy.

Durdles then gives the Dean a good evening, and adding, as he puts his hat on, 'You'll find me at home, Mister Jarsper, as agreed, when you want me; I'm a going home to clean myself,' soon slouches out of sight. This going home to clean himself is one of the man's incomprehensible compromises with inexorable facts; he, and his hat, and his boots, and his clothes, never showing any trace of cleaning, but being uniformly in one condition of dust and grit.

The lamplighter now dotting the quiet Close with specks of light, and running at a great rate up and down his little ladder with that object – his little ladder under the sacred shadow of whose inconvenience generations had grown up, and which all Cloisterham would have stood aghast at the idea of abolishing – the Dean withdraws to his dinner, Mr Tope to his tea, and Mr Jasper to his piano. There, with no light but that of the fire, he sits chanting choir-music in a low and beautiful voice, for two or three hours; in short, until it has been for some time dark, and the moon is about to rise.

Then he closes his piano softly, softly changes his coat for a pea-jacket with a goodly wicker-cased bottle in its largest pocket, and, putting on a low-crowned flap-brimmed hat, goes softly out. Why does he move so softly to-night? No outward reason is apparent for it. Can there be any sympathetic reason crouching darkly within him?

Repairing to Durdles's unfinished house, or hole in the city wall, and seeing a light within it, he softly picks his course among the gravestones, monuments, and stony lumber of the yard, already touched here and there, sidewise, by the rising moon. The two journeymen have left their two great saws sticking in their blocks of stone; and two skeleton journeymen out of the Dance of Death[2] might be grinning in the shadow of their sheltering sentry-boxes, about to slash away at cutting out the gravestones of the next two people destined to die in Cloisterham. Likely enough, the two think little of that now, being alive, and perhaps merry. Curious, to make a guess at the two; – or say at one of the two!

'Ho! Durdles!'

The light moves, and he appears with it at the door. He would seem to have been 'cleaning himself' with the aid of a bottle, jug, and tumbler; for no other cleansing instruments are visible in the bare brick room with rafters overhead and no plastered ceiling, into which he shows his visitor.

'Are you ready?'

'I am ready, Mister Jarsper. Let the old uns come out if they dare, when we go among their tombs. My spirits is ready for 'em.'

'Do you mean animal spirits, or ardent?'

'The one's the t'other,' answers Durdles, 'and I mean 'em both.'

He takes a lantern from a hook, puts a match or two in his pocket wherewith to light it, should there be need, and they go out together, dinner-bundle and all.

Surely an unaccountable sort of expedition! That Durdles himself, who is always prowling among old graves and ruins, like a Ghoule – that he should be stealing forth to climb, and dive, and wander without an object, is nothing extraordinary; but that the Choir Master or any one else should hold it worth his while to be with him, and to study moonlight effects in such company, is another affair. Surely an unaccountable sort of expedition, therefore!

''Ware that there mound by the yard-gate, Mister Jarsper.'

'I see it. What is it?'

'Lime.'

Mr Jasper stops, and waits for him to come up, for he lags behind. 'What you call quick-lime?'

'Aye!' says Durdles; 'quick enough to eat your boots. With a little handy stirring, quick enough to eat your bones.'

They go on, presently passing the red windows of the Travellers' Twopenny, and emerging into the clear moonlight of the Monks' Vineyard. This crossed, they come to Minor Canon Corner: of which the greater part lies in shadow until the moon shall rise higher in the sky.

The sound of a closing house-door strikes their ears, and two men come out. These are Mr Crisparkle and Neville. Jasper, with a strange and sudden smile upon his face, lays the palm of his hand upon the breast of Durdles, stopping him where he stands.

At that end of Minor Canon Corner the shadow is profound in the existing state of the light: at that end, too, there is a piece of old dwarf wall, breast high, the only remaining boundary of what was once a garden, but is now the thoroughfare. Jasper and Durdles would have turned this wall in another instant; but, stopping so short, stand behind it.

'Those two are only sauntering,' Jasper whispers; 'they will go out into the moonlight soon. Let us keep quiet here, or they will detain us, or want to join us, or what not.'

Durdles nods assent, and falls to munching some fragments from his bundle. Jasper folds his arms upon the top of the wall, and, with his chin resting on them, watches. He takes no note whatever of the Minor Canon, but watches Neville, as though his eye were at the trigger of a loaded rifle, and he had covered him, and were going to fire. A sense of destructive power is so expressed in his face, that even Durdles pauses in his munching, and looks at him, with an unmunched something in his cheek.

Meanwhile Mr Crisparkle and Neville walk to and fro, quietly talking together. What they say cannot be heard consecutively; but Mr Jasper has already distinguished his own name more than once.

'This is the first day of the week,' Mr Crisparkle can be distinctly heard to observe, as they turn back; 'and the last day of the week is Christmas Eve.'

'You may be certain of me, sir.'

The echoes were favorable at those points, but as the two approach, the sound of their talking becomes confused again. The word 'confidence,' shattered by the echoes, but still capable of being pieced together, is uttered by Mr Crisparkle. As they draw still nearer, this fragment of a reply is heard: 'Not deserved yet, but shall be, sir.' As they turn away again, Jasper again hears his own name, in connexion with the words from Mr Crisparkle: 'Remember that I said I answered for you confidently.' Then the sound of their talk becomes confused again; they halting for a little while, and some earnest action on the part of Neville succeeding. When they move once more, Mr Crisparkle is seen to look up at the sky, and to point before him. They then slowly disappear; passing out into the moonlight at the opposite end of the Corner.

It is not until they are gone that Mr Jasper moves. But then he turns to Durdles, and bursts into a fit of laughter. Durdles, who still has that suspended something in his cheek, and who sees nothing to laugh at, stares at him until Mr Jasper lays his face down on his arms to have his laugh out. Then Durdles bolts the something, as if desperately resigning himself to indigestion.

Among those secluded nooks there is very little stir or movement after dark. There is little enough in the high-tide of the day, but there is next to none at night. Besides that the cheerfully frequented High Street lies nearly parallel to the spot (the old Cathedral rising between the two), and is the natural channel in which the Cloisterham traffic flows, a certain awful hush pervades the ancient pile, the cloisters, and the churchyard, after dark, which not many people care to encounter. Ask the first hundred citizens of Cloisterham, met at random in the streets at noon, if they believed in Ghosts, they would tell you no; but put them to choose at night between these eerie Precincts and the thoroughfare of shops, and you would find that ninety-nine declared for the longer round and the more frequented way. The cause of this is not to be found in any local superstition that attaches to the Precincts – albeit a mysterious lady, with a child in her arms and a rope dangling from her neck, has been seen flitting about there by sundry witnesses as intangible as herself – but it is to be sought in the innate shrinking of dust with the breath of life in it from dust out of which the breath of life has passed; also, in the widely diffused, and almost as widely unacknowledged, reflection: 'If the dead do, under any circumstances, become visible to the living, these are such likely surroundings for the purpose that I, the living, will get out of them as soon as I can.'

Hence, when Mr Jasper and Durdles pause to glance around them, before descending into the crypt by a small side door, of which the latter has a key, the whole expanse of moonlight in their view is utterly deserted. One might fancy that the tide of life was stemmed by Mr Jasper's own Gate House. The murmur of the tide is heard beyond; but no wave passes the archway, over which his lamp burns red behind his curtain, as if the building were a Lighthouse.

They enter, locking themselves in, descend the rugged steps, and are down in the crypt. The lantern is not wanted, for the moonlight strikes in at the groined windows, bare of glass, the broken frames for which cast patterns on the ground. The heavy pillars which support the roof engender masses of black shade, but between them there are lanes of light. Up and down these lanes they walk, Durdles discoursing of the 'old uns' he yet counts on disinterring, and slapping a wall, in which he considers 'a whole family on 'em' to be stoned and earthed up, just as if he were a familiar friend of the family. The taciturnity of Durdles is for the time overcome by Mr Jasper's wicker bottle, which circulates freely; – in the sense, that is to say, that its contents enter freely into Mr Durdles's circulation, while Mr Jasper only rinses his mouth once, and casts forth the rinsing.

They are to ascend the great Tower. On the steps by which they rise to the Cathedral, Durdles pauses for new store of breath. The steps are very dark, but out of the darkness they can see the lanes of light they have traversed. Durdles seats himself upon a step. Mr Jasper seats himself upon another. The odor from the wicker bottle (which has somehow passed into Durdles's keeping) soon intimates that the cork has been taken out; but this is not ascertainable through the sense of sight, since neither can descry the other. And yet, in talking, they turn to one another, as though their faces could commune together.

'This is good stuff, Mister Jarsper!'

'It is very good stuff, I hope. I bought it on purpose.'

'They don't show, you see, the old uns don't, Mister Jarsper!'

'It would be a more confused world than it is, if they could.'

'Well, it *would* lead towards a mixing of things,' Durdles

acquiesces: pausing on the remark, as if the idea of ghosts had not previously presented itself to him in a merely inconvenient light, domestically, or chronologically. 'But do you think there may be Ghosts of other things, though not of men and women?'

'What things? Flower-beds and watering-pots? Horses and harness?'

'No. Sounds.'

'What sounds?'

'Cries.'

'What cries do you mean? Chairs to mend?'

'No. I mean screeches. Now, I'll tell you, Mister Jarsper. Wait a bit till I put the bottle right.' Here the cork is evidently taken out again, and replaced again. 'There! *Now* it's right! This time last year, only a few days later, I happened to have been doing what was correct by the season, in the way of giving it the welcome it had a right to expect, when them town-boys set on me at their worst. At length I gave 'em the slip, and turned in here. And here I fell asleep. And what woke me? The ghost of a cry. The ghost of one terrific shriek, which shriek was followed by the ghost of the howl of a dog: a long dismal woeful howl, such as a dog gives when a person's dead. That was *my* last Christmas Eve.'

'What do you mean?' is the very abrupt, and, one might say, fierce retort.

'I mean that I made enquiries everywhere about, and that no living ears but mine heard either that cry or that howl. So I say they was both ghosts; though why they came to me, I've never made out.'

'I thought you were another kind of man,' says Jasper, scornfully.

'So I thought, myself,' answers Durdles with his usual composure; 'and yet I was pricked out for it.'

Jasper had risen suddenly, when he asked him what he meant, and he now says, 'Come; we shall freeze here; lead the way.'

Durdles complies, not over-steadily; opens the door at the top of the steps with the key he has already used; and so emerges on the Cathedral level, in a passage at the side of the chancel. Here, the moonlight is so very bright again that the colors of the nearest stained-glass window are thrown upon their faces. The appearance of the unconscious Durdles, holding the door open for his companion to follow, as if from the grave, is ghastly enough, with a purple band across his face, and a yellow splash upon his brow; but he bears the close scrutiny of his companion in an insensible way, although it is prolonged while the latter fumbles among his pockets for a key confided to him that will open an iron gate, so to enable them to pass to the staircase of the great tower.

'That and the bottle are enough for you to carry,' he says, giving it to Durdles; 'hand your bundle to me; I am younger and longer-winded than you.' Durdles hesitates for a moment between bundle and bottle; but gives the preference to the bottle as being by far the better company, and consigns the dry weight to his fellow-explorer.

Then they go up the winding staircase of the great tower, toilsomely, turning and turning, and lowering their heads to avoid the stairs above, or the rough stone pivot around which they twist. Durdles has lighted his lantern, by drawing from the cold hard wall a spark of that mysterious fire which lurks in everything, and, guided by this speck, they clamber up among the cobwebs and the dust. Their way lies through strange places. Twice or thrice they emerge into level low-arched galleries, whence they can look down into the moonlit nave; and where Durdles, waving his lantern, shows the dim angels' heads upon the corbels of the roof, seeming to watch their progress. Anon, they turn into narrower and steeper staircases, and the night air begins to blow upon them, and the chirp of some startled jackdaw or frightened rook precedes the heavy beating of wings in a confined space, and the beating down of dust and straws upon their heads. At last, leaving their light behind a stair – for it blows fresh up here – they look down on Cloisterham, fair to see in the moonlight: its ruined habitations and sanctuaries of the dead, at the tower's base: its moss-softened red-tiled roofs and red-brick houses of the living, clustered beyond: its river winding down from the mist on the horizon, as though that were its source, and already heaving with a restless knowledge of its approach towards the sea.

Once again, an unaccountable expedition this! Jasper (always moving softly with no visible reason) contemplates the scene, and especially that stillest part of it which the Cathedral overshadows. But he contemplates Durdles quite as curiously, and Durdles is by times conscious of his watchful eyes.

Only by times, because Durdles is growing drowsy. As aëronauts lighten the load they carry, when they wish to rise, similarly Durdles has lightened the wicker bottle in coming up. Snatches of sleep surprise him on his legs, and stop him in his talk. A mild fit of calenture[3] seizes him, in which he deems that the ground, so far below, is on a level with the tower, and would as lief walk off the tower into the air as not. Such is his state when they begin to come down. And as aëronauts make themselves heavier when they wish to descend, similarly Durdles charges himself with more liquid from the wicker bottle, that he may come down the better.

The iron gate attained and locked – but not before Durdles has tumbled twice, and cut an eyebrow open once – they descend into the crypt again, with the intent of issuing forth as they entered. But, while returning among those lanes of light, Durdles becomes so very uncertain, both of foot and speech, that he half drops, half throws himself down, by one of the heavy pillars, scarcely less heavy than itself, and indistinctly appeals to his companion for forty winks of a second each.

'If you will have it so, or must have it so,' replies Jasper, 'I'll not leave you here. Take them, while I walk to and fro.'

Durdles is asleep at once; and in his sleep he dreams a dream.

It is not much of a dream, considering the vast extent of the domains of dreamland, and their wonderful productions; it is only remarkable for being unusually restless, and unusually real. He dreams of lying there, asleep, and yet counting his companion's footsteps as he walks to and fro. He dreams that the footsteps die away into distance of time and of space, and that something touches him, and that something falls from his hand. Then something clinks and gropes about, and he dreams that he is alone for so long a time, that the lanes of light take new directions as the moon advances in her course. From succeeding unconsciousness he passes into a dream of slow uneasiness from cold; and painfully awakes to a perception of the lanes of light – really changed, much as he had dreamed – and Jasper walking among them, beating his hands and feet.

'Holloa!' Durdles cries out, unmeaningly alarmed.

'Awake at last?' says Jasper, coming up to him. 'Do you know that your forties have stretched into thousands?'

'No.'

'They have though.'

'What's the time?'

'Hark! The bells are going in the Tower!'

They strike four quarters, and then the great bell strikes.

'Two!' cries Durdles, scrambling up; 'why didn't you try to wake me, Mister Jarsper?'

'I did. I might as well have tried to wake the dead: – your own family of dead, up in the corner there.'

'Did you touch me?'

'Touch you? Yes. Shook you.'

As Durdles recalls that touching something in his dream, he looks down on the pavement, and sees the key of the crypt door lying close to where he himself lay.

'I dropped you, did I?' he says, picking it up, and recalling that part of his dream. As he gathers himself again into an upright position, or into a position as nearly upright as he ever maintains, he is again conscious of being watched by his companion.

'Well?' says Jasper, smiling. 'Are you quite ready? Pray don't hurry.'

'Let me get my bundle right, Mister Jarsper, and I'm with you.'

As he ties it afresh, he is once more conscious that he is very narrowly observed.

'What do you suspect me of, Mister Jarsper?' he asks, with drunken displeasure. 'Let them as has any suspicions of Durdles, name 'em.'

'I've no suspicions of you, my good Mr Durdles; but I have suspicions that my bottle was filled with something stiffer than either of us supposed. And I also have suspicions,' Jasper adds, taking it from the pavement and turning it bottom upward, 'that it's empty.'

Durdles condescends to laugh at this. Continuing to chuckle when his laugh is over, as though remonstrant with himself on his drinking powers, he rolls to the door and unlocks it. They both pass out, and Durdles relocks it, and pockets his key.

'A thousand thanks for a curious and interesting night,' says Jasper, giving him his hand; 'you can make your own way home?'

'I should think so!' answers Durdles. 'If you was to offer Durdles the affront to show him his way home, he wouldn't go home.

> 'Durdles wouldn't go home till morning;[4]
> And then Durdles wouldn't go home,

Durdles wouldn't.' This, with the utmost defiance.

'Good-night, then.'

'Good-night, Mister Jarsper.'

Each is turning his own way, when a sharp whistle rends the silence, and the jargon is yelped out:

> 'Widdy widdy wen!
> I – ket – ches – Im – out – ar – ter – ten.
> Widdy widdy wy!
> Then – E – don't – go – then – I – shy –
> Widdy Widdy Wake-cock warning!'

Instantly afterwards, a rapid fire of stones rattles at the Cathedral wall, and the hideous small boy is beheld opposite, dancing in the moonlight.

'What! Is that baby-devil on the watch there!' cries Jasper in a fury: so quickly roused, and so violent, that he seems an older devil himself. 'I shall shed the blood of that Impish wretch! I know I shall do it!' Regardless of the fire, though it hits him more than once, he rushes at Deputy, collars him, and tries to bring him across. But Deputy is not to be so easily brought across. With a diabolical insight into the strongest part of his position, he is no sooner taken by the throat than he curls up his legs, forces his assailant to hang him, as it were, and gurgles in his throat, and screws his body, and twists, as already undergoing the first agonies of strangulation. There is nothing for it but to drop him. He instantly gets himself together, backs over to Durdles, and cries to his assailant, gnashing the great gap in front of his mouth with rage and malice:

'I'll blind yer, s'elp me! I'll stone yer eyes out, s'elp me! If I don't have yer eyesight, bellows me!' At the same time dodging behind Durdles, and snarling at Jasper, now from this side of him, and now from that: prepared, if pounced upon, to dart away in all manner of curvilinear directions, and, if run down after all, to grovel in the dust, and cry: 'Now, hit me when I'm down! Do it!'

'Don't hurt the boy, Mister Jarsper,' urges Durdles, shielding him. 'Recollect yourself.'

'He followed us to-night, when we first came here!'

'Yer lie, I didn't!' replies Deputy, in his one form of polite contradiction.

'He has been prowling near us ever since!'

'Yer lie, I haven't,' returns Deputy. 'I'd only just come out for my 'elth when I see you two a coming out of the Kinfreederel. If –

'I – ket – ches – Im – out – ar – ter – ten,'

(with the usual rhythm and dance, though dodging behind Durdles). 'it ain't *my* fault, is it?'

'Take him home, then,' retorts Jasper, ferociously, though with a strong check upon himself, 'and let my eyes be rid of the sight of you!'

Deputy, with another sharp whistle, at once expressing his relief, and his commencement of a milder stoning of Mr Durdles, begins stoning that respectable gentleman home, as if he were a reluctant ox. Mr Jasper goes to his Gate House, brooding. And thus, as everything comes to an end, the unaccountable expedition comes to an end – for the time.

*

CHAPTER 13

Both at their Best

MISS TWINKLETON'S establishment was about to undergo a serene hush. The Christmas recess was at hand. What had once, and at no remote period, been called, even by the erudite Miss Twinkleton herself, 'the half'; but what was now called, as being more elegant, and more chastely collegiate, 'the term'; would expire to-morrow. A noticeable relaxation of discipline had for some few days pervaded the Nuns' House. Club suppers had occurred in the bedrooms, and a dressed tongue had been carved with a pair of scissors, and handed round with the curling-tongs. Portions of marmalade had likewise been distributed on a service of plates constructed of curlpaper; and cowslip wine had been quaffed from the small squat measuring glass in which little Rickitts (a junior of weakly constitution) took her steel drops daily. The housemaids had been bribed with various fragments of riband, and sundry pairs of shoes more or less down at heel, to make no mention of crumbs in the beds; the airiest costumes had been worn on these festive occasions; and the daring Miss Ferdinand had even surprised the company with a sprightly solo on the comb-and-curlpaper, until suffocated in her own pillow by two flowing-haired executioners.

Nor were these the only tokens of dispersal. Boxes appeared in the bedrooms (where they were capital at other times), and a surprising amount of packing took place, out of all proportion to the amount packed. Largesse, in the form of odds and ends of cold cream and pomatum, and also of hairpins, was freely distributed among the attendants. On charges of inviolable secresy, confidences were interchanged respecting golden youth of England expected to call, 'at home,' on the first opportunity. Miss Giggles (deficient in sentiment) did indeed profess that she, for her part, acknowledged such homage by making faces at the golden youth; but this young lady was outvoted by an immense majority.

On the last night before a recess, it was always expressly made a point of honor that nobody should go to sleep, and that Ghosts should be encouraged by all possible means. This compact invariably broke down, and all the young ladies went to sleep very soon, and got up very early.

The concluding ceremony came off at twelve o'clock on the day of departure; when Miss Twinkleton, supported by Mrs Tisher, held a Drawing-Room in her own apartment (the globes already covered with brown holland), where glasses of white wine, and plates of cut pound-cake were discovered on the table. Miss Twinkleton then said, Ladies, another revolving year had brought us round to that festive period at which the first feelings of our nature bounded in our – Miss Twinkleton was annually going to add 'bosoms,' but annually stopped on the brink of that expression, and substituted 'hearts.' Hearts; our hearts. Hem! Again a revolving year, ladies, had brought us to a pause in our studies – let us hope our greatly advanced studies – and, like the mariner in his bark, the warrior in his tent, the captive in his dungeon, and the traveller in his various conveyances, we yearned for home. Did we say, on such an occasion, in the opening words of Mr Addison's impressive tragedy:[1]

'The dawn is overcast, the morning lowers,
    And heavily in clouds brings on the day,
    The great, th' important day——?'

Not so. From horizon to zenith all was *couleur de rose*, for all was redolent of our relations and friends. Might *we* find *them* prospering as *we* expected; might *they* find *us* prospering as *they* expected! Ladies, we would now, with our love to one another, wish one another good-bye, and happiness, until we met again. And when the time should come for our resumption of those pursuits which (here a general depression set in all round), pursuits which, pursuits which; – then let us ever remember what was said by the Spartan General, in words too trite for repetition, at the battle it were superfluous to specify.

The handmaidens of the establishment, in their best caps, then handed the trays, and the young ladies sipped and crumbled, and the bespoken coaches began to choke the street. Then, leave-taking was not long about, and Miss Twinkleton, in saluting each young lady's cheek, confided to her an exceedingly neat letter, addressed to her next friend at law, 'with Miss Twinkleton's best compliments' in the corner. This missive she handed with an air as if it had not the least connexion with the bill, but were something in the nature of a delicate and joyful surprise.

So many times had Rosa seen such dispersals, and so very little did she know of any other Home, that she was contented to remain where she was, and was even better contented than ever before, having her latest friend with her. And yet her latest friendship had a blank place in it of which she could not fail to be sensible. Helena Landless, having been a party to her brother's revelation about Rosa, and having entered into that compact of silence with Mr Crisparkle, shrank from any allusion to Edwin Drood's name. Why she so avoided it, was mysterious to Rosa, but she perfectly perceived the fact. But for the fact, she might have relieved her own little perplexed heart of some of its doubts and hesitations, by taking Helena into her confidence. As it was, she had no such vent: she could only ponder on her own difficulties, and wonder more and more why this avoidance of Edwin's name should last, now that she knew – for so much Helena had told her – that a good understanding was to be re-established between the two young men, when Edwin came down.

It would have made a pretty picture, so many pretty girls kissing Rosa in the cold porch of the Nuns' House, and that sunny little creature peeping out of it (unconscious of sly faces carved on spout and gable peeping at her), and waving farewells to the departing coaches, as if she represented the spirit of rosy youth abiding in the place to keep it bright and warm in its desertion. The hoarse High Street became musical with the cry, in various silvery voices, 'Good-bye, Rosebud, Darling!' and the effigy of Mr Sapsea's father over the opposite doorway seemed to say to mankind: 'Gentlemen, favor me with your attention to this charming little last lot left behind, and bid with a spirit worthy of the occasion!' Then the staid street, so unwontedly sparkling, youthful, and fresh for a few rippling moments, ran dry, and Cloisterham was itself again.

If Rosebud in her bower now waited Edwin Drood's coming with an uneasy heart, Edwin for his part was uneasy too. With far less force of purpose in his composition than the childish beauty, crowned by acclamation fairy queen of Miss Twinkleton's establishment, he had a conscience, and Mr Grewgious had pricked it. That gentleman's steady convictions of what was right and what was wrong in such a case as his, were neither to be frowned aside nor laughed aside. They would not be moved. But for the dinner in Staple Inn, and but for the ring he carried in the breast-pocket of his coat, he would have drifted into their wedding-day without another pause for real thought, loosely trusting that all would go well, left alone. But that serious putting him on his truth to the living and the dead had brought him to a check. He must either give the ring to Rosa, or he must take it back. Once put into this narrowed way of action, it was curious that he began to consider Rosa's claims upon him more unselfishly than he had ever considered them before, and began to be less sure of himself than he had ever been in all his easy-going days.

'I will be guided by what she says, and by how we get on,' was his decision, walking from the Gate House to the Nuns' House. 'Whatever comes of it, I will bear his words in mind, and try to be true to the living and the dead.'

Rosa was dressed for walking. She expected him. It was a bright frosty day, and Miss Twinkleton had already graciously sanctioned fresh air. Thus they got out together before it became necessary for either Miss Twinkleton, or the Deputy High Priest, Mrs Tisher, to lay even so much as one of those usual offerings on the shrine of Propriety.

'My dear Eddy,' said Rosa, when they had turned out of the High Street, and had got among the quiet walks in the neighbourhood of the Cathedral and the river: 'I want to say something very serious to you. I have been thinking about it for a long, long time.'

'I want to be serious with you too, Rosa dear. I mean to be serious and earnest.'

'Thank you, Eddy. And you will not think me unkind because I begin, will you? You will not think I speak for myself only, because I speak first? That would not be generous, would it? And I know you are generous!'

He said, 'I hope I am not ungenerous to you, Rosa.' He called her Pussy no more. Never again.

'And there is no fear,' pursued Rosa, 'of our quarrelling, is there? Because, Eddy,' clasping her hand on his arm, 'we have so much reason to be very lenient to each other!'

'We will be, Rosa.'

'That's a dear good boy! Eddy, let us be courageous. Let us change to brother and sister from this day forth.'

'Never be husband and wife?'

'Never!'

Neither spoke again for a little while. But after that pause he said, with some effort:

'Of course I know that this has been in both our minds, Rosa, and of course I am in honor bound to confess freely that it does not originate with you.'

'No, nor with you, dear,' she returned, with pathetic earnestness. 'It has sprung up between us. You are not truly happy in our engagement; I am not truly happy in it. Oh, I am so sorry, so sorry!' And there she broke into tears.

'I am deeply sorry too, Rosa! Deeply sorry for you.'

'And I for you, poor boy! And I for you!'

This pure young feeling, this gentle and forbearing feeling of each towards the other, brought with it its reward in a softening light that seemed to shine on their position. The relations between them did not look wilful, or capricious, or a failure, in such a light; they became elevated into something more self-denying, honorable, affectionate, and true.

'If we knew yesterday,' said Rosa, as she dried her eyes, 'and we did know yesterday, and on many, many yesterdays, that we were far from right together in those relations which were not of our own choosing, what better could we do to-day than change them? It is natural that we should be sorry, and you see how sorry we both are; but how much better to be sorry now than then?'

'When, Rosa?'

'When it would be too late. And then we should be angry, besides.'

Another silence fell upon them.

'And you know,' said Rosa, innocently, 'you couldn't like me then; and you can always like me now, for I shall not be a drag upon you, or a worry to you. And I can always like you now, and your sister will not tease or trifle with you. I often did when I was not your sister, and I beg your pardon for it.'

'Don't let us come to that, Rosa; or I shall want more pardoning than I like to think of.'

'No, indeed, Eddy; you are too hard, my generous boy, upon yourself. Let us sit down, brother, on these ruins, and let me tell you how it was with us. I think I know, for I have considered about it very much since you were here, last time. You liked me, didn't you? You thought I was a nice little thing?'

'Everybody thinks that, Rosa.'

'Do they?' She knitted her brow musingly for a moment, and then flashed out with the bright little induction: 'Well; but say they do. Surely it was not enough that you should think of me only as other people did; now, was it?'

The point was not to be got over. It was not enough.

'And that is just what I mean; that is just how it was with us,' said Rosa. 'You liked me very well, and you had grown used to me, and had grown used to the idea of our being married. You accepted the situation as an inevitable kind of thing, didn't you? It was to be, you thought, and why discuss or dispute it?'

It was new and strange to him to have himself presented to himself so clearly, in a glass of her holding up. He had always patronized her, in his superiority to her share of woman's wit. Was that but another instance of something radically amiss in the terms on which they had been gliding towards a life-long bondage?

'All this that I say of you, is true of me as well, Eddy. Unless it was, I might not be bold enough to say it. Only, the difference between us was, that by little and little there crept into my mind a habit of thinking about it, instead of dismissing it. My life is not so busy as yours, you see, and I have not so many things to think of. So I thought about it very much, and I cried about it very much too (though that was not your fault, poor boy); when all at once my guardian came down, to prepare for my leaving the Nuns' House. I tried to hint to him that I was not quite settled in my mind, but I hesitated and failed, and he didn't understand me. But he is a good, good man. And he put before me so kindly, and yet so strongly, how seriously we ought to consider, in our circumstances, that I resolved to speak to you the next moment we were alone and grave. And if I seemed to come to it easily just now, because I came to it all at once, don't think it was so really, Eddy, for Oh, it was very, very hard, and Oh, I am very, very sorry!'

Her full heart broke into tears again. He put his arm about her waist, and they walked by the river side together.

'Your guardian has spoken to me too, Rosa dear. I saw him before I left London.' His right hand was in his breast, seeking the ring; but he checked it, as he thought: 'If I am to take it back why should I tell her of it?'

'And that made you more serious about it, didn't it, Eddy? And if I had not spoken to you, as I have, you would have spoken to me? I hope you can tell me so? I don't like it to be *all* my doing, though it *is* so much better for us.'

'Yes, I should have spoken; I should have put everything before you; I came intending to do it. But I never could have spoken to you as you have spoken to me, Rosa.'

'Don't say you mean so coldly or unkindly, Eddy, please if you can help it.'

'I mean so sensibly and delicately, so wisely and affectionately.'

'That's my dear brother!' She kissed his hand in a little rapture. 'The dear girls will be dreadfully disappointed,' added Rosa, laughing, with the dew-drops glistening in her bright eyes. 'They have looked forward to it so, poor pets!'

'Ah! But I fear it will be a worse disappointment to Jack,' said Edwin Drood, with a start. 'I never thought of Jack!'

Her swift and intent look at him as he said the words could no more be recalled than a flash of lightning can. But it appeared as though she would have instantly recalled it, if she could; for she looked down, confused, and breathed quickly.

'You don't doubt its being a blow to Jack, Rosa?'

She merely replied, and that evasively and hurriedly: Why should she? She had not thought about it. He seemed, to her, to have so little to do with it.

'My dear child! Can you suppose that any one so wrapped up in another – Mrs Tope's expression: not mine – as Jack is in me, could fail to be struck all of a heap by such a sudden and complete change in my life? I say sudden, because it will be sudden to *him*, you know.'

She nodded twice or thrice, and her lips parted as if she would have assented. But she uttered no sound, and her breathing was no slower.

'How shall I tell Jack?' said Edwin, ruminating. If he had been less occupied with the thought, he must have seen her singular emotion. 'I never thought of Jack. It must be broken to him, before the town crier knows it. I dine with the dear fellow to-morrow and next day – Christmas Eve and Christmas Day – but it would never do to spoil his feast days. He always worries about me, and moddley-coddleys in the merest trifles. The news is sure to overset him. How on earth shall this be broken to Jack!'

'He must be told, I suppose?' said Rosa.

'My dear Rosa! Who ought to be in our confidence, if not Jack?'

'My guardian promised to come down, if I should write and ask him. I am going to do so. Would you like to leave it to him?'

'A bright idea!' cried Edwin. 'The other trustee. Nothing more natural. He comes down, he goes to Jack, he relates what we have agreed upon, and he states our case better than we could. He has already spoken feelingly to you, he has already spoken feelingly to me, and he'll put the whole thing feelingly to Jack. That's it!

I am not a coward, Rosa, but to tell you a secret, I am a little afraid of Jack.'

'No, no! You are not afraid of him?' cried Rosa, turning white and clasping her hands.

'Why, sister Rosa, sister Rosa, what do you see from the turret?'² said Edwin, rallying her. 'My dear girl!'

'You frightened me.'

'Most unintentionally, but I am sorry as if I had meant to do it. Could you possibly suppose for a moment, from any loose way of speaking of mine, that I was literally afraid of the dear fond fellow? What I mean is, that he is subject to a kind of paroxysm, or fit – I saw him in it once – and I don't know but that so great a surprise, coming upon him direct from me whom he is so wrapped up in, might bring it on perhaps. Which – and this is the secret I was going to tell you – is another reason for your guardian's making the communication. He is so steady, precise, and exact, that he will talk Jack's thoughts into shape, in no time: whereas with me Jack is always impulsive and hurried, and, I may say, almost womanish.'

Rosa seemed convinced. Perhaps from her own very different point of view of 'Jack,' she felt comforted and protected by the interposition of Mr Grewgious between herself and him.

And now, Edwin Drood's right hand closed again upon the ring in its little case, and again was checked by the consideration: 'It is certain, now, that I am to give it back to him; then why should I tell her of it?' That pretty sympathetic nature which could be so sorry for him in the blight of their childish hopes of happiness together, and could so quietly find itself alone in a new world to weave fresh wreaths of such flowers as it might prove to bear, the old world's flowers being withered, would be grieved by those sorrowful jewels; and to what purpose? Why should it be? They were but a sign of broken joys and baseless projects; in their very beauty they were (as the unlikeliest of men had said) almost a cruel satire on the loves, hopes, plans, of humanity, which are able to forecast nothing, and are so much brittle dust. Let them be. He would restore them to her guardian when he came down; he in his turn would restore them to the cabinet from which he had un-willingly taken them; and there, like old letters or old vows, or other records of old aspirations come to nothing, they would be disregarded, until, being valuable, they were sold into circulation again, to repeat their former round.

Let them be. Let them lie unspoken of, in his breast. However distinctly or indistinctly be entertained these thoughts, he arrived at the conclusion, Let them be. Among the mighty store of wonderful chains that are for ever forging, day and night, in the vast iron-works of time and circumstance, there was one chain forged in the moment of that small conclusion, riveted to the foundations of heaven and earth, and gifted with invincible force to hold and drag.

They walked on by the river. They began to speak of their separate plans. He would quicken his departure from England, and she would remain where she was, at least as long as Helena remained. The poor dear girls should have their disappointment broken to them gently, and, as the first preliminary, Miss Twinkleton should be confided in by Rosa, even in advance of the reappearance of Mr Grewgious. It should be made clear in all quarters that she and Edwin were the best of friends. There had never been so serene an understanding between them since they were first affianced. And yet there was one reservation on each side; on hers, that she intended through her guardian to withdraw herself immediately from the tuition of her music-master; on his, that he did already entertain some wandering speculations whether it might ever come to pass that he would know more of Miss Landless.

The bright frosty day declined as they walked and spoke together. The sun dipped in the river far behind them, and the old city lay red before them, as their walk drew to a close. The moaning water cast its seaweed duskily at their feet, when they turned to leave its margin; and the rooks hovered above them with hoarse cries, darker splashes in the darkening air.

'I will prepare Jack for my flitting soon,' said Edwin, in a low voice, 'and I will but see your guardian when he comes, and then go before they speak together. It will be better done without my being by. Don't you think so?'

'Yes.'

'We know we have done right, Rosa?'

'Yes.'

'We know we are better so, even now?'

'And shall be far, far better so, by-and-bye.'

Still, there was that lingering tenderness in their hearts towards the old positions they were relinquishing, that they prolonged their parting. When they came among the elm trees by the Cathedral, where they had last sat together, they stopped, as by consent, and Rosa raised her face to his, as she had never raised it in the old days; – for they were old already.

'God bless you, dear! Good-bye!'

'God bless you, dear! Good-bye!'

They kissed each other, fervently.

'Now, please take me home, Eddy, and let me be by myself.'

'Don't look round, Rosa,' he cautioned her, as he drew her arm through his, and led her away. 'Didn't you see Jack?'

'No! Where?'

'Under the trees. He saw us, as we took leave of each other. Poor fellow! he little thinks we have parted. This will be a blow to him, I am much afraid!'

She hurried on, without resting, and hurried on until they had passed under the Gate House into the street; once there, she asked:

'Has he followed us? You can look without seeming to. Is he behind?'

'No. Yes! he is! He has just passed out under the gateway. The dear sympathetic old fellow likes to keep us in sight. I am afraid he will be bitterly disappointed!'

She pulled hurriedly at the handle of the hoarse old bell, and the gate soon opened. Before going in, she gave him one last wide wondering look, as if she would have asked him with imploring emphasis: 'Oh! don't you understand?' And out of that look he vanished from her view.

CHAPTER 14

When Shall These Three Meet Again?[1]

CHRISTMAS Eve in Cloisterham. A few strange faces in the streets; a few other faces, half strange and half familiar, once the faces of Cloisterham children, now the faces of men and women who come back from the outer world at long intervals to find the city wonderfully shrunken in size, as if it had not washed by any means well in the meanwhile. To these, the striking of the Cathedral clock, and the cawing of the rooks from the Cathedral tower, are like voices of their nursery time. To such as these, it has happened in their dying hours afar off, that they have imagined their chamber floor to be strewn with the autumnal leaves[2] fallen from the elm trees in the Close: so have the rustling sounds and fresh scents of their earliest impressions revived when the circle of their lives was very nearly traced, and the beginning and the end were drawing close together.

Seasonable tokens are about. Red berries shine here and there in the lattices of Minor Canon Corner; Mr and Mrs Tope are daintily sticking sprigs of holly into the carvings and sconces of the Cathedral stalls, as if they were sticking them into the coat-buttonholes of the Dean and Chapter. Lavish profusion is in the shops: particularly in the articles of currants, raisins, spices, candied peel, and moist sugar. An unusual air of gallantry and dissipation is abroad; evinced in an immense bunch of mistletoe hanging in the greengrocer's shop doorway, and a poor little Twelfth Cake, culminating in the figure of a Harlequin – such a very poor little Twelfth Cake, that one would rather call it a Twenty-Fourth Cake, or a Forty-Eighth Cake – to be raffled for at the pastry-cook's, terms one shilling per member. Public amusements are not wanting. The Wax-Work which made so deep an impression on the reflective mind of the Emperor of China is to be seen by particular desire during Christmas Week only, on the premises of the bankrupt livery-stable keeper up the lane; and a new grand comic Christmas pantomime is to be produced at the Theatre: the latter heralded by the portra it of Signor Jacksonini the clown, saying 'How do you do to-morrow?' quite as large as life, and almost as miserably. In short, Cloisterham is up and doing: though from this description the High School and Miss Twinkleton's are to be excluded. From the former establishment, the scholars have gone home, every one of them in love with one of Miss Twinkleton's young ladies (who knows nothing about it); and only the handmaidens flutter occasionally in the windows of the latter. It is noticed, by-and-bye, that these damsels become, within the limits of decorum, more skittish when thus entrusted with the concrete representation of their sex, than when dividing the representation with Miss Twinkleton's young ladies.

Three are to meet at the Gate House to-night. How does each one of the three get through the day?

Neville Landless, though absolved from his books for the time by Mr Crisparkle – whose fresh nature is by no means insensible to the charms of a holiday – reads and writes in his quiet room, with a concentrated air, until it is two hours past noon. He then sets himself to clearing his table, to arranging his books, and to tearing up and burning his stray papers. He makes a clean sweep of all untidy accumulations, puts all his drawers in order, and leaves no note or scrap of paper undestroyed, save such memoranda as bear directly on his studies. This done, he turns to his wardrobe, selects a few articles of ordinary wear – among them, change of stout shoes and socks for walking – and packs these in a knapsack. This knapsack is new, and he bought it in the High Street yesterday. He also purchased, at the same time and at the same place, a heavy walking stick: strong in the handle for the grip of the hand, and iron-shod. He tries this, swings it, poises it, and lays it by, with the knapsack, on a window-seat. By this time his arrangements are complete.

He dresses for going out, and is in the act of going – indeed has left his room, and has met the Minor Canon on the staircase, coming out of his bedroom upon the same story – when he turns back again for his walking-stick, thinking he will carry it now. Mr Crisparkle, who has paused on the staircase, sees it in his hand on his immediately reappearing, takes it from him, and asks him with a smile how he chooses a stick?

'Really I don't know that I understand the subject,' he answers. 'I chose it for its weight.'

'Much too heavy, Neville; *much* too heavy.'

'To rest upon in a long walk, sir?'

'Rest upon?' repeats Mr Crisparkle, throwing himself into pedestrian form. 'You don't rest upon it; you merely balance with it.'

'I shall know better, with practice, sir. I have not lived in a walking country, you know.'

'True,' says Mr Crisparkle. 'Get into a little training, and we will have a few score miles together. I should leave you nowhere now. Do you come back before dinner?'

'I think not, as we dine early.'

Mr Crisparkle gives him a bright nod and a cheerful good-bye: expressing (not without intention) absolute confidence and ease.

Neville repairs to the Nuns' House, and requests that Miss Landless may be informed that her brother is there, by appointment. He waits at the gate, not even crossing the threshold; for he is on his parole not to put himself in Rosa's way.

His sister is at least as mindful of the obligation they have taken on themselves as he can be, and loses not a moment in joining him. They meet affectionately, avoid lingering there, and walk towards the upper inland country.

'I am not going to tread upon forbidden ground, Helena,' says Neville, when they have walked some distance and are turning; 'you will understand in another moment that I cannot help referring to – what shall I say? – my infatuation.'

'Had you not better avoid it, Neville? You know that I can hear nothing.'

'You can hear, my dear, what Mr Crisparkle has heard, and heard with approval.'

'Yes; I can hear so much.'

'Well, it is this. I am not only unsettled and unhappy myself, but I am conscious of unsettling and interfering with other people. How do I know that, but for my unfortunate presence, you, and – and – the rest of that former party, our engaging guardian excepted, might be dining cheerfully in Minor Canon Corner to-morrow? Indeed it probably would be so. I can see too well that I am not high in the old lady's opinion, and it is easy to understand what an irksome clog I must be upon the hospitalities of her orderly house – especially at this time of year – when I must be kept asunder from this person, and there is such a reason for my not being brought into contact with that person, and an unfavorable reputation has preceded me with such another person, and so on. I have put this very gently to Mr Crisparkle, for you know his self-denying ways; but still I have put it. What I have laid much greater stress upon at the same time is, that I am engaged in a miserable struggle with myself, and that a little change and absence may enable me to come through it the better. So, the weather being bright and hard, I am going on a walking expedition, and intend taking myself out of everybody's way (my own included, I hope) to-morrow morning.'

'When to come back?'

'In a fortnight.'

'And going quite alone?'

'I am much better without company, even if there were any one but you to bear me company, my dear Helena.'

'Mr Crisparkle entirely agrees, you say?'

'Entirely. I am not sure but that at first he was inclined to think it rather a moody scheme, and one that might do a brooding mind harm. But we took a moonlight walk, last Monday night, to talk it over at leisure, and I represented the case to him as it really is. I showed him that I do want to conquer myself, and that, this evening well got over, it is surely better that I should be away from here just now, than here. I could hardly help meeting certain people walking together here, and that could do no good, and is certainly not the way to forget. A fortnight hence, that chance will probably be over, for the time; and when it again arises for the last time, why, I can again go away. Further, I really do feel hopeful of bracing exercise and wholesome fatigue. You know that Mr Crisparkle allows such things their full weight in the preservation of his own sound mind in his own sound body, and that his just spirit is not likely to maintain one set of natural laws for himself and another for me. He yielded to my view of the matter, when convinced that I was honestly in earnest, and so, with his full consent, I start to-morrow morning. Early enough to be not only out of the streets, but out of hearing of the bells, when the good people go to church.'

Helena thinks it over, and thinks well of it. Mr Crisparkle doing so, she would do so; but she does originally, out of her own mind, think well of it, as a healthy project, denoting a sincere endeavor, and an active attempt at self-correction. She is inclined to pity him, poor fellow, for going away solitary on the great Christmas festival; but she feels it much more to the purpose to encourage him. And she does encourage him.

He will write to her?

He will write to her every alternate day, and tell her all his adventures.

Does he send clothes on, in advance of him?

'My dear Helena, no. Travel like a pilgrim, with wallet and staff. My wallet – or my knapsack – is packed, and ready for strapping on; and here is my staff!'

He hands it to her; she makes the same remark as Mr Crisparkle, that it is very heavy; and gives it back to him, asking what wood it is? Iron-wood.

Up to this point he has been extremely cheerful. Perhaps the having to carry his case with her, and therefore to present it in its brightest aspect, has roused his spirits. Perhaps the having done so with success is followed by a revulsion. As the day closes in, and the city lights begin to spring up before them, he grows depressed.

'I wish I were not going to this dinner, Helena.'

'Dear Neville, is it worth while to care much about it? Think how soon it will be over.'

'How soon it will be over!' he repeats, gloomily. 'Yes. But I don't like it.'

There may be a moment's awkwardness, she cheeringly represents to him, but it can only last a moment. He is quite sure of himself.

'I wish I felt as sure of everything else, as I feel of myself,' he answers her.

'How strangely you speak, dear! What do you mean?'

'Helena, I don't know. I only know that I don't like it. What a strange dead weight there is in the air!'

She calls his attention to those copperous clouds beyond the river, and says that the wind is rising. He scarcely speaks again, until he takes leave of her, at the gate of the Nuns' House. She does not immediately enter, when they have parted, but remains looking after him along the street. Twice he passes the Gate House, reluctant to enter. At length, the Cathedral clock chiming one quarter, with a rapid turn he hurries in.

And so *he* goes up the postern stair.

Edwin Drood passes a solitary day. Something of deeper moment than he had thought has gone out of his life; and in the silence of his own chamber he wept for it last night. Though the image of Miss Landless still hovers in the background of his mind, the pretty little affectionate creature, so much firmer and wiser than he had supposed, occupies its stronghold. It is with some misgivings of his own unworthiness that he thinks of her, and of what they might have been to one another, if he had been more in earnest some time ago; if he had set a higher value on her; if, instead of accepting his lot in life as an inheritance of course, he had studied the right way to its appreciation and enhancement. And still, for all this, and though there is a sharp heartache in all this, the vanity and caprice of youth sustain that handsome figure of Miss Landless in the background of his mind.

That was a curious look of Rosa's when they parted at the gate. Did it mean that she saw below the surface of his thoughts, and down into their twilight depths? Scarcely that, for it was a look of astonished and keen enquiry. He decides that he cannot understand it, though it was remarkably expressive.

As he only waits for Mr Grewgious now, and will depart immediately after having seen him, he takes a sauntering leave of the ancient city and its neighbourhood. He recalls the time when Rosa and he walked here or there, mere children, full of the dignity of being engaged. Poor children! he thinks, with a pitying sadness.

Finding that his watch has stopped, he turns into the jeweller's shop, to have it wound and set. The jeweller is knowing on the subject of a bracelet, which he begs leave to submit, in a general and quite aimless way. It would suit (he considers) a young bride to perfection; especially if of a rather diminutive style of beauty. Finding the bracelet but coldly looked at, the jeweller invites attention to a tray of rings for gentlemen; here is a style of ring, now, he remarks – a very chaste signet – which gentlemen are much given to purchasing, when changing their condition. A ring of a very responsible appearance. With the date of their wedding-day engraved inside, several gentlemen have preferred it to any other kind of memento.

The rings are as coldly viewed as the bracelet. Edwin tells the tempter that he wears no jewellery but his watch and chain, which were his father's; and his shirt-pin.

'That I was aware of,' is the jeweller's reply, 'for Mr Jasper dropped in for a watch-glass the other day, and, in fact, I showed these articles to him, remarking that if he *should* wish to make a present to a gentleman relative, on any particular occasion – But he said with a smile that he had an inventory in his mind of all the jewellery his gentleman relative ever wore; namely, his watch and chain, and shirt-pin.' Still (the jeweller considers) that might not apply to all times, though applying to the present time. 'Twenty minutes past two, Mr Drood, I set your watch at. Let me recommend you not to let it run down, sir.'

Edwin takes his watch, puts it on, and goes out, thinking: 'Dear old Jack! If I were to make an extra crease in my neck-cloth, he would think it worth noticing!'

He strolls about and about, to pass the time until the dinner hour. It somehow happens that Cloisterham seems reproachful to him to-day; has fault to find with him, as if he had not used it well; but is far more pensive with him than angry. His wonted carelessness is replaced by a wistful looking at, and dwelling upon, all the old landmarks. He will soon be far away, and may never see them again, he thinks. Poor youth! Poor youth!³

As dusk draws on, he paces the Monks' Vineyard. He has walked to and fro, full half an hour by the Cathedral chimes, and it has closed in dark, before he becomes quite aware of a woman crouching on the ground near a wicket gate in a corner. The gate commands a cross bye-path, little used in the gloaming; and the figure must have been there all the time, though he has but gradually and lately made it out.

He strikes into that path, and walks up to the wicket. By the light of a lamp near it, he sees that the woman is of a haggard appearance, and that her weazen chin is resting on her hands, and that her eyes are staring – with an unwinking, blind sort of stedfastness – before her.

Always kindly, but moved to be unusually kind this evening, and having bestowed kind words on most of the children and aged people he has met, he at once bends down, and speaks to this woman.

'Are you ill?'

'No, deary,' she answers, without looking at him, and with no departure from her strange blind stare.

'Are you blind?'

'No, deary.'

'Are you lost, homeless, faint? What is the matter, that you stay here in the cold so long, without moving?'

By slow and stiff efforts, she appears to contract her vision until it can rest upon him; and then a curious film passes over her, and she begins to shake.

He straightens himself, recoils a step, and looks down at her in a dread amazement; for he seems to know her.

'Good Heaven!' he thinks, next moment. 'Like Jack that night!'

As he looks down at her, she looks up at him, and whimpers: 'My lungs is weakly; my lungs is dreffle bad. Poor me, poor me, my cough is rattling dry!' And coughs in confirmation, horribly.

'Where do you come from?'

'Come from London, deary.' (Her cough still rending her.)

'Where are you going to?'

'Back to London, deary. I came here, looking for a needle in a haystack, and I ain't found it. Look'ee, deary; give me three and sixpence, and don't you be afeard for me. I'll get back to London then, and trouble no one. I'm in a business. – Ah, me! It's slack, it's slack, and times is very bad! – but I can make a shift to live by it.'

'Do you eat opium?'

'Smokes it,' she replies with difficulty, still racked by her cough. 'Give me three and sixpence, and I'll lay it out well, and get back. If you don't give me three and sixpence, don't give me a brass farden. And if you do give me three and sixpence, deary, I'll tell you something.'

He counts the money from his pocket, and puts it in her hand. She instantly clutches it tight, and rises to her feet with a croaking laugh of satisfaction.

'Bless ye! Hark'ee, dear genl'mn. What's your Chris'en name?'

'Edwin.'

'Edwin, Edwin, Edwin,' she repeats, trailing off into a drowsy repetition of the word; and then asks suddenly: 'Is the short of that name Eddy?'

'It is sometimes called so,' he replies, with the color starting to his face.

'Don't sweethearts call it so?' she asks, pondering.

'How should I know!'

'Haven't you a sweetheart, upon your soul?'

'None.'

She is moving away, with another 'Bless ye, and thank'ee, deary!' when he adds: 'You were to tell me something; you may as well do so.'

'So I was, so I was. Well, then. Whisper. You be thankful that your name ain't Ned.'

He looks at her, quite steadily, as he asks: 'Why?'

'Because it's a bad name to have just now.'

'How a bad name?'

'A threatened name. A dangerous name.'

'The proverb says that threatened men live long,' he tells her, lightly.

'Then Ned – so threatened is he, wherever he may be while I am a talking to you, deary – should live to all eternity!' replies the woman.

She has leaned forward, to say it in his ear, with her forefinger shaking before his eyes, and now huddles herself together, and with another 'Bless ye, and thank'ee!' goes away in the direction of the Travellers' Lodging House.

This is not an inspiriting close to a dull day. Alone, in a sequestered place, surrounded by vestiges of old time and decay, it rather has a tendency to call a shudder into being. He makes for the better lighted streets, and resolves as he walks on to say nothing of this to-night, but to mention it to Jack (who alone calls him Ned), as an odd coincidence, to-morrow; of course only as a coincidence, and not as anything better worth remembering.

Still, it holds to him, as many things much better worth remembering never did. He has another mile or so, to linger out before the dinner-hour; and, when he walks over the bridge and by the river, the woman's words are in the rising wind, in the angry sky, in the troubled water, in the flickering lights. There is some solemn echo of them even in the Cathedral chime, which strikes a sudden surprise to his heart as he turns in under the archway of the Gate House.

And so *he* goes up the postern stair.

John Jasper passes a more agreeable and cheerful day than either of his guests. Having no music-lessons to give in the holiday season, his time is his own, but for the Cathedral services. He is early among the shopkeepers, ordering little table luxuries that his nephew likes. His nephew will not be with him long, he tells his provision-dealers, and so must be petted and made much of. While out on his hospitable preparations, he looks in on Mr Sapsea; and

mentions that dear Ned, and that inflammable young spark of Mr
Crisparkle's, are to dine at the Gate House to-day, and make up
their difference. Mr Sapsea is by no means friendly towards the
inflammable young spark. He says that his complexion is 'Un-
English.' And when Mr Sapsea has once declared anything to be
Un-English, he considers that thing everlastingly sunk in the
bottomless pit.

John Jasper is truly sorry to hear Mr Sapsea speak thus, for he
knows right well that Mr Sapsea never speaks without a meaning,
and that he has a subtle trick of being right. Mr Sapsea (by a very
remarkable coincidence) is of exactly that opinion.

Mr Jasper is in beautiful voice this day. In the pathetic supplica-
tion to have his heart inclined to keep this law, he quite astonishes
his fellows by his melodious power. He has never sung difficult
music with such skill and harmony, as in this day's Anthem. His
nervous temperament is occasionally prone to take difficult music
a little too quickly; to-day, his time is perfect.

These results are probably attained through a grand composure
of the spirits. The mere mechanism of his throat is a little tender,
for he wears, both with his singing-robe and with his ordinary
dress, a large black scarf of strong close-woven silk, slung loosely
round his neck. But his composure is so noticeable, that Mr Crisparkle speaks of it as they come out from Vespers.

'I must thank you, Jasper, for the pleasure with which I have
heard you to-day. Beautiful! Delightful! You could not have so
outdone yourself, I hope, without being wonderfully well.'

'I *am* wonderfully well.'

'Nothing unequal,' says the Minor Canon, with a smooth
motion of his hand: 'nothing unsteady, nothing forced, nothing
avoided; all thoroughly done in a masterly manner, with perfect
self-command.'

'Thank you. I hope so, if it is not too much to say.'

'One would think, Jasper, you had been trying a new medicine
for that occasional indisposition of yours.'

'No, really? That's well observed; for I have.'

'Then stick to it, my good fellow,' says Mr Crisparkle, clapping
him on the shoulder with friendly encouragement, 'stick to it.'

'I will.'

'I congratulate you,' Mr Crisparkle pursues, as they come out of the Cathedral, 'on all accounts.'

'Thank you again. I will walk round to the Corner with you, if you don't object; I have plenty of time before my company come; and I want to say a word to you, which I think you will not be displeased to hear.'

'What is it?'

'Well. We were speaking, the other evening, of my black humors.'

Mr Crisparkle's face falls, and he shakes his head deploringly.

'I said, you know, that I should make you an antidote to those black humors; and you said you hoped I would consign them to the flames.'

'And I still hope so, Jasper.'

'With the best reason in the world! I mean to burn this year's Diary at the year's end.'

'Because you —?' Mr Crisparkle brightens greatly as he thus begins.

'You anticipate me. Because I feel that I have been out of sorts, gloomy, bilious, brain-oppressed, whatever it may be. You said I had been exaggerative. So I have.'

Mr Crisparkle's brightened face brightens still more.

'I couldn't see it then, because I *was* out of sorts; but I am in a healthier state now, and I acknowledge it with genuine pleasure. I made a great deal of a very little; that's the fact.'

'It does me good,' cries Mr Crisparkle, 'to hear you say it!'

'A man leading a monotonous life,' Jasper proceeds, 'and getting his nerves, or his stomach, out of order, dwells upon an idea until it loses its proportions. That was my case with the idea in question. So I shall burn the evidence of my case, when the book is full, and begin the next volume with a clearer vision.'

'This is better,' says Mr Crisparkle, stopping at the steps of his door to shake hands, 'than I could have hoped.'

'Why, naturally,' returns Jasper. 'You had but little reason to hope that I should become more like yourself. You are always training yourself to be, mind and body, as clear as crystal, and you always are, and never change; whereas I am a muddy, solitary, moping weed. However, I have got over that mope. Shall I wait, while you ask if Mr Neville has left for my place? If not, he and I may walk round together.'

'I think,' says Mr Crisparkle, opening the entrance door with his key, 'that he left some time ago; at least I know he left, and I think he has not come back. But I'll enquire. You won't come in?'

'My company wait,' says Jasper, with a smile.

The Minor Canon disappears, and in a few moments returns. As he thought, Mr Neville has not come back; indeed, as he remembers now, Mr Neville said he would probably go straight to the Gate House.

'Bad manners in a host!' says Jasper. 'My company will be there before me! What will you bet that I don't find my company embracing?'

'I will bet – or I would, if I ever did bet,' returns Mr Crisparkle, 'that your company will have a gay entertainer this evening.'

Jasper nods, and laughs Good Night!

He retraces his steps to the Cathedral door, and turns down past it to the Gate House. He sings, in a low voice and with delicate expression, as he walks along. It still seems as if a false note were not within his power to-night, and as if nothing could hurry or retard him. Arriving thus under the arched entrance of his dwelling, he pauses for an instant in the shelter to pull off that great black scarf, and hang it in a loop upon his arm. For that brief time, his face is knitted and stern. But it immediately clears, as he resumes his singing, and his way.

And so *he* goes up the postern stair.

The red light burns steadily all the evening in the lighthouse on the margin of the tide of busy life. Softened sounds and hum of traffic pass it and flow on irregularly into the lonely Precincts; but very little else goes by, save violent rushes of wind. It comes on to blow a boisterous gale.

The Precincts are never particularly well lighted; but the strong blasts of wind blowing out many of the lamps (in some instances shattering the frames too, and bringing the glass rattling to the ground), they are unusually dark to-night. The darkness is augmented and confused, by flying dust from the earth, dry twigs from the trees, and great ragged fragments from the rooks' nests up in the tower. The trees themselves so toss and creak, as this tangible part of the darkness madly whirls about, that they seem in peril of being torn out of the earth: while ever and again a crack, and a rushing fall, denote that some large branch has yielded to the storm.

No such power of wind has blown for many a winter-night. Chimneys topple in the streets, and people hold to posts and corners, and to one another, to keep themselves upon their feet. The violent rushes abate not, but increase in frequency and fury until at midnight, when the streets are empty, the storm goes thundering along them, rattling at all the latches, and tearing at all the shutters, as if warning the people to get up and fly with it, rather than have the roofs brought down upon their brains.

Still, the red light burns steadily. Nothing is steady but the red light.

All through the night the wind blows, and abates not. But early in the morning, when there is barely enough light in the east to dim the stars, it begins to lull. From that time, with occasional wild charges, like a wounded monster dying, it drops and sinks; and at full daylight it is dead.

It is then seen that the hands of the Cathedral clock are torn off; that lead from the roof has been stripped away, rolled up, and blown into the Close; and that some stones have been displaced upon the summit of the great tower. Christmas morning though it be, it is necessary to send up workmen, to ascertain the extent of the damage done. These, led by Durdles, go aloft; while Mr Tope and a crowd of early idlers gather down in Minor Canon Corner, shading their eyes and watching for their appearance up there.

This cluster is suddenly broken and put aside by the hands of Mr Jasper; all the gazing eyes are brought down to the earth by his loudly enquiring of Mr Crisparkle, at an open window:

'Where is my nephew?'

'He has not been here. Is he not with you?'

'No. He went down to the river last night, with Mr Neville, to look at the storm, and has not been back. Call Mr Neville!'

'He left this morning, early.'

'Left this morning, early? Let me in, let me in!'

There is no more looking up at the tower, now. All the assembled eyes are turned on Mr Jasper, white, half-dressed, panting, and clinging to the rail before the Minor Canon's house.

Impeached

NEVILLE Landless had started so early and walked at so good a pace, that when the church bells began to ring in Cloisterham for morning service, he was eight miles away. As he wanted his breakfast by that time, having set forth on a crust of bread, he stopped at the next road-side tavern to refresh.

Visitors in want of breakfast – unless they were horses or cattle, for which class of guests there was preparation enough in the way of water-trough and hay – were so unusual at the sign of The Tilted Wagon,[1] that it took a long time to get the wagon into the track of tea and toast and bacon. Neville, in the interval, sitting in a sanded parlor, wondering in how long a time after he had gone, the sneezy fire of damp fagots would begin to make somebody else warm.

Indeed, The Tilted Wagon, as a cool establishment on the top of a hill, where the ground before the door was puddled with damp hoofs and trodden straw; where a scolding landlady slapped a moist baby (with one red sock on and one wanting) in the bar; where the cheese was cast aground upon a shelf, in company with a mouldy tablecloth and a green-handled knife, in a sort of cast-iron canoe; where the pale-faced bread shed tears of crumb over its shipwreck in another canoe; where the family linen, half washed and half dried, led a public life of lying about; where everything to drink was drunk out of mugs, and everything else was suggestive of a rhyme to mugs; The Tilted Wagon, all these things considered, hardly kept its painted promise of providing good entertainment for Man and Beast. However, Man, in the present case, was not critical, but took what entertainment he could get, and went on again after a longer rest than he needed.

He stopped at some quarter of a mile from the house, hesitating whether to pursue the road, or to follow a cart-track between two high hedgerows, which led across the slope of a breezy heath, and evidently struck into the road again by-and-bye. He decided in favor of this latter track, and pursued it with some toil; the rise being steep, and the way worn into deep ruts.

He was laboring along, when he became aware of some other

pedestrians behind him. As they were coming up at a faster pace than his, he stood aside, against one of the high banks, to let them pass. But their manner was very curious. Only four of them passed. Other four slackened speed, and loitered as intending to follow him when he should go on. The remainder of the party (half a dozen perhaps) turned, and went back at a great rate.

He looked at the four behind him, and he looked at the four before him. They all returned his look. He resumed his way. The four in advance went on, constantly looking back; the four in the rear came closing up.

When they all ranged out from the narrow track upon the open slope of the heath, and this order was maintained, let him diverge as he would to either side, there was no longer room to doubt that he was beset by these fellows. He stopped, as a last test; and they all stopped.

'Why do you attend upon me in this way?' he asked the whole body. 'Are you a pack of thieves?'

'Don't answer him,' said one of the number; he did not see which. 'Better be quiet.'

'Better be quiet?' repeated Neville. 'Who said so?'

Nobody replied.

'It's good advice, whichever of you skulkers gave it,' he went on angrily. 'I will not submit to be penned in between four men there, and four men there. I wish to pass, and I mean to pass, those four in front.'

They were all standing still: himself included.

'If eight men, or four men, or two men, set upon one,' he proceeded, growing more enraged, 'the one has no chance but to set his mark upon some of them. And by the Lord I'll do it, if I am interrupted any further!'

. Shouldering his heavy stick, and quickening his pace, he shot on to pass the four ahead. The largest and strongest man of the number changed swiftly to the side on which he came up, and dexterously closed with him and went down with him; but not before the heavy stick had descended smartly.

'Let him be!' said this man in a suppressed voice, as they struggled together on the grass. 'Fair play! His is the build of a girl to mine, and he's got a weight strapped to his back besides. Let him alone. I'll manage him.'

After a little rolling about, in a close scuffle which caused the faces of both to be besmeared with blood, the man took his knee from Neville's chest, and rose, saying: 'There! Now take him arm-in-arm, any two of you!'

It was immediately done.

'As to our being a pack of thieves, Mr Landless,' said the man, as he spat out some blood, and wiped more from his face: 'you know better than that, at midday. We wouldn't have touched you, if you hadn't forced us. We're going to take you round to the high road, anyhow, and you'll find help enough against thieves there, if you want it. Wipe his face somebody; see how it's a-trickling down him!'

When his face was cleansed, Neville recognized in the speaker, Joe, driver of the Cloisterham omnibus, whom he had seen but once, and that on the day of his arrival.

'And what I recommend you for the present, is, don't talk, Mr Landless. You'll find a friend waiting for you, at the high road – gone ahead by the other way when we split into two parties – and you had much better say nothing till you come up with him. Bring that stick along, somebody else, and let's be moving!'

Utterly bewildered, Neville stared around him and said not a word. Walking between his two conductors, who held his arms in theirs, he went on, as in a dream: until they came again into the high road, and into the midst of a little group of people. The men who had turned back were among the group; and its central figures were Mr Jasper and Mr Crisparkle. Neville's conductors took him up to the Minor Canon, and there released him, as an act of deference to that gentleman.

'What is all this, sir? What is the matter? I feel as if I had lost my senses!' cried Neville, the group closing in around him.

'Where is my nephew?' asked Mr Jasper, wildly.

'Where is your nephew?' repeated Neville. 'Why do you ask me?'

'I ask you,' retorted Jasper, 'because you were the last person in his company, and he is not to be found.'

'Not to be found!' cried Neville, aghast.

'Stay, stay,' said Mr Crisparkle. 'Permit me, Jasper. Mr Neville, you are confounded; collect your thoughts; it is of great importance that you should collect your thoughts; attend to me.'

'I will try, sir, but I seem mad.'

'You left Mr Jasper's last night, with Edwin Drood?'

'Yes.'

'At what hour?'

'Was it at twelve o'clock?' asked Neville, with his hand to his confused head, and appealing to Jasper.

'Quite right,' said Mr Crisparkle; 'the hour Mr Jasper has already named to me. You went down to the river together?'

'Undoubtedly. To see the action of the wind there.'

'What followed? How long did you stay there?'

'About ten minutes; I should say not more. We then walked together to your house, and he took leave of me at the door.'

'Did he say that he was going down to the river again?'

'No. He said that he was going straight back.'

The bystanders looked at one another, and at Mr Crisparkle. To whom Mr Jasper, who had been intensely watching Neville, said: in a low distinct suspicious voice: 'What are those stains upon his dress?'

All eyes were turned towards the blood upon his clothes.

'And here are the same stains upon this stick!' said Jasper taking it from the hand of the man who held it. 'I know the stick to be his, and he carried it last night. What does this mean?'

'In the name of God, say what it means, Neville!' urged Mr Crisparkle.

'That man and I,' said Neville, pointing out his late adversary, 'had a struggle for the stick just now, and you may see the same marks on him, sir. What was I to suppose, when I found myself molested by eight people? Could I dream of the true reason when they would give me none at all?'

They admitted that they had thought it discreet to be silent, and that the struggle had taken place. And yet the very men who had seen it, looked darkly at the smears which the bright cold air had already dried.

'We must return, Neville,' said Mr Crisparkle; 'of course you will be glad to come back to clear yourself?'

'Of course, sir.'

'Mr Landless will walk at my side,' the Minor Canon continued, looking around him. 'Come, Neville!'

They set forth on the walk back; and the others, with one

exception, straggled after them at various distances. Jasper walked on the other side of Neville, and never quitted that position. He was silent, while Mr Crisparkle more than once repeated his former questions, and while Neville repeated his former answers; also, while they both hazarded some explanatory conjectures. He was obstinately silent, because Mr Crisparkle's manner directly appealed to him to take some part in the discussion, and no appeal would move his fixed face. When they drew near to the city, and it was suggested by the Minor Canon that they might do well in calling on the Mayor at once, he assented with a stern nod; but he spake no word until they stood in Mr Sapsea's parlor.

Mr Sapsea being informed by Mr Crisparkle of the circumstances under which they desired to make a voluntary statement before him, Mr Jasper broke silence by declaring that he placed his whole reliance, humanly speaking, on Mr Sapsea's penetration. There was no conceivable reason why his nephew should have suddenly absconded, unless Mr Sapsea could suggest one, and then he would defer. There was no intelligible likelihood of his having returned to the river, and been accidentally drowned in the dark, unless it should appear likely to Mr Sapsea, and then again he would defer. He washed his hands as clean as he could of all horrible suspicions, unless it should appear to Mr Sapsea that some such were inseparable from his last companion before his disappearance (not on good terms with previously), and then, once more, he would defer. His own state of mind, he being distracted with doubts, and laboring under dismal apprehensions, was not to be safely trusted; but Mr Sapsea's was.

Mr Sapsea expressed his opinion that the case had a dark look; in short (and here his eyes rested full on Neville's countenance), an Un-English complexion. Having made this grand point, he wandered into a denser haze and maze of nonsense than even a mayor might have been expected to disport himself in, and came out of it with the brilliant discovery that to take the life of a fellow-creature was to take something that didn't belong to you. He wavered whether or no he should at once issue his warrant for the committal of Neville Landless to jail, under circumstances of grave suspicion; and he might have gone so far as to do it but for the indignant protest of the Minor Canon: who undertook for the young man's remaining in his own house, and being produced by his own hands, whenever demanded. Mr Jasper then understood Mr Sapsea to suggest that the river should be dragged, that its banks should be rigidly examined, that particulars of the disappearance should be sent to all outlying places and to London, and that placards and advertisements should be widely circulated imploring Edwin Drood, if for any unknown reason he had withdrawn himself from his uncle's home and society, to take pity on that loving kinsman's sore bereavement and distress, and somehow inform him that he was yet alive. Mr Sapsea was perfectly understood, for this was exactly his meaning (though he had said nothing about it); and measures were taken towards all these ends immediately.

It would be difficult to determine which was the more oppressed with horror and amazement: Neville Landless, or John Jasper. But that Jasper's position forced him to be active, while Neville's forced him to be passive, there would have been nothing to choose between them. Each was bowed down and broken.

With the earliest light of the next morning, men were at work upon the river, and other men – most of whom volunteered for the service – were examining the banks. All the live-long day the search went on; upon the river, with barge and pole, and drag and net; upon the muddy and rushy shore, with jack-boot, hatchet, spade, rope, dogs, and all imaginable appliances. Even at night, the river was specked with lanterns, and lurid with fires; far-off creeks, into which the tide washed as it changed, had their knots of watchers, listening to the lapping of the stream, and looking out for any burden it might bear; remote shingly causeways near the sea, and lonely points off which there was a race of water, had their unwonted flaring cressets and rough-coated figures when the next day dawned; but no trace of Edwin Drood revisited the light of the sun.

All that day, again, the search went on. Now, in barge and boat; and now ashore among the osiers, or tramping amidst mud and stakes and jagged stones in low-lying places, where solitary watermarks and signals of strange shapes showed like spectres, John Jasper worked and toiled. But to no purpose; for still no trace of Edwin Drood revisited the light of the sun.

Setting his watches for that night again, so that vigilant eyes should be kept on every change of tide, he went home exhausted.

Unkempt and disordered, bedaubed with mud that had dried upon him, and with much of his clothing torn to rags, he had but just dropped into his easy chair, when Mr Grewgious stood before him.

'This is strange news,' said Mr Grewgious.

'Strange and fearful news.'

Jasper had merely lifted up his heavy eyes to say it, and now dropped them again as he drooped, worn out, over one side of his easy chair.

Mr Grewgious smoothed his head and face, and stood looking at the fire.

'How is your ward?' asked Jasper, after a time, in a faint, fatigued voice.

'Poor little thing! You may imagine her condition.'

'Have you seen his sister?' enquired Jasper, as before.

'Whose?'

The curtness of the counter-question, and the cool slow manner in which, as he put it, Mr Grewgious moved his eyes from the fire to his companion's face, might at any other time have been exasperating. In his depression and exhaustion, Jasper merely opened his eyes to say: 'The suspected young man's.'

'Do you suspect him?' asked Mr Grewgious.

'I don't know what to think. I cannot make up my mind.'

'Nor I,' said Mr Grewgious. 'But as you spoke of him as the suspected young man, I thought you *had* made up your mind. – I have just left Miss Landless.'

'What is her state?'

'Defiance of all suspicion, and unbounded faith in her brother.'

'Poor thing!'

'However,' pursued Mr Grewgious, 'it is not of her that I came to speak. It is of my ward. I have a communication to make that will surprise you. At least, it has surprised me.'

Jasper, with a groaning sigh, turned wearily in his chair.

'Shall I put it off till to-morrow?' said Mr Grewgious. 'Mind! I warn you, that I think it will surprise you!'

More attention and concentration came into John Jasper's eyes as they caught sight of Mr Grewgious smoothing his head again, and again looking at the fire; but now, with a compressed and determined mouth.

'What is it?' demanded Jasper, becoming upright in his chair.

'To be sure,' said Mr Grewgious, provokingly slowly and internally, as he kept his eyes on the fire: 'I might have known it sooner; she gave me the opening; but I am such an exceedingly Angular man, that it never occurred to me; I took all for granted.'

'What is it?' demanded Jasper, once more.

Mr Grewgious, alternately opening and shutting the palms of his hands as he warmed them at the fire, and looking fixedly at him sideways, and never changing either his action or his look in all that followed, went on to reply.

'This young couple, the lost youth and Miss Rosa, my ward, though so long betrothed, and so long recognizing their betrothal, and so near being married –'

Mr Grewgious saw a staring white face, and two quivering white lips, in the easy chair, and saw two muddy hands gripping its sides. But for the hands, he might have thought he had never seen the face.

'– This young couple came gradually to the discovery (made on both sides pretty equally, I think), that they would be happier and better, both in their present and their future lives, as affectionate friends, or say rather as brother and sister, than as husband and wife.'

Mr Grewgious saw a lead-colored face in the easy chair, and on its surface dreadful starting drops or bubbles, as if of steel.

'This young couple formed at length the healthy resolution of interchanging their discoveries, openly, sensibly, and tenderly. They met for that purpose. After some innocent and generous talk, they agreed to dissolve their existing, and their intended, relations, for ever and ever.'

Mr Grewgious saw a ghastly figure rise, open-mouthed, from the easy chair, and lift its outspread hands towards its head.

'One of this young couple, and that one your nephew, fearful, however, that in the tenderness of your affection for him you would be bitterly disappointed by so wide a departure from his projected life, forbore to tell you the secret, for a few days, and left it to be disclosed by me, when I should come down to speak to you, and he would be gone. I speak to you, and he IS gone.'

Mr Grewgious saw the ghastly figure throw back its head, clutch its hair with its hands, and turn with a writhing action from him.

'I have now said all I have to say: except that this young couple parted, firmly, though not without tears and sorrow, on the evening when you last saw them together.'

Mr Grewgious heard a terrible shriek, and saw no ghastly figure, sitting or standing; saw nothing but a heap of torn and miry clothes upon the floor.

Not changing his action even then, he opened and shut the palms of his hands as he warmed them, and looked down at it.

CHAPTER 16

Devoted

WHEN John Jasper recovered from his fit or swoon, he found himself being tended by Mr and Mrs Tope, whom his visitor had summoned for the purpose. His visitor, wooden of aspect, sat stiffly in a chair, with his hands upon his knees, watching his recovery.

'There! You've come to, nicely now, sir,' said the tearful Mrs Tope; 'you were thoroughly worn out, and no wonder!'

'A man,' said Mr Grewgious, with his usual air of repeating a lesson, 'cannot have his rest broken, and his mind cruelly tormented, and his body overtaxed by fatigue, without being thoroughly worn out.'

'I fear I have alarmed you?' Jasper apologized faintly, when he was helped into his easy chair.

'Not at all, I thank you,' answered Mr Grewgious.

'You are too considerate.'

'Not at all, I thank you,' answered Mr Grewgious again.

'You must take some wine, sir,' said Mrs Tope, 'and the jelly that I had ready for you, and that you wouldn't put your lips to at noon, though I warned you what would come of it, you know, and you not breakfasted; and you must have a wing of the roast fowl that has been put back twenty times if it's been put back once. It shall all be on table in five minutes, and this good gentleman belike will stop and see you take it.'

This good gentleman replied with a snort, which might mean

yes, or no, or anything, or nothing, and which Mrs Tope would have found highly mystifying, but that her attention was divided by the service of the table.

'You will take something with me?' said Jasper, as the cloth was laid.

'I couldn't get a morsel down my throat, I thank you,' answered Mr Grewgious.

Jasper both ate and drank almost voraciously. Combined with the hurry in his mode of doing it, was an evident indifference to the taste of what he took, suggesting that he ate and drank to fortify himself against any other failure of the spirits, far more than to gratify his palate. Mr Grewgious in the meantime sat upright, with no expression in his face, and a hard kind of imperturbably polite protest all over him: as though he would have said, in reply to some invitation to discourse: 'I couldn't originate the faintest approach to an observation on any subject whatever, I thank you.'

'Do you know,' said Jasper, when he had pushed away his plate and glass, and had sat meditating for a few minutes: 'do you know that I find some crumbs of comfort in the communication with which you have so much amazed me?'

'*Do* you?' returned Mr Grewgious; pretty plainly adding the unspoken clause, 'I don't, I thank you!'

'After recovering from the shock of a piece of news of my dear boy, so entirely unexpected, and so destructive of all the castles I had built for him; and after having had time to think of it; yes.'

'I shall be glad to pick up your crumbs,' said Mr Grewgious, dryly.

'Is there not, or is there – if I deceive myself, tell me so, and shorten my pain – is there not, or is there, hope that, finding himself in this new position, and becoming sensitively alive to the awkward burden of explanation, in this quarter, and that, and the other, with which it would load him, he avoided the awkwardness, and took to flight?'

'Such a thing might be,' said Mr Grewgious, pondering.

'Such a thing has been. I have read of cases in which people, rather than face a seven days' wonder, and have to account for themselves to the idle and impertinent, have taken themselves away, and been long unheard of.'

'I believe such things have happened,' said Mr Grewgious, pondering still.

'When I had, and could have, no suspicion,' pursued Jasper, eagerly following the new track, 'that the dear lost boy had withheld anything from me – most of all, such a leading matter as this – what gleam of light was there for me in the whole black sky? When I supposed that his intended wife was here, and his marriage close at hand, how could I entertain the possibility of his voluntarily leaving this place, in a manner that would be so unaccountable, capricious, and cruel? But now that I know what you have told me, is there no little chink through which day pierces? Supposing him to have disappeared of his own act, is not his disappearance more accountable and less cruel? The fact of his having just parted from your ward, is in itself a sort of reason for his going away. It does not make his mysterious departure the less cruel to me, it is true; but it relieves it of cruelty to her.'

Mr Grewgious could not but assent to this.

'And even as to me,' continued Jasper, still pursuing the new track, with ardor, and, as he did so, brightening with hope: 'he knew that you were coming to me; he knew that you were entrusted to tell me what you have told me; if your doing so has wakened a new train of thought in my perplexed mind, it reasonably follows that, from the same premises, he might have foreseen the inferences that I should draw. Grant that he did foresee them; and even the cruelty to me – and who am I! – John Jasper, Music Master! – vanishes.'

Once more, Mr Grewgious could not but assent to this.

'I have had my distrusts, and terrible distrusts they have been,' said Jasper; 'but your disclosure, overpowering as it was at first – showing me that my own dear boy had had a great disappointing reservation from me, who so fondly loved him – kindles hope within me. You do not extinguish it when I state it, but admit it to be a reasonable hope. I begin to believe it possible;' here he clasped his hands: 'that he may have disappeared from among us of his own accord, and that he may yet be alive and well!'

Mr Crisparkle came in at the moment. To whom Mr Jasper repeated:

'I begin to believe it possible that he may have disappeared of his own accord, and may yet be alive and well!'

Mr Crisparkle taking a seat, and enquiring: 'Why so?' Mr
Jasper repeated the arguments he had just set forth. If they had
been less plausible than they were, the good Minor Canon's mind
would have been in a state of preparation to receive them, as ex-
culpatory of his unfortunate pupil. But he, too, did really attach
great importance to the lost young man's having been, so immediately before his disappearance, placed in a new and em-
barrassing relation towards every one acquainted with his projects
and affairs; and the fact seemed to him to present the question in a
new light.

'I stated to Mr Sapsea, when we waited on him,' said Jasper: as
he really had done: 'that there was no quarrel or difference between
the two young men at their last meeting. We all know that their
first meeting was, unfortunately, very far from amicable; but all
went smoothly and quietly when they were last together at my
house. My dear boy was not in his usual spirits; he was depressed –
I noticed that – and I am bound henceforth to dwell upon the
circumstance the more now that I know there was a special reason
for his being depressed: a reason, moreover, which may possibly
have induced him to absent himself.'

'I pray to Heaven it may turn out so!' exclaimed Mr Crisparkle.

'*I* pray to Heaven it may turn out so!' repeated Jasper. 'You
know – and Mr Grewgious should now know likewise – that I
took a great prepossession against Mr Neville Landless, arising
out of his furious conduct on that first occasion. You know that I
came to you, extremely apprehensive, on my dear boy's behalf,
of his mad violence. You know that I even entered in my Diary,
and showed the entry to you, that I had dark forebodings against
him. Mr Grewgious ought to be possessed of the whole case. He
shall not, through any suppression of mine, be informed of a part
of it, and kept in ignorance of another part of it. I wish him to be
good enough to understand that the communication he had made
to me has hopefully influenced my mind, in spite of its having been,
before this mysterious occurrence took place, profoundly impressed
against young Landless.'

This fairness troubled the Minor Canon much. He felt that he
was not as open in his own dealing. He charged against himself
reproachfully that he had suppressed, so far, the two points of a
second strong outbreak of temper against Edwin Drood on the

part of Neville, and of the passion of jealousy having, to his own certain knowledge, flamed up in Neville's breast against him. He was convinced of Neville's innocence of any part in the ugly disappearance, and yet so many little circumstances combined so wofully against him, that he dreaded to add two more to their cumulative weight. He was among the truest of men; but he had been balancing in his mind, much to its distress, whether his volunteering to tell these two fragments of truth, at this time, would not be tantamount to a piecing together of falsehood in the place of truth.

However, here was a model before him. He hesitated no longer. Addressing Mr Grewgious, as one placed in authority by the revelation he had brought to bear on the mystery (and surpassingly Angular Mr Grewgious became when he found himself in that unexpected position), Mr Crisparkle bore his testimony to Mr Jasper's strict sense of justice, and, expressing his absolute confidence in the complete clearance of his pupil from the least taint of suspicion, sooner or later, avowed that his confidence in that young gentleman had been formed, in spite of his confidential knowledge that his temper was of the hottest and fiercest, and that it was directly incensed against Mr Jasper's nephew, by the circumstance of his romantically supposing himself to be enamored of the same young lady. The sanguine reaction manifest in Mr Jasper was proof even against this unlooked-for declaration. It turned him paler; but he repeated that he would cling to the hope he had derived from Mr Grewgious; and that if no trace of his dear boy were found, leading to the dreadful inference that he had been made away with, he would cherish unto the last stretch of possibility the idea, that he might have absconded of his own wild will.

Now, it fell out that Mr Crisparkle, going away from this conference still very uneasy in his mind, and very much troubled on behalf of the young man whom he held as a kind of prisoner in his own house, took a memorable night walk.

He walked to Cloisterham Weir.

He often did so, and consequently there was nothing remarkable in his footsteps tending that way. But the preoccupation of his mind so hindered him from planning any walk, or taking heed of the objects he passed, that his first consciousness of being near the Weir was derived from the sound of the falling water close at hand.

'How did I come here!'[1] was his first thought, as he stopped.

'Why did I come here!' was his second.

Then he stood intently listening to the water. A familiar passage in his reading, about airy tongues that syllable men's names,[2] rose so unbidden to his ear, that he put it from him with his hand, as if it were tangible.

It was starlight. The Weir was full two miles above the spot to which the young men had repaired to watch the storm. No search had been made up here, for the tide had been running strongly down, at that time of the night of Christmas Eve, and the likeliest places for the discovery of a body, if a fatal accident had happened under such circumstances, all lay – both when the tide ebbed, and when it flowed again – between that spot and the sea. The water came over the Weir, with its usual sound on a cold starlight night, and little could be seen of it; yet Mr Crisparkle had a strange idea that something unusual hung about the place.

He reasoned with himself: What was it? Where was it? Put it to the proof. Which sense did it address?

No sense reported anything unusual there. He listened again, and his sense of hearing again checked the water coming over the Weir, with its usual sound on a cold starlight night.

Knowing very well that the mystery with which his mind was occupied, might of itself give the place this haunted air, he strained those hawk's eyes of his for the correction of his sight. He got closer to the Weir, and peered at its well-known posts and timbers. Nothing in the least unusual was remotely shadowed forth. But he resolved that he would come back early in the morning.

The Weir ran through his broken sleep, all night, and he was back again at sunrise. It was a bright frosty morning. The whole composition before him, when he stood where he had stood last night, was clearly discernible in its minutest details. He had surveyed it closely for some minutes, and was about to withdraw his eyes, when they were attracted keenly to one spot.

He turned his back upon the Weir, and looked far away at the sky, and at the earth, and then looked again at that one spot. It caught his sight again immediately, and he concentrated his vision upon it. He could not lose it now, though it was but such a speck in the landscape. It fascinated his sight. His hands began plucking off his coat. For it struck him that at that spot – a corner of the

Weir – something glistened, which did not move and come over with the glistening water-drops, but remained stationary.

He assured himself of this, he threw off his clothes, he plunged into the icy water, and swam for the spot. Climbing the timbers, he took from them, caught among their interstices by its chain, a gold watch, bearing engraved upon its back, E. D.

He brought the watch to the bank, swam to the Weir again, climbed it, and dived off. He knew every hole and corner of all the depths, and dived and dived and dived, until he could bear the cold no more. His notion was, that he would find the body; he only found a shirt-pin sticking in some mud and ooze.

With these discoveries he returned to Cloisterham, and, taking Neville Landless with him, went straight to the Mayor. Mr Jasper was sent for, the watch and shirt-pin were identified, Neville was detained, and the wildest frenzy and fatuity of evil report arose against him. He was of that vindictive and violent nature, that but for his poor sister, who alone had influence over him, and out of whose sight he was never to be trusted, he would be in the daily commission of murder. Before coming to England he had caused to be whipped to death sundry 'Natives' – nomadic persons, encamping now in Asia, now in Africa, now in the West Indies, and now at the North Pole – vaguely supposed in Cloisterham to be always black, always of great virtue, always calling themselves Me, and everybody else Massa or Missie (according to sex), and always reading tracts of the obscurest meaning, in broken English, but always accurately understanding them in the purest mother tongue. He had nearly brought Mrs Crisparkle's grey hairs with sorrow to the grave. (Those original expressions were Mr Sapsea's.) He had repeatedly said he would have Mr Crisparkle's life. He had repeatedly said he would have everybody's life, and become in effect the last man. He had been brought down to Cloisterham, from London, by an eminent Philanthropist, and why? Because that Philanthropist had expressly declared: 'I owe it to my fellow-creatures that he should be, in the words of BENTHAM, where he is the cause of the greatest danger to the smallest number.'[3]

These dropping shots from the blunderbusses of blunder-headedness might not have hit him in a vital place. But he had to stand against a trained and well-directed fire of arms of precision too. He had notoriously threatened the lost young man, and had,

according to the showing of his own faithful friend and tutor who
strove so hard for him, a cause of bitter animosity (created by
himself, and stated by himself), against that ill-starred fellow. He
had armed himself with an offensive weapon for the fatal night,
and he had gone off early in the morning, after making preparations
for departure. He had been found with traces of blood on him;
truly, they might have been wholly caused as he represented, but
they might not, also. On a search-warrant being issued for the
examination of his room, clothes, and so forth, it was discovered
that he had destroyed all his papers, and rearranged all his possessions, on the very afternoon of the disappearance. The watch
found at the Weir was challenged by the jeweller as one he had
wound and set for Edwin Drood, at twenty minutes past two on
that same afternoon; and it had run down, before being cast into
the water; and it was the jeweller's positive opinion that it had
never been re-wound. This would justify the hypothesis that the
watch was taken from him not long after he left Mr Jasper's house
at midnight, in company with the last person seen with him, and
that it had been thrown away after being retained some hours. Why
thrown away? If he had been murdered, and so artfully disfigured,
or concealed, or both, as that the murderer hoped identification to
be impossible, except from something that he wore, assuredly the
murderer would seek to remove from the body the most lasting,
the best known, and the most easily recognizable, things upon it.
Those things would be the watch and shirt-pin. As to his opportunities of casting them into the river; if he were the object of
these suspicions, they were easy. For, he had been seen by many
persons, wandering about on that side of the city – indeed on all
sides of it – in a miserable and seemingly half-distracted manner.
As to the choice of the spot, obviously such criminating evidence
had better take its chance of being found anywhere, rather than
upon himself, or in his possession. Concerning the reconciliatory
nature of the appointed meeting between the two young men, very
little could be made of that in young Landless's favor; for it
distinctly appeared that the meeting originated, not with him, but
with Mr Crisparkle, and that it had been urged on by Mr Crisparkle;
and who could say how unwillingly, or in what ill-conditioned
mood, his enforced pupil had gone to it? The more his case was
looked into, the weaker it became in every point. Even the broad

suggestion that the lost young man had absconded, was rendered additionally improbable on the showing of the young lady from whom he had so lately parted; for, what did she say, with great earnestness and sorrow, when interrogated? That he had, expressly and enthusiastically, planned with her, that he would await the arrival of her guardian, Mr Grewgious. And yet, be it observed, he disappeared before that gentleman appeared.

On the suspicions thus urged and supported, Neville was detained and re-detained, and the search was pressed on every hand, and Jasper labored night and day. But nothing more was found. No discovery being made, which proved the lost man to be dead, it at length became necessary to release the person suspected of having made away with him. Neville was set at large. Then, a consequence ensued which Mr Crisparkle had too well foreseen. Neville must leave the place, for the place shunned him and cast him out. Even had it not been so, the dear old china shepherdess would have worried herself to death with fears for her son, and with general trepidation occasioned by their having such an inmate. Even had that not been so, the authority to which the Minor Canon deferred officially, would have settled the point.

'Mr Crisparkle,' quoth the Dean, 'human justice may err, but it must act according to its lights. The days of taking sanctuary are past. This young man must not take sanctuary with us.'

'You mean that he must leave my house, sir?'

'Mr Crisparkle,' returned the prudent Dean, 'I claim no authority in your house. I merely confer with you, on the painful necessity you find yourself under, of depriving this young man of the great advantages of your counsel and instruction.'

'It is very lamentable, sir,' Mr Crisparkle represented.

'Very much so,' the Dean assented.

'And if it be a necessity –' Mr Crisparkle faltered.

'As you unfortunately find it to be,' returned the Dean.

Mr Crisparkle bowed submissively: 'It is hard to prejudge his case, sir, but I am sensible that –'

'Just so. Perfectly. As you say, Mr Crisparkle,' interposed the Dean, nodding his head smoothly, 'there is nothing else to be done. No doubt, no doubt. There is no alternative, as your good sense has discovered.'

'I am entirely satisfied of his perfect innocence, sir, nevertheless.'

'We-e-ell!' said the Dean, in a more confidential tone, and slightly glancing around him, 'I would not say so, generally. Not
generally. Enough of suspicion attaches to him to – no, I think I
would not say so, generally.'

Mr Crisparkle bowed again.

'It does not become us, perhaps,' pursued the Dean, 'to be
partizans. Not partizans. We clergy keep our hearts warm and our
heads cool, and we hold a judicious middle course.'

'I hope you do not object, sir, to my having stated in public,
emphatically, that he will reappear here, whenever any new
suspicion may be awakened, or any new circumstance may come
to light in this extraordinary matter?'

'Not at all,' returned the Dean. 'And yet, do you know, I
don't think,' with a very nice and neat emphasis on those two
words: 'I *don't think* I would state it emphatically. State it?
Ye-e-es! But emphatically? No-o-o. I *think* not. In point of fact,
Mr Crisparkle, keeping our hearts warm and our heads cool, we
clergy need do nothing emphatically.'

So Minor Canon Row knew Neville Landless no more; and he
went whithersoever he would, or could, with a blight upon his
name and fame.

It was not until then that John Jasper silently resumed his place
in the choir. Haggard and red-eyed, his hopes plainly had deserted
him, his sanguine mood was gone, and all his worst misgivings
had come back. A day or two afterwards, while unrobing, he took
his Diary from a pocket of his coat, turned the leaves, and with an
impressive look, and without one spoken word, handed this
entry to Mr Crisparkle to read:

My dear boy is murdered. The discovery of the watch and shirt-pin
convinces me that he was murdered that night, and that his jewellery
was taken from him to prevent identification by its means. All the
delusive hopes I had founded on his separation from his betrothed
wife, I give to the winds. They perish before this fatal discovery. I now
swear, and record the oath on this page, That I nevermore will discuss
this mystery with any human creature, until I hold the clue to it in my
hand. That I never will relax in my secresy or in my search. That I
will fasten the crime of the murder of my dear dead boy upon the
murderer. And That I devote myself to his destruction.

*

CHAPTER 17

Philanthropy, Professional and Unprofessional[1]

FULL half a year had come and gone, and Mr Crisparkle sat in a waiting-room in the London chief offices of the Haven of Philanthropy, until he could have audience of Mr Honeythunder.

In his college-days of athletic exercises, Mr Crisparkle had known professors of the Noble Art of fisticuffs, and had attended two or three of their gloved gatherings. He had now an opportunity of observing that as to the phrenological formation[2] of the backs of their heads, the Professing Philanthropists were uncommonly like the Pugilists. In the development of all those organs which constitute, or attend, a propensity to 'pitch into' your fellow-creatures, the Philanthropists were remarkably favored. There were several Professors passing in and out, with exactly the aggressive air upon them of being ready for a turn-up with any Novice who might happen to be on hand, that Mr Crisparkle well remembered in the circles of the Fancy. Preparations were in progress for a moral little Mill somewhere on the rural circuit, and other Professors were backing this or that Heavy-Weight as good for such or such speech-making hits, so very much after the manner of the sporting publicans, that the intended Resolutions might have been Rounds. In an official manager of these displays much celebrated for his platform tactics, Mr Crisparkle recognized (in a suit of black) the counterpart of a deceased benefactor of his species, an eminent public character, once known to fame as Frosty-faced Fogo, who in days of yore superintended the formation of the magic circle with the ropes and stakes. There were only three conditions of resemblance wanting between these Professors and those. Firstly, the Philanthropists were in very bad training: much too fleshy, and presenting, both in face and figure, a superabundance of what is known to Pugilistic Experts as Suet Pudding. Secondly, the Philanthropists had not the good temper of the Pugilists, and used worse language. Thirdly, their fighting code stood in great need of revision, as empowering them not only to bore their man to the ropes, but to bore him to the confines of distraction; also to hit him when he was down, hit him anywhere and anyhow, kick him, stamp upon him, gouge him, and maul him behind his back without mercy. In these last particulars the Professors of the Noble Art were much nobler than the Professors of Philanthropy.

Mr Crisparkle was so completely lost in musing on these similarities and dissimilarities, at the same time watching the crowd which came and went, always, as it seemed, on errands of antagonistically snatching something from somebody, and never giving anything to anybody: that his name was twice called before he heard it. On his at length responding, he was shown by a miserably shabby and underpaid stipendiary Philanthropist (who could hardly have done worse if he had taken service with a declared enemy of the human race) to Mr Honeythunder's room.

'Sir,' said Mr Honeythunder, in his tremendous voice, like a schoolmaster issuing orders to a boy of whom he had a bad opinion, 'sit down.'

Mr Crisparkle seated himself.

Mr Honeythunder, having signed the remaining few score of a few thousand circulars, calling upon a corresponding number of families without means to come forward, stump up instantly, and be Philanthropists, or go to the Devil, another shabby stipendiary Philanthropist (highly disinterested, if in earnest) gathered these into a basket and walked off with them.

'Now, Mr Crisparkle,' said Mr Honeythunder, turning his chair half round towards him when they were alone, and squaring his arms with his hands on his knees, and his brows knitted, as if he added, I am going to make short work of *you:* 'Now, Mr Crisparkle, we entertain different views, you and I, sir, of the sanctity of human life.'

'Do we?' returned the Minor Canon.

'We do, sir.'

'Might I ask you,' said the Minor Canon: 'what are your views on that subject?'

'That human life is a thing to be held sacred, sir.'

'Might I ask you,' pursued the Minor Canon as before: 'what you suppose to be my views on that subject?'

'By George, sir!' returned the Philanthropist, squaring his arms still more, as he frowned on Mr Crisparkle: 'they are best known to yourself.'

'Readily admitted. But you began by saying that we took different views, you know. Therefore (or you could not say so) you must have set up some views as mine. Pray, what views *have* you set up as mine?'

'Here is a man – and a young man,' said Mr Honeythunder, as if that made the matter infinitely worse, and he could have easily borne the loss of an old one: 'swept off the face of the earth by a deed of violence. What do you call that?'

'Murder,' said the Minor Canon.

'What do you call the doer of that deed, sir?'

'A murderer,' said the Minor Canon.

'I am glad to hear you admit so much, sir,' retorted Mr Honeythunder, in his most offensive manner; 'and I candidly tell you that I didn't expect it.' Here he lowered heavily at Mr Crisparkle again.

'Be so good as to explain what you mean by those very unjustifiable expressions.'

'I don't sit here, sir,' returned the Philanthropist, raising his voice to a roar, 'to be browbeaten.'

'As the only other person present, no one can possibly know that better than I do,' returned the Minor Canon very quietly. 'But I interrupt your explanation.'

'Murder!' proceeded Mr Honeythunder, in a kind of boisterous reverie, with his platform folding of his arms, and his platform nod of abhorrent reflection after each short sentiment of a word. 'Bloodshed! Abel! Cain! I hold no terms with Cain. I repudiate with a shudder the red hand when it is offered me.'

Instead of instantly leaping into his chair and cheering himself hoarse, as the Brotherhood in public meeting assembled would infallibly have done on this cue, Mr Crisparkle merely reversed the quiet crossing of his legs, and said mildly: 'Don't let me interrupt your explanation – when you begin it.'

'The Commandments say no murder. NO murder, sir!' proceeded Mr Honeythunder, platformally pausing as if he took Mr Crisparkle to task for having distinctly asserted that they said, You may do a little murder and then leave off.

'And they also say, you shall bear no false witness,' observed Mr Crisparkle.

'Enough!' bellowed Mr Honeythunder, with a solemnity and severity that would have brought the house down at a meeting. 'E – e – nough! My late wards being now of age, and I being released from a trust which I cannot contemplate without a thrill of horror, there are the accounts which you have undertaken to accept on their behalf, and there is a statement of the balance which you have undertaken to receive, and which you cannot receive too soon. And let me tell you, sir, I wish, that as a man and a Minor Canon, you were better employed,' with a nod. 'Better employed,' with another nod. 'Bet – ter em – ployed!' with another and the three nods added up.

Mr Crisparkle rose; a little heated in the face, but with perfect command of himself.

'Mr Honeythunder,' he said, taking up the papers referred to: 'my being better or worse employed than I am at present is a matter of taste and opinion. You might think me better employed in enrolling myself a member of your Society.'

'Ay, indeed, sir!' retorted Mr Honeythunder, shaking his head in a threatening manner. 'It would have been better for you if you had done that long ago!'

'I think otherwise.'

'Or,' said Mr Honeythunder, shaking his head again, 'I might think one of your profession better employed in devoting himself to the discovery and punishment of guilt than in leaving that duty to be undertaken by a layman.'

'I may regard my profession from a point of view which teaches me that its first duty is towards those who are in necessity and tribulation, who are desolate and oppressed,'[3] said Mr Crisparkle. 'However, as I have quite clearly satisfied myself that it is no part of my profession to make professions, I say no more of that. But I owe it to Mr Neville, and to Mr Neville's sister (and in a much lower degree to myself), to say to you that I *know* I was in the full possession and understanding of Mr Neville's mind and heart at the time of this occurrence; and that, without in the least coloring or concealing what was to be deplored in him and required to be corrected, I feel certain that his tale is true. Feeling that certainty, I befriend him. As long as that certainty shall last, I will befriend him. And if any consideration could shake me in this resolve, I should be so ashamed of myself for my meanness that no man's good opinion – no, nor no woman's – so gained, could compensate me for the loss of my own.'

Good fellow! Manly fellow! And he was so modest, too. There was no more self-assertion in the Minor Canon than in the schoolboy who had stood in the breezy playing-fields keeping a wicket. He was simply and staunchly true to his duty alike in the large case and in the small. So all true souls ever are. So every true soul ever was, ever is, and ever will be. There is nothing little to the really great in spirit.

'Then who do you make out did the deed?' asked Mr Honeythunder, turning on him abruptly.

'Heaven forbid,' said Mr Crisparkle, 'that in my desire to clear one man I should lightly criminate another! I accuse no one.'

'Tcha!' ejaculated Mr Honeythunder with great disgust; for this was by no means the principle on which the Philanthropic Brotherhood usually proceeded. 'And, sir, you are not a disinterested witness, we must bear in mind.'

'How am I an interested one?' enquired Mr Crisparkle, smiling innocently, at a loss to imagine.

'There was a certain stipend, sir, paid to you for your pupil, which may have warped your judgment a bit,' said Mr Honeythunder, coarsely.

'Perhaps I expect to retain it still?' Mr Crisparkle returned, enlightened; 'do you mean that too?'

'Well, sir,' returned the professional Philanthropist, getting up, and thrusting his hands down into his trousers pockets; 'I don't go about measuring people for caps. If people find I have any about me that fit 'em, they can put 'em on and wear 'em, if they like. That's their look out: not mine.'

Mr Crisparkle eyed him with a just indignation, and took him to task thus:

'Mr Honeythunder, I hoped when I came in here that I might be under no necessity of commenting on the introduction of platform manners or platform manœuvres among the decent forbearances of private life. But you have given me such a specimen of both, that I should be a fit subject for both if I remained silent respecting them. They are detestable.'

'They don't suit *you*, I dare say, sir.'

'They are,' repeated Mr Crisparkle, without noticing the interruption, 'detestable. They violate equally the justice that should belong to Christians, and the restraints that should belong to gentlemen. You assume a great crime to have been committed by one whom I, acquainted with the attendant circumstances, and having numerous reasons on my side, devoutly believe to be innocent of it. Because I differ from you on that vital point, what is your platform resource? Instantly to turn upon me, charging that I have no sense of the enormity of the crime itself, but am its aider and abettor! So, another time – taking me as representing your opponent in other cases – you set up a platform credulity: a moved and seconded and carried unanimously profession of faith in some ridiculous delusion or mischievous imposition. I decline to believe it, and you fall back upon your platform resource of proclaiming that I believe nothing; that because I will not bow down to a false God of your making, I deny the true God! Another time, you make the platform discovery that War is a calamity, and you propose to abolish it by a string of twisted resolutions tossed into the air like the tail of a kite. I do not admit the discovery to be yours in the least, and I have not a grain of faith in your remedy. Again, your platform resource of representing me as revelling in the horrors of a battle field like a fiend incarnate! Another time, in another of your undiscriminating platform rushes, you would punish the sober for the drunken. I claim consideration for the comfort, convenience, and refreshment of the sober; and you presently make platform proclamation that I have a depraved desire to turn Heaven's creatures into swine and wild beasts! In all such cases your movers, and your seconders, and your supporters – your regular Professors of all degrees – run amuck like so many mad Malays; habitually attributing the lowest and basest motives with the utmost recklessness (let me call your attention to a recent instance in yourself for which you should blush), and quoting figures which you know to be as wilfully onesided as a statement of any complicated account that should be all Creditor side and no Debtor, or all Debtor side and no Creditor. Therefore it is, Mr Honeythunder, that I consider the platform a sufficiently bad example and a sufficiently bad school, even in public life; but hold that, carried into private life, it becomes an unendurable nuisance.'

'These are strong words, sir!' exclaimed the Philanthropist.

'I hope so,' said Mr Crisparkle. 'Good morning.'

He walked out of the Haven at a great rate, but soon fell into his regular brisk pace, and soon had a smile upon his face as he went along, wondering what the china shepherdess would have said if she had seen him pounding Mr Honeythunder in the late little lively affair. For Mr Crisparkle had just enough of harmless vanity to hope that he had hit hard, and to glow with the belief that he had trimmed the Philanthropic jacket pretty handsomely.

He took himself to Staple Inn, but not to P. J. T. and Mr Grewgious. Full many a creaking stair he climbed before he reached some attic rooms in a corner, turned the latch of their unbolted door, and stood beside the table of Neville Landless.

An air of retreat and solitude hung about the rooms, and about their inhabitant. He was much worn, and so were they. Their sloping ceilings, cumbrous rusty locks and grates, and heavy wooden bins and beams, slowly mouldering withal, had a prisonous look, and he had the haggard face of a prisoner. Yet the sunlight shone in at the ugly garret window, which had a penthouse to itself thrust out among the tiles; and on the cracked and smoke-blackened parapet beyond, some of the deluded sparrows of the place rheumatically hopped, like little feathered cripples who had left their crutches in their nests; and there was a play of living leaves at hand that changed the air, and made an imperfect sort of music in it that would have been melody in the country.

The rooms were sparely furnished, but with good store of books. Everything expressed the abode of a poor student. That Mr Crisparkle had been either chooser, lender, or donor of the books, or that he combined the three characters, might have been easily seen in the friendly beam of his eyes upon them as he entered.

'How goes it, Neville?'

'I am in good heart, Mr Crisparkle, and working away.'

'I wish your eyes were not quite so large and not quite so bright,' said the Minor Canon, slowly releasing the hand he had taken in his.

'They brighten at the sight of you,' returned Neville. 'If you were to fall away from me, they would soon be dull enough.'

'Rally, rally!' urged the other, in a stimulating tone. 'Fight for it, Neville!'

'If I were dying, I feel as if a word from you would rally me; if my pulse had stopped, I feel as if your touch would make it beat again,' said Neville. 'But I *have* rallied, and am doing famously.'

Mr Crisparkle turned him with his face a little more towards the light.

'I want to see a ruddier touch here, Neville,' he said, indicating his own healthy cheek by way of pattern; 'I want more sun to shine upon you.'

Neville drooped suddenly, as he replied in a lowered voice: 'I am not hardy enough for that, yet. I may become so, but I cannot bear it yet. If you had gone through those Cloisterham streets as I did; if you had seen, as I did, those averted eyes, and the better sort of people silently giving me too much room to pass, that I might not touch them or come near them, you wouldn't think it quite unreasonable that I cannot go about in the daylight.'

'My poor fellow!' said the Minor Canon, in a tone so purely sympathetic that the young man caught his hand: 'I never said it was unreasonable: never thought so. But I should like you to do it.'

'And that would give me the strongest motive to do it. But I cannot yet. I cannot persuade myself that the eyes of even the stream of strangers I pass in this vast city look at me without suspicion. I feel marked and tainted, even when I go out – as I do only – at night. But the darkness covers me then, and I take courage from it.'

Mr Crisparkle laid a hand upon his shoulder, and stood looking down at him.

'If I could have changed my name,' said Neville, 'I would have done so. But as you wisely pointed out to me, I can't do that, for it would look like guilt. If I could have gone to some distant place, I might have found relief in that, but the thing is not to be thought of, for the same reason. Hiding and escaping would be the construction in either case. It seems a little hard to be so tied to a stake, and innocent; but I don't complain.'

'And you must expect no miracle to help you, Neville,' said Mr Crisparkle, compassionately.

'No, sir, I know that. The ordinary fulness of time and circumstance is all I have to trust to.'

'It will right you at last, Neville.'

'So I believe, and I hope I may live to know it.'

But perceiving that the despondent mood into which he was falling cast a shadow on the Minor Canon, and (it may be) feeling that the broad hand upon his shoulder was not then quite as steady as its own natural strength had rendered it when it first touched him just now, he brightened and said:

'Excellent circumstances for study, anyhow! and you know, Mr Crisparkle, what need I have of study in all ways. Not to mention that you have advised me to study for the difficult profession of the law, specially, and that of course I am guiding myself by the advice of such a friend and helper. Such a good friend and helper!'

He took the fortifying hand from his shoulder, and kissed it. Mr Crisparkle beamed at the books, but not so brightly as when he had entered.

'I gather from your silence on the subject that my late guardian is adverse, Mr Crisparkle?'

The Minor Canon answered: 'Your late guardian is a – a most unreasonable person, and it signifies nothing to any reasonable person whether he is *ad*verse or *per*verse, or the *re*verse.'

'Well for me that I have enough with economy to live upon,' sighed Neville, half wearily and half cheerily, 'while I wait to be learned, and wait to be righted! Else I might have proved the proverb, that while the grass grows, the steed starves!'

He opened some books as he said it, and was soon immersed in their interleaved and annotated passages, while Mr Crisparkle sat beside him, expounding, correcting, and advising. The Minor Canon's Cathedral duties made these visits of his difficult to accomplish, and only to be compassed at intervals of many weeks. But they were as serviceable as they were precious to Neville Landless.

When they had got through such studies as they had in hand, they stood leaning on the window-sill, and looking down upon the patch of garden. 'Next week,' said Mr Crisparkle, 'you will cease to be alone, and will have a devoted companion.'

'And yet,' returned Neville, 'this seems an uncongenial place to bring my sister to!'

'I don't think so,' said the Minor Canon. 'There is duty to be done here; and there are womanly feeling, sense, and courage wanted here.'

'I meant,' explained Neville, 'that the surroundings are so dull and unwomanly, and that Helena can have no suitable friend or society here.'

'You have only to remember,' said Mr Crisparkle, 'that you are here yourself, and that she has to draw you into the sunlight.'

They were silent for a little while, and then Mr Crisparkle began anew.

'When we first spoke together, Neville, you told me that your sister had risen out of the disadvantages of your past lives as superior to you as the tower of Cloisterham Cathedral is higher than the chimneys of Minor Canon Corner. Do you remember that?'

'Right well!'

'I was inclined to think it at the time an enthusiastic flight. No matter what I think it now. What I would emphasize is, that under the head of Pride your sister is a great and opportune example to you.'

'Under *all* heads that are included in the composition of a fine character, she is.'

'Say so; but take this one. Your sister has learnt how to govern what is proud in her nature. She can dominate it even when it is wounded through her sympathy with you. No doubt she has suffered deeply in those same streets where you suffered deeply. No doubt her life is darkened by the cloud that darkens yours. But bending her pride into a grand composure that is not haughty or aggressive, but is a sustained confidence in you and in the truth, she has won her way through those streets until she passes along them as high in the general respect as any one who treads them. Every day and hour of her life since Edwin Drood's disappearance, she has faced malignity and folly – for you – as only a brave nature well directed can. So it will be with her to the end. Another and weaker kind of pride might sink broken-hearted, but never such a pride as hers: which knows no shrinking, and can get no mastery of her.'

The pale cheek beside him flushed under the comparison and the hint implied in it. 'I will do all I can to imitate her,' said Neville.

'Do so, and be a truly brave man as she is a truly brave woman,' answered Mr Crisparkle, stoutly. 'It is growing dark. Will you go my way with me, when it is quite dark? Mind! It is not I who wait for darkness.'

Neville replied that he would accompany him directly. But Mr Crisparkle said he had a moment's call to make on Mr Grewgious as an act of courtesy, and would run across to that gentleman's chambers, and rejoin Neville on his own doorstep, if he would come down there to meet him.

Mr Grewgious, bolt upright as usual, sat taking his wine in the dusk at his open window; his wineglass and decanter on the round table at his elbow; himself and his legs on the windowseat; only one hinge in his whole body, like a bootjack.

'How do you do, reverend sir?' said Mr Grewgious, with abundant offers of hospitality, which were as cordially declined as made. 'And how is your charge getting on over the way in the set that I had the pleasure of recommending to you as vacant and eligible?'

Mr Crisparkle replied suitably.

'I am glad you approve of them,' said Mr Grewgious, 'because I entertain a sort of fancy for having him under my eye.'

As Mr Grewgious had to turn his eye up considerably, before he could see the chambers, the phrase was to be taken figuratively and not literally.

'And how did you leave Mr Jasper, reverend sir?' said Mr Grewgious.

Mr Crisparkle had left him pretty well.

'And where did you leave Mr Jasper, reverend sir?'

Mr Crisparkle had left him at Cloisterham.

'And when did you leave Mr Jasper, reverend sir?'

That morning.

'Umps!' said Mr Grewgious. 'He didn't say he was coming, perhaps?'

'Coming where?'

'Anywhere, for instance?' said Mr Grewgious.

'No.'

'Because here he is,' said Mr Grewgious, who had asked all these questions, with his preoccupied glance directed out at window. 'And he don't look agreeable, does he?'

Mr Crisparkle was craning towards the window, when Mr Grewgious added:

'If you will kindly step round here behind me, in the gloom of the room, and will cast your eye at the second-floor landing window, in yonder house, I think you will hardly fail to see a slinking individual in whom I recognize our local friend.'

'You are right!' cried Mr Crisparkle.

'Umps!' said Mr Grewgious. Then he added, turning his face so abruptly that his head nearly came into collision with Mr Crisparkle's: 'what should you say that our local friend was up to?'

The last passage he had been shown in the Diary returned on Mr Crisparkle's mind with the force of a strong recoil, and he asked Mr Grewgious if he thought it possible that Neville was to be harassed by the keeping of a watch upon him?

'A watch,' repeated Mr Grewgious, musingly. 'Aye!'

'Which would not only of itself haunt and torture his life,' said Mr Crisparkle, warmly, 'but would expose him to the torment of a perpetually reviving suspicion, whatever he might do, or wherever he might go?'

'Aye!' said Mr Grewgious, musingly still. 'Do I see him waiting for you?'

'No doubt you do.'

'Then *would* you have the goodness to excuse my getting up to see you out, and to go out to join him, and to go the way that you were going, and to take no notice of our local friend?' said Mr Grewgious. 'I entertain a sort of fancy for having *him* under my eye to-night, do you know?'

Mr Crisparkle, with a significant nod, complied, and rejoining Neville, went away with him. They dined together and parted at the yet unfinished and undeveloped railway station: Mr Crisparkle to get home; Neville to walk the streets, cross the bridges, make a wide round of the city in the friendly darkness, and tire himself out.

It was midnight when he returned from his solitary expedition, and climbed his staircase. The night was hot, and the windows of the staircase were all wide open. Coming to the top, it gave him a passing chill of surprise (there being no rooms but his up there) to find a stranger sitting on the window-sill, more after the manner of a venturesome glazier than an amateur ordinarily careful of his neck; in fact, so much more outside the window than inside, as to suggest the thought that he must have come up by the water-spout instead of the stairs.

The stranger said nothing until Neville put his key in his door;

then, seeming to make sure of his identity from the action, he spoke:

'I beg your pardon,' he said, coming from the window with a frank and smiling air, and a prepossessing address; 'the beans.'

Neville was quite at a loss.

'Runners,' said the visitor. 'Scarlet. Next door at the back.'

'Oh!' returned Neville. 'And the mignonette and wallflower?'

'The same,' said the visitor.

'Pray walk in.'

'Thank you.'

Neville lighted his candles, and the visitor sat down. A handsome gentleman, with a young face, but with an older figure in its robustness and its breadth of shoulder; say a man of eight-and-twenty, or at the utmost thirty: so extremely sunburnt that the contrast between his brown visage and the white forehead shaded out of doors by his hat, and the glimpse of white throat below the neckerchief, would have been almost ludicrous but for his broad temples, bright blue eyes, clustering brown hair, and laughing teeth.

'I have noticed,' said he; '– my name is Tartar.'

Neville inclined his head.

'I have noticed (excuse me) that you shut yourself up a good deal, and that you seem to like my garden aloft here. If you would like a little more of it, I could throw out a few lines and stays between my windows and yours, which the runners would take to directly. And I have some boxes, both of mignonette and wallflower, that I could shove on along the gutter (with a boat-hook I have by me) to your windows, and draw back again when they wanted watering or gardening, and shove on again when they were ship-shape, so that they would cause you no trouble. I couldn't take this liberty without asking your permission, so I venture to ask it. Tartar, corresponding set, next door.'

'You are very kind.'

'Not at all. I beg you will not think so. I ought to apologize for looking in so late. But having noticed (excuse me) that you generally walk out at night, I thought I should inconvenience you least by awaiting your return. I am always afraid of inconveniencing busy men, being an idle man.'

'I should not have thought so, from your appearance.'

'No? I take it as a compliment. In fact, I was bred in the Royal Navy and was First Lieutenant when I quitted it. But an uncle disappointed in the service leaving me his property on condition that I left the Navy, I accepted the fortune and resigned my commission.'

'Lately, I presume?'

'Well, I had had twelve or fifteen years of knocking about first. I came here some nine months before you; I had had one crop before you came. I chose this place, because, having served last in a little Corvette, I knew I should feel more at home where I had a constant opportunity of knocking my head against the ceiling. Besides: it would never do for a man who had been aboard ship from his boyhood to turn luxurious all at once. Besides, again: having been accustomed to a very short allowance of land all my life, I thought I'd feel my way to the command of a landed estate, by beginning in boxes.'

Whimsically as this was said, there was a touch of merry earnestness in it that made it doubly whimsical.

'However,' said the Lieutenant, 'I have talked quite enough about myself. It is not my way, I hope; it has merely been to present myself to you naturally. If you will allow me to take the liberty I have described, it will be a charity, for it will give me something more to do. And you are not to suppose that it will entail any interruption or intrusion on you, for that is far from my intention.'

Neville replied that he was greatly obliged, and that he thankfully accepted the kind proposal.

'I am very glad to take your windows in tow,' said the Lieutenant. 'From what I have seen of you when I have been gardening at mine, and you have been looking on, I have thought you (excuse me) rather too studious and delicate! May I ask, is your health at all affected?'

'I have undergone some mental distress,' said Neville, confused, 'which has stood me in the stead of illness.'

'Pardon me,' said Mr Tartar.

With the greatest delicacy he shifted his ground to the windows again, and asked if he could look at one of them. On Neville's opening it, he immediately sprang out, as if he were going aloft with a whole watch in an emergency, and were setting a bright example.

'For Heaven's sake!' cried Neville, 'don't do that! Where are you going, Mr Tartar? You'll be dashed to pieces!'

'All well!' said the Lieutenant, coolly looking about him on the housetop. 'All taut and trim here. Those lines and stays shall be rigged before you turn out in the morning. May I take this short cut home and say, Good-night?'

'Mr Tartar!' urged Neville. 'Pray! It makes me giddy to see you!'

But Mr Tartar, with a wave of his hand and the deftness of a cat, had already dipped through his scuttle of scarlet runners without breaking a leaf, and 'gone below.'

Mr Grewgious, his bedroom window-blind held aside with his hand, happened at that moment to have Neville's chambers under his eye for the last time that night. Fortunately his eye was on the front of the house and not the back, or this remarkable appearance and disappearance might have broken his rest as a phenomenon. But, Mr Grewgious seeing nothing there, not even a light in the windows, his gaze wandered from the windows to the stars, as if he would have read in them something that was hidden from him. Many of us would, if we could; but none of us so much as know our letters in the stars yet – or seem likely to, in this state of existence – and few languages can be read until their alphabets are mastered.

CHAPTER 18

A Settler in Cloisterham[1]

At about this time a stranger appeared in Cloisterham; a white-haired personage with black eyebrows. Being buttoned up in a tightish blue surtout, with a buff waistcoat and grey trousers, he had something of a military air; but he announced himself at the Crozier[2] (the orthodox hotel, where he put up with a portmanteau) as an idle dog who lived upon his means; and he further announced that he had a mind to take a lodging in the picturesque old city for a month or two, with a view of settling down there altogether. Both announcements were made in the coffee-room of the Crozier, to all whom it might, or might not, concern, by the stranger as he stood with his back to the empty fireplace, waiting for his fried sole, veal cutlet, and pint of sherry. And the waiter (business being chronically slack at the Crozier) represented all whom it might or might not concern, and absorbed the whole of the information.

This gentleman's white head was unusually large, and his shock of white hair was unusually thick and ample. 'I suppose, waiter,' he said, shaking his shock of hair, as a Newfoundland dog might shake his before sitting down to dinner, 'that a fair lodging for a single buffer might be found in these parts, eh?'

The waiter had no doubt of it.

'Something old,' said the gentleman. 'Take my hat down for a moment from that peg, will you? No, I don't want it; look into it. What do you see written there?'

The waiter read: 'Datchery.'

'Now you know my name,' said the gentleman; 'Dick Datchery. Hang it up again. I was saying something old is what I should prefer, something odd and out of the way; something venerable, architectural, and inconvenient.'

'We have a good choice of inconvenient lodgings in the town, sir, I think,' replied the waiter, with modest confidence in its resources that way; 'indeed, I have no doubt that we could suit you that far, however particular you might be. But a architectural lodging!' That seemed to trouble the waiter's head, and he shook it.

'Anything Cathedraly, now,' Mr Datchery suggested.

'Mr Tope,' said the waiter, brightening, as he rubbed his chin with his hand, 'would be the likeliest party to inform in that line.'

'Who is Mr Tope?' enquired Dick Datchery.

The waiter explained that he was the Verger, and that Mrs Tope had indeed once upon a time let lodgings herself – or offered to let them; but that as nobody had ever taken them, Mrs Tope's window-bill, long a Cloisterham Institution, had disappeared; probably had tumbled down one day, and never been put up again.

'I'll call on Mrs Tope,' said Mr Datchery, 'after dinner.'

So when he had done his dinner, he was duly directed to the spot, and sallied out for it. But the Crozier being an hotel of a most retiring disposition, and the waiter's directions being fatally precise, he soon became bewildered, and went boggling about and about the Cathedral Tower, whenever he could catch a glimpse of it, with a general impression on his mind that Mrs Tope's was somewhere very near it, and that, like the children in the game of hot boiled beans and very good butter, he was warm in his search when he saw the Tower, and cold when he didn't see it.

He was getting very cold indeed when he came upon a fragment of burial-ground in which an unhappy sheep was grazing. Unhappy, because a hideous small boy was stoning it through the railings, and had already lamed it in one leg, and was much excited by the benevolent sportsmanlike purpose of breaking its other three legs, and bringing it down.

"It 'im agin!' cried the boy, as the poor creature leaped; 'and made a dint in 'is wool.'

'Let him be!' said Mr Datchery. 'Don't you see you have lamed him?'

'Yer lie,' returned the sportsman. 'E went and lamed 'isself. I see 'im do it, and I giv' 'im a shy as a Widdy-warning to 'im not to go a bruisin 'is master's mutton any more.'

'Come here.'

'I won't; I'll come when yer can ketch me.'

'Stay there then, and show me which is Mr Tope's.'

'Ow can I stay here and show you which is Topeseses, when Topeseses is t'other side the Kinfreederal, and over the crossings, and round ever so many corners? Stoo-pid! Ya-a-ah!'

'Show me where it is, and I'll give you something.'

'Come on, then!'

This brisk dialogue concluded, the boy led the way, and by-and-bye stopped at some distance from an arched passage, pointing.

'Look'ee yonder. You see that there winder and door?'

'That's Tope's?'

'Yer lie; it ain't. That's Jarsper's.'

'Indeed?' said Mr Datchery, with a second look of some interest.

'Yes, and I ain't a goin no nearer 'IM, I tell yer.'

'Why not?'

"Cos I ain't a goin to be lifted off my legs and 'ave my braces bust and be choked; not if I knows it, and not by 'Im. Wait till I

set a jolly good flint a flyin at the back o' 'is jolly old 'ed some day!
Now look t'other side the harch; not the side where Jarsper's door
is; t'other side.'

'I see.'

'A little way in, o' that side, there's a low door, down two steps.
That's Topeseses with 'is name on a hoval plate.'

'Good. See here,' said Mr Datchery, producing a shilling. 'You
owe me half of this.'

'Yer lie; I don't owe yer nothing; I never seen yer.'

'I tell you you owe me half of this, because I have no sixpence
in my pocket. So the next time you meet me you shall do something else for me, to pay me.'

'All right, give us 'old.'

'What is your name, and where do you live?'

'Deputy. Travellers' Twopenny, 'cross the green.'

The boy instantly darted off with the shilling, lest Mr Datchery
should repent, but stopped at a safe distance, on the happy chance
of his being uneasy in his mind about it, to goad him with a demon
dance expressive of its irrevocability.

Mr Datchery, taking off his hat to give that shock of white hair
of his another shake, seemed quite resigned, and betook himself
whither he had been directed.

Mr Tope's official dwelling, communicating by an upper stair
with Mr Jasper's (hence Mrs Tope's attendance on that gentleman),
was of very modest proportions, and partook of the character of a
cool dungeon. Its ancient walls were massive and its rooms rather
seemed to have been dug out of them, than to have been designed
beforehand with any reference to them. The main door opened at
once on a chamber of no describable shape, with a groined roof,
which in its turn opened on another chamber of no describable
shape, with another groined roof: their windows small, and in the
thickness of the walls. These two chambers, close as to their
atmosphere and swarthy as to their illumination by natural light,
were the apartments which Mrs Tope had so long offered to an
unappreciative city. Mr Datchery, however, was more appreciative.
He found that if he sat with the main door open he would enjoy
the passing society of all comers to and fro by the gateway, and
would have light enough. He found that if Mr and Mrs Tope, living
overhead, used for their own egress and ingress a little side stair

that came plump into the Precincts by a door opening outward, to the surprise and inconvenience of a limited public of pedestrians in a narrow way, he would be alone, as in a separate residence. He found the rent moderate, and everything as quaintly inconvenient as he could desire. He agreed therefore to take the lodging then and there, and money down, possession to be had next evening, on condition that reference was permitted him to Mr Jasper as occupying the Gate House, of which, on the other side of the gateway, the Verger's hole-in-the-wall was an appanage or subsidiary part.

The poor dear gentleman was very solitary and very sad, Mrs Tope said, but she had no doubt he would 'speak for her.' Perhaps Mr Datchery had heard something of what had occurred there last winter?

Mr Datchery had as confused a knowledge of the event in question, on trying to recall it, as he well could have. He begged Mrs Tope's pardon when she found it incumbent on her to correct him in every detail of his summary of the facts, but pleaded that he was merely a single buffer getting through life upon his means as idly as he could, and that so many people were so constantly making away with so many other people, as to render it difficult for a buffer of an easy temper to preserve the circumstances of the several cases unmixed in his mind.

Mr Jasper proving willing to speak for Mrs Tope, Mr Datchery, who had sent up his card, was invited to ascend the postern staircase. The Mayor was there, Mrs Tope said; but he was not to be regarded in the light of company, as he and Mr Jasper were great friends.

'I beg pardon,' said Mr Datchery, making a leg with his hat under his arm, as he addressed himself equally to both gentlemen; 'a selfish precaution on my part, and not personally interesting to anybody but myself. But as a buffer living on his means, and having an idea of doing it in this lovely place in peace and quiet, for remaining span of life, beg to ask if the Tope family are quite respectable?'

Mr Jasper could answer for that without the slightest hesitation.

'That is enough, sir,' said Mr Datchery.

'My friend the Mayor,' added Mr Jasper, presenting Mr Datchery with a courtly motion of his hand towards that potentate; 'whose recommendation is actually much more important to a stranger than that of an obscure person like myself, will testify in their behalf, I am sure.'

'The Worshipful the Mayor,' said Mr Datchery, with a low bow, 'places me under an infinite obligation.'

'Very good people, sir, Mr and Mrs Tope,' said Mr Sapsea, with condescension. 'Very good opinions. Very well behaved. Very respectful. Much approved by the Dean and Chapter.'

'The Worshipful the Mayor gives them a character,' said Mr Datchery, 'of which they may indeed be proud. I would ask His Honor (if I might be permitted) whether there are not many objects of great interest in the city which is under his beneficent sway?'

'We are, sir,' returned Mr Sapsea, 'an ancient city, and an ecclesiastical city. We are a constitutional city, as it becomes such a city to be, and we uphold and maintain our glorious privileges.'

'His Honor,' said Mr Datchery, bowing, 'inspires me with a desire to know more of the city, and confirms me in my inclination to end my days in the city.'

'Retired from the Army, sir?' suggested Mr Sapsea.

'His Honor the Mayor does me too much credit,' returned Mr Datchery.

'Navy, sir?' suggested Mr Sapsea.

'Again,' repeated Mr Datchery, 'His Honor the Mayor does me too much credit.'

'Diplomacy is a fine profession,' said Mr Sapsea, as a general remark.

'There, I confess, His Honor the Mayor is too many for me,' said Mr Datchery, with an ingenuous smile and bow; 'even a diplomatic bird must fall to such a gun.'

Now, this was very soothing. Here was a gentleman of a great – not to say a grand – address, accustomed to rank and dignity, really setting a fine example how to behave to a Mayor. There was something in that third person style of being spoken to, that Mr Sapsea found particularly recognisant of his merits and position.

'But I crave pardon,' said Mr Datchery. 'His Honor the Mayor will bear with me, if for a moment I have been deluded into occupying his time, and have forgotten the humble claims upon my own, of my hotel, the Crozier.'

'Not at all, sir,' said Mr Sapsea. 'I am returning home, and if you would like to take the exterior of our Cathedral in your way, I shall be glad to point it out.'

'His Honor the Mayor,' said Mr Datchery, 'is more than kind and gracious.'

As Mr Datchery, when he had made his acknowledgments to Mr Jasper, could not be induced to go out of the room before the Worshipful, the Worshipful led the way down stairs; Mr Datchery following with his hat under his arm, and his shock of white hair streaming in the evening breeze.

'Might I ask His Honor,' said Mr Datchery, 'whether that gentleman we have just left is the gentleman of whom I have heard in the neighbourhood as being much afflicted by the loss of a nephew, and concentrating his life on avenging the loss?'

'That is the gentleman. John Jasper, sir.'

'Would His Honor allow me to enquire whether there are strong suspicions of any one?'

'More than suspicions, sir,' returned Mr Sapsea, 'all but certainties.'

'Only think now!' cried Mr Datchery.

'But proof, sir, proof must be built up stone by stone,' said the Mayor. 'As I say, the end crowns the work. It is not enough that Justice should be morally certain; she must be *im*morally certain – legally, that is.'

'His Honor,' said Mr Datchery, 'reminds me of the nature of the law. Immoral. How true!'

'As I say, sir,' pompously went on the Mayor, 'the arm of the law is a strong arm, and a long arm. That is the way *I* put it. A strong arm and a long arm.'

'How forcible! – And yet, again, how true!' murmured Mr Datchery.

'And without betraying what I call the secrets of the prison-house,'[3] said Mr Sapsea; 'the secrets of the prison-house is the term I used on the bench.'

'And what other term than His Honor's would express it?' said Mr Datchery.

'Without, I say, betraying them, I predict to you, knowing the iron will of the gentleman we have just left (I take the bold step of calling it iron, on account of its strength), that in this case the long arm will reach, and the strong arm will strike. – This is our

Cathedral, sir. The best judges are pleased to admire it, and the best among our townsmen own to being a little vain of it.'

All this time Mr Datchery had walked with his hat under his arm, and his white hair streaming. He had an odd momentary appearance upon him of having forgotten his hat, when Mr Sapsea now touched it; and he clapped his hand up to his head as if with some vague expectation of finding another hat upon it.

'Pray be covered, sir,' entreated Mr Sapsea; magnificently implying: 'I shall not mind it, I assure you.'

'His Honor is very good, but I do it for coolness,' said Mr Datchery.

Then Mr Datchery admired the Cathedral, and Mr Sapsea pointed it out as if he himself had invented and built it; there were a few details indeed of which he did not approve, but those he glossed over, as if the workmen had made mistakes in his absence. The Cathedral disposed of, he led the way by the churchyard, and stopped to extol the beauty of the evening – by chance – in the immediate vicinity of Mrs Sapsea's epitaph.

'And by-the-bye,' said Mr Sapsea, appearing to descend from an elevation to remember it all of a sudden; like Apollo shooting down from Olympus to pick up his forgotten lyre; '*that* is one of our small lions. The partiality of our people has made it so, and strangers have been seen taking a copy of it now and then. I am not a judge of it myself, for it is a little work of my own. But it was troublesome to turn, sir; I may say, difficult to turn with elegance.'

Mr Datchery became so ecstatic over Mr Sapsea's composition that, in spite of his intention to end his days in Cloisterham, and therefore his probably having in reserve many opportunities of copying it, he would have transcribed it into his pocket-book on the spot, but for the slouching towards them of its material producer and perpetuator, Durdles, whom Mr Sapsea hailed, not sorry to show him a bright example of behavior to superiors.

'Ah, Durdles! This is the mason, sir; one of our Cloisterham worthies; everybody here knows Durdles. Mr Datchery, Durdles; a gentleman who is going to settle here.'

'I wouldn't do it if I was him,' growled Durdles. 'We're a heavy lot.'

'You surely don't speak for yourself, Mr Durdles,' returned Mr Datchery, 'any more than for His Honor.'

'Who's His Honor?' demanded Durdles.

'His Honor the Mayor.'

'I never was brought afore him,' said Durdles, with anything but the look of a loyal subject of the mayoralty, 'and it'll be time enough for me to Honor him when I am. Until which, and when, and where:

> 'Mister Sapsea is his name[4]
> England is his nation,
> Cloisterham's his dwelling-place,
> Aukshneer's his occupation.'

Here, Deputy (preceded by a flying oyster-shell) appeared upon the scene, and requested to have the sum of threepence instantly 'chucked' to him by Mr Durdles, whom he had been vainly seeking up and down, as lawful wages overdue. While that gentleman, with his bundle under his arm, slowly found and counted out the money, Mr Sapsea informed the new settler of Durdles's habits, pursuits, abode, and reputation. 'I suppose a curious stranger might come to see you, and your works, Mr Durdles, at any odd time?' said Mr Datchery upon that.

'Any gentleman is welcome to come and see me any evening if he brings liquor for two with him,' returned Durdles, with a penny between his teeth and certain halfpence in his hands. 'Or if he likes to make it twice two, he'll be double welcome.'

'I shall come. Master Deputy, what do you owe me?'

'A job.'

'Mind you pay me honestly with the job of showing me Mr Durdles's house when I want to go there.'

Deputy, with a piercing broadside of whistle through the whole gap in his mouth, vanished.

The Worshipful and the Worshipper then passed on together until they parted, with many ceremonies, at the Worshipful's door; even then, the Worshipper carried his hat under his arm, and gave his streaming white hair to the breeze.

Said Mr Datchery to himself that night, as he looked at his white hair in the gas-lighted looking-glass over the coffee-room chimneypiece at the Crozier, and shook it out: 'For a single buffer, of an easy temper, living idly on his means, I have had a rather busy afternoon!'

CHAPTER 19

Shadow on the Sun-Dial [1]

AGAIN Miss Twinkleton has delivered her valedictory address, with the accompaniments of white wine and pound cake, and again the young ladies have departed to their several homes. Helena Landless has left the Nuns' House to attend her brother's fortunes, and pretty Rosa is alone.

Cloisterham is so bright and sunny in these summer days, that the Cathedral and the monastery-ruin show as if their strong walls were transparent. A soft glow seems to shine from within them, rather than upon them from without, such is their mellowness as they look forth on the hot corn-fields and the smoking roads that distantly wind among them. The Cloisterham gardens blush with ripening fruit. Time was when travel-stained pilgrims rode in clattering parties through the city's welcome shades; time is when wayfarers, leading a gipsy life between haymaking time and harvest, and looking as if they were just made of the dust of the earth, so very dusty are they, lounge about on cool doorsteps, trying to mend their unmendable shoes, or giving them to the city kennels as a hopeless job, and seeking others in the bundles that they carry, along with their yet unused sickles swathed in bands of straw. At all the more public pumps there is much cooling of bare feet, together with much bubbling and gurgling of drinking with hand to spout on the part of these Bedouins; the Cloisterham police meanwhile looking askant from their beats with suspicion, and manifest impatience that the intruders should depart from within the civic bounds, and once more fry themselves on the simmering highroads.

On the afternoon of such a day, when the last Cathedral service is done, and when that side of the High Street on which the Nuns' House stands is in grateful shade, save where its quaint old garden opens to the west between the boughs of trees, a servant informs Rosa, to her terror, that Mr Jasper desires to see her.

If he had chosen his time for finding her at a disadvantage, he could have done no better. Perhaps he has chosen it. Helena Landless is gone, Mrs Tisher is absent on leave, Miss Twinkleton (in her amateur state of existence) has contributed herself and a veal pie to a picnic.

'Oh why, why, why, did you say I was at home!' cries Rosa, helplessly.

The maid replies, that Mr Jasper never asked the question. That he said he knew she was at home, and begged she might be told that he asked to see her.

'What shall I do, what shall I do?' thinks Rosa, clasping her hands.

Possessed by a kind of desperation, she adds in the next breath that she will come to Mr Jasper in the garden. She shudders at the thought of being shut up with him in the house; but many of its windows command the garden, and she can be seen as well as heard there, and can shriek in the free air and run away. Such is the wild idea that flutters through her mind.

She has never seen him since the fatal night, except when she was questioned before the Mayor, and then he was present in gloomy watchfulness, as representing his lost nephew and burning to avenge him. She hangs her garden-hat on her arm, and goes out. The moment she sees him from the porch, leaning on the sun-dial, the old horrible feeling of being compelled by him, asserts its hold upon her. She feels that she would even then go back, but that he draws her feet towards him. She cannot resist, and sits down, with her head bent, on the garden-seat beside the sun-dial. She cannot look up at him for abhorrence, but she has perceived that he is dressed in deep mourning. So is she. It was not so at first; but the lost has long been given up, and mourned for, as dead.

He would begin by touching her hand. She feels the intention, and draws her hand back. His eyes are then fixed upon her, she knows, though her own see nothing but the grass.

'I have been waiting,' he begins, 'for some time, to be summoned back to my duty near you.'

After several times forming her lips, which she knows he is closely watching, into the shape of some other hesitating reply, and then into none, she answers: 'Duty, sir?'

'The duty of teaching you, serving you as your faithful music-master.'

'I have left off that study.'

'Not left off, I think. Discontinued. I was told by your guardian that you discontinued it under the shock that we have all felt so acutely. When will you resume?'

'Never, sir.'

'Never? You could have done no more if you had loved my dear boy.'

'I did love him!' cries Rosa, with a flash of anger.

'Yes; but not quite – not quite in the right way, shall I say? Not in the intended and expected way. Much as my dear boy was, unhappily, too self-conscious and self-satisfied (but I draw no parallel between him and you in that respect) to love as he should have loved, or as any one in his place would have loved – must have loved!'

She sits in the same still attitude, but shrinking a little more.

'Then, to be told that you discontinued your study with me, was to be politely told that you abandoned it altogether?' he suggests.

'Yes,' says Rosa, with sudden spirit. 'The politeness was my guardian's, not mine. I told him that I was resolved to leave off, and that I was determined to stand by my resolution.'

'And you still are?'

'I still am, sir. And I beg not to be questioned any more about it. At all events, I will not answer any more; I have that in my power.'

She is so conscious of his looking at her with a gloating admiration of the touch of anger on her, and the fire and animation it brings with it, that even as her spirit rises, it falls again, and she struggles with a sense of shame, affront, and fear, much as she did that night at the piano.

'I will not question you any more, since you object to it so much; I will confess.'

'I do not wish to hear you, sir,' cries Rosa, rising.

This time he does touch her with his outstretched hand. In shrinking from it, she shrinks into her seat again.

'We must sometimes act in opposition to our wishes,' he tells her in a low voice. 'You must do so now, or do more harm to others than you can ever set right.'

'What harm?'

'Presently, presently. You question *me*, you see, and surely that's not fair when you forbid me to question you. Nevertheless, I will answer the question presently. Dearest Rosa! Charming Rosa!'

She starts up again.

This time he does not touch her. But his face looks so wicked and menacing, as he stands leaning against the sun-dial – setting, as it were, his black mark upon the very face of day – that her flight is arrested by horror as she looks at him.

'I do not forget how many windows command a view of us,' he says, glancing towards them. 'I will not touch you again, I will come no nearer to you than I am. Sit down, and there will be no mighty wonder in your music-master's leaning idly against a pedestal and speaking with you, remembering all that has happened and our shares in it. Sit down, my beloved.'

She would have gone once more – was all but gone – and once more his face, darkly threatening what would follow if she went, has stopped her. Looking at him with the expression of the instant frozen on her face, she sits down on the seat again.

'Rosa, even when my dear boy was affianced to you, I loved you madly; even when I thought his happiness in having you for his wife was certain, I loved you madly; even when I strove to make him more ardently devoted to you, I loved you madly; even when he gave me the picture of your lovely face so carelessly traduced by him, which I feigned to hang always in my sight for his sake, but worshipped in torment for yours, I loved you madly. In the distasteful work of the day, in the wakeful misery of the night, girded by sordid realities, or wandering through Paradises and Hells of visions in which I rushed, carrying your image in my arms, I loved you madly.'

If anything could make his words more hideous to her than they are in themselves, it would be the contrast between the violence of his look and delivery, and the composure of his assumed attitude.

'I endured it all in silence. So long as you were his, or so long as I supposed you to be his, I hid my secret loyally. Did I not?'

This lie, so gross, while the mere words in which it is told are so true, is more than Rosa can endure. She answers with kindling indignation: 'You were as false throughout, sir, as you are now. You were false to him, daily and hourly. You know that you made my life unhappy by your pursuit of me. You know that you made me afraid to open his generous eyes, and that you forced me, for his own trusting, good, good sake, to keep the truth from him, that you were a bad, bad man!'

His preservation of his easy attitude rendering his working features and his convulsive hands absolutely diabolical, he returns, with a fierce extreme of admiration:

'How beautiful you are! You are more beautiful in anger than in repose. I don't ask you for your love; give me yourself and your hatred; give me yourself and that pretty rage; give me yourself and that enchanting scorn; it will be enough for me.'

Impatient tears rise to the eyes of the trembling little beauty, and her face flames; but as she again rises to leave him in indignation, and seek protection within the house, he stretches out his hand towards the porch, as though he invited her to enter it.

'I told you, you rare charmer, you sweet witch, that you must stay and hear me, or do more harm than can ever be undone. You asked me what harm. Stay, and I will tell you. Go, and I will do it!'

Again Rosa quails before his threatening face, though innocent of its meaning, and she remains. Her panting breathing comes and goes as if it would choke her; but with a repressive hand upon her bosom, she remains.

'I have made my confession that my love is mad. It is so mad that, had the ties between me and my dear lost boy been one silken thread less strong, I might have swept even him from your side when you favored him.'

A film comes over the eyes she raises for an instant, as though he had turned her faint.

'Even him,' he repeats. 'Yes, even him! Rosa, you see me and you hear me. Judge for yourself whether any other admirer shall love you and live, whose life is in my hand.'

'What do you mean, sir?'

'I mean to show you how mad my love is. It was hawked through the late enquiries by Mr Crisparkle, that young Landless had confessed to him that he was a rival of my lost boy.[2] That is an inexpiable offence in my eyes. The same Mr Crisparkle knows under my hand that I have devoted myself to the murderer's discovery and destruction, be he who he might, and that I determined to discuss the mystery with no one until I should hold the clue in which to entangle the murderer as in a net. I have since worked patiently to wind and wind it round him; and it is slowly winding as I speak.'

'Your belief, if you believe in the criminality of Mr Landless, is not Mr Crisparkle's belief, and he is a good man,' Rosa retorts.

'My belief is my own; and I reserve it, worshipped of my soul! Circumstances may accumulate so strongly *even against an innocent man*, that, directed, sharpened, and pointed, they may slay him. One wanting link discovered by perseverance against a guilty man, proves his guilt, however slight its evidence before, and he dies. Young Landless stands in deadly peril either way.'

'If you really suppose,' Rosa pleads with him, turning paler, 'that I favor Mr Landless, or that Mr Landless has ever in any way addressed himself to me, you are wrong.'

He puts that from him with a slighting action of his hand and a curled lip.

'I was going to show you how madly I love you. More madly now than ever, for I am willing to renounce the second object that has arisen in my life to divide it with you; and henceforth to have no object in existence but you only. Miss Landless has become your bosom friend. You care for her peace of mind?'

'I love her dearly.'

'You care for her good name?'

'I have said, sir, I love her dearly.'

'I am unconsciously,' he observes with a smile, as he folds his hands upon the sun-dial and leans his chin upon them, so that his talk would seem from the windows (faces occasionally come and go there) to be of the airiest and playfullest: 'I am unconsciously giving offence by questioning again. I will simply make statements, therefore, and not put questions. You do care for your bosom friend's good name, and you do care for her peace of mind. Then remove the shadow of the gallows from her, dear one!'

'You dare propose to me to –'

'Darling, I dare propose to you. Stop there. If it be bad to idolize you, I am the worst of men; if it be good, I am the best. My love for you is above all other love, and my truth to you is above all other truth. Let me have hope and favor, and I am a forsworn man for your sake.'

Rosa puts her hands to her temples, and, pushing back her hair, looks wildly and abhorrently at him, as though she were trying to piece together what it is his deep purpose to present to her only in fragments.

'Reckon up nothing at this moment, angel, but the sacrifices that I lay at those dear feet, which I could fall down among the vilest ashes and kiss, and put upon my head as a poor savage might. There is my fidelity to my dear boy after death. Tread upon it!'

With an action of his hands, as though he cast down something precious.

'There is the inexpiable offence against my adoration of you. Spurn it!'

With a similar action.

'There are my labors in the cause of a just vengeance for six toiling months. Crush them!'

With another repetition of the action.

'There is my past and my present wasted life. There is the desolation of my heart and my soul. There is my peace; there is my despair. Stamp them into the dust, so that you take me, were it even mortally hating me!'

The frightful vehemence of the man, now reaching its full height, so additionally terrifies her as to break the spell that has held her to the spot. She swiftly moves towards the porch; but in an instant he is at her side, and speaking in her ear.

'Rosa, I am self-repressed again. I am walking calmly beside you to the house. I shall wait for some encouragement and hope. I shall not strike too soon. Give me a sign that you attend to me.'

She slightly and constrainedly moves her hand.

'Not a word of this to any one, or it will bring down the blow, as certainly as night follows day. Another sign that you attend to me.'

She moves her hand once more.

'I love you, love you, love you. If you were to cast me off now — but you will not — you would never be rid of me. No one should come between us. I would pursue you to the death.'

The handmaid coming out to open the gate for him, he quietly pulls off his hat as a parting salute, and goes away with no greater show of agitation than is visible in the effigy of Mr Sapsea's father opposite. Rosa faints in going up-stairs, and is carefully carried to her room and laid down on her bed. A thunderstorm is coming on, the maids say, and the hot and stifling air has overset the pretty dear; no wonder; they have felt their own knees all of a tremble all day long.

CHAPTER 20

Divers Flights[1]

ROSA no sooner came to herself than the whole of the late interview was before her. It even seemed as if it had pursued her into
her insensibility, and she had not had a moment's unconsciousness
of it. What to do, she was at a frightened loss to know: the only
one clear thought in her mind was, that she must fly from this
terrible man.

But where could she take refuge, and how could she go? She
had never breathed her dread of him to any one but Helena. If
she went to Helena, and told her what had passed, that very act
might bring down the irreparable mischief that he threatened he
had the power, and that she knew he had the will, to do. The more
fearful he appeared to her excited memory and imagination, the
more alarming her responsibility appeared: seeing that a slight
mistake on her part, either in action or delay, might let his male-
volence loose on Helena's brother.

Rosa's mind throughout the last six months had been stormily
confused. A half-formed, wholly unexpressed suspicion tossed in
it, now heaving itself up, and now sinking into the deep; now
gaining palpability, and now losing it. Jasper's self-absorption in
his nephew when he was alive, and his unceasing pursuit of the
enquiry how he came by his death, if he were dead, were themes so
rife in the place, that no one appeared able to suspect the possibility
of foul play at his hands. She had asked herself the question, 'Am
I so wicked in my thoughts as to conceive a wickedness that others
cannot imagine?' Then she had considered, Did the suspicion
come of her previous recoiling from him before the fact? And if so,
was not that a proof of its baselessness? Then she had reflected.
'What motive could he have, according to my accusation?' She
was ashamed to answer in her mind, 'The motive of gaining *me!*'
And covered her face, as if the lightest shadow of the idea of
founding murder on such an idle vanity were a crime almost as
great.

She ran over in her mind again, all that he had said by the sun-
dial in the garden. He had persisted in treating the disappearance

as murder, consistently with his whole public course since the
finding of the watch and shirt-pin. If he were afraid of the crime
being traced out, would he not rather encourage the idea of a
voluntary disappearance? He had even declared that if the ties
between him and his nephew had been less strong, he might have
swept 'even him' away from her side. Was that like his having
really done so? He had spoken of laying his six months' labors in
the cause of a just vengeance at her feet. Would he have done
that, with that violence of passion, if they were a pretence? Would
he have ranged them with his desolate heart and soul, his wasted
life, his peace, and his despair? The very first sacrifice that he
represented himself as making for her, was his fidelity to his dear
boy after death. Surely these facts were strong against a fancy that
scarcely dared to hint itself. And yet he was so terrible a man!
In short, the poor girl (for what could she know of the criminal
intellect, which its own professed students perpetually misread,
because they persist in trying to reconcile it with the average
intellect of average men, instead of identifying it as a horrible
wonder apart) could get by no road to any other conclusion than
that he *was* a terrible man, and must be fled from.

She had been Helena's stay and comfort during the whole time.
She had constantly assured her of her full belief in her brother's
innocence, and of her sympathy with him in his misery. But she
had never seen him since the disappearance, nor had Helena ever
spoken one word of his avowal to Mr Crisparkle in regard of
Rosa, though as a part of the interest of the case it was well known
far and wide. He was Helena's unfortunate brother, to her, and
nothing more. The assurance she had given her odious suitor was
strictly true, though it would have been better (she considered
now) if she could have restrained herself from giving it. Afraid
of him as the bright and delicate little creature was, her spirit
swelled at the thought of his knowing it from her own lips.

But where was she to go? Anywhere beyond his reach, was no
reply to the question. Somewhere must be thought of. She determined to go to her guardian, and to go immediately. The feeling
she had imparted to Helena on the night of their first confidence,
was so strong upon her – the feeling of not being safe from him,
and of the solid walls of the old convent being powerless to keep
out his ghostly following of her – that no reasoning of her own

could calm her terrors. The fascination of repulsion had been upon her so long, and now culminated so darkly, that she felt as if he had power to bind her by a spell. Glancing out at window, even now, as she rose to dress, the sight of the sun-dial on which he had leaned when he declared himself, turned her cold, and made her shrink from it, as though he had invested it with some awful quality from his own nature.

She wrote a hurried note to Miss Twinkleton, saying that she had sudden reason for wishing to see her guardian promptly, and had gone to him; also, entreating the good lady not to be uneasy, for all was well with her. She hurried a few quite useless articles into a very little bag, left the note in a conspicuous place, and went out, softly closing the gate after her.

It was the first time she had ever been even in Cloisterham High Street alone. But knowing all its ways and windings very well, she hurried straight to the corner from which the omnibus departed. It was, at that very moment, going off.

'Stop and take me, if you please, Joe. I am obliged to go to London.'

In less than another minute she was on her road to the railway, under Joe's protection. Joe waited on her when she got there, put her safely into the railway carriage, and handed in the very little bag after her, as though it were some enormous trunk, hundred-weights heavy, which she must on no account endeavour to lift.

'Can you go round when you get back, and tell Miss Twinkleton that you saw me safely off, Joe?'

'It shall be done, Miss.'

'With my love, please, Joe.'

'Yes, Miss – and I wouldn't mind having it myself!' But Joe did not articulate the last clause; only thought it.

Now that she was whirling away for London in real earnest, Rosa was at leisure to resume the thoughts which her personal hurry had checked. The indignant thought that his declaration of love soiled her; that she could only be cleansed from the stain of its impurity by appealing to the honest and true; supported her for a time against her fears, and confirmed her in her hasty resolution. But as the evening grew darker and darker, and the great city impended nearer and nearer, the doubts usual in such cases began to arise. Whether this was not a wild proceeding, after all; how Mr Grewgious might regard it; whether she should find him at the journey's end; how she would act if he were absent; what might become of her, alone, in a place so strange and crowded; how if she had but waited and taken counsel first; whether, if she could now go back, she would not do it thankfully: a multitude of such uneasy speculations disturbed her, more and more as they accumulated. At length the train came into London over the housetops; and down below lay the gritty streets with their yet un-needed lamps aglow, on a hot light summer night.

'Hiram Grewgious, Esquire, Staple Inn, London.' This was all Rosa knew of her destination; but it was enough to send her rattling away again in a cab, through deserts of gritty streets, where many people crowded at the corners of courts and byways to get some air, and where many other people walked with a miserably mono-tonous noise of shuffling feet on hot paving-stones, and where all the people and all their surroundings were so gritty and so shabby.

There was music playing here and there, but it did not enliven the case. No barrel-organ mended the matter, and no big drum beat dull care away. Like the chapel bells that were also going here and there, they only seemed to evoke echoes from brick surfaces, and dust from everything. As to the flat wind-instruments, they seemed to have cracked their hearts and souls in pining for the country.

Her jingling conveyance stopped at last at a fast-closed gateway, which appeared to belong to somebody who had gone to bed very early, and was much afraid of housebreakers; Rosa, discharging her conveyance, timidly knocked at this gateway, and was let in, very little bag and all, by a watchman.

'Does Mr Grewgious live here?'

'Mr Grewgious lives there, Miss,' said the watchman, pointing further in.

So Rosa went further in, and, when the clocks were striking ten, stood on P. J. T.'s doorsteps, wondering what P. J. T. had done with his street door.

Guided by the painted name of Mr Grewgious, she went up-stairs and softly tapped and tapped several times. But no one answering, and Mr Grewgious's door-handle yielding to her touch, she went in, and saw her guardian sitting on a windowseat at an open window, with a shaded lamp placed far from him on a table in a corner.

Rosa drew nearer to him in the twilight of the room. He saw her, and he said in an under-tone: 'Good Heaven!'

Rosa fell upon his neck, with tears, and then he said, returning her embrace:

'My child, my child! I thought you were your mother!

'But what, what, what,' he added, soothingly, 'has happened? My dear, what has brought you here? Who has brought you here?'

'No one. I came alone.'

'Lord bless me!' ejaculated Mr Grewgious. 'Came alone! Why didn't you write to me to come and fetch you?'

'I had no time. I took a sudden resolution. Poor, poor Eddy!'

'Ah, poor fellow, poor fellow!'

'His uncle has made love to me. I cannot bear it,' said Rosa, at once with a burst of tears, and a stamp of her little foot; 'I shudder with horror of him, and I have come to you to protect me and all of us from him, if you will?'

'I will!' cried Mr Grewgious, with a sudden rush of amazing energy. 'Damn him!

> 'Confound his politics!
> Frustrate his knavish tricks!
> On Thee his hopes to fix?
> Damn him again!'

After this most extraordinary outburst, Mr Grewgious, quite beside himself, plunged about the room, to all appearance undecided whether he was in a fit of loyal enthusiasm, or combative denunciation.

He stopped and said, wiping his face: 'I beg your pardon, my dear, but you will be glad to know I feel better. Tell me no more just now, or I might do it again. You must be refreshed and cheered. What did you take last? Was it breakfast, lunch, dinner, tea, or supper? And what will you take next? Shall it be breakfast, lunch, dinner, tea, or supper?'

The respectful tenderness with which, on one knee before her, he helped her to remove her hat, and disentangle her pretty hair from it, was quite a chivalrous sight. Yet who, knowing him only on the surface, would have expected chivalry – and of the true sort, too: not the spurious – from Mr Grewgious?

'Your rest too must be provided for,' he went on; 'and you shall have the prettiest chamber in Furnival's. Your toilet must be provided for, and you shall have everything that an unlimited head chambermaid – by which expression I mean a head chambermaid not limited as to outlay – can procure. Is that a bag?' he looked hard at it; sooth to say, it required hard looking at to be seen at all in a dimly-lighted room: 'and is it your property, my dear?'

'Yes, sir. I brought it with me.'

'It is not an extensive bag,' said Mr Grewgious, candidly, 'though admirably calculated to contain a day's provision for a canary bird. Perhaps you brought a canary bird?'

Rosa smiled, and shook her head.

'If you had, he should have been made welcome,' said Mr Grewgious, 'and I think he would have been pleased to be hung upon a nail outside and pit himself against our Staple sparrows; whose execution must be admitted to be not quite equal to their intention. Which is the case with so many of us! You didn't say what meal, my dear. Have a nice jumble of all meals.'

Rosa thanked him, but said she could only take a cup of tea. Mr Grewgious, after several times running out, and in again, to mention such supplementary items as marmalade, eggs, watercresses, salted fish, and frizzled ham, ran across to Furnival's without his hat, to give his various directions. And soon afterwards they were realized in practice, and the board was spread.

'Lord bless my soul!' cried Mr Grewgious, putting the lamp upon it, and taking his seat opposite Rosa; 'what a new sensation for a poor old Angular bachelor, to be sure!'

Rosa's expressive little eyebrows asked him what he meant!

'The sensation of having a sweet young presence in the place that whitewashes it, paints it, papers it, decorates it with gilding, and makes it Glorious!' said Mr Grewgious. 'Ah me! Ah me!'

As there was something mournful in his sigh, Rosa, in touching him with his tea-cup, ventured to touch him with her small hand too.

'Thank you, my dear,' said Mr Grewgious. 'Ahem! Let's talk!'

'Do you always live here, sir?' asked Rosa.

'Yes, my dear.'

'And always alone?'

'Always alone; except that I have daily companion in a gentleman by the name of Bazzard; my clerk.'

'*He* doesn't live here?'

'No, he goes his ways after office hours. In fact, he is off duty here, altogether, just at present;[2] and a Firm down stairs, with which I have business relations, lend me a substitute. But it would be extremely difficult to replace Mr Bazzard.'

'He must be very fond of you,' said Rosa.

'He bears up against it with commendable fortitude if he is,' returned Mr Grewgious, after considering the matter. 'But I doubt if he is. Not particularly so. You see, he is discontented, poor fellow.'

'Why isn't he contented?' was the natural enquiry.

'Misplaced,' said Mr Grewgious, with great mystery.

Rosa's eyebrows resumed their inquisitive and perplexed expression.

'So misplaced,' Mr Grewgious went on, 'that I feel constantly apologetic towards him. And he feels (though he doesn't mention it) that I have reason to be.'

Mr Grewgious had by this time grown so very mysterious, that Rosa did not know how to go on. While she was thinking about it Mr Grewgious suddenly jerked out of himself for the second time:

'Let's talk. We were speaking of Mr Bazzard. It's a secret, and moreover it is Mr Bazzard's secret; but the sweet presence at my table makes me so unusually expansive, that I feel I must impart it in inviolable confidence. What do you think Mr Bazzard has done?'

'Oh dear!' cried Rosa, drawing her chair a little nearer, and her mind reverting to Jasper, 'nothing dreadful, I hope?'

'He has written a play,' said Mr Grewgious, in a solemn whisper. 'A tragedy.'

Rosa seemed much relieved.

'And nobody,' pursued Mr Grewgious in the same tone, 'will hear, on any account whatever, of bringing it out.'

Rosa looked reflective, and nodded her head slowly; as who should say: 'Such things are, and why are they!'

'Now, you know,' said Mr Grewgious, '*I* couldn't write a play.'

'Not a bad one, sir?' asked Rosa, innocently, with her eyebrows again in action.

'No. If I was under sentence of decapitation, and was about to be instantly decapitated, and an express arrived with a pardon for the condemned convict Grewgious if he wrote a play, I should be under the necessity of resuming the block and begging the executioner to proceed to extremities, – meaning,' said Mr Grewgious, passing his hand under his chin, 'the singular number, and this extremity.'

Rosa appeared to consider what she would do if the awkward supposititious case were hers.

'Consequently,' said Mr Grewgious, 'Mr Bazzard would have a sense of my inferiority to himself under any circumstances; but when I am his master, you know, the case is greatly aggravated.'

Mr Grewgious shook his head seriously, as if he felt the offence to be a little too much, though of his own committing.

'How came you to be his master, sir?' asked Rosa.

'A question that naturally follows,' said Mr Grewgious. 'Let's talk. Mr Bazzard's father, being a Norfolk farmer, would have furiously laid about him with a flail, a pitchfork, and every agricultural implement available for assaulting purposes, on the slightest hint of his son's having written a play. So the son, bringing to me the father's rent (which I receive), imparted his secret, and pointed out that he was determined to pursue his genius, and that it would put him in peril of starvation, and that he was not formed for it.'

'For pursuing his genius, sir?'

'No, my dear,' said Mr Grewgious, 'for starvation. It was impossible to deny the position that Mr Bazzard was not formed to be starved, and Mr Bazzard then pointed out that it was desirable that I should stand between him and a fate so perfectly unsuited to his formation. In that way Mr Bazzard became my clerk, and he feels it very much.'

'I am glad he is grateful,' said Rosa.

'I didn't quite mean that, my dear. I mean that he feels the degradation. There are some other geniuses that Mr Bazzard has become acquainted with, who have also written tragedies, which likewise nobody will on any account whatever hear of bringing out, and these choice spirits dedicate their plays to one another in a highly panegyrical manner. Mr Bazzard has been the subject of one of these dedications. Now, you know, *I* never had a play dedicated to *me*!'

Rosa looked at him as if she would have liked him to be the recipient of a thousand dedications.

'Which again, naturally, rubs against the grain of Mr Bazzard,' said Mr Grewgious. 'He is very short with me sometimes, and then I feel that he is meditating "This blockhead is my master! A fellow who couldn't write a tragedy on pain of death, and who will never have one dedicated to him with the most complimentary congratulations on the high position he has taken in the eyes of posterity!" Very trying, very trying. However, in giving him directions, I reflect beforehand: "Perhaps he may not like this," or "He might take it ill if I asked that," and so we get on very well. Indeed, better than I could have expected.'

'Is the tragedy named, sir?' asked Rosa.

'Strictly between ourselves,' answered Mr Grewgious, 'it has a dreadfully appropriate name. It is called The Thorn of Anxiety. But Mr Bazzard hopes – and I hope – that it will come out at last.'

It was not hard to divine that Mr Grewgious had related the Bazzard history thus fully, at least quite as much for the recreation of his ward's mind from the subject that had driven her there, as for the gratification of his own tendency to be social and communicative. 'And now, my dear,' he said at this point, 'if you are not too tired to tell me more of what passed to-day – but only if you feel quite able – I should be glad to hear it. I may digest it the better, if I sleep on it to-night.'

Rosa, composed now, gave him a faithful account of the interview. Mr Grewgious often smoothed his head while it was in progress, and begged to be told a second time those parts which bore on Helena and Neville. When Rosa had finished, he sat grave, silent, and meditative, for a while.

'Clearly narrated,' was his only remark at last, 'and, I hope, clearly put away here,' smoothing his head again. 'See, my dear,' taking her to the open window, 'where they live! The dark windows over yonder.'

'I may go to Helena to-morrow?' asked Rosa.

'I should like to sleep on that question to-night,' he answered, doubtfully. 'But let me take you to your own rest, for you must need it.'

With that, Mr Grewgious helped her to get her hat on again, and hung upon his arm the very little bag that was of no earthly use, and led her by the hand (with a certain stately awkwardness, as if he were going to walk a minuet) across Holborn, and into Furnival's Inn. At the hotel door, he confided her to the Unlimited head chambermaid, and said that while she went up to see her room, he would remain below, in case she should wish it exchanged for another, or should find that there was anything she wanted.

Rosa's room was airy, clean, comfortable, almost gay. The Unlimited had laid in everything omitted from the very little bag (that is to say, everything she could possibly need), and Rosa tripped down the great many stairs again, to thank her guardian for his thoughtful and affectionate care of her.

'Not at all, my dear,' said Mr Grewgious, infinitely gratified; 'it is I who thank you for your charming confidence and for your charming company. Your breakfast will be provided for you in a neat, compact, and graceful little sitting-room (appropriate to your figure), and I will come to you at ten o'clock in the morning. I hope you don't feel very strange indeed, in this strange place.'

'Oh no, I feel so safe!'

'Yes, you may be sure that the stairs are fire-proof,' said Mr Grewgious, 'and that any outbreak of the devouring element would be perceived and suppressed by the watchmen.'

'I did not mean that,' Rosa replied. 'I mean, I feel so safe from him.'

'There is a stout gate of iron bars to keep him out,' said Mr Grewgious, 'and Furnival's is specially watched and lighted, and *I* live over the way!' In the stoutness of his knight-errantry, he seemed to think the last-named protection all-sufficient. In the same spirit, he said to the gate-porter as he went out, 'If some one staying in the hotel should wish to send across the road to me in the night, a crown will be ready for the messenger.' In the same spirit, he walked up and down outside the iron gate for the best part of an hour, with some solicitude: occasionally looking in between the bars, as if he had laid a dove in a high roost in a cage of lions, and had it on his mind that she might tumble out.

Nothing occurred in the night[3] to flutter the tired dove, and the dove arose refreshed. With Mr Grewgious, when the clock struck ten in the morning, came Mr Crisparkle, who had come at one plunge out of the river at Cloisterham.

'Miss Twinkleton was so uneasy, Miss Rosa,' he explained to her, 'and came round to Ma and me with your note, in such a state of wonder, that, to quiet her, I volunteered on this service by the very first train to be caught in the morning. I wished at the time that you had come to me; but now I think it best that you did *as* you did, and came to your guardian.'

'I did think of you,' Rosa told him; 'but Minor Canon Corner was so near him –'

'I understand. It was quite natural.'

'I have told Mr Crisparkle,' said Mr Grewgious, 'all that you told me last night, my dear. Of course I should have written it to him immediately; but his coming was most opportune. And it was particularly kind of him to come, for he had but just gone.'

'Have you settled,' asked Rosa, appealing to them both, 'what is to be done for Helena and her brother?'

'Why, really,' said Mr Crisparkle, 'I am in great perplexity. If even Mr Grewgious, whose head is much longer than mine and who is a whole night's cogitation in advance of me, is undecided, what must I be!'

The Unlimited here put her head in at the door – after having rapped, and been authorized to present herself – announcing that a gentleman wished for a word with another gentleman named Crisparkle, if any such gentleman were there. If no such gentleman were there, he begged pardon for being mistaken.

'Such a gentleman is here,' said Mr Crisparkle, 'but is engaged just now.'

'Is it a dark gentleman?' interposed Rosa, retreating on her guardian.

'No, Miss, more of a brown gentleman.'

'You are sure not with black hair?' asked Rosa, taking courage.

'Quite sure of that, Miss. Brown hair and blue eyes.'

'Perhaps,' hinted Mr Grewgious, with habitual caution, 'it might be well to see him, reverend sir, if you don't object. When one is in a difficulty, or at a loss, one never knows in what direction a way out may chance to open. It is a business principle of mine, in such a case, not to close up any direction, but to keep an eye on every direction that may present itself. I could relate an anecdote in point, but that it would be premature.'

'If Miss Rosa will allow me, then? Let the gentleman come in,' said Mr Crisparkle.

The gentleman came in; apologized, with a frank but modest grace, for not finding Mr Crisparkle alone; turned to Mr Crisparkle, and smilingly asked the unexpected question: 'Who am I?'

'You are the gentleman I saw smoking under the trees in Staple Inn a few minutes ago.'

'True. There I saw you. Who else am I?'

Mr Crisparkle concentrated his attention on a handsome face, much sunburnt; and the ghost of some departed boy seemed to rise, gradually and dimly, in the room.

The gentleman saw a struggling recollection lighten up the Minor Canon's features, and smiling again, said: 'What will you have for breakfast this morning? You are out of jam.'

'Wait a moment!' cried Mr Crisparkle, raising his right hand. 'Give me another instant! Tartar!'

The two shook hands with the greatest heartiness, and then went the wonderful length – for Englishmen – of laying their hands each on the other's shoulders, and looking joyfully each into the other's face.

'My old fag!' said Mr Crisparkle.

'My old master!' said Mr Tartar.

'You saved me from drowning!' said Mr Crisparkle.

'After which you took to swimming, you know!' said Mr Tartar.

'God bless my soul!' said Mr Crisparkle.

'Amen!' said Mr Tartar.

And then they fell to shaking hands most heartily again.

'Imagine,' exclaimed Mr Crisparkle, with glistening eyes: 'Miss Rosa Bud and Mr Grewgious, imagine Mr Tartar, when he was the smallest of juniors, diving for me, catching me, a big heavy senior, by the hair of the head, and striking out for the shore with me like a water-giant!'

'Imagine my not letting him sink, as I was his fag!' said Mr Tartar. 'But the truth being that he was my best protector and friend, and did me more good than all the masters put together, an irrational impulse seized me to pick him up, or go down with him.'

'Hem! Permit me, sir, to have the honor,' said Mr Grewgious, advancing with extended hand, 'for an honor I truly esteem it. I am proud to make your acquaintance. I hope you didn't take cold. I hope you were not inconvenienced by swallowing too much water. How have you been since?'

It was by no means apparent that Mr Grewgious knew what he said, though it was very apparent that he meant to say something highly friendly and appreciative.

If Heaven, Rosa thought, had but sent such courage and skill to her poor mother's aid! And he to have been so slight and young then!

'I don't wish to be complimented upon it, I thank you, but I think I have an idea,' Mr Grewgious announced, after taking a jog-trot or two across the room, so unexpected and unaccountable that they had all stared at him, doubtful whether he was choking or had the cramp. 'I *think* I have an idea. I believe I have had the pleasure of seeing Mr Tartar's name as tenant of the top set in the house next the top set in the corner?'

'Yes, sir,' returned Mr Tartar. 'You are right so far.'

'I am right so far,' said Mr Grewgious. 'Tick that off,' which he did, with his right thumb on his left. 'Might you happen to know the name of your neighbour in the top set on the other side of the party-wall?' coming very close to Mr Tartar, to lose nothing of his face, in his shortness of sight.

'Landless.'

'Tick that off,' said Mr Grewgious, taking another trot, and then coming back. 'No personal knowledge, I suppose, sir?'

'Slight, but some.'

'Tick that off,' said Mr Grewgious, taking another trot, and again coming back. 'Nature of knowledge, Mr Tartar?'

'I thought he seemed to be a young fellow in a poor way, and I asked his leave – only within a day or so – to share my flowers up there with him; that is to say, to extend my flower-garden to his windows.'

'Would you have the kindness to take seats?' said Mr Grewgious. '*I have* an idea!'

They complied; Mr Tartar none the less readily, for being all abroad; and Mr Grewgious, seated in the centre, with his hands upon his knees, thus stated his idea, with his usual manner of having got the statement by heart.

'I cannot as yet make up my mind whether it is prudent to hold open communication under present circumstances, and on the part of the fair member of the present company, with Mr Neville or Miss Helena. I have reason to know that a local friend of ours (on whom I beg to bestow a passing but a hearty malediction, with the kind permission of my reverend friend) sneaks to and fro, and dodges up and down. When not doing so himself, he may have some informant skulking about, in the person of a watchman, porter, or such-like hanger-on of Staple. On the other hand, Miss Rosa very naturally wishes to see her friend Miss Helena, and it would seem important that at least Miss Helena (if not her brother too, through her) should privately know from Miss Rosa's lips what has occurred, and what has been threatened. Am I agreed with generally in the views I take?'

'I entirely coincide with them,' said Mr Crisparkle, who had been very attentive.

'As I have no doubt I should,' added Mr Tartar, smiling, 'if I understood them.'

'Fair and softly, sir,' said Mr Grewgious; 'we shall fully confide in you directly, if you will favor us with your permission. Now, if our local friend should have any informant on the spot, it is tolerably clear that such informant can only be set to watch the chambers in the occupation of Mr Neville. He reporting, to our local friend, who comes and goes there, our local friend would supply for himself, from his own previous knowledge, the identity of the parties. Nobody can be set to watch all Staple, or to concern himself with comers and goers to other sets of chambers: unless, indeed, mine.'

'I begin to understand to what you tend,' said Mr Crisparkle, 'and highly approve of your caution.'

'I needn't repeat that I know nothing yet of the why and wherefore,' said Mr Tartar; 'but I also understand to what you tend, so let me say at once that my chambers are freely at your disposal.'

'There!' cried Mr Grewgious, smoothing his head triumphantly. 'Now we have all got the idea. You have it, my dear?'

'I think I have,' said Rosa, blushing a little as Mr Tartar looked quickly towards her.

'You see, you go over to Staple with Mr Crisparkle and Mr Tartar,' said Mr Grewgious; 'I going in and out and out and in, alone, in my usual way; you go up with those gentlemen to Mr Tartar's rooms; you look into Mr Tartar's flower-garden; you wait for Miss Helena's appearance there, or you signify to Miss Helena that you are close by; and you communicate with her freely, and no spy can be the wiser.'

'I am very much afraid I shall be –'

'Be what, my dear?' asked Mr Grewgious, as she hesitated. 'Not frightened?'

'No, not that,' said Rosa, shyly; – 'in Mr Tartar's way. We seem to be appropriating Mr Tartar's residence so very coolly.'

'I protest to you,' returned that gentleman, 'that I shall think the better of it for evermore, if your voice sounds in it only once.'

Rosa, not quite knowing what to say about that, cast down her eyes, and turning to Mr Grewgious, dutifully asked if she should put her hat on? Mr Grewgious being of opinion that she could not do better, she withdrew for the purpose. Mr Crisparkle took the opportunity of giving Mr Tartar a summary of the distresses of Neville and his sister; the opportunity was quite long enough, as the hat happened to require a little extra fitting on.

Mr Tartar gave his arm to Rosa, and Mr Crisparkle walked, detached, in front.

'Poor, poor Eddy!' thought Rosa, as they went along.

Mr Tartar waved his right hand as he bent his head down over Rosa, talking in an animated way.

'It was not so powerful or so sun-browned when it saved Mr Crisparkle,' thought Rosa, glancing at it; 'but it must have been very steady and determined even then.'

Mr Tartar told her he had been a sailor, roving everywhere for years and years.

'When are you going to sea again?' asked Rosa.

'Never!'

Rosa wondered what the girls would say if they could see her crossing the wide street on the sailor's arm. And she fancied that the passers-by must think her very little and very helpless, contrasted with the strong figure that could have caught her up and carried her out of any danger, miles and miles without resting.

She was thinking further, that his far-seeing blue eyes looked as if they had been used to watch danger afar off, and to watch it without flinching, drawing nearer and nearer: when, happening to raise her own eyes, she found that he seemed to be thinking something about *them*.

This a little confused Rosebud, and may account for her never afterwards quite knowing how she ascended (with his help) to his garden in the air,[4] and seemed to get into a marvellous country that came into sudden bloom like the country on the summit of the magic bean-stalk. May it flourish for ever!

*

CHAPTER 21

A Gritty State of Things comes on

MR Tartar's chambers were the neatest, the cleanest, and the best-ordered chambers ever seen under the sun, moon, and stars. The floors were scrubbed to that extent, that you might have supposed the London blacks[1] emancipated for ever, and gone out of the land for good. Every inch of brass-work in Mr Tartar's possession was polished and burnished, till it shone like a brazen mirror. No speck, nor spot, nor spatter soiled the purity of any of Mr Tartar's household gods, large, small, or middle sized. His sitting-room was like the admiral's cabin, his bath room was like a dairy, his sleeping chamber, fitted all about with lockers and drawers, was like a seedsman's shop; and his nicely-balanced cot just stirred in the midst, as if it breathed. Everything belonging to Mr Tartar had quarters of its own assigned to it: his maps and charts had their quarters; his books had theirs; his brushes had theirs; his boots had theirs; his clothes had theirs; his case-bottles had theirs; his telescopes and other instruments had theirs. Everything was readily accessible. Shelf, bracket, locker, hook, and drawer were equally within reach, and were equally contrived with a view to avoiding waste of room, and providing some snug inches of stowage for something that would have exactly fitted nowhere else. His gleaming little service of plate was so arranged upon his sideboard as that a slack

salt-spoon would have instantly betrayed itself; his toilet imple-
ments were so arranged upon his dressing-table as that a toothpick
of slovenly deportment could have been reported at a glance. So
with the curiosities he had brought home from various voyages.
Stuffed, dried, repolished, or otherwise preserved, according to
their kind; birds, fishes, reptiles, arms, articles of dress, shells,
seaweeds, grasses, or memorials of coral reef; each was displayed
in its especial place, and each could have been displayed in no
better place. Paint and varnish seemed to be kept somewhere out
of sight, in constant readiness to obliterate stray finger-marks
wherever any might become perceptible in Mr Tartar's chambers.
No man-of-war was ever kept more spick and span from careless
touch. On this bright summer day, a neat awning was rigged over
Mr Tartar's flower-garden as only a sailor could rig it; and there
was a sea-going air upon the whole effect, so delightfully complete,
that the flower-garden might have appertained to stern-windows
afloat, and the whole concern might have bowled away gallantly
with all on board, if Mr Tartar had only clapped to his lips the
speaking trumpet that was slung in a corner, and given hoarse
orders to have the anchor up, look alive there, men, and get all
sail upon her!

Mr Tartar doing the honors[2] of this gallant craft was of a piece
with the rest. When a man rides an amiable hobby that shies at
nothing and kicks nobody, it is always agreeable to find him riding
it with a humorous sense of the droll side of the creature. When the
man is a cordial and an earnest man by nature, and withal is perfectly fresh and genuine, it may be doubted whether he is ever seen
to greater advantage than at such a time. So Rosa would have
naturally thought (even if she *hadn't* been conducted over the ship
with all the homage due to the First Lady of the Admiralty, or
First Fairy of the Sea), that it was charming to see and hear Mr
Tartar half laughing at, and half rejoicing in, his various con-
trivances. So Rosa would have naturally thought, anyhow, that the
sunburnt sailor showed to great advantage when, the inspection
finished, he delicately withdrew out of his admiral's cabin, beseeching her to consider herself its Queen, and waving her free of
his flower-garden with the hand that had had Mr Crisparkle's
life in it.

'Helena! Helena Landless! Are you there?'

'Who speaks to me? Not Rosa?' Then a second handsome face appearing.

'Yes, my darling!'

'Why, how did you come here, dearest?'

'I – I don't quite know,' said Rosa with a blush; 'unless I am dreaming!'

Why with a blush? For their two faces were alone with the other flowers. Are blushes among the fruits of the country of the magic bean-stalk?

'*I* am not dreaming,' said Helena, smiling. 'I should take more for granted if I were. How do we come together – or so near together – so very unexpectedly?'

Unexpectedly indeed, among the dingy gables and chimney-pots of P. J. T.'s connexion, and the flowers that had sprung from the salt sea. But Rosa, waking, told in a hurry how they came to be together, and all the why and wherefore of that matter.

'And Mr Crisparkle is here,' said Rosa, in rapid conclusion; 'and, could you believe it? Long ago, he saved his life!'

'I could believe any such thing of Mr Crisparkle,' returned Helena, with a mantling face.

(More blushes in the bean-stalk country!)

'Yes, but it wasn't Mr Crisparkle,' said Rosa, quickly putting in the correction.

'I don't understand, love.'

'It was very nice of Mr Crisparkle to be saved,' said Rosa, 'and he couldn't have shown his high opinion of Mr Tartar more expressively. But it was Mr Tartar who saved him.'

Helena's dark eyes looked very earnestly at the bright face among the leaves, and she asked, in a slower and more thoughtful tone:

'Is Mr Tartar with you now, dear?'

'No; because he has given up his rooms to me – us, I mean. It *is* such a beautiful place!'

'Is it?'

'It is like the inside of the most exquisite ship that ever sailed. It is like – it is like –!'

'Like a dream?' suggested Helena.

Rosa answered with a little nod, and smelled the flowers.

Helena resumed, after a short pause of silence, during which she seemed (or it was Rosa's fancy) to compassionate somebody: 'My poor Neville is reading in his own room, the sun being so very bright on this side just now. I think he had better not know that you are so near.'

'Oh, I think so too!' cried Rosa very readily.

'I suppose,' pursued Helena, doubtfully, 'that he must know by-and-bye all you have told me; but I am not sure. Ask Mr Crisparkle's advice, my darling. Ask him whether I may tell Neville as much or as little of what you have told me as I think best.'

Rosa subsided into her State Cabin, and propounded the question. The Minor Canon was for the free exercise of Helena's judgment.

'I thank him very much,' said Helena, when Rosa emerged again with her report. 'Ask him whether it would be best to wait until any new maligning and pursuing of Neville on the part of this wretch shall disclose itself, or to try to anticipate it: I mean, so far as to find out whether any such goes on darkly about us?'

The Minor Canon found this point so difficult to give a confident opinion on, that, after two or three attempts and failures, he suggested a reference to Mr Grewgious. Helena acquiescing, he betook himself (with a most unsuccessful assumption of lounging indifference) across the quadrangle to P. J. T.'s, and stated it. Mr Grewgious held decidedly to the general principle, that if you could steal a march upon a brigand or a wild beast, you had better do it; he also held decidedly to the special case, that John Jasper was a brigand *and* a wild beast in combination.

Thus advised, Mr Crisparkle came back again and reported to Rosa, who in her turn reported to Helena. She, now steadily pursuing her train of thought at her window, considered thereupon.

'We may count on Mr Tartar's readiness to help us, Rosa?' she enquired.

O yes! Rosa shyly thought so. O yes, Rosa shyly believed she could almost answer for it. But should she ask Mr Crisparkle? 'I think your authority on the point as good as his, my dear,' said Helena, sedately, 'and you needn't disappear again for that.' Odd of Helena!

'You see: Neville,' Helena pursued after more reflection, 'knows no one else here: he has not so much as exchanged a word with any one else here. If Mr Tartar would call to see him openly and often;

if he would spare a minute for the purpose, frequently; if he would even do so, almost daily; something might come of it.'

'Something might come of it, dear?' repeated Rosa, surveying her friend's beauty with a highly perplexed face. 'Something might?'

'If Neville's movements are really watched, and if the purpose really is to isolate him from all friends and acquaintance and wear his daily life out grain by grain (which would seem to be in the threat to you), does it not appear likely,' said Helena, 'that his enemy would in some way communicate with Mr Tartar to warn him off from Neville? In which case, we might not only know the fact, but might know from Mr Tartar what the terms of the communication were.'

'I see!' cried Rosa. And immediately darted into her State Cabin again.

Presently her pretty face reappeared, with a heightened color, and she said that she had told Mr Crisparkle, and that Mr Crisparkle had fetched in Mr Tartar, and that Mr Tartar – 'who is waiting now, in case you want him,' added Rosa, with a half look back, and in not a little confusion between the inside of the State Cabin and the out – had declared his readiness to act as she had suggested, and to enter on his task that very day.

'I thank him from my heart,' said Helena. 'Pray tell him so.'

Again not a little confused between the Flower Garden and the Cabin, Rosa dipped in with her message, and dipped out again with more assurances from Mr Tartar, and stood wavering in a divided state between Helena and him, which proved that confusion is not always necessarily awkward, but may sometimes present a very pleasant appearance.

'And now, darling,' said Helena, 'we will be mindful of the caution that has restricted us to this interview for the present, and will part. I hear Neville moving too. Are you going back?'

'To Miss Twinkleton's?' asked Rosa.

'Yes.'

'Oh, I could never go there any more. I couldn't indeed, after that dreadful interview!' said Rosa.

'Then where *are* you going, pretty one?'

'Now I come to think of it, I don't know,' said Rosa. 'I have settled nothing at all yet, but my guardian will take care of me.

Don't be uneasy, dear. I shall be sure to be somewhere.'

(It did seem likely.)

'And I shall hear of my Rosebud from Mr Tartar?' enquired Helena.

'Yes, I suppose so; from –' Rosa looked back again in a flutter, instead of supplying the name. 'But tell me one thing before we part, dearest Helena. Tell me that you are sure, sure, sure, I couldn't help it.'

'Help it, love?'

'Help making him malicious and revengeful. I couldn't hold any terms with him, could I?'

'You know how I love you, darling,' answered Helena, with indignation; 'but I would sooner see you dead at his wicked feet.'

'That's a great comfort to me! And you will tell your poor brother so, won't you? And you will give him my remembrance and my sympathy? And you will ask him not to hate me?'

With a mournful shake of the head, as if that would be quite a superfluous entreaty, Helena lovingly kissed her two hands to her friend, and her friend's two hands were kissed to her; and then she saw a third hand (a brown one) appear among the flowers and leaves, and help her friend out of sight.

The refection that Mr Tartar produced in the Admiral's Cabin by merely touching the spring knob of a locker and the handle of a drawer, was a dazzling enchanted repast. Wonderful macaroons, glittering liqueurs, magically preserved tropical spices, and jellies of celestial tropical fruits, displayed themselves profusely at an instant's notice. But Mr Tartar could not make time stand still; and time, with his hard-hearted fleetness, strode on so fast, that Rosa was obliged to come down from the bean-stalk country to earth and her guardian's chambers.

'And now, my dear,' said Mr Grewgious, 'what is to be done next? To put the same thought in another form; what is to be done with you?'

Rosa could only look apologetically sensible of being very much in her own way, and in everybody else's. Some passing idea of living, fireproof, up a good many stairs in Furnival's Inn for the rest of her life, was the only thing in the nature of a plan that occurred to her.

'It has come into my thoughts,' said Mr Grewgious, 'that the respected lady, Miss Twinkleton, occasionally repairs to London in the recess, with the view of extending her connexion, and being available for interviews with metropolitan parents, if any; whether, until we have time in which to turn ourselves round, we might invite Miss Twinkleton to come and stay with you for a month?'

'Stay where, sir?'

'Whether,' explained Mr Grewgious, 'we might take a furnished lodging in town for a month, and invite Miss Twinkleton to assume the charge of you in it for that period?'

'And afterwards?' hinted Rosa.

'And afterwards,' said Mr Grewgious, 'we should be no worse off than we are now.'

'I think that might smooth the way,' assented Rosa.

'Then let us,' said Mr Grewgious, rising, 'go and look for a furnished lodging. Nothing could be more acceptable to me than the sweet presence of last evening, for all the remaining evenings of my existence; but these are not fit surroundings for a young lady. Let us set out in quest of adventures, and look for a furnished lodging. In the meantime, Mr Crisparkle here, about to return home immediately, will no doubt kindly see Miss Twinkleton, and invite that lady to co-operate in our plan.'

Mr Crisparkle, willingly accepting the commission, took his departure; Mr Grewgious and his ward set forth on their expedition.

As Mr Grewgious's idea of looking at a furnished lodging was to get on the opposite side of the street to a house with a suitable bill in the window, and stare at it; and then work his way tortuously to the back of the house and stare at that; and then not go in, but make similar trials of another house, with the same result; their progress was but slow. At length he bethought himself of a widowed cousin, divers times removed, of Mr Bazzard's, who had once solicited his influence in the lodger world, and who lived in Southampton Street, Bloomsbury Square. This lady's name, stated in uncompromising capitals of considerable size on a brass door-plate, and yet not lucidly stated as to sex or condition, was BILLICKIN.

Personal faintness, and an overpowering personal candour, were

the distinguishing features of Mrs Billickin's organization. She
came languishing out from her own exclusive back parlor, with the
air of having been expressly brought-to for the purpose, from an
accumulation of several swoons.

'I hope I see you well, sir,' said Mrs Billickin, recognizing her
visitor with a bend.

'Thank you, quite well. And you, ma'am?' returned Mr
Grewgious.

'I am as well,' said Mrs Billickin, becoming aspirational with
excess of faintness, 'as I hever ham.'

'My ward and an elder lady,' said Mr Grewgious, 'wish to find
a genteel lodging for a month or so. Have you any apartments
available, ma'am?'

'Mr Grewgious,' returned Mrs Billickin, 'I will not deceive you;
far from it. I *have* apartments available.'

This with the air of adding: 'Convey me to the stake, if you will;
but while I live, I will be candid.'

'And now, what apartments, ma'am?' asked Mr Grewgious,
cosily. To tame a certain severity apparent on the part of Mrs
Billickin.

'There is this sitting-room – which, call it what you will, it is
the front parlor, Miss,' said Mrs Billickin, impressing Rosa into
the conversation: 'the back parlor being what I cling to and never
part with; and there is two bedrooms at the top of the ouse with
gas laid on. I do not tell you that your bedroom floors is firm, for
firm they are not. The gas-fitter himself allowed that to make a
firm job, he must go right under your jistes,[3] and it were not
worth the outlay as a yearly tenant so to do. The piping is
carried above your jistes, and it is best that it should be made
known to you.'

Mr Grewgious, and Rosa exchanged looks of some dismay,
though they had not the least idea what latent horrors this carriage
of the piping might involve. Mrs Billickin put her hand to her
heart, as having eased it of a load.

'Well! The roof is all right, no doubt,' said Mr Grewgious,
plucking up a little.

'Mr Grewgious,' returned Mrs Billickin, 'if I was to tell you, sir,
that to have nothink above you is to have a floor above you, I
should put a deceptin upon you which I will not do. No, sir. Your

slates WILL rattle loose at that elewation in windy weather, do your utmost, best or worst! I defy you, sir, be you who you may, to keep your slates tight, try how you can.' Here Mrs Billickin, having been warm with Mr Grewgious, cooled a little, not to abuse the moral power she held over him. 'Consequent,' proceeded Mrs Billickin, more mildly, but still firmly in her incorruptible candour; 'consequent it would be worse than of no use for me to trapse and travel up to the top of the ouse with you, and for you to say, "Mrs Billickin, what stain do I notice in the ceiling, for a stain I do consider it?" and for me to answer, "I do not understand you, sir." No, sir; I will not be so underhand. I *do* understand you before you pint it out. It is the wet, sir. It do come in, and it do not come in. You may lay dry there half your lifetime; but the time will come, and it is best that you should know it, when a dripping sop would be no name for you.'

Mr Grewgious looked much disgraced by being prefigured in this pickle.

'Have you any other apartments, ma'am?' he asked.

'Mr Grewgious,' returned Mrs Billickin, with much solemnity, 'I have. You ask me have I, and my open and my honest answer air, I have. The first and second floors is wacant, and sweet rooms.'

'Come, come! There's nothing against *them*,' said Mr Grewgious, comforting himself.

'Mr Grewgious,' replied Mrs Billickin, 'pardon me, there is the stairs. Unless your mind is prepared for the stairs, it will lead to inevitable disapintmink. You cannot, Miss,' said Mrs Billickin, addressing Rosa reproachfully, 'place a first floor, and far less a second, on the level footing of a parlior. No, you cannot do it, Miss, it is beyond your power, and wherefore try?'

Mrs Billickin put it very feelingly, as if Rosa had shown a head-strong determination to hold the untenable position.

'Can we see these rooms, ma'am?' enquired her guardian.

'Mr Grewgious,' returned Mrs Billickin, 'you can. I will not disguise it from you, sir, you can.'

Mrs Billickin then sent into her back parlor for her shawl (it being a state fiction, dating from immemorial antiquity, that she could never go anywhere without being wrapped up), and having been enrobed by her attendant, led the way. She made various genteel pauses on the stairs for breath, and clutched at her heart in the drawing-room as if it had very nearly got loose, and she had caught it in the act of taking wing.

'And the second floor?' said Mr Grewgious, on finding the first satisfactory.

'Mr Grewgious,' replied Mrs Billickin, turning upon him with ceremony, as if the time had now come when a distinct under-standing on a difficult point must be arrived at, and a solemn confidence established: 'the second floor is over this.'

'Can we see that too, ma'am?'

'Yes, sir,' returned Mrs Billickin, 'it is open as the day.'

That also proving satisfactory, Mr Grewgious retired into a window with Rosa for a few words of consultation, and then asking for pen and ink, sketched out a line or two of agreement. In the meantime Mrs Billickin took a seat, and delivered a kind of Index to, or Abstract of, the general question.

'Five-and-forty shillings per week by the month certain at the time of year,' said Mrs Billickin, 'is only reasonable to both parties. It is not Bond Street nor yet St James's Palace; but it is not pre-tended that it is. Neither is it attempted to be denied – for why should it? – that the Archway leads to a Mews. Mewses must exist. Respectin' attendance; two is kep', at liberal wages. Words *has* arisen as to tradesmen, but dirty shoes on fresh hearthstoning was attributable, and no wish for a commission on your orders. Coals is either *by* the fire, or *per* the scuttle.' She emphasized the pre-positions as marking a subtle but immense difference. 'Dogs is not viewed with faviour. Besides litter, they gets stole and sharing suspicions is apt to creep in, and unpleasantness takes place.'

By this time Mr Grewgious had his agreement-lines and his earnest-money ready. 'I have signed it for the ladies, ma'am,' he said, 'and you'll have the goodness to sign it for yourself, Christian and Surname, here, if you please.'

'Mr Grewgious,' said Mrs Billickin in a new burst of candour, 'no, sir! You must excuse the Chris'en name.'

Mr Grewgious stared at her.

'The door plate is used as a protection,' said Mrs Billickin, 'and acts as such, and go from it I will not!'

Mr Grewgious stared at Rosa.

'No, Mr Grewgious, you must excuse me. So long as this ouse

is known indefinite as Billickin's, and so long as it is a doubt with
the riff-raff where Billickin may be hidin', near the street door or
down the airy, and what his weight and size, so long I feel safe.
But commit myself to a solitary female statement, no, Miss! Nor
would you for a moment wish,' said Mrs Billickin, with a strong
sense of injury, 'to take that advantage of your sex, if you was
not brought to it by inconsiderate example.'

Rosa reddening as if she had made some most disgraceful
attempt to over-reach the good lady, besought Mr Grewgious
to rest content with any signature. And accordingly, in a baronial
way, the sign-manual BILLICKIN got appended to the document.

Details were then settled for taking possession on the next day
but one, when Miss Twinkleton might be reasonably expected, and
Rosa went back to Furnival's Inn on her guardian's arm.

Behold Mr Tartar walking up and down Furnival's Inn, checking
himself when he saw them coming, and advancing towards them!

'It occurred to me,' hinted Mr Tartar, 'that we might go up
the river, the weather being so delicious and the tide serving. I have
a boat of my own at the Temple Stairs.'

'I have not been up the river for this many a day,' said Mr
Grewgious, tempted.

'I was never up the river,' added Rosa.

Within half an hour they were setting this matter right by going
up the river. The tide was running with them, the afternoon was
charming. Mr Tartar's boat was perfect. Mr Tartar and Lobley
(Mr Tartar's man) pulled a pair of oars. Mr Tartar had a yacht, it
seemed, lying somewhere down by Greenhithe; and Mr Tartar's
man had charge of this yacht, and was detached upon his present
service. He was a jolly-favored man, with tawny hair and whiskers,
and a big red face. He was the dead image of the sun in old wood-
cuts, his hair and whiskers answering for rays all round him.
Resplendent in the bow of the boat, he was a shining sight, with a
man-of-war's man's shirt on – or off, according to opinion – and
his arms and breast tattoo'd all sorts of patterns. Lobley seemed to
take it easily, and so did Mr Tartar; yet their oars bent as they
pulled, and the boat bounded under them. Mr Tartar talked as if
he were doing nothing, to Rosa who was really doing nothing, and
to Mr Grewgious who was doing this much that he steered all
wrong – but what did that matter, when a turn of Mr Tartar's

skilful wrist, or a mere grin of Mr Lobley's over the bow, put all to rights! The tide bore them on in the gayest and most sparkling manner, until they stopped to dine in some everlastingly green garden, needing no matter of fact identification here; and then the tide obligingly turned – being devoted to that party alone for that day – and as they floated idly among some osier beds, Rosa tried what she could do in the rowing way, and came off splendidly, being much assisted; and Mr Grewgious tried what he could do, and came off on his back, doubled up with an oar under his chin, being not assisted at all. Then there was an interval of rest under boughs (such rest!) what time Mr Lobley mopped, and, arranging cushions, stretchers, and the like, danced the tight-rope the whole length of the boat like a man to whom shoes were a superstition and stockings slavery; and then came the sweet return among delicious odours of limes in bloom, and musical ripplings; and, all too soon, the great black city cast its shadow on the waters, and its dark bridges spanned them as death spans life, and the everlastingly green garden seemed to be left for everlasting, unregainable and far away.

'Cannot people get through life without gritty stages, I wonder!' Rosa thought next day, when the town was very gritty again, and everything had a strange and an uncomfortable appearance on it of seeming to wait for something that wouldn't come. No. She began to think, that, now the Cloisterham school days had glided past and gone, the gritty stages would begin to set in at intervals and make themselves wearily known.

Yet what did Rosa expect? Did she expect Miss Twinkleton? Miss Twinkleton duly came. Forth from her back parlor issued the Billickin to receive Miss Twinkleton, and War was in the Billickin's eye from that fell moment.

Miss Twinkleton brought a quantity of luggage with her, having all Rosa's as well as her own. The Billickin took it ill that Miss Twinkleton's mind, being sorely disturbed by this luggage, failed to take in her personal identity with that clearness of perception which was due to its demands. Stateliness mounted her gloomy throne upon the Billickin's brow in consequence. And when Miss Twinkleton, in agitation taking stock of her trunks and packages, of which she had seventeen, particularly counted in the Billickin herself as number eleven, the B found it necessary to repudiate.

'Things cannot too soon be put upon the footing,' said she, with a candour so demonstrative as to be almost obtrusive, 'that the person of the Ouse is not a box nor yet a bundle, nor a carpet bag – no, I am ily obleeged to you, Miss Twinkleton, nor yet a beggar.' This last disclaimer had reference to Miss Twinkleton's distractedly pressing two and sixpence on her, instead of the cabman.

Thus cast off, Miss Twinkleton wildly enquired 'which gentleman' was to be paid? There being two gentlemen in that position (Miss Twinkleton having arrived with two cabs), each gentleman on being paid held forth his two and sixpence on the flat of his open hand, and, with a speechless stare and a dropped jaw, displayed his wrong to Heaven and Earth. Terrified by this alarming spectacle, Miss Twinkleton placed another shilling in each hand, at the same time appealing to the law in flurried accents, and recounting her luggage; this time with the two gentlemen in, who caused the total to come out complicated. Meanwhile the two gentlemen, each looking very hard at the last shilling, as if it might become eighteenpence if he kept his eyes on it, grumblingly descended the doorsteps, ascended their carriages, and drove away, leaving Miss Twinkleton bewildered on a bonnet-box in tears.

The Billickin beheld this manifestation of weakness without sympathy, and gave directions for 'a young man to be got in,' to wrestle with the luggage. When that gladiator had disappeared from the arena, peace ensued, and the new lodgers dined.

But the Billickin had somehow come to the knowledge that Miss Twinkleton kept a school. The leap from that knowledge to the inference that Miss Twinkleton would set herself to teach *her* something, was easy. 'But you don't do it,' soliloquized the Billickin; '*I* am not your pupil, whatever she,' meaning Rosa, 'may be, poor thing!'

Miss Twinkleton, on the other hand, having changed her dress and recovered her spirits, was animated by a bland desire to improve the occasion in all ways, and to be as serene a model as possible. In a happy compromise between her two states of existence, she had already become, with her work-basket before her, the equably vivacious companion with a slight judicious flavoring of information, when the Billickin announced herself.

'I will not hide from you, ladies,' said the B, enveloped in the shawl of state, 'for it is not my character to hide neither my motives nor my actions, that I take the liberty to look in upon you to express a ope that your dinner was to your liking. Though not Professed but Plain, still her wages should be a sufficient object to her to stimilate to soar above mere roast and biled.'

'We dined very well indeed,' said Rosa, 'thank you.'

'Accustomed,' said Miss Twinkleton, with a gracious air which to the jealous ears of the Billickin seemed to add 'my good woman': — 'Accustomed to a liberal and nutritious, yet plain and salutary diet, we have found no reason to bemoan our absence from the ancient city, and the methodical household, in which the quiet routine of our lot has been hitherto cast.'

'I did think it well to mention to my cook,' observed the Billickin with a gush of candour, 'which I ope you will agree with me, Miss Twinkleton, was a right precaution, that the young lady being used to what we should consider here but poor diet, had better be brought forard by degrees. For a rush from scanty feeding to generous feeding, and from what you may call messing to what you may call method, do require a power of constitution which is not often found in youth, particular when undermined by boarding-school.'

It will be seen that the Billickin now openly pitted herself against Miss Twinkleton, as one whom she had fully ascertained to be her natural enemy.

'Your remarks,' returned Miss Twinkleton, from a remote moral eminence, 'are well meant, I have no doubt; but you will permit me to observe that they develop a mistaken view of the subject, which can only be imputed to your extreme want of accurate information.'

'My informiation,' retorted the Billickin, throwing in an extra syllable for the sake of an emphasis at once polite and powerful; 'my informiation, Miss Twinkleton, were my own experience, which I believe is usually considered to be good guidance. But whether so or not, I was put in youth to a very genteel boarding-school, the mistress being no less a lady than yourself, of about your own age or it may be some years younger, and a poorness of blood flowed from the table which has run through my life.'

'Very likely,' said Miss Twinkleton, still from her distant eminence; 'and very much to be deplored. Rosa, my dear, how are you getting on with your work?'

'Miss Twinkleton,' resumed the Billickin, in a courtly manner, 'before retiring on the Int, as a lady should, I wish to ask of yourself, as a lady, whether I am to consider that my words is doubted?'

'I am not aware on what ground you cherish such a supposition,' began Miss Twinkleton, when the Billickin neatly stopped her.

'Do not, if you please, put suppositions betwixt my lips where none such have been imported by myself. Your flow of words is great, Miss Twinkleton, and no doubt is expected from you by your pupils, and no doubt is considered worth the money. *No* doubt, I am sure. But not paying for flows of words, and not asking to be faviored with them here, I wish to repeat my question.'

'If you refer to the poverty of your circulation –' began Miss Twinkleton again, when again the Billickin neatly stopped her.

'I have used no such expressions.'

'If you refer, then, to the poorness of your blood –'

'Brought upon me,' stipulated the Billickin, expressly, 'at a boarding-school.'

'Then,' resumed Miss Twinkleton, 'all I can say is, that I am bound to believe, on your asseveration, that it is very poor indeed. I cannot forbear adding, that if that unfortunate circumstance influences your conversation, it is much to be lamented, and it is eminently desirable that your blood were richer. Rosa, my dear, how are you getting on with your work?'

'Hem! Before retiring, Miss,' proclaimed the Billickin to Rosa, loftily cancelling Miss Twinkleton, 'I should wish it to be understood between yourself and me that my transactions in future is with you alone. I know no elderly lady here, Miss; none older than yourself.'

'A highly desirable arrangement, Rosa my dear,' observed Miss Twinkleton.

'It is not, Miss,' said the Billickin, with a sarcastic smile, 'that I possess the Mill I have heard of, in which old single ladies could be ground up young (what a gift it would be to some of us!), but that I limit myself to you totally.'

'When I have any desire to communicate a request to the person of the house, Rosa my dear,' observed Miss Twinkleton with majestic cheerfulness, 'I will make it known to you, and you will kindly undertake, I am sure, that it is conveyed to the proper quarter.'

'Good-evening, Miss,' said the Billickin, at once affectionately and distantly. 'Being alone in my eyes, I wish you good-evening with best wishes, and do not find myself drove, I am truly 'appy to say, into expressing my contempt for any indiwidual, unfortunately for yourself, belonging to you.'

The Billickin gracefully withdrew with this parting speech, and from that time Rosa occupied the restless position of shuttlecock between these two battledores. Nothing could be done without a smart match being played out. Thus, on the daily-arising question of dinner, Miss Twinkleton would say; the three being present together:

'Perhaps, my love, you will consult with the person of the house, whether she could procure us a lamb's fry; or, failing that, a roast fowl.'

On which the Billickin would retort (Rosa not having spoken a word), 'If you was better accustomed to butcher's-meat, Miss, you would not entertain the idea of a lamb's fry. Firstly, because lambs has long been sheep, and secondly, because there is such things as killing-days, and there is not. As to roas* fowls, Miss, why you must be quite surfeited with roast fowls, letting alone your buying, when you market for yourself, the agedest of poultry with the scaliest of legs, quite as if you was accustomed to picking 'em out for cheapness. Try a little inwention, Miss. Use yourself to ousekeeping a bit. Come now, think of somethink else.'

To this encouragement, offered with the indulgent toleration of a wise and liberal expert, Miss Twinkleton would rejoin, reddening:

'Or, my dear, you might propose to the person of the house, a duck.'

'Well, Miss!' the Billickin would exclaim (still no word being spoken by Rosa), 'you do surprise me when you speak of ducks! Not to mention that they're getting out of season and very dear, it really strikes to my heart to see you have a duck; for the breast, which is the only delicate cuts in a duck, always goes in a direction which I cannot imagine where, and your own plate comes down so miserable skin-and-bony! Try again, Miss. Think more of yourself and less of others. A dish of sweetbreads, now, or a bit of mutton. Somethink at which you can get your equal chance.'

Occasionally the game would wax very brisk indeed, and would be kept up with a smartness rendering such an encounter as this quite tame. But the Billickin almost invariably made by far the higher score; and would come in with side hits of the most unexpected and extraordinary description, when she seemed without a chance.

All this did not improve the gritty state of things in London, or the air that London had acquired in Rosa's eyes of waiting for something that never came. Tired of working and conversing with Miss Twinkleton, she suggested working and reading: to which Miss Twinkleton readily assented, as an admired reader, of tried powers. But Rosa soon made the discovery that Miss Twinkleton didn't read fairly. She cut the love scenes, interpolated passages in praise of female celibacy, and was guilty of other glaring pious frauds. As an instance in point, take the glowing passage: 'Ever dearest and best adored, said Edward, clasping the dear head to his breast, and drawing the silken hair through his caressing fingers, from which he suffered it to fall like golden rain; ever dearest and best adored, let us fly from the unsympathetic world and the sterile coldness of the stony-hearted, to the rich warm Paradise of Trust and Love.' Miss Twinkleton's fraudulent version tamely ran thus: 'Ever engaged to me with the consent of our parents on both sides, and the approbation of the silver-haired rector of the district, said Edward, respectfully raising to his lips the taper fingers so skilful in embroidery, tambour, crochet, and other truly feminine arts; let me call on thy papa ere to-morrow's dawn has sunk into the west, and propose a suburban establishment, lowly it may be, but within our means, where he will be always welcome as an evening guest, and where every arrangement shall invest economy and the constant interchange of scholastic acquirements with the attributes of the ministering angel to domestic bliss.'

As the days crept on and nothing happened, the neighbours began to say that the pretty girl at Billickin's, who looked so wistfully and so much out of the gritty windows of the drawing-room, seemed to be losing her spirits. The pretty girl might have lost them but for the accident of lighting on some books of voyages and sea-adventure. As a compensation against their romance, Miss Twinkleton, reading aloud, made the most of all the latitudes and longitudes, bearings, winds, currents, offsets, and other statistics (which she felt to be none the less improving because they expressed nothing whatever to her); while Rosa, listening intently, made the most of what was nearest to her heart. So they both did better than before.

CHAPTER 22

The Dawn Again

ALTHOUGH Mr Crisparkle and John Jasper met daily under the Cathedral roof, nothing at any time passed between them bearing reference to Edwin Drood after the time, more than half a year gone by, when Jasper mutely showed the Minor Canon the conclusion and the resolution entered in his Diary. It is not likely that they ever met, though so often, without the thoughts of each reverting to the subject. It is not likely that they ever met, though so often, without a sensation on the part of each that the other was a perplexing secret to him. Jasper as the denouncer and pursuer of Neville Landless, and Mr Crisparkle as his consistent advocate and protector, must at least have stood sufficiently in opposition to have speculated with keen interest each on the steadiness and next direction of the other's designs. But neither ever broached the theme.

False pretence not being in the Minor Canon's nature, he doubtless displayed openly that he would at any time have revived the subject, and even desired to discuss it. The determined reticence of Jasper, however, was not to be so approached. Impassive, moody, solitary, resolute, concentrated on one idea, and on its attendant fixed purpose that he would share it with no fellow creature, he lived apart from human life. Constantly exercising an Art which brought him into mechanical harmony with others, and which could not have been pursued unless he and they had been in the nicest mechanical relations and unison, it is curious to consider that the spirit of the man was in moral accordance or interchange with nothing around him. This indeed he had confided to his lost nephew, before the occasion for his present inflexibility arose.

That he must know of Rosa's abrupt departure, and that he must divine its cause, was not to be doubted. Did he suppose that he had terrified her into silence, or did he suppose that she had imparted to any one – to Mr Crisparkle himself, for instance – the particulars of his last interview with her? Mr Crisparkle could not determine this in his mind. He could not but admit, however, as a just man, that it was not, of itself, a crime to fall in love with Rosa, any more than it was a crime to offer to set love above revenge.

The dreadful suspicion of Jasper, which Rosa was so shocked to have received into her imagination, appeared to have no harbour in Mr Crisparkle's. If it ever haunted Helena's thoughts or Neville's, neither gave it one spoken word of utterance. Mr Grewgious took no pains to conceal his implacable dislike of Jasper, yet he never referred it, however distantly, to such a source. But he was a reticent as well as an eccentric man; and he made no mention of a certain evening when he warmed his hands at the Gate House fire, and looked steadily down upon a certain heap of torn and miry clothes upon the floor.

Drowsy Cloisterham, whenever it awoke to a passing reconsideration of a story above six months old and dismissed by the bench of magistrates, was pretty equally divided in opinion whether John Jasper's beloved nephew had been killed by his passionate rival treacherously, or in an open struggle; or had, for his own purposes, spirited himself away. It then lifted up its head, to notice that the bereaved Jasper was still ever devoted to discovery and revenge; and then dozed off again. This was the condition of matters, all round, at the period to which the present history has now attained.

The Cathedral doors have closed for the night; and the Choir-Master, on a short leave of absence for two or three services, sets his face towards London. He travels thither by the means by which Rosa travelled, and arrives, as Rosa arrived, on a hot, dusty evening.

His travelling baggage is easily carried in his hand, and he repairs with it, on foot, to a hybrid hotel in a little square behind Aldersgate Street, near the General Post Office. It is hotel, boarding-house, or lodging-house, at its visitor's option. It announces itself as a novel enterprise in the new Railway Advertisers timidly beginning to spring up. It bashfully, almost apologetically, gives the traveller to understand that it does not expect him, on the good old constitutional hotel plan, to order a pint of sweet blacking[1] for his drinking, and throw it away; but insinuates that he may have his boots blacked instead of his stomach, and maybe also have bed, breakfast, attendance, and a porter up all night, for a certain fixed charge. From these and similar premises, many true Britons in the lowest spirits deduce that the times are levelling times, except in the article of high roads, of which there will shortly be not one in England.

He eats without appetite, and soon goes forth again. Eastward and still eastward through the stale streets he takes his way, until he reaches his destination: a miserable court, specially miserable among many such.

He ascends a broken staircase, opens a door, looks into a dark stifling room, and says: 'Are you alone here?'

'Alone, deary; worse luck for me, and better for you,' replies a croaking voice. 'Come in, come in, whoever you be: I can't see you till I light a match, yet I seem to know the sound of your speaking. I am acquainted with you; ain't I?'

'Light your match, and try.'

'So I will, deary, so I will; but my hand that shakes, as I can't lay it on a match all in a moment. And I cough so, that, put my matches where I may, I never find 'em there. They jump and start as I cough and cough, like live things. Are you off a voyage, deary?'

'No.'

'Not seafaring?'

'No.'

'Well, there's land customers, and there's water customers. I'm a mother to both. Different from Jack Chinaman t'other side the court. He ain't a father to neither. It ain't in him. And he ain't got the true secret of mixing, though he charges as much as me that has, and more if he can get it. Here's a match, and now where's the candle? If my cough takes me, I shall cough out twenty matches afore I gets a light.'

But she finds the candle, and lights it, before the cough comes on. It seizes her in the moment of success, and she sits down rocking herself to and fro, and gasping at intervals, 'Oh, my lungs is awful bad, my lungs is wore away to cabbage-nets!' until the fit is over.

During its continuance she has had no power of sight, or any other power not absorbed in the struggle; but as it leaves her, she begins to strain her eyes, and as soon as she is able to articulate, she cries, staring:

'Why, it's you!'

'Are you so surprised to see me?'

'I thought I never should have seen you again, deary. I thought you was dead, and gone to Heaven.'

'Why?'

'I didn't suppose you could have kept away, alive, so long, from the poor old soul with the real receipt for mixing it! And you are in mourning too! Why didn't you come and have a pipe or two of comfort? Did they leave you money, perhaps, and so you didn't want comfort?'

'No!'

'Who was they as died, deary?'

'A relation.'

'Died of what, lovey?'[2]

'Probably, Death.'

'We are short to-night!' cries the woman, with a propitiatory laugh. 'Short and snappish, we are! But we're out of sorts for want of a smoke. We've got the all-overs, haven't us, deary? But this is the place to cure 'em in; this is the place where the all-overs is smoked off.'

'You may make ready, then,' replies the visitor, 'as soon as you like.'

He divests himself of his shoes, loosens his cravat, and lies across the foot of the squalid bed, with his head resting on his left hand.

'Now, you begin to look like yourself,' says the woman, approvingly. 'Now I begin to know my old customer indeed! Been trying to mix for yourself this long time, poppet?'

'I have been taking it now and then in my own way.'

'Never take it your own way. It ain't good for trade and it ain't good for you. Where's my ink bottle, and where's my thimble, and where's my little spoon? He's going to take it in a artful form now, my deary dear!'

Entering on her process, and beginning to bubble and blow at the faint spark enclosed in the hollow of her hands, she speaks from time to time, in a tone of snuffing satisfaction, without breaking off; when he speaks, he does so without looking at her, and as if his thoughts were already roaming away by anticipation.

'I've got a pretty many smokes ready for you, first and last; haven't I, chuckey?'

'A good many.'

'When you first come, you was quite new to it; warn't ye?'

'Yes, I was easily disposed of, then.'

'But you got on in the world, and was able by-and-bye to take your pipes with the best of 'em, warn't ye?'

'Aye. And the worst.'

'It's just ready for you. What a sweet singer you was when you first come! Used to drop your head, and sing yourself off, like a bird! It's ready for you now, deary.'

He takes it from her with great care, and puts the mouthpiece to his lips. She seats herself beside him, ready to refill the pipe. After inhaling a few whiffs in silence, he doubtingly accosts her with:

'Is it as potent as it used to be?'

'What do you speak of, deary?'

'What should I speak of, but what I have in my mouth!'

'It's just the same. Always the identical same.'

'It doesn't taste so. And it's slower.'

'You've got more used to it, you see.'

'That may be the cause, certainly. Look here.' He stops, becomes dreamy, and seems to forget that he has invited her attention. She bends over him, and speaks in his ear.

'I'm attending to you. Says you just now, look here. Says I now, I am attending to ye. We was talking just before of your being used to it.'

'I know all that. I was only thinking. Look here. Suppose you had something in your mind; something you were going to do.'

'Yes, deary; something I was going to do?'

'But had not quite determined to do.'

'Yes, deary.'

'Might or might not do, you understand.'

'Yes.' With the point of a needle she stirs the contents of the bowl.

'Should you do it in your fancy, when you were lying here doing this?'

She nods her head. 'Over and over again.'

'Just like me! I did it over and over again. I have done it hundreds of thousands of times in this room.'

'It's to be hoped it was pleasant to do, deary.'

'It *was* pleasant to do!'

He says this with a savage air, and a spring or start at her. Quite unmoved, she retouches or replenishes the contents of the bowl with her little spatula. Seeing her intent upon the occupation, he sinks into his former attitude.

'It was a journey, a difficult and dangerous journey. That was the subject in my mind. A hazardous and perilous journey, over abysses where a slip would be destruction. Look down, look down! You see what lies at the bottom there?'

He has darted forward to say it, and to point at the ground, as though at some imaginary object far beneath. The woman looks at him, as his spasmodic face approaches close to hers, and not at his pointing. She seems to know what the influence of her perfect quietude will be; if so, she has not miscalculated it, for he subsides again.

'Well; I have told you. I did it, here, hundreds of thousands of times. What do I say? I did it millions and billions of times. I did it so often, and through such vast expanses of time, that when it was really done, it seemed not worth the doing, it was done so soon.'

'That's the journey you have been away upon?' she quietly remarks.

He glares at her as he smokes; and then, his eyes becoming filmy, answers: 'That's the journey.'

Silence ensues. His eyes are sometimes closed and sometimes open. The woman sits beside him, very attentive to the pipe, which is all the while at his lips.

'I'll warrant,' she observes, when he has been looking fixedly at her for some consecutive moments, with a singular appearance in his eyes of seeming to see her a long way off, instead of so near him: 'I'll warrant you made the journey in a many ways, when you made it so often?'

'No, always in one way.'

'Always in the same way?'

'Aye.'

'In the way in which it was really made at last?'

'Aye.'

'And always took the same pleasure in harping on it?'

'Aye.'

For the time he appears unequal to any other reply than this lazy monosyllabic assent. Probably to assure herself that it is not the assent of a mere automaton, she reverses the form of her next sentence.

'Did you never get tired of it, deary, and try to call up something else for a change?'

He struggles into a sitting posture, and retorts upon her: 'What do you mean? What did I want? What did I come for?'

She gently lays him back again, and, before returning him the instrument he has dropped, revives the fire in it with her own breath; then says to him, coaxingly:

'Sure, sure, sure! Yes, yes, yes! Now I go along with you. You was too quick for me. I see now. You come o' purpose to take the journey. Why, I might have known it, through its standing by you so.'

He answers, first with a laugh, and then with a passionate setting of his teeth: 'Yes, I came on purpose. When I could not bear my life, I came to get the relief, and I got it. It WAS one! It WAS one!' This repetition with extraordinary vehemence, and the snarl of a wolf.

She observes him very cautiously, as though mentally feeling her way to her next remark. It is: 'There was a fellow-traveller, deary.'

'Ha ha ha!' He breaks into a ringing laugh, or rather yell.

'To think,' he cries, 'how often fellow-traveller, and yet not know it! To think how many times he went the journey, and never saw the road!'

The woman kneels upon the floor, with her arms crossed on the coverlet of the bed, close by him, and her chin upon them. In this crouching attitude she watches him. The pipe is falling from his mouth. She puts it back, and, laying her hand upon his chest, moves him slightly from side to side. Upon that lie speaks, as if she had spoken.

'Yes! I always made the journey first, before the changes of colors and the great landscapes and glittering processions began. They couldn't begin till it was off my mind. I had no room till then for anything else.'

Once more he lapses into silence. Once more she lays her hand upon his chest, and moves him slightly to and fro, as a cat might stimulate a half-slain mouse. Once more he speaks, as if she had spoken.

'What? I told you so. When it comes to be real at last, it is so short that it seems unreal for the first time. Hark!'

'Yes, deary. I'm listening.'

'Time and place are both at hand.'

He is on his feet, speaking in a whisper, and as if in the dark.

'Time, place, and fellow-traveller,' she suggests, adopting his tone, and holding him softly by the arm.

'How could the time be at hand unless the fellow-traveller was? Hush! The journey's made. It's over.'

'So soon?'

'That's what I said to you. So soon. Wait a little. This is a vision. I shall sleep it off. It has been too short and easy. I must have a better vision than this; this is the poorest of all. No struggle, no consciousness of peril, no entreaty – and yet I never saw *that* before.' With a start.

'Saw what, deary?'

'Look at it! Look what a poor, mean, miserable thing it is! *That* must be real. It's over!'

He has accompanied this incoherence with some wild un-meaning gestures; but they trail off into the progressive inaction of stupor, and he lies a log upon the bed.

The woman, however, is still inquisitive. With a repetition of her catlike action she slightly stirs his body again, and listens; stirs it again, and listens; whispers to it, and listens. Finding it past all rousing for the time, she slowly gets upon her feet, with an air of disappointment, and flicks the face with the back of her hand in turning from it.

But she goes no further away[3] from it than the chair upon the hearth. She sits in it, with an elbow on one of its arms, and her chin upon that hand, intent upon him. 'I heard ye say once,' she croaks under her breath, 'I heard ye say once, when I was lying where you're lying, and you were making your speculations upon me, "Unintelligible!" I heard you say so, of two more than me. But don't ye be too sure always; don't ye be too sure, beauty!'

Unwinking, catlike, and intent, she presently adds: 'Not so

potent as it once was? Ah! Perhaps not at first. Ye may be more right there. Practice makes perfect. I may have learned the secret how to make ye talk, my deary.'

He talks no more, whether or no. Twitching in an ugly way from time to time, both as to his face and limbs, he lies heavy and silent. The wretched candle burns down; the woman takes its expiring end between her fingers, lights another at it, crams the guttering frying morsel deep into the candlestick, and rams it home with the new candle, as if she were loading some ill-savoured and unseemly weapon of witchcraft; the new candle in its turn burns down; and still he lies insensible. At length what remains of the last candle is blown out, and daylight looks into the room.

It has not looked very long, when he sits up, chilled and shaking, slowly recovers consciousness of where he is, and makes himself ready to depart. The woman receives what he pays her with a grateful 'Bless ye, bless ye, deary!' and seems, tired out, to begin making herself ready for sleep as he leaves the room.

But seeming may be false or true. It is false in this case, for the moment the stairs had ceased to creak under his tread, she glides after him, muttering emphatically: 'I'll not miss ye twice!'

There is no egress from the court but by its entrance. With a weird peep from the doorway, she watches for his looking back. He does not look back before disappearing, with a wavering step. She follows him, peeps from the court, sees him still faltering on without looking back, and holds him in view.

He repairs to the back of Aldersgate Street, where a door immediately opens to his knocking. She crouches in another doorway, watching that one, and easily comprehending that he puts up temporarily at that house. Her patience is unexhausted by hours. For sustenance she can, and does, buy bread within a hundred yards, and milk as it is carried past her.

He comes forth again at noon, having changed his dress, but carrying nothing in his hand, and having nothing carried for him. He is not going back into the country, therefore, just yet. She follows him a little way, hesitates instantaneously, turns confidently and goes straight into the house he has quitted.

Is the gentleman from Cloisterham indoors?

Just gone out.

Unlucky. When does the gentleman return to Cloisterham?

At six this evening.

Bless ye and thank ye. May the Lord prosper a business where a civil question, even from a poor soul, is so civilly answered!

'I'll not miss ye twice!' repeats the poor soul in the street, and not so civilly. 'I lost ye last, where that omnibus you got into nigh your journey's end plied betwixt the station and the place. I wasn't so much as certain that you even went right on to the place. Now I know ye did. My gentleman from Cloisterham, I'll be there before ye and bide your coming. I've swore my oath that I'll not miss ye twice!'

Accordingly, that same evening the poor soul stands in Cloisterham High Street, looking at the many quaint gables of the Nuns' House, and getting through the time as she best can until nine o'clock; at which hour she has reason to suppose that the arriving omnibus passengers may have some interest for her. The friendly darkness, at that hour, renders it easy for her to ascertain whether this be so or not; and it is so, for the passenger not to be missed twice arrives among the rest.

'Now, let me see what becomes of you. Go on!'

An observation addressed to the air. And yet it might be addressed to the passenger, so compliantly does he go on along the High Street until he comes to an arched gateway, at which he unexpectedly vanishes. The poor soul quickens her pace; is swift, and close upon him in turning under the gateway; but only sees a postern staircase on one side of it, and on the other side an ancient vaulted room, in which a large-headed, grey-haired gentleman is writing, under the odd circumstances of sitting open to the thoroughfare and eyeing all who pass, as if he were toll-taker at the gateway: though the way is free.

'Halloa!' he cries in a low voice, seeing her brought to a standstill: 'Who are you looking for?'

'There was a gentleman passed in here this minute, sir. Gentleman in mourning.'

'Of course there was. What do you want with him?'

'Where do he live, deary?'

'Live? Up that staircase.'

'Bless ye! Whisper. What's his name, deary?'

'Surname Jasper, Christian name John. Mr John Jasper.'

'Has he a calling, good gentleman?'

'Calling? Yes. Sings in the choir.'

'In the spire?'

'Choir.'

'What's that?'

Mr Datchery rises from his papers, and comes to his doorstep. 'Do you know what a cathedral is?' he asks, jocosely.

The woman nods.

'What is it?'

She looks puzzled, casting about in her mind to find a definition, when it occurs to her that it is easier to point out the substantial object itself, massive against the dark-blue sky and the early stars.

'That's the answer. Go in there at seven to-morrow morning, and you may see Mr John Jasper, and hear him too.'

'Thank ye! Thank ye!'

The burst of triumph in which she thanks him does not escape the notice of the single buffer of an easy temper living idly on his means. He glances at her; clasps his hands behind him, as the wont of such buffers is, and lounges along the echoing Precincts at her side.

'Or,' he suggests, with a backward hitch of his head, 'you can go up at once to Mr Jasper's rooms there.'

The woman eyes him with a cunning smile, and shakes her head.

'Oh! You don't want to speak to him?'

She repeats her dumb reply, and forms with her lips a soundless 'No.'

'You can admire him at a distance three times a day, whenever you like. It's a long way to come for that, though.'

The woman looks up quickly. If Mr Datchery thinks she is to be so induced to declare where she comes from, he is of a much easier temper than she is. But she acquits him of such an artful thought, as he lounges along, like the chartered bore of the city, with his uncovered grey hair blowing about, and his purposeless hands rattling the loose money in the pockets of his trousers.

The chink of the money has an attraction for her greedy ears. 'Wouldn't you help me to pay for my traveller's lodging, dear gentleman, and to pay my way along? I am a poor soul, I am indeed, and troubled with a grievous cough.'

'You know the travellers' lodging, I perceive, and are making direct for it,' is Mr Datchery's bland comment, still rattling his loose money. 'Been here often, my good woman?'

'Once in all my life.'

'Aye, aye?'

They have arrived at the entrance to the Monks' Vineyard. An appropriate remembrance, presenting an exemplary model for imitation, is revived in the woman's mind by the sight of the place. She stops at the gate, and says energetically:

'By this token, though you mayn't believe it, That a young gentleman gave me three and sixpence as I was coughing my breath away on this very grass. I asked him for three and sixpence, and he gave it me.'

'Wasn't it a little cool to name your sum?' hints Mr Datchery, still rattling. 'Isn't it customary to leave the amount open? Mightn't it have had the appearance, to the young gentleman – only the appearance – that he was rather dictated to?'

'Look'ee here, deary,' she replies, in a confidential and persuasive tone, 'I wanted the money to lay it out on a medicine as does me good, and as I deal in. I told the young gentleman so, and he gave it me, and I laid it out honest to the last brass farden. I want to lay out the same sum in the same way now; and if you'll give it me, I'll lay it out honest to the last brass farden again, upon my soul!'

'What's the medicine?'

'I'll be honest with you beforehand, as well as after. It's opium.'

Mr Datchery, with a sudden change of countenance, gives her a sudden look.

'It's opium, deary. Neither more nor less. And it's like a human creetur so far, that you always hear what can be said against it, but seldom what can be said in its praise!'

Mr Datchery begins very slowly to count out the sum demanded of him. Greedily watching his hands, she continues to hold forth on the great example set him.

'It was last Christmas Eve, just arter dark, the once that I was here afore, when the young gentleman gave me the three and six.'

Mr Datchery stops in his counting, finds he has counted wrong, shakes his money together, and begins again.

'And the young gentleman's name,' she adds, 'was Edwin.'

Mr Datchery drops some money, stoops to pick it up, and reddens with the exertion as he asks:

'How do you know the young gentleman's name?'

'I asked him for it, and he told it me. I only asked him the two questions, what was his Chris'en name, and whether he'd a sweet-heart? And he answered, Edwin, and he hadn't.'

Mr Datchery pauses with the selected coins in his hand, rather as if he were falling into a brown study of their value, and couldn't bear to part with them. The woman looks at him distrustfully, and with her anger brewing for the event of his thinking better of the gift; but he bestows it on her as if he were abstracting his mind from the sacrifice, and with many servile thanks she goes her way.

John Jasper's lamp is kindled, and his Lighthouse is shining when Mr Datchery returns alone towards it. As mariners on a dangerous voyage, approaching an iron-bound coast, may look along the beams of the warning light to the haven lying beyond it that may never be reached, so Mr Datchery's wistful gaze is directed to this beacon, and beyond.

His object in now revisiting his lodging is merely to put on the hat which seems so superfluous an article in his wardrobe. It is half-past ten by the Cathedral clock when he walks out into the Precincts again; he lingers and looks about him, as though, the enchanted hour when Mr Durdles may be stoned home having struck, he had some expectation of seeing the Imp who is appointed to the mission of stoning him.

In effect, that Power of Evil is abroad. Having nothing living to stone at the moment, he is discovered by Mr Datchery in the unholy office of stoning the dead, through the railings of the churchyard. The Imp finds this a relishing and piquing pursuit; firstly, because their resting-place is announced to be sacred; and secondly, because the tall headstones are sufficiently like themselves, on their beat in the dark, to justify the delicious fancy that they are hurt when hit.

Mr Datchery hails him with: 'Halloa, Winks!'

He acknowledges the hail with: 'Halloa, Dick!' Their acquaintance seemingly having been established on a familiar footing.

'But, I say,' he remonstrates, 'don't yer go a making my name public. I never means to plead to no name, mind yer. When they says to me in the Lock-up, a goin to put me down in the book, "What's your name?" I says to them "Find out." Likeways when they says "What's your religion?" I says "Find out."' Which, it may be observed in passing, it would be immensely difficult for the State, however Statistical, to do.

'Asides which,' adds the boy, 'there ain't no family of Winkses.'

'I think there must be.'

'Yer lie, there ain't. The travellers give me the name on account of my getting no settled sleep and being knocked up all night; whereby I gits one eye roused open afore I've shut the other. That's what Winks means. Deputy's the nighest name to indict me by: but yer wouldn't catch me pleading to that, neither.'

'Deputy be it always, then. We two are good friends; eh, Deputy?'

'Jolly good.'

'I forgave you the debt you owed me when we first became acquainted, and many of my sixpences have come your way since; eh, Deputy?'

'Ah! And what's more, yer ain't no friend o' Jarsper's. What did he go a histing me off my legs for?'

'What indeed! But never mind him now. A shilling of mine is coming your way to-night, Deputy. You have just taken in a lodger I have been speaking to; an infirm woman with a cough.'

'Puffer,' assents Deputy, with a shrewd leer of recognition, and smoking an imaginary pipe with his head very much on one side and his eyes rolling very much out of their places: 'Hopeum Puffer.'

'What is her name?'

'Er Royal Highness the Princess Puffer.'[4]

'She has some other name than that. Where does she live?'

'Up in London. Among the Jacks.'

'The sailors?'

'I said so; Jacks. And Chaynermen. And hother Knifers.'

'I should like to know, through you, exactly where she lives.'

'All right. Give us 'old.'

A shilling passes; and, in that spirit of confidence which should pervade all business transactions between principals of honor, this piece of business is considered done.

'But here's a lark!' cries Deputy. 'Where do yer think Er Royal Highness is a goin to to-morrow morning? Blest if she ain't a goin to the KIN-FREE-DER-EL!' He greatly prolongs the word in his ecstasy, and smites his leg, and doubles himself up in a fit of shrill laughter.

'How do you know that, Deputy?'

'Cos she told me so just now. She said she must be hup and hout o' purpose. She ses, "Deputy, I must 'ave a early wash, and make myself as swell as I can, for I'm a goin to take a turn at the KIN-FREE-DER-EL!"' He separates the syllables with his former zest, and, not finding his sense of the ludicrous sufficiently relieved by stamping about on the pavement, breaks into a slow and stately dance, perhaps supposed to be performed by the Dean.

Mr Datchery receives the communication with a well satisfied though a pondering face, and breaks up the conference. Returning to his quaint lodging, and sitting long over the supper of bread and cheese and salad and ale which Mrs Tope has left prepared for him, he still sits when his supper is finished. At length he rises, throws open the door of a corner cupboard, and refers to a few uncouth chalked strokes on its inner side.

'I like,' says Mr Datchery, 'the old tavern way of keeping scores. Illegible except to the scorer. The scorer not committed, the scored debited with what is against him. Humph! A very small score this, a very poor score!'

He sighs over the contemplation of its poverty, takes a bit of chalk from one of the cupboard shelves, and pauses with it in his hand, uncertain what addition to make to the account. 'I think a moderate stroke,' he concludes, 'is all I am justified in scoring up;' so, suits the action to the word, closes the cupboard, and goes to bed.

A brilliant morning shines on the old city. Its antiquities and ruins are surpassingly beautiful, with the lusty ivy gleaming in the sun, and the rich trees waving in the balmy air. Changes of glorious light from moving boughs, songs of birds, scents from gardens, woods, and fields – or, rather, from the one great garden of the whole cultivated island in its yielding time – penetrate into the Cathedral, subdue its earthy odour, and preach the Resurrection and the Life. The cold stone tombs of centuries ago grow warm, and flecks of brightness dart into the sternest marble corners of the building, fluttering there like wings.

Comes Mr Tope with his large keys, and yawningly unlocks and sets open. Come Mrs Tope and attendant sweeping sprites. Come, in due time, organist and bellows-boy, peeping down from the red curtains in the loft, fearlessly flapping dust from books up at that remote elevation, and whisking it from stops and pedals. Come sundry rooks, from various quarters of the sky, back to the great tower; who may be presumed to enjoy vibration, and to know that bell and organ are going to give it them. Come a very small and straggling congregation indeed: chiefly from Minor Canon Corner and the Precincts. Come Mr Crisparkle, fresh and bright; and his ministering brethren, not quite so fresh and bright. Come the Choir in a hurry (always in a hurry, and struggling into their nightgowns at the last moment, like children shirking bed), and comes John Jasper leading their line.[5] Last of all comes Mr Datchery into a stall, one of a choice empty collection very much at his service, and glancing about him for Her Royal Highness the Princess Puffer.

The service is pretty well advanced before Mr Datchery can discern Her Royal Highness. But by that time he has made her out, in the shade. She is behind a pillar, carefully withdrawn from the Choir Master's view, but regards him with the closest attention. All unconscious of her presence, he chants and sings. She grins when he is most musically fervid, and -- yes, Mr Datchery sees her do it! – shakes her fist at him behind the pillar's friendly shelter.

Mr Datchery looks again to convince himself. Yes, again! As ugly and withered as one of the fantastic carvings on the under brackets of the stall seats, as malignant as the Evil One, as hard as the big brass eagle holding the sacred books upon his wings (and, according to the sculptor's presentation of his ferocious attributes, not at all converted by them), she hugs herself in her lean arms, and then shakes both fists at the leader of the Choir.

And at that moment, outside the grated door of the Choir, having eluded the vigilance of Mr Tope by shifty resources in which he is an adept, Deputy peeps, sharp-eyed, through the bars, and stares astounded from the threatener to the threatened.

The service comes to an end, and the servitors disperse to breakfast. Mr Datchery accosts his last new acquaintance outside, when the Choir (as much in a hurry to get their bedgowns off, as they were but now to get them on) have scuffled away.

'Well, mistress. Good morning. You have seen him?'

'*I*'ve seen him, deary; *I*'ve seen him!'

'And you know him?'

'Know him! Better far, than all the Reverend Parsons put together know him.'

Mrs Tope's care has spread a very neat, clean breakfast ready for her lodger. Before sitting down to it, he opens his corner-cupboard door; takes his bit of chalk from its shelf; adds one thick line to the score, extending from the top of the cupboard-door to the bottom; and then falls to with an appetite.

APPENDIX A

Dickens's Notes and Number Plans

BEGINNING with *Dombey and Son* (1846–8), it became Dickens's practice to make notes for those of his novels which were published in monthly parts, or numbers, and to bind the notes with his manuscripts. He made separate notes for each number. Taking a sheet of his wonted stationery, he would fold it vertically; then, using the crease down the centre as a dividing line, he would jot down on the left-hand side various memoranda as to what was to go into the current number – the leading incidents, and the characters who were to be introduced or re-introduced – and on the right-hand side the name of the book, the chapter numbers and titles, and the notes particularly applicable to each chapter. Thus he could see at a glance the contents and organization of each monthly part. He apparently made most of his notes for each number just prior to, or during, the actual writing of the number, but a few notes were made some months ahead (and he would seem to have made a few others even *after* he had written the chapter or number with which they were concerned).

Dickens's notes and number plans for *The Mystery of Edwin Drood* are reproduced in type in the pages which follow; the first such page representing his attempts to 'fix' the title of the book and the names of a few of its characters. The reader will observe that there are two discrepancies between Dickens's plans for the book and the finished (or unfinished) product: 'Mr Durdles and Friend', which we know as Chapter 5, is shown here as Chapter 8, and there are no notes for Chapter 9, 'Birds in the Bush'. The explanation is that, after Dickens had written the first two numbers and delivered them together to his printers, it was discovered – 'to my horror', as he later told Forster – that they were each six printed pages too short. (He usually judged more accurately the amount of manuscript needed.) To correct the deficiency, he transferred the five-page 'Mr Durdles and Friend' from the second number to the first, and wrote an extra page of text which he inserted into the middle of Chapter 3, 'The Nuns' House'. This solved the problem of the first monthly part but left the second eleven pages short. So he wrote 'Birds in the Bush', using material which he had meant to use in the third number, as is shown by the query 'Rosa's guardian?' on the left-hand side of the plan for that month, which is followed by the notation 'DONE IN Nº II'. The use of this material meant advancing and contracting the story somewhat beyond his original intentions, as may be deduced from various other notes in the plans for the third, fourth and fifth numbers.

So much, and much else, may be learned from a careful perusal. But, although the relation of the story's 'finer threads to the whole pattern' may have been 'always before the eyes of the story-weaver at his loom', as Dickens said in the Postscript to *Our Mutual Friend* (1864–5), it doesn't follow that one can easily, or fully, discern that pattern by looking over the author's notes. For he didn't feel it necessary to explicitly mention to himself the leading ideas, or first principles, of his story – as will be evident to anyone examining the notes for *The Mystery of Edwin Drood*. They are fascinating. They are suggestive. But they are curiously cryptic, as if the author wished to conceal, even at the privacy of his desk, the solution to his Mystery.

Friday Twentieth August, 1869.

Gilbert   Alfred

Edwin

Jasper   Edwyn

Michael   Oswald

Arthur

The loss of James Wakefield

Selwyn

Edwyn

Edgar

Mr Honeythunder

Mr Honeyblast

James's Disappearance

The Dean

Mrs Dean

Miss Dean

Flight And Pursuit

Sworn to avenge it

One object in Life

A Kinsman's Devotion

The Two Kinsmen

The loss of Edwyn Brood

The loss of Edwin Brude

The Mystery in the Drood Family

The loss of Edwyn Drood

The flight of Edwyn Drood

Edwin Drood in hiding

The loss of Edwin Drude

The Disappearance of Edwin Drood

The Mystery of Edwin Drood

Dead? Or alive?

Opium-Smoking
     Touch the key note
          'When the Wicked Man' ——
The Uncle and Nephew:
          'Pussy's' Portrait
  You won't take warning then?

Dean   Mr Jasper
  Minor Canon, Mr Crisparkle   Verger Peptune
  Uncle and Nephew   change to Tope
Gloves for the Nuns' House
      churchyard
        Cathedral town running throughout

  Inside the Nuns' House
     Miss Twinkleton and her double existence
              Mrs Tisher
              Rosebud
The affianced young people. Every love scene of theirs, a
                          quarrel more or less

     Mr Sapsea. old Tory Jackass
                  His wife's epitaph

    Jasper and the keys
         Durdles down in the crypt and among
the graves. His dinner bundle.

(Mystery of Edwin Drood. —— Nº I.)

Chapter I.

~~Prologue~~   The Dawn

> change title to The Dawn
>
> opium smoking and Jasper
> Lead up to Cathedral

Chapter II.

> a Dean and a Chapter also

Cathedral and Cathedral town   / Mr Crisparkle
and the Dean.   Uncle and Nephew.
            Murder very far off
Edwin's story and Pussy

Chapter III.

The Nuns' House

Still picturesque suggestions of Cathedral Town
  The Nuns' House and the young couple's first love scene

Chapter IV.

Mr Sapsea

Connect Jasper with him.   (He will want a solemn donkey
bye and bye.)
            Epitaph brings them together, and
            brings Durdles with them.
   The keys.   Stony Durdles

Bring in the other young couple.   <u>Yes</u>

or

Neville and Olympia Heyridge —_∧Heyfort?

Philanthropy in Minor Canon Corner

<u>Neville and Helena Landless</u>

Mixture of Oriental blood – or imperceptibly acquired mixture
in them.   <u>Yes</u>

<u>No</u>

(Mystery of Edwin Drood. —— No II.)

Chapter V.

The Blustrous Philanthropist
Mr Honeythunder

Old Mrs Crisparkle
China Shepherdess

Minor Canon Corner

Chapter VI.

More Confidences than One

Neville's to Mr Crisparkle,
Rosa's to Helena

/ Piano scene with
Jasper. She singing,
he following her lips.

Chapter VII.

Daggers Drawn

quarrel (Fomented by Jasper) Goblet. And then
confession to Mr Crisparkle
Jasper lays his ground

Chapter VIII.

Mr Durdles and friend

Deputy engaged to stone Durdles nightly
Carry through the woman of the 1st chapter

Carry through Durdles's calling – and the
bundle & the keys
John Jasper looks at Edwin asleep

Pursue Edwin Drood and Rosa?
    Lead on to final scene between them in Nº V?   IV?
                                            <u>Yes</u>

    How many more scenes between them?
    Way to be paved for their marriage —
                  ————————and parting   ~~fore~~ instead.   <u>Yes</u>

      Miss Twinkleton's?   No.   Next Nº
      Rosa's guardian?   <u>Done in Nº II.</u>

      Mr Sapsea?   Yes. last chapter
      Neville Landless at Mr Crisparkle's |
                   And Helena? | <u>Yes</u>

        Neville admires Rosa. That comes out
      from himself.

(Mystery of Edwin Drood. —— N<u>o</u> III.)

Chapter ~~IX~~

Smoothing the Way

——That is, for Jasper's plan, through Mr Crisparkle;
   who takes new ground on Neville's new
   confidence.

      Minor Canon Corner. The closet I
remember there as a child.

      Edwin's appointment for Xmas Eve.

Chapter XI

A Picture and a Ring

P.

J.   T.

1747

Dinner in chambers. | The two waiters |

      Bazzard the clerk

Mr Grewgious's past story.

'A ring of diamonds and rubies delicately set in gold.'

                Edwin takes it

Chapter XII.

A Night with Durdles

Lay the ground for the manner of the murder, to
   come out at last.

      Keep the boy suspended.

      Night picture of the Cathedral.

Once more carry through Edwin and Rosa?
                                    or, Last time?   <u>Last time</u>

~~Last scene but one between them.~~
Then   outside
Last meeting of Rosa and Edwin ~~in~~ the Cathedral?
                                    ^
                                                    <u>Yes</u>

                                    Kiss at parting.
                                        'Jack.'

Edwin goes to the dinner.
        The Windy night.
            The Surprise and Alarm.
                    Jasper's failure in the one great
    object made known by Mr Grewgious.

                    Jasper's Diary? <u>Yes</u>

(Mystery of Edwin Drood. —— Nº IV.)

Chapter XIII.

Both at their Best

The Last Interview

And Parting

Chapter XIV.

When shall these three meet again?

How each passes the day.

	Neville	
Watch and shirt pin all Edwin's jewellery	Edwin	Watch to the jeweller
	Jasper	

'And so <u>he</u> goes up the Postern stair'   Storms of Wind

Chapter XV.

Impeached

Neville away early.

Pursued and brought back.

Mr Grewgious's communication: And his scene with Jasper

Chapter XVI.

Devoted

Jasper's artful use of the communication on his recovery.
  Cloisterham Weir, Mr Crisparkle, and the Watch and pin.
Jasper's artful turn
<u>The Dean</u>.   Neville cast out.

Jasper's Diary. 'I devote myself to his destruction.'

Edwin and Rosa for the last time?   Done already.

Kinfrederel

Edwin Disappears

                                    Done already

The mystery

(Mystery of Edwin Drood. —— Nº V.)

Chapter XVII.

professional and

Philanthropy ~~in divers places~~   unprofessional

Chapter XVIII.

~~Shadow on the Sun Dial~~

A Settler in Cloisterham

Chapter XIX.

~~A Settler in Cloisterham~~

Shadow on the Sun Dial

Chapter XX.

~~'Let's Talk.'~~

~~Various Flights~~   Divers Flights

[Dickens made no notes for the sixth monthly part . . .

(Mystery of Edwin Drood. —— N⁰ VI.)

Chapter XXI.

A Gritty State of Things comes on

Chapter XXII.

The Dawn again

Chapter XXIII.

. . . Nor for any of the three chapters he planned for it.]

APPENDIX B

The 'Sapsea Fragment'

ONE of the several small mysteries connected with *The Mystery of Edwin Drood* is represented by a partial manuscript found among the author's papers after his death. John Forster, in describing this discovery in his *Life of Charles Dickens*, misleadingly assigned to these few pages a title, 'How Mr Sapsea ceased to be a Member of the Eight Club. Told by Himself', without informing the reader that it was not Dickens's title and that we do not have the actual opening of the 'chapter', as he called it. The fragment, in the form in which it has been preserved, consists of five sheets, half the size of those of the manuscript proper, and numbered at the top by Dickens as pages 6 to 10; and numbered in the upper right-hand corners, presumably by Forster for the benefit of the printer, as pages 2 to 6 (the missing page 1 very likely bearing the title Forster gave the production). The writing breaks off suddenly in the midst of a sentence on page 10, with the words 'Or if I was to deny'. But it could not have been death which lifted the author's pen from his page, for we know that he was working on and finished Chapter 22, 'The Dawn Again', on the last afternoon of his writing life. It must have been some less drastic interruption – perhaps a thought, the recognition of some new possibility.

It has been assumed that this broken bit of manuscript was something written ahead, but the evidence would rather seem to indicate that it is something discarded. We must suppose, knowing the author's thrifty and efficient writing habits, that if he ever wrote anything ahead it would be his practice to write such pages on sheets of paper the same size as the rest of his manuscript, leaving the pages unnumbered until such time as he could fit them into their proper place. His invariable practice was to write his text on sheets of blue stationery slightly smaller than what is now called 'letter size' ($7\frac{1}{4}$ inches by 9), and to write his notes on such sheets folded in half – that is, on sheets the same size as the Sapsea pages.

This alone might be enough to suggest the speculative, exploratory character of the fragment (the writing of which, it will be noted, is somewhat unpremeditated), but there is another circumstance which hints that Dickens was merely trying out an idea: which is, that it was composed very early. Forster seemed to think it was written about the time of the fifth and sixth numbers, not observing that there are considerations which date the composition earlier. One of these is that Mr Sapsea is nowhere addressed in the fragment as 'Mayor', a distinction he acquired in Chapter 12. Dickens originally wrote 'Mr Sapsea's importance has received enhancement, for it is settled that he will be the next Mayor of Cloisterham'– but he later altered the last clause, changing it to the past tense: '. . . for he has become Mayor of Cloisterham'. He must have realized after writing the sentence that the action described in the chapter had to be taking place in the middle of December (the 18th, to be specific), and Lord Mayor's Day is 9 November; and, as Mr Sapsea was shortly to be called upon to act in his official capacity, it was necessary that he should have been elected Mayor already. The fact that he is never spoken of as the Mayor in the fragment – and he surely would be, if he were such – shows that it was written before Dickens appointed him to that position: in other words, some time before 25 February 1870, the date on which he read the third number (containing Chapter 12) to his friends.

My own conclusion is that Dickens must have written these half-pages after being warned by his printers in December that his first two numbers were deficient in length. This meant using material in the second number which he had planned for the third, and generally contracting and advancing the story beyond his original plans. He must have felt that the introduction of new material would be necessary. When we connect this with something he wrote at about the same time, we see, or so I think, what he was working towards, in 'trying out' the deferential young man Poker who so unmercifully chaffs Mr Sapsea. In his letter of 14 January 1870 to James T. Fields, he says, remarking upon his new book, that 'the 5th and 6th Nos. will turn upon an interest suspended until the end.' We can hardly take this as being other than a reference to the mysterious Datchery, who figures so prominently in those numbers (Chapters 17 to 22).

The extant text of the 'Sapsea Fragment' follows.

Wishing to take the air, I proceeded by a circuitous route to the Club, it being our weekly night of meeting. I found that we mustered our full strength. We were enrolled under the denomination of the Eight Club. We were eight in number; we met at eight o'clock during eight months of the year; our annual subscription was eight shillings each; we played eight games of four handed cribbage, at eightpence the game; our frugal supper was composed of eight rolls, eight mutton chops, eight pork sausages, eight baked potatoes, eight marrow bones with eight toasts, and eight bottles of ale. There may or may not be a certain harmony of color in the ruling idea of this (to adopt a phrase of our lively neighbours) reunion. It was a little idea of mine.

A somewhat popular member of the Eight Club was a member by the name of Kimber. By profession, dancing-master. A commonplace hopeful sort of man, wholly destitute of dignity or knowledge of the world.

As I entered the Club-room, Kimber was making the remark: 'And he still half believes him to be very high in the Church.'

In the act of hanging up my hat on the Eighth peg by the door, I caught Kimber's visual ray. He lowered it, and passed a remark on the next change of the moon. I did not take particular notice of this at the moment, because the world was often pleased to be a little shy of Ecclesiastical topics in my presence. For I felt that I was picked out (though perhaps only through a coincidence) to a certain extent to represent what I call our glorious constitution in church and state. The phrase may be objected to by captious minds; but I own to it as mine. I threw it off in argument some little time back. I said, Our Glorious Constitution in Church and State.

Another member of the Eight Club was Peartree, also member of the Royal College of Surgeons. Mr Peartree is not accountable to me for his opinions, and I say no more of them here than that he attends the poor gratis whenever they want him, and is not the parish doctor. Mr Peartree may justify it to the grasp of *his* mind thus to do his republican utmost to bring an appointed officer into contempt. Suffice it that Mr Peartree can never justify it to the grasp of *mine*.

Between Peartree and Kimber there was a sickly sort of feeble-minded alliance. It came under my particular notice when I sold off Kimber by auction. (Goods taken in execution.) He was a widower in a white under waistcoat and slight shoes with bows, and had two daughters not ill-looking. Indeed, the reverse. Both daughters taught dancing in Scholastic Establishments for Young Ladies – had done so at Mrs Sapsea's; nay, Twinkleton's – and both, in giving lessons, presented the unwomanly spectacle of having little fiddles tucked under their chins. In spite of which the younger one might, if I am correctly informed – I will raise the veil so far as to say I KNOW she might – have soared for life from this degrading taint, but for having the class of mind allotted to what I call the common herd, and being so incredibly devoid of veneration as to become painfully ludicrous.

When I sold off Kimber without reserve, Peartree (as poor as he can hold together) had several prime household lots knocked down to him. *I* am not to be blinded, and of course it was as plain to me what he was going to do with them, as it was that he was a brown hulking sort of revolutionary subject who had been in India with the soldiers and ought (for the sake of society) to have his neck broke. I saw the lots shortly afterwards in Kimber's lodging – through the windows – and I easily made out that there had been a sneaking pretence of lending them 'till better times. A man with a smaller knowledge of the world than myself might have been led to suspect that Kimber had held back money from his creditors and fraudulently bought the goods. But besides that I knew for certain he had no money, I knew that this would involve a species of forethought not to be made compatible with the frivolity of a caperer, inoculating other people with capering, for his bread.

As it was the first time I had seen either of those two since the Sale, I kept myself in what I call Abeyance. When selling him up, I had delivered a few remarks – shall I say a little homily? – concerning Kimber, which the world did regard as more than usually worth notice. I had come up into my pulpit, it was said, uncommonly like; and a murmur of recognition had repeated his (I will not name whose) title, before I spoke. I had then gone on to say that all present would find, in the first page of the Catalogue that was lying before them, in the last paragraph before the first lot, the following words: 'Sold in pursuance of a Writ of execution issued by a Creditor'. I had then proceeded to remind my Friends that however frivolous, not to say contemptible, the pursuits by which a man got his goods together, still his goods were as dear to him, and as cheap to society (if sold without reserve) as though his pursuits had been of character that would bear serious contemplation. I had then divided my text (if I may be allowed so to call it) into three heads: firstly, Sold; secondly, In pursuance of a writ of execution; thirdly, Issued by a creditor; with a few moral reflections on each, and winding up with 'Now to the first lot' in a manner that was complimented when I afterwards mingled with my hearers.

So not being certain on what terms I and Kimber stood, I was grave, I was chilling. Kimber, however, moving to me, I moved to Kimber. (I was the creditor who had issued the writ. Not that it matters.)

'I was alluding, Mr Sapsea,' said Kimber, 'when you came in, to a stranger who entered into conversation with me in the street as I came to the club. He had been speaking to you just before, it seemed, by the churchyard; and though you had told him who you were, I could hardly persuade him that you were not high in the Church.'

'Idiot!' said Peartree.

'Ass!' said Kimber.

'Idiot and Ass!' said the other five members.

'Idiot and Ass, gentlemen,' I remonstrated, looking around me, 'are strong expressions to apply to a young man of good appearance and address.' My generosity was roused. I own it.

'You'll admit that he must be a Fool,' said Peartree.

'You can't deny that he must be a Blockhead,' said Kimber.

Their tone of disgust amounted to being offensive. Why should the young man be so calumniated? What had he done? He had only made an innocent and natural mistake. I controlled my generous indignation, and said so.

'Natural,' repeated Kimber. '*He*'s a Natural!'

The remaining six members of the Eight Club laughed unanimously. It stung me. It was a scornful laugh. My anger was roused in behalf of an absent friendless stranger. I rose (for I had been sitting down).

'Gentlemen,' I said with dignity, 'I will not remain one of this club allowing opprobrium to be cast on an unoffending person in his absence. I will not so violate what I call the sacred rites of hospitality. Gentlemen, until you know how to behave yourselves better, I leave you. Gentlemen, until then I withdraw from this place of meeting whatever personal qualifications I may have brought into it. Gentlemen, until then you cease to be the Eight Club, and must make the best you can of becoming the Seven.'

I put on my hat and retired. As I went down stairs I distinctly heard them give a suppressed cheer. Such is the power of demeanour and knowledge of mankind. – I had forced it out of them.

II

Whom should I meet in the street, within a few yards of the door of the inn where the Club was held, but the selfsame young man whose cause I had felt it my duty so warmly – and I will add so disinterestedly – to take up!

'Is it Mr Sapsea,' he said doubtfully, 'or is it –'

'It is Mr Sapsea,' I replied.

'Pardon me, Mr Sapsea; you appear warm, Sir.'

'I have been warm,' I said, 'and on your account.' Having stated the circumstances at some length (my generosity almost overpowered him), I asked him his name.

'Mr Sapsea,' he answered, looking down, 'your penetration is so acute, your glance into the souls of your fellow men is so penetrating, that if I was hardy enough to deny that my name is Poker, what would it avail me?'

I don't know that I had quite exactly made out to a fraction that his name *was* Poker, but I dare say I had been pretty near doing it.

'Well, well,' said I, trying to put him at his ease by nodding my head in a soothing way. 'Your name is Poker, and there is no harm in being named Poker.'

'Oh Mr Sapsea!' cried the young man in a very well behaved manner. 'Bless you for those words!' He then, as if ashamed of having given way to his feelings, looked down again.

'Come, Poker,' said I, 'let me hear more about you. Tell me. Where are you going to, Poker, and where do you come from?'

'Ah Mr Sapsea!' exclaimed the young man. 'Disguise from you is impossible. You know already that I come from somewhere, and am going somewhere else. If I was to deny it, what would it avail me?'

'Then don't deny it,' was my remark.

'Or,' pursued Poker, in a kind of despondent rapture, 'or if I was to deny that I came to this town to see and hear you, Sir, what would it avail me? Or if I was to deny

NOTES

The editor acknowledges the help of 'Notes to *Edwin Drood*' by T. W. Hill, in the *Dickensian*, XL (1944), pp. 198–203; XLI (1945), pp. 30–37.

CHAPTER 1

1 (p. 37). *this woman*. In May 1869 Dickens guided some friends through the criminal haunts and thieves' quarters of the Ratcliffe Highway. 'In a miserable court,' writes James T. Fields, 'we found the haggard old woman blowing at a kind of pipe made of an old penny ink-bottle. The identical words which Dickens puts into the mouth of this wretched creature in "Edwin Drood" we heard her croon as we leaned over the tattered bed on which she was lying . . . and the Chinamen and Lascars made never-to-be-forgotten pictures in the scene.' *Yesterdays with Authors* (1900), *circa* p. 202; also see *Life of Charles Dickens* by John Forster, J. W. T. Ley edn (1928), p. 844.

2 (p. 40). *When the Wicked Man –*. The importance the author attached to these 'intoned words' is attested by a notation in the plan of the first monthly number (see Appendix A):

Touch the keynote
'When the Wicked Man'—

The quoted phrase is from Ezekiel 18.27: 'Again, when the wicked man turneth away from his wickedness that he hath committed and doeth that which is lawful and right, he shall save his soul alive.' These are the opening words of the Morning Prayer and the Evening Prayer in the Anglican Church liturgy.

CHAPTER 2

1 (p. 41). *an old stone gatehouse*. The original of this (in Rochester: see note 1, Chapter 3, below) would be College Gate, or College Yard Gate, a fifteenth-century stone construction with an upper storey of wood. The gateway beneath is the entrance from the High Street into the Cathedral precincts. But Dickens would seem to have appropriated, for Jasper's residence, a feature or so from the two other gatehouses in Rochester: the postern staircase of the Priory Gate and the spacious interior of the Deanery Gatehouse.

2 (p. 43). *Tell me, shep-herds*. Mr Crisparkle is singing his part in a glee by Joseph Mazzinghi (1765–1844): 'Ye Shepherds, tell me' (or 'The Wreath').

3 (p. 45). *Begone dull care*. 'Author unknown. The tune is seventeenth

century ... The words were set as a glee by John Sale and this may be the music Dickens knew.' James T. Lightwood, *Charles Dickens and Music* (1912), p. 138. Later in this chapter, Edwin quotes from the second verse of the same song: 'My wife shall dance, and I shall sing, so merrily pass the day.'

4   (p. 47). *opium for a pain.* In the MS., the passage beginning with these words and ending with the phrase 'thus addresses him' is written on a wafer originally pasted over another piece of writing but since removed to the facing sheet. The once-obscured passage reads:

'opium for a pain. . . Its effects steal over me like a blight or cloud, and pass. You see them in the act of passing. Put the knives out at the door – both of them.'

'My dear Jack, why?'

'It's going to lighten: they may attract the lightning: put them in the dark.'

With a scared and confounded face the younger man complies. No flash ensues, nor was there, for the moment, any passing likelihood of a thunderstorm. He gently and assiduously tends his kinsman who by slow degrees recovers and clears away that cloud or blight. When he (Jasper) is quite himself, and is, as it were, once more all resolved into that concentrated look, he lays a tender hand on his nephew's shoulder and thus addresses him:

(There is a reference to knives attracting lightning in *Martin Chuzzlewit*, Chapter 43.)

Opium was widely used as a medicine during the eighteenth and nineteenth centuries, most often as a specific for headaches and sleeplessness. It was usually taken as a powder, or mixed with wine or some other alcoholic drink (laudanum).

5   (p. 50). *Nothing half so sweet in life.* From 'Love's Young Dream' by Thomas Moore (1779–1852).

CHAPTER 3

1   (p. 51). *Cloisterham.* The original of this 'old Cathedral town' is obviously Dickens's boyhood home, Rochester. The likeness is unmistakable; but it would be an error to insist upon too literal a correspondence between the town of fiction and that of fact. The actual locations and objects of Rochester would seem to be suggestive only: Dickens used or ignored them, depending upon how they contributed to the atmosphere, plot and thematic character of his story, making such changes as he saw fit.

2   (p. 52). *the Nuns' House.* The 'model' for this is Eastgate House in Rochester (which also sat for Westgate House in *Pickwick Papers*). A handsome sixteenth-century red-brick house, it was never a convent, but it was a School for Young Ladies at the time Dickens was writing the story. It is now a museum.

3 (p. 55). *And how did you pass your birthday, Pussy?* The passage of some
400 words beginning with this sentence and ending with the phrase 'He
checks the look, and asks' is not in the MS., even in the form of an interpolated slip. It was very likely written at the printers, so as to bring the
text of the number up to the full thirty-two printed pages.

4 (p. 59). *Belzoni or somebody.* Belzoni, actually. At the opening of the
second pyramid at Gizeh, the 6' 6" Giovanni Battista Belzoni (1778–1823)
became lodged in one of the tiny passages leading down into the burial
chamber and was extricated with great difficulty. See also note 2, Chapter 4,
below.

CHAPTER 4

1 (p. 63). *wooden effigy.* There was such a figure in Rochester; but 'I
found', says Mr Woodford Sowray in a note in the *Dickensian*, II (1906),
p. 167, 'that it did not stand over the doorway of the ancient three-gabled
house in the High Street, as described in *Edwin Drood*, but that its actual
position was over the door of a house further on in the direction of
Chatham . . . that the house when the story was written was occupied by
a Mr Batten, a builder (now dead), who was at one time mayor of the city
and that in the course of alterations to the house the effigy was removed.'

Dickens also claimed this 'ancient three-gabled house' as Uncle Pumble-
chook's premises in *Great Expectations*.

2 (p. 68). *sounding and tapping.* Belzoni, and various antiquarians, explorers
and tomb robbers, had used this method to locate hollow spaces behind
seemingly solid walls. See Belzoni's *Narrative of the Operation and Recent
Discoveries in Egypt and Nubia* (1820), p. 180.

3 (p. 71). *and he gets out of the room, deigning no word of answer.* This paragraph, and the chapter, originally had a different ending:

and finally he gets out of the room with the sulky retort, 'How does
the fact stand, Mr Jasper? The fact stands six to one side to half a dozen
on t'other. So fur as Durdles sees the fact with *his* eyes, it has took up
that position as near as may be.'

When Dickens found it necessary to change 'Mr Durdles and Friend'
from the eighth chapter to the fifth (see note 1, Chapter 5, below), he
deleted the above lines and added the present ending, in which Mr Sapsea
'proposes a hit at backgammon' and 'beguiles the golden evening until
pretty late.' This is so that the late-night action of 'Mr Durdles and
Friend' can follow plausibly.

CHAPTER 5

1 (p. 71). *Mr Durdles and Friend.* This was originally Chapter 8, the last
chapter of the second number. When Dickens was informed by his

printer that his first two numbers were, together, twelve printed pages too
short, he found it necessary to transfer this chapter to the first number,
where it became Chapter 5, and to write a new chapter, 'Birds in the
Bush', to fill out the second number.

This change was not altogether a happy one. The opening sentence
begins 'John Jasper, on his way home through the Close . . .'; which would
be in order if he had just left Mr Crisparkle's house, as at the end of
Chapter 7, for he then would have to walk back through the Close to his
bachelor gatehouse. But on his way home from Mr Sapsea's house, the
obvious – that is, the shortest – route would be directly up the Cloisterham
High Street. If we take Cloisterham as a loose sketch of Rochester, it is
apparent that Jasper, to go through the Close on his way home from
Sapsea's, would have to turn down a side lane and walk for some distance
and through several turnings before coming to the Close. But perhaps,
like his recent host Mr Sapsea (in the Fragment), he 'wished to take the
air' and so 'proceeded by a circuitous route'.

2 (p. 73). *the monument of that devoted wife.* These words are followed in
the MS. by the phrase 'with inscription finished'; but the author struck it
out of the printed text, on removing the chapter to its present position, as
Durdles could hardly have finished the inscription the same evening that
Mr Sapsea gave him the copy – 'wonderful workman' though he may be.

3 (p. 76). *As Durdles and Jasper come near.* The matter following this
originally differed from what we now have. The passage cancelled from
the MS. reads:

As Durdles and Jasper come near, a woman is seen crouching and smoking in the cold night air on a seat just outside the door which stands ajar.
Of a sudden Jasper stops and looks at this woman – the lighter colored
figure of Durdles being between himself and her – very keenly.

'Is that Deputy?' she croaks out in a whimpering and feeble way.
'Where have you been, you young good-for-nothing wretch?'

'Out for my 'elth,' returns the hideous sprite.

'I'll claw you,' retorts the woman, 'when I can lay my fingers on you.
I'll be bad for your 'elth. (O me, O me, my breath is very short.) I wanted
my pipe and my little spoon, and ye'd been and put 'em on a shelf I couldn't
find.'

'Wot did yer go to bed for then?' retorts Deputy, quite unabashed.
'Who'd ha' thought yer was going to get up again?'

'You! You might ha' known I was like to do it.'

'Yer lie,' says Deputy in his only form of contradiction.

Jasper touches Durdles on the shoulder, and, laying his finger on his
lips when that worthy looks round, leads the way onward gingerly
enough. He more than once or twice looks back, but utters no word until
they have reached the corner of the lane, then he casually remarks in a
subdued voice that he is well out of any unseemly quarrel or discussion in
such a place, and glances back again.

In the notes for this chapter, there is a line: '*Carry through the woman of the*

1st chapter'. This sentence is underscored and there is placed before it an emphatic '*No*'.

CHAPTER 6

1 (p. 78). *the old lady's cap into Chancery*. The last word, as used by 'the learned in the Noble Art', means: 'Of the head of an antagonist, in a secure position under one's arm so that one can pommel it without fear of effective retaliation; – in allusion to the helplessness of a person involved in a chancery suit' (*Webster's Dictionary*). Dickens made a famous attack on Court of Chancery in *Bleak House*.

2 (p. 79). *Minor Canon Corner*. The original, in Rochester, would be Minor Canon Row, St Margaret's Street, on the south side of the Cathedral Close.

3 (p. 83). *In those days*. Mr T. W. Hill has argued (in an essay '*Drood* Time in Cloisterham' in the *Dickensian*, XL (1944), pp. 113–17) that it is impossible, because of various inconsistencies, to assign any date to the story. But the development of the railway to the Rochester neighbourhood (again, taking Cloisterham as representing Rochester), to which perhaps the greatest weight should be given in determining the period of the story, was in the 1840s.

4 (p. 84). *Joe, Joe, Joe!* Thus Mr Crisparkle admonishes the Cloisterham omnibus driver. But, curiously enough, he had himself been named Joe in the MS., until this chapter.

5 (p. 85). *Then they came to Minor Canon Corner.* This sentence does not appear in previous editions of *The Mystery of Edwin Drood*. It is written on the back of MS. page 6 of the second number, and I conjecture that it was meant to open the crowded first paragraph at the top of page 6, which begins, a trifle abruptly: 'Mrs Crisparkle had need of her own share of philanthropy' etc. The printers must either have overlooked it or have been uncertain what to do with it; and, as it was not Dickens's habit to consult his MS. when correcting the proofs, he could easily have overlooked it too.

6 (p. 87). *that distinguished man*. K. J. Fielding has suggested that the radical politician John Bright (1811–89) was the original of Mr Honeythunder ('Edwin Drood and Governor Eyre', *Listener*, 25 December 1952; pp. 1083–4). And compare the description of Bright given in *The Education of Henry Adams* (Riverside edn, 1918), pp. 190 ff. For instance: 'Even among friends at the dinner-table he talked as though he were denouncing them, or someone else, on a platform.'

CHAPTER 7

1 (p. 90). *abject and servile dependents, of an inferior race*. Dickens at first wrote: 'an inferior and servile eastern race, abjectly devoted to my step-father's title', perhaps altering it to delete the reference to the title – about

which he gives no further information – and perhaps also to emphasize Neville's racial judgement (which is not necessarily the author's, as is shown by Mr Crisparkle's following inward comment).

CHAPTER 8

1 (p. 105). *You, my dear sir ... have accepted a dangerous charge*. This is followed in the MS. by some further words of Jasper's. The complete paragraph read:

'You, my dear sir,' pursues Jasper, taking his hand, 'even you have accepted a dangerous charge. You must sometimes, no doubt often, have to put yourself in opposition to his fierce nature, and suppress it. After what I have seen to-night, I am fearful even for you.'

These lines were not obliterated in the MS., but were struck out of the proofs: for reasons of space, very likely, as the number was over-long.

CHAPTER 9

1 (p. 105). *Birds in the Bush*. See note 1, Chapter 5, above. This chapter made the number slightly over-long, and Dickens removed a few lines from the end, mostly from the peripatetic conversation between Grewgious and Jasper.

2 (p. 108). *Tilbury Fort*. Where Elizabeth I reviewed the army and navy on 8 August 1588, after the defeat of the Spanish Armada.

3 (p. 108). *Monsieur La`Fontaine*. Jean de La Fontaine (1621–95), author of a poetic version of Aesop's *Fables*.

4 (p. 112). *Cotillon*. A square dance; quadrille; or a series of round dances.

5 (p. 117). *pen-and-ink-ubus*. Hill says that this was an 'old pun, even in Dickens's day' (*Dickensian*, XL (1944), p. 203). John Forster was apparently unaware of its age, as he extracts it as a sample (though a small one) of Dickens's ready wit, from one of his conversations. *Life of Charles Dickens*, J. W. T. Ley edn (1928), p. 840.

6 (p. 119). *observed Jasper*. Between this observation and the words closely following, 'Mr Grewgious, as you quite fairly said just now . . .', Dickens omitted these lines – the largest number dropped from this chapter:

'Eh?' said the other, expressionlessly innocent. But not without adding internally, 'This is a very quick watchdog!'

'So, you have settled with her that you would come back at Christmas?' repeated Jasper.

'At Christmas? Certainly. Oh, dear yes. I settled with her that I would come back at Christmas,' replied Mr Grewgious, as if the question had previously lain between Lady Day, Midsummer Day, and Michaelmas.

By this time, sometimes walking slowly, and sometimes standing still, they had reached the Gate House.

'Will you not walk up,' said Jasper, 'and refresh?'

'Thank you, no. I have a horse and chaise here, and have not much time to get across and catch the new railroad yonder.'

Jasper pressed his hand.

CHAPTER 10

1 (p. 122). *beetling fragment of monastery ruin.* In the corresponding topography of Rochester, this would be Rochester Castle. But Dickens has completely 'ecclesiasticized' the setting, and so the castle becomes a monastery. The title-page vignette by Luke Fildes shows Rochester Castle in the middle-ground, with the square-pinnacled tower of the Cathedral in the background.

2 (p. 124). *like the highly-popular lamb.* A Mr J. M. Makeham wrote to the author after the appearance of this monthly number (the third), objecting to this figure of speech as distasteful, 'as it is drawn from a passage of Holy Writ which is greatly reverenced . . . as a prophetic description of the sufferings of our Saviour.' Dickens replied in a letter dated Wednesday, 8 June 1870, one of the last two letters, and possibly the very last, he wrote:

It would be quite inconceivable to me – but for your letter – that any reasonable reader could possibly attach a scriptural reference to a passage in a book of mine, reproducing a much abused social figure of speech . . . I am truly shocked to find that any reader can make the mistake.

I have always striven in my writings to express veneration for the life and lessons of our Saviour; because I feel it . . . But I have never made proclamation of this from the house tops.

The Nonesuch Dickens: Letters, Vol. 3, p. 784.

CHAPTER 11

1 (p. 134). *Perhaps John Thomas.* Not a bad guess. The inscription represents the initials and date of one of the presidents of Staple Inn: 'Principal John Thompson, 1747.'

2 (p. 135). *the hotel in Furnival's Inn.* This would be Wood's Hotel, within the archway of the Inn. Dickens lived in chambers at Furnival's from some time in 1834 (probably December) to February 1837; and he may have lived in Wood's Hotel itself for some six months before moving to Furnival's (or so says Percy Fitzgerald, *Dickensian*, III (1907), pp. 215–19). Furnival's had not been used as an Inn of Chancery since 1817, and was demolished in 1895. The site is now occupied by the Prudential Assurance Company, which owns Staple Inn.

3 (p. 136). *baleful tree of Java.* The upas tree (*antiaris toxicaria*), which was

reputed to be so poisonous that nothing which its shadow fell upon would grow. Its bark produces a gum used by the natives of Java to make poison for their arrowheads.

4 (p. 139). *Circumlocutional Department.* One of Dickens's most famous satirical thrusts was his attack in *Little Dorrit* on what he called the 'Circumlocution Office': see Chapter 10, 'Containing the whole Science of Government'.

CHAPTER 12

1 (p. 150). *It'll grow upon you.* The original paragraph was longer, reading in its entirety:

'Don't you get into a bad habit of boasting,' retorts Durdles, with a grave cautionary nod. 'It'll grow upon you. You'll be boasting before long tl ·t His Reverence the Dean is your friend; and if you don't check yourse , we shall have you next claiming the Bishop.'

This is rather a fine discourse for Durdles, especially as his speech is otherwise thickening: Jasper becomes 'Jarsper' in this chapter and continues so to the end.

2 (p. 151). *Dance of Death.* Dickens almost certainly had in mind the satirical drawings of Hans Holbein (1497?–1543), in which Death is represented, in the shape of skeletal figures, as mockingly taking part in every form of human activity.

3 (p. 157). *calenture.* A fever afflicting persons in hot climates, 'giving rise', says T. W. Hill, 'to delirious fancies, and hence sometimes applied to a desire to leap from a height, as from a ship's deck into the sea or from a high tower or cliff' (*Dickensian*, XLI (1945), p. 32).

4 (p. 159). *Durdles wouldn't go home till morning.* A parody of 'We Won't Go Home till Morning'. Author uncertain. 'The tune is founded on an air known as Malbrough, or Malbrook, which originated during the Duke of Marlborough's Campaign.' James T. Lightwood, *Charles Dickens and Music* (1912), p. 159. The unparodied chorus is given at the end of Chapter 7, *Pickwick Papers.*

CHAPTER 13

1 (p. 161). *Addison's impressive tragedy. Cato* (1713).
2 (p. 168). *sister Rosa, sister Rosa, what do you see from the turret?* From Bluebeard: 'Sister Anne, Sister Anne, what do you see from the tower?'

CHAPTER 14

1 (p. 170). *When Shall These Three Meet Again?* From the opening lines of *Macbeth*:

When shall we three meet again
In thunder, lightning, or in rain?

2 (p. 171). *chamber floor ... strewn with the autumnal leaves.* Dickens was
speaking here from personal experience: 'A day or so before her death,
that little sister [Fanny Dickens Burnett] told me that, in the night, the
smell of the fallen leaves in the woods where we had habitually walked as
very young children, had come upon her with such strength of reality
that she had moved her weak head to look for strewn leaves on the floor
at her bedside.' 'New Year's Day', *Household Words*, 1 January 1859;
also published in *Miscellaneous Papers.*

3 (p. 177). *Poor youth! Poor youth!* These mournful exclamations were
substituted for a line which read: 'And he little, little knows how near a
case he has for thinking so.'

CHAPTER 15

1 (p. 184). *The Tilted Wagon.* 'Tilted', in this connection, means 'tented'.
Dickens first called this tavern 'The Fox and Goose', and then 'The Hare
and Hounds'.

CHAPTER 16

1 (p. 197). *How did I come here!* ... This and the next two sentences are not
in the MS.; they were added to the proofs, as were these:
   The short paragraph beginning 'He reasoned with himself', and the
paragraph following.
   The passage beginning 'He turned his back upon the Weir' and ending
'His hands began plucking off his coat'.
   The sentence beginning 'It is very lamentable, sir', and the three sub-
sequent sentences.
By adding these four passages, Dickens lengthened the number by
twenty-one lines. It would otherwise have been too short.

2 (p. 197). *airy tongues that syllable men's names.* From Milton's *Comus*,
lines 205-9.

3 (p. 198). *greatest danger to the smallest number.* A parody of the famous
formula of Jeremy Bentham (1748-1832): 'that the greatest happiness of
the greatest number is the foundation of morals and legislation.'

CHAPTER 17

1 (p. 202). *Philanthropy, Professional and Unprofessional.* This chapter
opens the fifth number, which also includes Chapters 18, 19 and 20.
Dickens found that he had overwritten the number by 154 lines and so

had to remove at least that many, if its four chapters were to fit into the
thirty-two printed pages. In this chapter, he trimmed the conversation
between Mr Crisparkle and Honeythunder, and removed about one half
of the lines in which Crisparkle praises Helena's character to Neville
Landless. But he died before the number went into print, and his literary
executor John Forster, in order to place before the readers everything he
possibly could of the story, reinstated the excisions (which are still to be
found in the texts of all editions, including this one). When it was discovered by scholars some decades later that Forster had put back into the
book passages 'which the mature judgement of the author had rejected',
there was a good deal of indignation – for it was wrongly supposed that
the only reason Dickens could have had for removing the lines was that
they 'gave away' too much of his story.

For a complete listing of all excisions the reader may consult *The
Problem of Edwin Drood* by W. Robertson Nicoll (1912), pp. 4–13.

2 (p. 202). *phrenological formation.* The organ of combativeness is just
behind the ear.

3 (p. 205). *necessity and tribulation . . . desolate and oppressed.* 'An instance',
says T. W. Hill (*Dickensian*, XLI (1945), p. 34), 'of Dickens's effective
use of quotation from the Book of Common Prayer: these phrases occur
in the litany.'

CHAPTER 18

1 (p. 216). *A Settler in Cloisterham.* John Y. Watt refers to this chapter (in
the introduction to his unpublished study of the MS. of *Edwin Drood*, a
copy of which is at the Victoria and Albert Museum) as 'that most discussed chapter of any book of modern times.' This startling statement
may very well have been true in England during the years 1905–20, when
the *Drood* controversy was widely discussed and argued.

The excisions from the proofs of this chapter are numerous, and of
peculiar interest as they affect that mysterious personage Datchery. Dickens
had pruned from the number (see note 1, Chapter 17, above) everything
which could be most easily dispensed with; but this was insufficient,
amounting only to some 120 lines. As he had to remove another thirty-
four lines, he had no recourse but to sacrifice something of the story itself:
which he did by cutting out of the present chapter every line which un-
mistakably showed that Datchery was interested in Jasper, and that he had
never before been in Cloisterham. This not only left the narrative sequence
intact but harmlessly enhanced the mystery of the monthly part. The more
interesting of the deletions are cited below:

The following passage:

with a general impression on his mind that Mrs Tope's was somewhere
very near it, and that, like the children in the game of hot boiled beans
and very good butter, he was warm in his search when he saw the Tower,
and cold when he didn't see it.

He was getting very cold indeed when

The sentence ' "Indeed ?" said Mr Datchery, with a second look of some interest.'

The sentence beginning 'Mr Datchery, taking off his hat'.

The sentence beginning 'Perhaps Mr Datchery had heard', and the whole of the subsequent paragraph.

And the long passage beginning ' "Might I ask His Honor' and ending with the sentence: 'All this time Mr Datchery had walked with his hat under his arm, and his white hair streaming.'

2   (p. 216). *the Crozier*. Probably suggested by the Mitre in nearby Chatham.

3   (p. 222). *secrets of the prison-house*. Mr Sapsea is unwittingly quoting *Hamlet*, Act 1, Scene 5.

4   (p. 224). *Mister Sapsea is his name*. A variant of some doggerel lines which schoolboys were fond of writing on the fly-leaves of their books, that there might be no mistake as to the owner.

CHAPTER 19

1   (p. 225). *Shadow on the Sun-Dial*. This was originally Chapter 18; but Dickens decided, after he had written two MS. pages of 'A Settler in Cloisterham' (which was then Chapter 19), that the positions of the two chapters should be reversed: a change most likely made in the interest of the time-sequence of the story. There were no excisions from the proofs of this chapter.

2   (p. 229). *a rival of my lost boy*. This declaration by Jasper was followed in the MS. by two further sentences, which in their earliest form read: 'I charge him with the murder of my lost boy. I was slow of belief at first, but the circumstances [*undecipherable*] aloud is against him, and I fully believed.' Dickens made several small alterations in these lines, then obliterated them entirely, interpolating the sentence we now have: 'That is an inexpiable offence in my eyes.'

CHAPTER 20

1   (p. 232). *Divers Flights*. Forster changed the title of the present chapter to 'A Flight', a name which it bears in all editions published prior to this one. (See note 4 below.)

There were a few excisions from this chapter, most of these being from the conversations towards the end.

2   (p. 238). *he is off duty here, altogether, just at present*. This statement by Grewgious has been much commented on – some readers assuming that if Bazzard is 'off duty', he is not at Staple Inn and so must be at the book's other scene of action, Cloisterham: i.e., as Datchery. It is worth noting, perhaps, that the statement was not originally so emphatic:

In fact, he is off duty at present . . .

But the author saw fit to interpolate the words 'here' and 'altogether' into the sentence in the manuscript and the word 'just' into the same sentence in the proofs, so that it reads as we now have it.

3 (p. 242). *Nothing occurred in the night*. A new chapter is begun here in all editions published prior to this one. When Forster reinstated Dickens's excisions (as explained above), he created a surplusage of text, which he carried forward into the next monthly part in the guise of a chapter – Chapter 21, 'A Recognition'. The present edition restores the author's chapter numbers and titles.

4 (p. 247). *she ascended . . . to his garden in the air*. This is one of the divers flights referred to in the title. When Forster divided the chapter into two parts, he necessarily separated this fanciful ascent from Rosa's earlier flight from Jasper (and her coming into London by train 'over the rooftops'). It was apparently for this reason that he changed 'Divers Flights' to the singular in his title for the first part.

CHAPTER 21

1 (p. 247). *London blacks*. The chimney-sweeps, one might think. But in *Great Expectations*, Chapter 20, Dickens uses the word 'blacks' to mean specks of soot deposited by the London smoke and fog.

2 (p. 248). *Mr Tartar doing the honors*. The passage beginning with these words and ending with 'Helena! Helena Landless! Are you there?' is written on a wafer pasted over a previously-written passage. The following is offered as a partial reading of the latter:

There ministered to Mr Tartar . . . his servant in these chambers, a . . . with a shaggy red beard and whiskers . . . his big head . . . the conventional hair as with rays . . . appeared to be shining . . . pantaloons of canvas, with shoes of buff . . . when first seen by the visitors.

. . . Said Mr Tartar, 'He is a Triton.'

'Don't you mean a sailor?' said Mr Crisparkle . . .

'I don't indeed. He is a jack of all trades, but he was apprenticed to [*end of page*]

The sailor – or Triton – referred to is, of course, Mr Tartar's man Lobley introduced a few pages later into the published version. The name 'Lobley' is possibly derived from 'loblolly', a thick oatmeal gruel at that time traditionally served to sailors; and/or from 'loblolly boy', a ship-surgeon's assistant and dispenser.

3 (p. 254). *jistes*. See Forster's *Life of Charles Dickens*, J. W. T. Ley edn (1928), p. 747:

More rarely, entry is made [in his notebook] of some oddity of speech, and he has preserved in it . . . what he declared to have been as startling a message as he ever received: 'The gas-fitter says, sir, that he can't alter the fitting of your gas in your bedroom without taking out almost the ole of your bedroom floor, and pulling your room to pieces. He says, of course, you can have it done if you wish ... but he would have to destroy your room first, and go entirely under the jistes.'

CHAPTER 22

1 (p. 266). *pint of sweet blacking*. T. W. Hill says (in the *Dickensian*, XLI (1945), p. 36): 'Dickens probably means the very dark treacly port wine (so called) obtainable on draught at many second-rate inns'.

2 (p. 267). *Died of what, lovey?* Jasper first said, in reply to this question: 'Not of what we take. Death. I'm out of sorts. Get to work. Get to work.'

3 (p. 271). *But she goes no further away*. The passage beginning with these words and ending with 'and daylight looks into the room', is written on a wafer pasted over a similar passage, which has some variant wording:

'So far, I might a'most as well have never found out how to set you talking,' is her commentary. 'You are too sleepy to talk too plain, and you hold your secrets tight, you do.'

4 (p. 277). *Er Royal Highness the Princess Puffer*. Deputy's first impulse was to call her 'Mother Puffer', but the author suppressed that. The original of the character was undoubtedly 'Lascar Sal', or 'Sally the opium-eater', who was well known to the Metropolitan Police and slumming 'swells'. According to Frederick Wellesley (*Recollections of a Soldier-Diplomat* (1947), pp. 75–6), who visited her some time during the years 1863–6, this woman, who appeared to be about eighty, was actually only twenty-six years old. Dickens's friend James T. Fields evidently had not been put in possession of this incredible fact (see note 1, Chapter 1, above), but it will be observed that Dickens himself nowhere, in the notes, MS., or published text of *The Mystery of Edwin Drood*, refers to the woman's fictive counterpart as aged or old. (In this connection, see Philip Collins, 'Inspector Bucket visits the Princess Puffer', in the *Dickensian*, LX (1964), pp. 88–90; and Arthur J. Cox, 'The Haggard Woman', in *The Mystery and Detection Annual 1972*, pp. 65–77.)

5 (p. 279). *John Jasper leading their line*. This has been objected to by more than one writer. That place of honour belongs to the smaller boys.

READ MORE IN PENGUIN

In every corner of the world, on every subject under the sun, Penguin represents quality and variety – the very best in publishing today.

For complete information about books available from Penguin – including Puffins, Penguin Classics and Arkana – and how to order them, write to us at the appropriate address below. Please note that for copyright reasons the selection of books varies from country to country.

In the United Kingdom: Please write to *Dept. EP, Penguin Books Ltd, Bath Road, Harmondsworth, West Drayton, Middlesex UB7 ODA*

In the United States: Please write to *Consumer Sales, Penguin USA, P.O. Box 999, Dept. 17109, Bergenfield, New Jersey 07621-0120.* VISA and MasterCard holders call 1-800-253-6476 to order Penguin titles

In Canada: Please write to *Penguin Books Canada Ltd, 10 Alcorn Avenue, Suite 300, Toronto, Ontario M4V 3B2*

In Australia: Please write to *Penguin Books Australia Ltd, P.O. Box 257, Ringwood, Victoria 3134*

In New Zealand: Please write to *Penguin Books (NZ) Ltd, Private Bag 102902, North Shore Mail Centre, Auckland 10*

In India: Please write to *Penguin Books India Pvt Ltd, 706 Eros Apartments, 56 Nehru Place, New Delhi 110 019*

In the Netherlands: Please write to *Penguin Books Netherlands bv, Postbus 3507, NL-1001 AH Amsterdam*

In Germany: Please write to *Penguin Books Deutschland GmbH, Metzlerstrasse 26, 60594 Frankfurt am Main*

In Spain: Please write to *Penguin Books S. A., Bravo Murillo 19, 1° B, 28015 Madrid*

In Italy: Please write to *Penguin Italia s.r.l., Via Felice Casati 20, I–20124 Milano*

In France: Please write to *Penguin France S. A., 17 rue Lejeune, F–31000 Toulouse*

In Japan: Please write to *Penguin Books Japan, Ishikiribashi Building, 2–5–4, Suido, Bunkyo-ku, Tokyo 112*

In Greece: Please write to *Penguin Hellas Ltd, Dimocritou 3, GR–106 71 Athens*

In South Africa: Please write to *Longman Penguin Southern Africa (Pty) Ltd, Private Bag X08, Bertsham 2013*

PENGUIN AUDIOBOOKS

A Quality of Writing that Speaks for Itself

Penguin Books has always led the field in quality publishing. Now you can listen at leisure to your favourite books, read to you by familiar voices from radio, stage and screen. Penguin Audiobooks are ideal as gifts, for when you are travelling or simply to enjoy at home. They are produced to an excellent standard, and abridgements are always faithful to the original texts. From thrillers to classic literature, biography to humour, with a wealth of titles in between, Penguin Audiobooks offer you quality, entertainment and the chance to rediscover the pleasure of listening.

You can order Penguin Audiobooks through Penguin Direct by telephoning (0181) 899 4036. The lines are open 24 hours every day. Ask for Penguin Direct, quoting your credit card details.

Published or forthcoming:

Emma by Jane Austen, read by Fiona Shaw

Persuasion by Jane Austen, read by Joanna David

Pride and Prejudice by Jane Austen, read by Geraldine McEwan

The Tenant of Wildfell Hall by Anne Brontë, read by Juliet Stevenson

Jane Eyre by Charlotte Brontë, read by Juliet Stevenson

Villette by Charlotte Brontë, read by Juliet Stevenson

Wuthering Heights by Emily Brontë, read by Juliet Stevenson

The Woman in White by Wilkie Collins, read by Nigel Anthony and Susan Jameson

Heart of Darkness by Joseph Conrad, read by David Threlfall

Tales from the One Thousand and One Nights, read by Souad Faress and Raad Rawi

Moll Flanders by Daniel Defoe, read by Frances Barber

Great Expectations by Charles Dickens, read by Hugh Laurie

Hard Times by Charles Dickens, read by Michael Pennington

Martin Chuzzlewit by Charles Dickens, read by John Wells

The Old Curiosity Shop by Charles Dickens, read by Alec McCowen

PENGUIN AUDIOBOOKS

Crime and Punishment by Fyodor Dostoyevsky, read by Alex Jennings

Middlemarch by George Eliot, read by Harriet Walter

Silas Marner by George Eliot, read by Tim Pigott-Smith

The Great Gatsby by F. Scott Fitzgerald, read by Marcus D'Amico

Madame Bovary by Gustave Flaubert, read by Claire Bloom

Jude the Obscure by Thomas Hardy, read by Samuel West

The Return of the Native by Thomas Hardy, read by Steven Pacey

Tess of the D'Urbervilles by Thomas Hardy, read by Eleanor Bron

The Iliad by Homer, read by Derek Jacobi

Dubliners by James Joyce, read by Gerard McSorley

The Dead and Other Stories by James Joyce, read by Gerard McSorley

On the Road by Jack Kerouac, read by David Carradine

Sons and Lovers by D. H. Lawrence, read by Paul Copley

The Fall of the House of Usher by Edgar Allan Poe, read by Andrew Sachs

Wide Sargasso Sea by Jean Rhys, read by Jane Lapotaire and Michael Kitchen

The Little Prince by Antoine de Saint-Exupéry, read by Michael Maloney

Frankenstein by Mary Shelley, read by Richard Pasco

Of Mice and Men by John Steinbeck, read by Gary Sinise

Travels with Charley by John Steinbeck, read by Gary Sinise

The Pearl by John Steinbeck, read by Hector Elizondo

Dr Jekyll and Mr Hyde by Robert Louis Stevenson, read by Jonathan Hyde

Kidnapped by Robert Louis Stevenson, read by Robbie Coltrane

The Age of Innocence by Edith Wharton, read by Kerry Shale

The Buccaneers by Edith Wharton, read by Dana Ivey

Mrs Dalloway by Virginia Woolf, read by Eileen Atkins

READ MORE IN PENGUIN

CHARLES DICKENS

'A popular and fecund, but yet profound, serious and wonderfully resourceful practising novelist, a master of it' – Q. D. Leavis

'He was successful beyond any English novelist, probably beyond any novelist that has ever lived, in exactly hitting off the precise tone of thought and feeling' – Leslie Stephen

'All the political futility which has forced men of the calibre of Mussolini, Kemal and Hitler to assume dictatorship might have been saved if people had only believed what Dickens told them in *Little Dorrit*' – Bernard Shaw

'Heaven for the just: for the wicked, Hell. Herein Dickens is true to the opinion of his countrymen and of his time' – André Gide

'Language and morality add dimensions to his cartoons and turn them into literature' – Anthony Burgess

Barnaby Rudge
The Christmas Books
Dombey and Son
Hard Times
Martin Chuzzlewit
Nicholas Nickleby
Oliver Twist
The Pickwick Papers
American Notes for General
  Circulation

Bleak House
David Copperfield
Great Expectations
Little Dorrit
The Mystery of Edwin
  Drood
The Old Curiosity Shop
Out Mutual Friend
A Tale of Two Cities
Selected Short Fiction